CELESTIAL AWAKENING

CELESTIAL AWAKENING

By Frank LoBue

PROLOGUE

Unknown Galactic Coordinates

Summary of Terrian Hominid Events

A solitary figure sat in a large, darkened corner of an unexplored region of the galaxy. The being smiled, bearing rows of sharklike teeth, as the news that has traveled so far was projected into her mind.

The Terrian sun seemed to levitate above the horizon of the North Pole, as it has since those many years from first arrival. Solar radiation and atmospheric gases collide, creating a visually spectacular array of greens, reds, and violets in the evening sky of the now truly blue planet, the self-deemed intelligence of the Human species formerly called Earth. The carbon footprint so definitively marking the existence of mankind on the planet has been slowly reversed. Just as upon first arrival, the blue oceans are free of pollutants and teeming with life from the old world and the new, the land masses that remain harbor the infinitesimal animal life that can tolerate the harsh climates, and the skies again belong to the avians of this reborn planet but still remain intolerant to the other children she birthed. Earth—or Gaia, as it is now known among them—has now brought herself back from the brink of extinction by eliminating the very thing that plagued her: the Human species.

Some 1,494 years ago, Humans discovered that their time on Earth had come to an end. The species, in all of their infinite wisdom, could not see their own demise in front of them until it was too late. For billions of years, Earth grew and flourished without the presence of these hominids. Creatures as tall as their skyscrapers once roamed the blue planet, oceans receding while ice ages formed, the terrain altering constantly with shifts of tectonic plates and cosmic collisions, the Earth ever-changing. When Earth's primordial essence gave birth to her child, the symbiosis between the blue planet and the early Humans was cohesive, mutually beneficial for both but only for a time. Humanity was nurtured by their Mother Earth like a child nestled into a mother's warm embrace. Humanity thrived, their intelligence growing by leaps and bounds. Learning, teaching, building, procreating, all to strengthen their resolve and grow as a species. Intelligence—these Humans have not broken the seam on what an intelligence can accomplish.

With all of their intellect, they could not fathom what would become of their species, let alone what they called their home. With the dawn of their Industrial Age, Humans began to turn the symbiotic relationship into a parasitic infestation. Fossil fuels were used to power their grand mechanisms, the metal and ore of the planet upheaved to build towers of glass and steel, and the atoms of their dimension split and collided upon to produce grim, but useful, results. Soon enough, Humans multiplied to extraordinary numbers, nearly exceeding the planet's resources. Wars, famine, and pestilence steadily remained, despite the advances in their medicines, genetic sequencing, and chemical, mechanical, and biological engineering. Humanity has always had an innate ability to be blinded by their own fortitude, creating as well as destroying without acknowledgment of the consequences until it beckons them to recognize their follies. Their creative destruction sped up natural phenomena that should not have occurred for more than a million years in Earth's life cycle.

The effluence produced by their intentional, wasteful ways caused Earth's atmosphere to thin, increasing the solar radiation absorbed onto the surface of the planet. The global climate shifted. Temperature increases, erratic weather patterns, bizarre animal behavior, and radiation spikes throughout the globe became noticeable to some and ignored by most. The Earth's solar rotation in Human designated Earth year AD 2000 became a year of unprecedented change in the eyes of Humanity, for it was realized that the polar ice caps were melting, and oceanic waters began to slowly but inevitably rise. It could not be stopped, for all of their wasted efforts.

Humanity, as they had been doing for millennia, fought

among each other, denying their scientists' evidence and claiming paranoia was to blame. The years passed, earthquakes shook cities to rubble, tsunamis and hurricanes swallowed small islands back into the sea, and tornadoes grew in size enough to seem as if black holes existed in the eyes of the storms. Earth, mother to the Human race, had finally exposed the world from which they created.

Humanity had seen the end of days on their home planet—

A chronological report clicked on as the creature sat in an eager silence.

Galaxy 0132.7: Deemed Harvest Worthy
Species: Terrian
Viable Coding: Terrian QNC subcoding relayed to bionic interfaces. Subcoding requires tactile accumulation, subjects problematic.
Terrian Biomakeup: Insipid evolution, biped formulary, emotional and logistical thought processes, diversionary stratum intellect, decision making, and reasoning. Current hindrance assessment: queryful. Mutations abundant, species suited for interface. Harvest number 0132.7.453.
Status: Monitor and report. Time elapsed status of primary species event logs. Send to receive. Current timeline concurrent with primary species. Orbit of Terrian 3 in Terrian species years 100.23 million. Terrian years in flux from Terrian home planet 1,494.
Synoptic Compendium ID: 923.0132.7

Earth year 2025: An electrical superstorm decimates the electrical grid across the Eastern Seaboard of the United States and as far inland as the Midwestern states, plummeting the infrastructure and economics into chaos. As a result came the decimation of the global stock market; all global commerce turned onto its belly, exposing the frailties of capitalism among Human collaboration in a time that soon would be essential to survival.

India is rocked by the largest magnitude earthquake

known in Earth's recorded history, causing geothermal plates to shift, increasing volcanic activities in the region. India's primary governing body is evacuated to a safe haven in the Northern Rocky Mountain region in the United States. The Northern Hemisphere's temperature has risen five degrees Celsius since Earth year 2000. The Greenland ice sheath has begun to melt, causing the Arctic Ocean to change the terrain of the continents drastically. Seventy-three percent of the Earth's surface is water.

Earth years 2035–2039: Humanity is immensely unprepared for such a radical change in environmental conditions. Iceland, Norway, Sweden, Finland, and Great Britain are reclaimed by the surrounding oceans, being swallowed into the gullet of Mother Earth. Millions attempt to flee from coastal Europe further inland to Africa, Russia, the Middle East, and some to North America by any means necessary, but most perish. Millions more die from disease and pestilence. The British Parliament is evacuated within hours of the first floods and is the third government to sit alongside the United States at the now-named Rocky Mountain Safe Haven (RMSH). Humanity, in most respects, has realized the imminent destruction that is presented in their forefront. Seventy-nine percent of the Earth's surface is swathed by ocean by the year 2037. The year 2039 shows Humanity in the midst of total chaos. Most of the cities are burning to ashen rumble, famine has spread globally, clean water has become endangered, and the death toll continues to rise. Papua New Guinea, the Solomon Islands, and the eastern half of Australia are decimated as superhurricanes claim them back into the sea. No known survivors. Tsunamis plunge Japan back into the sea, killing millions and spreading disease among refugees fleeing to China, then swiftly through the Asian continent. The remaining Korean, Vietnamese, Taiwanese, and Japanese political leaders, high ranking military, and leading scientific minds are evacuated to the RMSH in North America to participate in a think tank to solve the global threat. The Vietnamese and Taiwanese delegates do not reach the safe haven for still-unknown reasons. The Chinese government elects that citizens are to stay in country; the proceeding subzero winter tempests devour the continent, and it is unknown whether any survived. Very few Japanese and Korean delegates survive, but those who do join the other survivors at the RMSH. The Russian government has militarized, closing borders and using deadly force to prevent Asian and Middle Eastern refugees from entering. War ensues between the nations. Millions of lives are extinguished; it is unknown whether there are any survivors. Eighty-three percent of the Earth's surface is covered in water by year's end.

Earth year 2040: The faults along the West Coast become great chasms. California, Oregon, Washington, and the western half of Nevada now are a feature deep within the Earth as well as the lives residing among them. The Pacific Ocean has now claimed all the existing islands. The increase in solar radiation to the Earth's surface has made global temperatures erratic. The Middle Eastern deserts become scorching wastelands, uninhabitable to the majority of biological life. Pakistan and Iran refuse to communicate with each other or surrounding governing entities. Mere days after reports of no refugees seeking solace from either country, all communications are lost; no survivors are known from either country. The Saudi Arabian government is the only surviving governing body in the Middle East to flee to the RMSH. As suddenly as the temperature rose in the deserts, the seas responded in kind; much of the coastal land masses become ocean reef. Africa is in the midst of returning to the Atlantic and Indian Oceans; earthquakes and volcanic activity have increased throughout the region. Mexico and South America have either been claimed by the rising waters or made into marshlands, habitable only to amphibian and marine life. A total of 85 percent of the Earth's surface is covered with water.

Earth year 2045: Coastal cities around the globe have become devoid of Human life; little animal life is known to have survived. The increase in thermal expansion has caused the sea levels to quadruple the speed of the rising tide. The atmosphere grows thinner, as evident by the increase in global radiation levels. The Earth's average surface temperature has risen ten degrees Fahrenheit. New York City, once a city of global recognition and Human socialization, is now an uninhabitable and unrecognizable swampland. Florida and all Southern states venturing into mid-Texas have been eradicated by superstorms and claimed by the surrounding seas. Humans in all regions of North America have either fled to the RMSH or have met their demise from the elements, pestilence, or starvation. The Northern Hemisphere has begun to cool; Russia and Asia plunge into an eternal winter. Temperatures have drastically decreased in the region, becoming intolerable for life. Global communication has broken down; the internet and most forms of communication have been exhausted. Any attempt by the safe haven to reach the remnants of the Russian or Asian governments has failed. Eighty-seven percent of the Earth's surface is now covered in water.

Earth year 2079: An estimated 5.5 billion Humans have died. Scattered pockets of Humanity have survived on the remaining land masses by burrowing deep into the mountainous terrains to escape the ever-growing toxic environment. The land masses that remain exist at the high ascension points around the planet: Mount Elbrus in Russia, Mount Everest in Asia, Mount Kilimanjaro in Africa, and the Rocky Mountain region from Mount Elbert in Colorado to Mount Robson in Canada. However, these regions are slowly being claimed to the waters of the planet. The Humans seek to thrive, but their options are slowly dwindling.

Query notation: Resilience in species; suggest swift action to acquire submission. All latitudes and longitudes recorded for future reconnaissance.

The Humans, now knowing they cannot preserve their life on the planet, begin to develop methods for living off-planet. A new governing body is formed out of the seven remaining prominent governments that successfully fled to the

RMSH. The vestiges of the US, Canadian, Japanese, Korean, British, Saudi Arabian, and Indian governments form what Humans have deemed the Morsus Mihi, a translation of their ancient language of Latin, meaning "alliance." The species believes with the formation of a unified Human collaborative that an unprecedented peace and age of prosperity can begin for Humanity.

Query notation: In the midst of impending annihilation, the species holds on to aspects of hope—hope for not only survival but for a way to thrive and expand. This has not been seen in other species. Others have seen aspects of hope and faith as detrimental to their survival and resort to their bestial savagery, which in turn leads to their inevitable submission.

Knowing time is dangerously limited on the planet, the Morsus Mihi order all extraorbital shuttles that have been constructed in preparation for this inevitable event to be launched. Numerous engineering crews, medical personnel, and much of the scientific community launch in synchronous orbit to salvage the derelict satellites and space stations in a massive conglomerate to construct the first colonial space station. Habitat domes are erected on the Moon's surface, all in an attempt to survive in space. In the later months of 2079, construction begins on the largest space port in recorded Human history for the transition of the vestiges of the species into space in hopes of survival. A total of 91 percent of the Earth's surface is now covered in water.

Earth years 2084–2090: The surface of the Earth has drastically changed in the years since what Humans have come to call the Convergence. Isolated land masses hold pockets of the dwindling species beneath the surface. Radiation levels have risen to such heights that Humanity cannot survive on the surface of their mother planet without suffering physiological chemical and radioactive ailments. Unknown numbers in these areas, global coordinates were recorded and sent to primary interfaces for future reference.

The RMSH is surrounded by newly formed ocean; only because of the elevation has it managed to preserve Humanity.

Construction of the Overlook is completed in Earth year 2084. The migration of the Humans to the space station has been ongoing for approximately 1.5 Earth years. The Morsus Mihi implement a mandate to establish more permanent residences on the lunar surface. The scientific community sends DNA samples of plant and animal life to the Overlook for future development of the lost species of Earth. Since the Convergence, Humanity has downsized drastically; fewer than three million Human beings remain at this point in history. All surface work and maintenance must be conducted in biohazard containment suits. Ninety-two percent of the Earth's surface is now covered in water, with radiation levels rising steadily as the atmosphere continues to thin, allowing massive amounts of solar radiation onto the surface of the planet.

With the Morsus Mihi on station in the summer of 2085, they begin to formulate a new government and plan to build a society in which work garners rewards and all work is for the betterment of Humankind as a whole. New standards of regulations and policies are put in place to maintain civility among the people as the new governing body takes shape. A new era of biological and technological breakthroughs commences throughout society.

Query notation: Human ingenuity and development are a threat.

Human science progresses rapidly following the transition to space. In 2086, Humans begin to identify skill sets on a genomic level. The Morsus Mihi give choices to their populace. Some Humans blend to their destined skill sets, while others maintain their solidarity of existence. Under a veil of secrecy, the Morsus Mihi conduct genomic experimentation. Subtle class systems develop with unspoken words; upheavals formulate, and discontent ensues among the Human race, but the ultimate goal of survival and expansion is maintained for the time past.

Query notation: Of any species interfaced, none require more recognition of individualistic identification as does the Human species. The species' mind-set dictates swift application.

In the same year, as the Humans strive to move forward to solidify their survival, the scientific community begins planning and preparation for *terraforma*, or worldbuilding, operations and colonization of the red planet, Mars. Shuttles, equipment, and personnel begin to make the journey to Mars to begin the terraforma operations. Humanity has become self-sustaining in the spatial orbit around their Mother Earth and on the surface of the moon by 2089 but seek further expansion into the cosmos, which they call the Auctius. The lunar domes have been reserved for the families and nonessential personnel not involved with the Auctius. Only higher-echelon individuals have authority over Auctius operations. The Overlook at this time remains the base of operations for the Morsus Mihi and terraforma operations.

In Earth year 2090, also known as Exim Gaia 1 (EG 1), most of the Humans have left Earth, now called Gaia. Less than one hundred thousand Humans elect to stay behind, as they believe Humans were never meant to leave the planet. Communication with the RMSH is severed in the winter of EG 1. A total of 96 percent of the Earth's surface is now covered in water and will no longer nourish the Human species.

RMSH location recorded for primary reserve interfaces.

EG 21–EG 60: Humans have had immense success in the terraformation of Mars. This species is nothing if not ingenious in their methodologies. EG 21 drilling commences to the core of the red planet as Humans unleash the icy nucleus so that it ascends into the thin atmosphere of the desolate planet. Once drilling completed around the planet, EG 28, Humans on the surface were evacuated to the safety of the various space stations orbiting Mars and lunar domes on the Martian moons, Phobos and Deimos.

In EG 31, utilizing magnetic rail technology positioned

among the asteroid belt, Humans proceed to conduct timed cataclysmic impactions with the Martian surface. By utilizing the asteroids in a type of slingshot technique toward various key locations around the planet during its orbital cycle, the asteroids struck the Martian surface with world-ending force, creating a thick cloud of various noxious gases around the planet and thus creating a breathable atmosphere for sustaining Human life. Humanity's creativity has given them another avenue of hope that they would reside in the embrace of a planet once again. Humanity had predicted it would take more than half a century for the atmosphere to thin and detoxify to optimal conditions for colonization.

With this time, the species took advantage and combined their efforts once again in a mass collaboration between many of the great minds produced by the species to improve in many different areas scientifically, agriculturally, and technologically, advancing themselves significantly in many areas for the betterment of all, as they claim. Humans harness the power of fusion technology to make traversing the stars quicker and vastly more efficient. They make many immense steps for the intellectual progress of their species, advancing in many areas with success not seen in other species. Regardless of Humanity's joint venture, the populace remains defiant. As surveyed previously, Humans have a need for self-identification. It seems essential to the existence of this species. Regardless of the growing unrest, the species maintains its goals of progression, procreation, and colonization of their system. Unpredicted findings in this species suggest heightened threat assessments. Hindrance level increased, precarious. The Human race must be interfaced swiftly to prevent uprising.

Among the genetic, agricultural, and engineering advances, Humans have made profound progress with microrobotics and artificial intelligence, and the applications of such have been expansive. Enhancements in the Human bioform with genetic and technological modifications are now a main-

13

stay among the Gaian Interplanetary Alliance (GIA). The Morsus Mihi, over the years since EG 1, created the GIA to govern and police the people as the Morsus Mihi themselves act as a conjunctive tribunal. Together they introduce new defense initiatives as radicals, religious zealots, and rebellions naturally develop against an authoritative entity.

Track progress of unrest; utilize as vantage stratagem.

With the development of nanomachines and cybernetic modifications, Humanity propels the age of technology forward by leaps and bounds. Biological enhancements, medical technological advancements, and spatial technology enhancements take progressive steps forward with the new developments. Humanity has made the introduction of these nanomachines into their terraforma processes. The utilization of the newly created photosynthetic artificial lifeforms, or PALS, into the terraforma process has substantially decreased the expected time frame of the formation of breathable atmospheric gases and the habitation of the Martian surface. Minimal testing of the technology is initiated before application.

EG 68–EG 231: EG 71, Mars becomes habitable decades before predictions. Humanity revels in their success and proceeds to colonize the former red planet. Industrial complexes, rural communities, metropolises, and governmental facilities are constructed over the course of years. Culture, commerce, government, and society have slowly manifested to establish a further sense of stability in the Human race. The GIA establishes the capital of their governmental imperium on Olympus Mons, the highest and most prominent peak in Mars. Within years the species has adapted to their new home; new generations are born to their Martian mother. They introduce former vegetation and animal life from Gaia to supplement the planet; PALs assist in speed of agricultural and ecological development. Scientists are fascinated with the abundance of genetic change that occurs with biological organisms as they are introduced to the Martian environment.

Mars becomes their beacon of light in the many years of strife and darkness the Humans feel they have endured. Internal recordings report the Morsus Mihi has expressed concern on limiting themselves to one solar system. There has been discussion in recent years of taking the Auctius further; with the many advancements in stellar technology, they feel Humanity can survive for longer durations in what they now call the Celestial. The Morsus Mihi are unanimous in the decision that they must further the Auctius to amplify the success of Humanity's survival.

Others among the GIA, mostly the civilian leadership, want to conform to Mars, fearing what the Auctius could do to the Human condition, as "playing God" (as they say) has not worked in the past. EG 120 terraforma operations are launched, under protest from the dividing factions, to Mercury, Venus, and Pluto. Utilizing the asteroid belt as a source of catastrophic terraformation material, along with the iron ore and other precious metals along their asteroid belt, they have near-limitless resources for expansion into the Solaris, what they now call their solar system. Humanity's divisions become more prominent as independent factions maintain their individual beliefs, thus linking to their individual survival. Record psychological impingement, and exploit for ease of harvest and transition.

EG 243–EG 303: Pluto terraforma operations fail. The dwarf planet remains dormant as the dual orbit with its moon, Charon, prevent an atmosphere from being maintained. The planet has since been subsidized for industrial operations of the GIA. Venus has been terraformed and is nearly identical to Gaia when the planet was young, before mankind's carbon footprint. Colonization of Gaia's sister planet commences without haste. EG 256: Mercury is unsuccessful, as the Terrian sun burns through any atmospheric layers formed. The planet becomes isolated by the Morsus Mihi for unknown reasons. Isolation status and location verified; revisit and investigate in future time frame. Humanity continues to search beyond their Solaris for habitable systems.

EG 300: Continue prime directive; record and report augmentation of Humanity in their solar system and beyond.

EG 493: For over a century, mankind was unable traverse the stars in a fashion that would allow for progressive development of the GIA. However, Human imagination creates advances in hypersleep and enhanced stellar engine technology that give them the opportunity to travel beyond their Solaris to neighboring systems. Humans have developed a stable nuclear quantum-fission stellar engine capable of speeds faster than traditional and close to the speed of light. Planning and preparation commence for traversing the Celestial.

Query notation: The species has continued to express aptitude for high advancement in a variety of logistical, spatial, biotechnical fields, as well as problem solving in areas critical for survival and progression of supplementing base knowledge.

Industrial, logistical, and communication stellar stations are constructed on the outer rim of the now-deemed Gaian Solaris. Military research and recruitment, stellar travel, and scientific experimentation in the areas of quantum physics, biotechnology, and robotics become among the highest priorities for the progression of Humanity within the GIA.

Query notation: Humans fear the unknown and thus will go extreme lengths for their sense of security.

Various rebellious movements, chief among them being the Liber Mortales movement, have announced their succession from the GIA to oppose the genetic predispositions and augmentations as well as the Auctius throughout the galaxy. The Humans become divided among themselves further, war inevitable.

EG 508–EG 550: Civil war erupts among the Humans in EG 511. Because of the dividing factions, Mars becomes a battleground for the first time in billions of years. Thousands of casualties on both sides. The civilian population suffers from strife and famine as the war devastates agricultural sites and farming communities throughout Mars.

EG 538 sees the end of the civil discontent, as treaties are signed among the GIA and the Liber Mortales. The treaty entails a lasting individuality among Humanity. The GIA and Liber Mortales have agreed to individual development from the Gaian Interplanetary Alliance. Terms are reached among the factions as long as the overall outcome benefits mankind as a whole. The Liber Mortales and many among the civilian sect see separation from the GIA and Morsus Mihi as another milestone for Humanity. The Liber Mortales establishes a council that constructs dialogue with the Morsus Mihi and GIA delegates. The Morsus Mihi remains an observing party with continuing influence in operations of Humanity and government among the GIA. A tenuous peace is formed. Terraforma and colonization operations launch to multiple Solari among the galaxy EG 542.

EG 698–EG 902: The first stellar system traversed, EG 698, was, after all, the closest to their home Solaris, Alpha Centauri. The Humans predicted they would be able to terraform and colonize half of the system, with the aid of the PALs technology, within a hundred of their Gaian years. Nevertheless, with all the preparation, setbacks were abundant in the wake of universal causations. The immense gravitational pull of the system's binary suns caused catastrophic system failures to every stellar cruiser that approached the system. Some cruisers are now derelict forever, floating in space as a mass grave or pulled into the black hole that exists between binary suns. Efforts to colonize the system are abandoned. While most of the galaxy remains unknown to Humans, as historic records were fragmented during the Convergence, this did not deter the species. Humanity as a whole commenced forward, undeterred by their losses, launching multiple probes and stellarcraft into other sectors of the Celestial.

Humans successfully reach another Solaris mere light years away from Alpha Centauri, which is established in EG

782, canonized Crescat. Crescat contains three planets and four moons, all planets and one moon suitable for terraforma. The Humans make haste in colonization of the Solaris. The Morsus Mihi maintain their goal to create a society of unified ideals and perpetual growth throughout the Celestial. A series of tenets are created as a guide for Humanity's advancement, not only throughout the galaxy but within their own intellect.

The planets and moons of Crescat contain dormant biological constructs that potentiated the PALs AI, in turn quadrupling the speed of the terraforma processes; colonization of the planets commences in EG 789. The biological abnormalities are integrated into the PALs technology, further developing their terraforma techniques. Continuing their technological advancements, a new stellar engine is developed EG 825, bringing them even closer to FSL, faster than light, travel. The species has advanced quicker than predicted. Their quantum drives utilize the manipulation of quantum energy and fission in such obscure formalities that, as such, all specifics, blueprints, and formularies are uploaded to primary and secondary interfaces.

Query notation: Humanity's ability to progress intellectually is requiring recalculation of assimilation timeline. Retarding intellectual growth will lead to a more submissive nature with future generations that will be procreated.

EG 901–EG 1100: Crescat Solaris is fully established with a new Solaris called Ipsum in the midst of terraformation. Humans continue to find that many more Solaris have either habitable planets and moons or those suitable for terraforma. Continual advances in quantum stellar engine and hypersleep technology are abundant at this stage of Human development. As such, multiple deep space missions are put in motion for further terraforma operations and colonization. Through continuous progression of their biological and technological understandings, the species pioneers from Solaris to Solaris within these years, utilizing the quantum drives and Quisthium, a chemical manipulator developed for advanced hypersleep. Humanity's harmonization within the masses, for the time, seems to be the survival of the species through mass migration throughout the cosmos. Humans' division within the populace remains steady; further rebellions develop throughout the GIA.

EG 1181: The species has now colonized five of their so-called Solaris. The Auctius has proven fruitful for the species. The leadership has fermented the Tenets of the Auctius, which continue to guide the mainstream of the species.

Humanity's rebellious nature is again noted as troublesome as the Liber Vultus, remnants of the Liber Mortales, call for the Morsus Mihi to quell the GIA in the wake of claims of secret military experimentation involving psionic manipulation. Many rebel for fear of entrapment of their individuality minor skirmishes and rebellions emerge throughout the GIA territories. The rebels claim the GIA has been keeping their policies of transparency cloaked from the masses since the signing of the treaty hundreds of years before for reasons of security and intelligence gathering to control aspects of Human development. The GIA claims to have abandoned the new avenues of research and continues to monitor this aspect closely.

A curious advancement the species has made not only to revitalize the aspects of the whole to Humanity but yet another admirable technological feat is the creation of a techno-biological quantum computer dubbed the Gnanimus. In tandem with the Gnanimus, a transmitter is developed to allow a near-limitless reach to almost any Human anywhere in the Celestial, the nanophage. The Gnanimus acts as a central hub for communication, culmination of acquired knowledge, and a beacon for the continuing evolution of the species.

Query notation: Despite the history of essential world-ending events of the Convergence and the many civil, global, and Celestial wars among themselves, Humans continue to belittle their growing intellect with internal conflicts of morality and aspiration. Species themselves will not expand unless ridding themselves of individual appetites, thus making them susceptible for psychological manipulation and harvest.

EG 1288: An evolution in the Gnanimus leads to the realization of interdimensional realms. Contact is made with an energy-based species, the Caiets. Skeptics among Humans debate whether the beings are the purest form of imagination brought into existence through the Gnanimus connection or whether they really are interdimensional, sentient, energy-based entities. Along with the discovery of the energy-based beings came further developments into their biocomputer technology—in particular, the manipulation of the quantum energy, or what Humans have come to call Vis, that is embodied in the Caiets' dimension. The energy species claims the Vis flows throughout the dimensions and is an expansive interconnectivity of, as they call it, the Realms of Reality. Humans develop various modalities for application and manipulation of the Vis. Through the energy manipulation, the Humans have been able to synthesize various technologies: palpable holographic interfaces, genetic regeneration, and various mechanical engineering applications, including digital engine modifications and thin-layered polymers, for advanced solar shielding. Technology, bioform and otherwise, must be integrated into the harvest.

EG 1394: Along with their home system, the Gaian Solaris, the Human species have emigrated to seven solar systems; thus far, with the Tenets of the Auctius there to "guide all of Humanity into the breadth of the Celestial," as quoted by the Morsus Mihi, Humanity's tenets guide their quest throughout the cosmos but leave them strategically and psychologically vulnerable to manipulation and subjugation. Full analytical analysis of psychological components and logistical strategies downloading to primary interfaces. Summaries of each Solaris function are as follows:

Gaian Imperial Solaris: Base of operations for the

Human species, Mars primary TerraOrbis of Gaian Interplanetary Alliance. The Morsus Mihi and the delegates of Gaian Interplanetary Alliance are based out of the Olympus Mons capital on Mars, the bureaucratic and military extremities of the GIA.

Crescat Solaris: Xegriculture, terraforma operations, interplanetary horticulture, agriculture, and other agronomic, cultivation, and farmstead operations.

Ipsum Solaris: Engineering; mechanical, chemical, and biological, spatial design, architecture and fabrication, robotics and cybernetics. Main proponent of Gnanimus and nanophage operations.

Bellatorius Solaris: Military design, strategy, and defensive operations, xenocombat, and security preparedness for GIA.

Ducovímus Solaris: "The Philosopher's Solaris"—mathematics, logistics, philosophy, communications, xenolinguistics.

Vitachlora Solaris: Xenomedicine, psychology, microbiology, pharmacology, genetic manipulation, health and wellness.

Sapietás Solaris: Xenohistory, archaeology, sociology, religious ideology, Celestial theology.

Tracaelus Solaris: Terraforma operations ongoing, Solaris still in development. Quantum theory, spatial physics, deep space travel, interdimensional theory.

Humanity has delved deep into their home galaxy. With their new Solaris, Tracaelus, being the beacon of their accomplishments as one species united, the species have set their sights on the deeper horizons past their own galaxy. The Human intellect continues to surpass previous reports of their insipid evolution. With the majority of Humanity working to better their species, they have sped their evolution in ways that were unpredicted. Theories have been surmised that Vis can be manipulated to bring Humanity to the new era of FSL travel. Experimentation with Vis energy, quantum engines, and deep space travel becomes priority among the GIA. Numerous drones and satellites were launched toward the deepest points light-years into their galaxy and beyond.

EG 1423: Incoming Priority Report...High-priority intercept with Human species at navigational waypoint in Tracaelus Solaris within five Gaian years.

EG 1428: Humanity has finally discovered that they are not the only sentient species in their universe in EG 1428. The Humans have come in contact with the species named the Noanoagans—or, at least, the name Humans have come to terms with, given their crude translation of the Noanoagan native language—just on the outskirts of the Tracaelus Solaris. Humanity learns of the Noanoagans' thousand-year journey through the vastness of the Celestial to find a sustainable planet for their species. Humanity donates a luna to the refugees located in the Tracaelus Solaris, which the Noanoagans name Tasóa, meaning "peaceful habitation." Terraforma commences EG 1430. The terraforma of the moon is the most substantial in Human history, as the alien species breathes a noxious gas harmful to Human fetuses and children who have not reached pubescent age. Terraformation of luna complete EG 1448. The Noanoagans introduce a method for faster than light speed travel, also known in Human terms as aethra travel, and construction of Aethra Gateway underway EG 1453.

Current timestamp for record EG 1479: Current location, Tracaelus Solaris. Priority mission parameters continue as follows: Observe construction of Aethra Gateway. Observe Human and Noanoagan interaction. Siphon critical information as interspecies collaboration furthers and the use of Noanoagan technology is implemented to expedite construction operations. Construction of gateway nearing completion estimate full operation of Aethra Gateway in eight Gaian months. Current threat assessment recommends exercising extreme caution in assimilation of species. Continue relation with agents inside...incoming stellar vessel. Target acquired.

Impact likely...damage substantial. End transmission.

A subtle hiss emanates from the darkness: "It has begun."

CHAPTER 1

Tracaelus Solaris, Twenty Thousand Light-Years from the Edge of the Milky Way Galaxy
0.3 AU outside Aethra Gateway Construction Zone

"Sadie, what the hell did we just hit?" shouted the pilot as a bright neon-red light spastically blinked to his left and a persistent beeping pinged from the holographic radar screen that popped up in front of the pilot's face, indicating a small impact off the starboard hull of his stellar cruiser.

"It seems as if we have struck a small metallic object off the port bow," a soft, silky invisible voice said. "It could be anything from an asteroid fragment to a piece of space shrapnel from the Aethra. It is difficult to surmise at this point in time, Nachman."

With a precise conscious thought, an incentum, Sadie sent an elongated robotic arm from a porthole of the ship and quickly grabbed a chunk of the unverified metal as the ship silently swam through space, specifically the Tracaelus Solaris. "I will save a sample for further investigation," said the voice.

"Thanks, Sadie; keep me posted," said the pilot as he turned to face the Vis monitor display. "I told you, you little chump, don't make me chase you. Now you see what happens when I have to chase a trog like you."

"Kiss my ass, you rock-dwelling piece of alvum. When I get loose, I'm gonna tear you a new portal, son!" yelled the aging and armless man strapped to a cargo chair.

"Not a whole lot you can do when I have your arms as my copilot, bud," Nachman said as he smirked at the prisoner, waved goodbye with the prisoner's cybernetic left arm, and blinked, muting the console just as the prisoner spouted off a slew of profanities. The pilot tossed the arm onto the worn copilot seat; it landed with a soft thud. Nachman noted that the left arm did appear more worn than the right, as patches of synthetic dermis were missing from the knuckles and fingertips of his left hand. *Scumbag is left-handed*, thought Nachman.

As Nachman scanned the left arm, admiring the rustic sheen as it didn't glint off the light, his eyes caught a glimpse of the forearm of the right lying just underneath the left. A bar code was laser-cut into the forearm, bits of grime and dirt stuck in the etched grooves, telling Nachman it had been there for a while. With age and noticeably improper care, bits of biorust could form in scarred alloy in any organic enhancement. *This guy has been behind laser bars for a good while.* Nachman lifted the right arm, the other falling to the floor; he just let it rest where it landed. Just above the bar code inlaid in the titiconium alloy were the numbers 674. The numbers were a bright-metallic orange. Nachman smiled. He was a prisoner of Tenebrae, all right.

All Luna Tholus, incarceration moons, had a color-coding system that permanently stained the alloy of any biological or synthetic substance. A GIA treat—if you were ever a prisoner anywhere in the Alliance, you were branded for life. Nachman looked at the bar code and scanned it with an internal retinal scanner in his ocumech; the prisoner information blinked into existence on a holo-page in front of him.

Nachman leaned back in his chair watching two Vis-rendered displays. The Vis displays took whatever shape, size, and color scheme a user could project with their incentum. Nachman preferred the spherical shapes with a color mix of blues and greens in the display and text; those colors didn't sting the nanomechs in his left eye as much. The display on the left, a small oval, sifted through the data files of Tenebrae's QQ block with an algorithm programmed by Sadie to find any keywords, phrases, or events relating to the escaped prisoners or the knowledge of a prison break. The other, a large circle, showed the screaming torso without arms that was Prisoner 674, bound with titiconium-laced restraints to a reinforced cargo chair. Nachman mused at the crinkle in prisoner 674's forehead; it looked quite like a crooked smile every time the vulgarisms came spewing out.

The Gaian Interplanetary Alliance (GIA), Nachman's former employers, had put out a multisystem retributio to capture, detain, and return fourteen escapees of the Luna Tholus Tenebrae in the Bellatorius Solaris. All the prisoners had various wants and warrants from unsanctioned Gnanimus hacks to phage theft. Nothing special about any of them—as far as Nachman could tell anyway. However, it was highly odd that out of Tenebrae, a Tholus I class moon—meaning it was highly tenable and excessively fortified, as it housed some of the Alliance's worst of the worst in an underground portion of the fortress, with some of the techiest mech to come out of Ipsum—these various criminals could and would so easily escape.

Work was slow with the Liber Vultus, the movement built upon the remnants of the Liber Mortales rebellion, becoming increasingly more brazen in their protests against the Aethra construction. Nachman figured since the sovereign sector was looking a little bleak for work these days, it wouldn't hurt to do a bit of cleanup for his former employer. Nachman did have to watch those jobs even closer still. Not many of the upper echelon of the GIA wanted to hire an Arquis, a GIA-sanctioned private investigator, with possible familial ties to the unrest between the GIA and the Liber Vultus. Besides, risky as they were, Celestial-wide retributios were guaranteed to keep the lights on.

There were also a couple of things a bit quirky about the retributio in Nachman's eyes. The obvious one to Nachman was that it was open to any and all contractors. Among the various Arquis and other private contractors responding to the retributio, other not-so-reputable types often answered, those being the Vorcalus. And, by Gaia, Nachman despised being associated with those space hunters; not one of them was right in the head. Thieving, untrustworthy, disreputable space pirates. Do business with a select few of them if you absolutely had to, but keep the distance as much as you can. The lot of them spent too much time awake in the open cosmos too often. Without inducing a Qusom, you might end up on the wrong side of crazy; the pilot could vouch for the latter. The Vorcalus really could not care less that any Arquis or GIA stooge had captured 674 or any of the other thirteen escapees. They would just as soon tear the *Satyr* apart for scrap, take the clothes off Nachman's back, thieve the retributio, and leave him floating in open space to suffocate on his own sullied air. *Still worth it*, Nachman thought, *if it keeps the purifiers swirling*.

The second thing itching at Nachman, like that itch in your back you just can't seem to scratch, was that this retributio was just too easy. But like Nachman's mother always said, "Don't let your ego get in the way of survival." Openended, easy, GIA, Vorcalus all had to be tolerated if Nachman wanted to keep the *Satyr* running to traverse the Celestial and not make landfall. The open Celestial seemed like the type of peace he needed these days, regardless of the insanity risk.

Five Gaian years had passed since Nachman Rosenblatt decided to leave the GIA's elite guerrilla squads in an attempt to gain some solidarity from the institution and refresh his direction in life. Having served his mandated time in the GIA, Nachman wanted to be free of the restraints that were cast upon him even before he was even born. He had been given the option to extend his contract—but under strict observation for an incident that should have never happened. Nachman would rather keep that short story buried in the back of his incentum for a while. Before all went to alvum, he would have accepted a commission as an officer in the GIA's elite forces, the Naibus. He would have been more than willing to command his own squad. But, Nachman chose option B: he left.

The strict periodic observations throughout his free state would remain in place for the Elitists in the Bellatorius Solaris, central command for the Naibus. In Nachman's opinion, the periodic observations were less than subtle and more than periodic. The GIA still claimed him as a special case—property, more or less—among the scientific and military communities, and it was pursuant of his former employer to monitor vital GIA personnel with a former security clearance such as Nachman's. Nachman always thought if his genes hadn't had played tricks on him, he would probably have some semblance of a normal life. Instead, he was low on credits and in dire need of a decent meal that wasn't served at an outpost bar and maybe a dip in the healing fountains of a Vitachloris orbis or luna. Yeah, the spring spas of Lortaris with a nice stiff drink sounded great to Nachman right now. The GIA were nothing but pain in Nachman's side, both literally and figuratively.

Nachman's mother, Delylah, had signed a contract with the Alliance in order to save Nachman's life before it could even take shape. Nachman was unfortunately destined to be born with many congenital deformities, too many to sustain life, as a result of his mother's contact with atmospheric gases of the Noanoagan lunar outpost, Tasóa. What Noanoagans breathe as oxygen was discovered to be harmful to fetuses and prepubescents. The new element the Noanoagans introduced, iogyn, interacted with the amniotic fluid of Humans with very unfortunate genetic side effects to the fetus; otherwise, the exposure was harmless. Nachman's mother had not known she was pregnant at the time. The GIA took advantage of her blight and offered her a Paevum, a timed contract in which the GIA acquired whatever asset they deemed fortuitous to the progression of the Human species. As written in the Paevum, the GIA would inject experimental nanorobots into the womb and install a nanophage, if applicable, into the fetus in an attempt to rebuild Nachman on a cellular level.

Traditionally, a nanophage was implanted when a child came of pubescent age; however, with the abundance of nanomachines and extensive reconstruction modalities necessary, the fetus was rejecting the nanomachines, and a nanophage became applicable in the twenty-first week of Delylah's pregnancy. It was a risky procedure, painful to both mother and fetus, but she had signed the Paevum, giving the GIA permission to save her baby by any means required, which essentially gave the GIA plenty of room for experimentation. Bonding the biological components of baby Nachman with the technology of the nanomachines allowed the fetus to be rebuilt on a cellular level. The encoding and symbiosis of man and machine on this level was so intricate that only the complexity of the nanophage, implanted in the youngest recorded Human being to date, had essentially provided Nachman with his life. Nachman figured he owed the GIA a little smear of gratitude for that aspect at least—and he meant very little.

Another resulting effect of the Paevum required Delylah to "voluntarily" relinquish custody of Nachman two weeks after his thirteenth birthday to serve in the GIA for the minimum required length of service of fifteen years for the greater good of Humankind. Normally the youth of Humanity were drafted into the GIA upon their nineteenth years to serve the greater good of mankind through a variety of genetically predisposed skill surveys unless they elected for independent status. For Nachman, though, he was what was considered a special circumstance. He was automatically assigned to the Naibus Institutum, the training academy for the elite of the GIA. Everything from military tactics to geological terraforma survey was taught at this training facility.

Nachman had always felt like a science experiment his entire time in service. Test after test, the poking and prodding to his rebuilt cellular structure, the nanorobots that lay dormant in his system always gave him the sense they were going to take over, and his nanophage was the first to be placed in a fetus—*Yay*, he always thought. His nanophage, right. *And Gaia has suddenly become habitable again*, thought Nachman. The GIA scientists always praised themselves for the discovery, but Nachman was always left as an afterthought. After all, the lab coats always claimed that Nachman had "the most complex nanophage to ever adapt to a Human cerebellum." Nachman felt a bitter feeling writhe in his gut, like a snake slithering through his intestinal tunnels, as he recalled the psi-stability training in the early years of the Naibus Institutum. Hovering between the gravity tables like a fish awaiting the gutting knife. Vis wrist and ankle restraints held him down while cerebellar probes, two, sometimes three, at a time inserted themselves into the base of Nachman's skull. Stability training felt more like they were making soup of his sanity. Nachman rubbed the base of his neck as the memory caused near-perceptible pain. Nachman shook off the memory to focus on the task at hand.

"Hey, Sadie, you up?"

"Of course, Nachman, always," said his partner.

"Sadie, will you ever just call me Nach like, well, everyone else?"

"Now, Nachman, I am inside your head. I know your innermost thoughts, and I can assuredly say that you have never acquired a taste for your social moniker," said Sadie.

To the higher elite of the GIA and a majority of members of the Morsus Mihi, Sadie was a second-generation bonded perception engine, BPE, or as the beings prefer to be called, Caiets; they were capable of communicating and rendering individual thought with the programmed user. But to Nachman, Sadie was a friend, partner, and confidant who had been there almost his whole life, sometimes enduring some of the same trials as Nachman.

There were some among the GIA that have a running theory, a theory that had since been proven that Caiets were a sentient species made up entirely of the Celestial quantum energy Vis. Yet there were those who still believed that the Caiets were a mere essence of thought produced from the depths of the Human imagination. Nachman and many others contend that Caiets required a willing, symbiotic liaison with a Human in order to make their existence known in their dimension and that they are most assuredly independent sentient beings in the Human and their own dimension. Not much was known about where they are from, and no Human, as far as the GIA is aware, has yet to set foot or incentum in that dimension.

Nachman could feel the warm glow of the nanomechs in his eyes as they projected a spectacular array of color spectrum imaging, utilizing the retina as a projector so that the user could render the Caiet's avatar and manipulate the nonsentient Vis via nerve responses with the nanophage, acting as a conduit for the Vis. Any Human could see and interact with a Caiet, but only those with a nanophage could manipulate the Celestial energy. Those who had chosen to live without the Gnanimus connection relied on other palpable means of Celestial survival. Nachman's enhancements made the connection with Sadie much stronger than that of the standard bond. The GIA still found it a mystery, as did Nachman. In light of this heightened connection, Nachman learned, over time, that it also strengthened the incorporeal bond with Sadie.

A swirling mixture of green and purple Vis, like colliding gases of a distant Celestial nebula appeared in front of Nachman, and with an audible pop, Sadie's avatar appeared. Sadie rendered herself as tall and slender—"leggy," as Humans would say—with distinct and purposeful feminine features. Nachman often wondered why she chose such a forming female form, but Sadie never would say. Her body was framed by a neon-green hue encapsulating the color-changing Vis that ebbed and flowed throughout her body like a swirling, digitized mist that periodically collided with itself, bursting with bright incandescence. Her long, flowing, purple-neon hair always appeared as if the wind was slowly breezing through her locks. Sadie walked—or, rather, glided—across Nachman's field of vision, passing through the flight console as if it wasn't there and snatching the small oval holo-page from Nachman's view. Nachman shooed her away, much like he would a tervol, a pesky little skin-nibbling insect.

Sadie glided down the stairs to the open assembly area behind Nachman's pilot chair with the joyful sass of an irritating sister and snapped her fingers. She could just as easily send an incentum to manipulate the Vis, but Sadie did prefer spectacle often—too often for Nachman. A large desk—transparent brown, made to appear oaken in the vein of sixteenth-century England, complete with ornate etchings of knights in the midst of a grand celebration of mead and hog—appeared just in front of where she was standing. Sadie had always had, from the day Nachman saw her behind his incentum, a fascination with ancient Human history. She would create as many facsimiles as her incentum could produce—from ancient kettle ovens from the pioneer days of the Americas to Ushanka hats from the Soviet Union. Lucky for her, Sadie had become a mature Caiet a year ago, and only mature Caiets could manipulate Vis in the Human realm in such a manner. It wasn't established by those who believed in the Caiets' sentience how old the species are or what constituted a young or mature Caiet, but a user knew when their Caiet matured. Call it a noda —a gut feeling, Nachman always said. Sadie walked toward the desk, each footfall producing different colors of neon, Sadie's favorite tone of color. Purple, pink, green, any color in random sequence, but it was always neon. Sadie sat at the desk, crossed her legs, and began to read the files from Tenebrae as they virtually stacked up in the Vis-rendered inbox.

Nachman tilted his head up, glancing at his recaptured prisoner's file. "Sadie, continue to run through the archives of each prisoner, their stat data, criminal profiles, the works. Oh, and sift through Tenebrae's acquisition, transfer, and personnel data. Got that noda in the pit that tells me something isn't kosher."

"Give you results as quick as an incentum, Nachman," said Sadie.

With the smallest conscious thought, Nachman could interact with a biosynthetic central intelligence, the Gnanimus, governed and operated with strict oversight by the GIA. The Gnanimus was essentially the fundamental culmination of the Human experience. The Gnanimus grew along with Humanity's Auctius throughout the Celestial. As the Morsus Mihi exalted, "As our species discovers the Gnanimus discovers and with discovery the shared knowledge to all who choose to connect to the inherited data." Nachman only wished that statement rung true. The general public barely knew the half of what was going on behind closed portholes. Although any Human user could upload any information—from the discovery of the smallest rodent in the tropic planets of the Vitachlora Solaris to instructions on how to repair a demolished quantum stellar engine in deep space with life support failing, and only a sonar-driver for a tool—there was, of course, a filtering and dissemination process the GIA put all information through. Everyone knew the GIA sanctioned an abundant amount of Gnanimus outgoing data, but no one, except the Vultus and maybe a few Vorcalus pirates, spoke up about it. Nachman hadn't officially joined the Vultus movement, but he kept his ear to the ground on such matters. Anybody possessing the nanophage could connect to the Gnanimus and in turn gain the wealth of knowledge Humanity possesses. Who got that knowledge was a subject Nachman refused to debate any further, another reason he was glad to be away from the Gaian's constraints. The Gnanimus contained the capability of linking with a Human user on a level not only physiological but incorporeal. Nachman had heard the experience described as swimming through a sugar field on Venus. To Nachman, it was nothing more than opening an access port and downloading data, redundant most days.

This connection was established through a user's nanophage, a microscopic quantum computer implanted in the cerebellum, that provided an intra-Celestial connection to the Gnanimus and thus the rest of the Human race. The range seemed limitless since the discovery of the Caiets. As the user grew and matured, the Gnanimus allowed the nanophage (some simply call it a phage), to grow with the knowledge stored for the user. Nachman still believed that with this essential growth comes the continued survey of the Human experience and the infinite discoveries throughout the Celestial for all connected, but his pessimism in the standard had taken the forefront lately. *What about the rest?* he had been asking of late.

All were given a choice to have a phage—well, most anyway. With this choice, there were those that opposed the mainstream ideals and refused a phage, not trusting those in elite status, for the elite can betray trust at times, from Nachman's personal experience. Among the people, conspiracy and resistance naturally arose against an apparent oppression —the Liber Vultus being the main voice—but all, as far as Nachman knew, were still given the choice to connect to the Gnanimus. In most cases, anyone could choose to live without a phage, and any Human, barring some medical abnormality, could have a nanophage implanted any time after pubescence. Life in the Celestial could be rigorous without a phage, but those who were determined did manage. Nachman half thought those in the minority were right in refusing a phage; he had been feeling the pressing need for solitude these days.

Choice. Good, bad—Nachman always felt as if choice was something that was foreign territory in his Naibus years. Oh, and being the only known fetal bonded nanophage user had a lot to do with the path that was chosen for him. Nachman knew his mother had meant well and didn't blame her for anything. He didn't blame the GIA either (well, anymore), and frankly he was over the bitterness toward them. He just wanted to move on and be left to his own accord.

Nachman, as any connected user, could disconnect from the Gnanimus at any given time; however, once a brain became connected to the nanophage, regardless of accessing the Gnanimus, the phage must remain implanted, intact, and assimilated to the brain stem. If the nanophage was removed any time after activation, it could inflict permanent damage to the user that would ultimately lead to the user's death. These days, Nachman found being connected worthwhile, as he needed to eat; Sadie, on the other hand, could not care less about eating but would miss swimming through Human history inside the Gnanimus.

Nachman and his partner scanned through the public access files of the Tenebrae prison moon. Sadie could sense Nachman grumbling about taking on a GIA cleanup job as he scanned the files. Nachman loathed being associated with them, but "when one needs to eat, one doesn't get picky anymore," as she had heard Nachman say on occasion. Sadie took a peek beyond certain GIA firewalls in the prison system to see what was happening behind the scenes; Sadie always suspected an inside job until proven otherwise in these situations. With his eyes open, Nachman faced the *Satyr*'s forward window, but his eyes had a glazed look to them, as if he were in the midst of a dream. Nachman sifted through the prisoner records using the Gnanimus to key into specifics about prisoner 674, while Sadie continued to research every interaction each prisoner had with each other, every prisoner, visitor, and guard in the facility.

Nachman's eyes maintained the glazed cloudiness as his mind was connected to the Gnanimus. While connected, his body began to run in a state of self-conduction known as SuiMori. *Just another tool in his arsenal*, as Nachman thought; Sadie would say it was a unique talent. Most users must leave their body in a state of hibernation, vulnerable in a soldier's mind, while searching the Gnanimus. Only the Morsus Mihi, those enlisted in certain echelons of the GIA, a Naibus elite operator, or the Elitists in command could attain this skill of self-conductive awareness. While in SuiMori, the body continued to maintain autonomic functions as well as conduct activities of daily living—even those as complex as piloting the *Satyr*. Nachman connected to the Gnanimus, studying the prisoner files, all the while, behind the automaticity, Nachman's subconsciousness was still in full control, allowing him to complete multiple tasks within seconds. Nachman always wondered why the Morsus Mihi won't let the mainstream learn SuiMori; it wasn't that difficult, and it saved loads of time.

The incandescence dimmed in the cabin to a soft glow. Sadie nodded in Nachman's direction and became silent, less than a whisper. She could hear the hum from the Vis holo-monitor with how quiet she felt. Nachman felt active nanites in the left ocumech dilate his pupil and begin deciphering the code on the screen, sending the algorithms to his phage, receiving all the information at speeds he could only imagine. It felt like a tickle inside the nape of his neck every time. Nachman's nano-filaments attached to his phage sensed the binary interfaces in the *Satyr*'s control console, and before the alarm sounded, indicating that flaring in the aging quantum stellar engine of the *Satyr*, Nachman's body was already reacting. Still glossy-eyed, he reached for a toggle switch on the Vis interface that activated a coolant flow into the Genus 2v dual quantum engines. Nachman thought it was a far cry from the Genus 6d synchronous quantum engines the GIA had floating in the cosmos these days. The engines on the *Satyr* had been due for an upgrade six cycles ago; however, Nachman thought he was savvy enough with a sonar wrench that he could keep the engines running for at least another cycle.

"You know full well they are going to give out within half that time, Nachman," replied Sadie as she read through the documents, glimpsing the incentum across her processes.

Nachman rolled his eyes purposefully while his mind was still scanning Prisoner 674's profile, plucking the information from the Gnanimus as if he were searching through a filing cabinet. Sadie recognized Nachman's juvenile gesture, known to happen when a Human is more annoyed than upset. Sadie smirked as she knew too well that after all this time with Nachman, she was still amused by the irrational complexities of the Human emotional spectrum. Sadie sat at the holo-desk, forever bemused by Nachman's infantile actions, thumbing through documents from Tenebrae she had synthesized from the Gnanimus. All the while Nachman had already finished compiling all the prisoner information, including personal and professional histories and in chronological order, quick and efficient.

Nachman knew Sadie was a methodical being when it suited her mood—timely, precise, and extremely efficient—but she loved to slow herself down, to a fault at times, and absorb all around her rather than rely on the Gnanimus to directly feed her information in less than a nanosecond. Nachman usually enjoyed her recreations, the melding of time periods, but sometimes he needed her to just focus on the job. For this occasion, Sadie not only chose the grand sixteenth-century oak table but a brown leather high-back cushioned chair, one with the rivets inlaid around the seat back and armrests. Nachman swore she rendered the damned thing every other day. On the corner was an old-style banker's lamp, just like the one from the old detective novels she likes to read, and a parallel stack of manila filing folders were overpiled and tilting on one corner of the desk. Nachman often related his level of annoyance with her in these situations to a sister poking at her brother just because he has a toy she wants.

"Sadie, I swear, the more time you spend fabricating those elaborate images, the less is spent doing actual casework."

"You have your process, and I have mine," said Sadie as she straightened in her chair, her eyes widening as she read one of her faux printouts. "And I believe that I have found something of a minuscule breach in Tenebrae's fortitude, Nachman."

Nachman shifted his right hand on his armrest, easing a joystick that turned his chair to face Sadie on the far side of the cabin. With his left, he reached for a long, unkempt beard. Nachman's beard was stringy and long, flowing to the crest of his sternum. His eyes were youthful, hiding the wisdom and strength of a seasoned soldier, deceptive to those who do not know him. A pearl-white adhesion bisecting his left ocular cavity protruded ever so slightly from the dermis. The ocu-mech that was now his left eye, replaced when he was still a toddler, was spliced directly into his oculomotor nerve; it silently whirred as it focused on Sadie across the *Satyr*.

Fabricating the cockpit of the *Satyr* was the most complicated but the most fun part of the overhaul. The refit took away all likeness of a traditional Parixia bomber. Nachman, Sadie, and a substantial set of Ipsum rep-mechs had spent the better part of the autumn season stationed coolly underground on the only derelict planet in Sapietás Solaris, Sandere, with the exception of the monks of course, fabricating and customizing the rusted space junker into a home. The titiconium hatch that separated the cockpit stairs and cabin had been removed, as well as all the partitions that had separated each compartment of the *Satyr*, with the exception of the quantum engine room, to shield from particulates exhausting from the older model engines, the visitor's quarters, and Nachman's quarters. The only area of privacy Nachman needed were in his quarters, a place to rest and contemplate when needed. Nachman figured since he had to make a home out of a rusted bombardier stellarcraft, he wanted the fewest walls possible. What better way than to keep an eye on passengers than in an open ship? Nachman had major trust issues indeed. The openness appealed to Nachman anyway; one day he would have that...one day he would retire on a deserted island on a lush Vitachloran orbis. For now, his ship would have to do as a home, office, and sanctuary.

"The culprit is an ether-virus, now dormant, embedded in Tenebrae's mainframe. It was only set to target the locking mechanisms of the fourteen prisoners' containment units as well as the cameras in each hall for the specific time allotted to make escape undetected," Sadie said as the corner of her lip curled into a curious smirk. "And coincidentally the virus was not that hard to find, as if it were overlooked with intent."

"What do you think Sadie? Inside job?" grunted Nachman.

"Seems as such from the coincidental oversight," Sadie commented.

"It's no wonder the retributio is open and Celestial-wide; most of these guys claiming it don't ask too many questions. Alvum, I can't stand when my gut is right," Nachman said.

Nachman turned back toward the main console, resting his right elbow on the armrest, still stroking his thickly peppered goatee, twirling the tip in earnest with his index finger while peering out of the double pane forward window at the Tracaelus Solaris, the youngest colonized solaris in the GIA. Well, if you would call just over a hundred years old young. The deepest into the Celestial yet, nothing but an abyss waiting to welcome or annihilate the Human race. *To travel deeper into the Celestial would be a feat beyond imagination—and down-right frightening*, Nachman thought.

Nachman thought carefully about where to go from here with the evidence presented: a) Was keeping the lights on worth the risk of being stabbed in the back, again? Because that noda was telling him it would happen again with the swelling conspiracy brewing with this case. And b) Were these measly credits, the credits he needed to keep the *Satyr* afloat and keep the galley stocked with provisions for the treks ahead, that his gracious former handlers were offering for this piece of alvum in his cargo hold—was that worth taking the risk? Nachman shrugged, smiled, and sat up a little straighter in his worn, high-backed and bucketed, faded, nebula-blue captain's chair. *Well, at least it's not my ego this time, Ma*, Nachman thought.

Nachman glanced at the flight display, checking the engine status—the coolant seemed to have calmed them for now—and the video feed of the prisoner who appeared to have nodded off. The neon-blue Vis display defied gravity as it floated like leaves skidding on a pond during a breezy autumn morning in familiar patterns of flight controls, and a blend of

Human languages spoken by most throughout the Gaian Inter-planetary Alliance. The Vis display projecting from the console showed navigation controls and stellar-mapping coordinates, quantum fuel, Vis storage meters, and hull integrity to the left and to the right all radar and sensor readout and lexcom communication arrays. Beneath the console were the manual fight controls in case of emergency or when Nachman wanted to slow down himself. Those times seemed few and far between to him these days. The Vis was fully contained inside the hardened console with transparency shielding to allow for ease of manipulation but containment of the Vis. Nachman could sculpt the Vis with his hands or an incentum; most of the time, Nachman preferred the hands-on method. The console, the main flight deck of the *Satyr*, served as the entire upper deck of the main cabin. Wide windows showed a panoramic view of the Celestial as he swam through the stars. Nachman's chair was retrofitted with zero-gravity technology (ZG tech). Three small pads covered the underside of the chair with three other pads attached to a two-meter-wide zero-gravity track, allowing the chair to glide along the base of the console as if it were the grand chair at the organ of the Aedis Caelesti, the Church of the Celestial, with Nachman as the maestro of the *Satyr*'s orchestra.

A large colorful news logo flashed on the display Sadie didn't snatch away. Nachman glanced at the media broadcast to the left and above the flight controls. A tall, lanky Noanoagan with dull green and teal coloring and a short, pudgy Human served as the news anchoring team. They gave an intense briefing on a situation that had unfolded on Tasóa a few hours ago. Nachman always had the interstellar news broadcast running, specifically ICB, Independent Celestial Broadcasters—no-muss-no-fuss reporting, and their reputation preceded them. Nachman had a few journalist acquaintances from Ducovímus he kept handy for the tight, undisclosed situations. Nachman paid no mind to the broadcast unless there was relevance to a current caseload. This newscast, though, was a touchy one. He kept it muted but couldn't help but glance at the bold magenta underwriting scrolling smoothly on the bottom of the feed: *Tragedy in Tasóa—Twelve Hours Ago, One Half of Noanoagan Orimer Assassinated Moments before Unification Speech.*

"That's such a shame. Orimers Buhai and Tejwenn were a driven force for good and showed such promise in bringing Humanity together, stronger again," Sadie said from across the cabin, already sensing the news feed through her link with the *Satyr*.

"Yeah, maybe they shouldn't have been so public about it," Nachman responded. "And isn't it funny how it took aliens to get the Elitists and the Vultus to sit back down at the negotiation table?"

"You can be too cynical sometimes, my dear Nachman."

"Well, if you look at it, they are fighting over something that doesn't even require death and destruction to get the point across," Nachman said.

"Much as your species has been doing since the beginning." Sadie smirked at the anticipated rhetoric.

Nachman looked in Sadie's direction but ignored her and continued as if uninterrupted. "Look, if you don't want to go out past the rim of the known and see what is out in the deep, deep Celestial, then don't. Stay at home, do your job, and stay out of it. If they want to go, then let them go; there is absolutely no need to pick up a weapon and blast somebody because they want to go explore the rest of the universe. Alvum, I don't want to go out there, and I'm perfectly content not killing anybody over it."

Sadie said nothing. She knew Nachman had his own philosophies on life and the universe, and most she agreed with, which is one among many reasons she had been with him so long. Sadie let Nachman stew, saying nothing, and continued researching the prisoners' backgrounds, which happened to be quite intriguing in a historical sense.

Nachman stewed, knowing it was the same old rant he

has always told. Nachman always tried to play the neutral but always leaned on the side of what was right. Nachman sat back stroking his goatee, his chalky eyes stutter-stepping in his sockets as he sifted through the Tenebrae database. The mugshots of the fourteen prisoners appeared at the end of the file stack. Nachman sent the incentum to pull all mugshots with criminal history, known associates, and relatives and moved them to the table display in front of his chair; the current detainee, Prisoner 674, was at the top of the stack. Nachman perused through the file and allowed the Gnanimus to link to his nanophage and download all other information into his mind-files. The rest he preferred to read; it seemed more intimate for Nachman on these up-close occasions. He felt he could get to know the case a bit better if he saw the eyes of those involved—a key to the mind, the eyes always are, the monks said.

Nachman shook his head. He sure didn't like the fact Sadie got him riled up at times. Sadie could get into Nachman's head as easy as he could get into a perp's. The fact that Sadie spent 60 percent of her time inside Nachman's mind was beside the point, but she only did that when she was trying to point something out. That thought prompted Nachman to look at the news feed, and it enlarged into a smooth but oblong oval. Nachman turned up the volume with a brainwave.

The scene had moved from the newsroom to that of the incident. The reporter, a young man in his early twenties, was standing outside of the brightly colored Noanoagan dignitary offices in the parliament of Tasóa. Small buildings, smooth and angular to represent the planet of Noanoaga from ancient times, where there were masses of GIA magistrates; Noanoagan delegates and members of the Fale'aloa (Fale for short—the Noanoagan peacekeepers); and hundreds of civilians from both species. Naibus recruits, in the Bellatorius dust-red body armor and white cargo pants, were being used as perimeter guards keeping the crowd at bay but were beginning to have a hard time keeping the Noanoagan civilians behind the titiconium barricades, as they were twice the size of an average adult male with the strength and endurance to bolster the size.

The Noanoagans resembled what ancient Humans would link to the legend of the Sasquatch or Yeti from the tales of pre-GIA history. The Noanoagans said long-range scout ships were launched prior to the mother ship launch from their home planet had managed to make it to pre-Convergence Gaia, where they hid out among the ice and forest, collecting research data and identifying various cultural and biological facts to one day adapt to the ways of life on Gaia with Humans—that is, until the Convergence.

The Gaian Noas, as they came to be referred to, lived out their days on Gaia, communications severed with their mother ship, and became the legend Humans know still to this day with truth brought into the legend. Some were brown and white like the stories, but the species is a sea of color—blues, purples, oranges—and all were full of hairlike follicles from pointed ears to three-toed feet. The species stood from the shortest recorded of 1.5 to tallest of 4.5 meters tall. Their snouts varied from short to long, but all of their cranial structures could be compared to that of an ape, like the Yeti and Sasquatch. The piercing of the ears with large jewels or hoops and a colorful array of body art were common among the species for various cultural reasons, such as identifying a family's lineage or a cultural title. They were usually known as a docile species with not much of a threatening temperament unless provoked. Unfortunately, today one of their most revered and respected high council members was murdered. And out of all six members, the one killed was the Orimer, who represented sentient peace among the vast dark of the sacred sea, the Fayaía (Fā-yā-ee-ā). Today they had reason to feel provoked.

The noticeably short on-site reporter flicked back a lock of neon-yellow hair that had been covering his ear, tapped the small earpiece, and with his with his best attempt not to look as jittery as a kid singing his first solo, pointed over his shoulder and broke the news to the masses: "The scene behind us is one of confusion, sadness, and discontent, as we have witnessed the unpredicted and unprecedented assassination of one of the most prominent crusaders in the unification between not only Noanoagan and Human but Humanity within itself."

The camera cut to the crowd behind the barricades and security forces. Humans and Noa alike wept for the fallen ambassador. The camera cut back to the reporter, now looking media solemn. "The female half of the Orimer, one of the six of the high council of Noanoagans, Buhai has been slain and her male *Nafusma*." At the bottom of the feed in italics, the translation of the Noanoagan word and proper pronunciation in English read *Nafusma* (Nā-foos-mā), meaning *bonded*. "Tejwenn has been designated as missing without contact. The Naibus and Fale have initiated intelligence gathering into the whereabouts of the assassin. With search teams out among the terraluna and surrounding orbit, it is only a matter of time before both Human and Noanoagan councils have answers for the civilian populace."

The news report continued with flashes of footage from the assassination, crowd reactions, and political interviews, as Nachman muted the feed again. *The kid is quite articulate for being that nervous*, Nachman thought.

Nachman leaned back in his chair, letting all of the information he had just received from the intelligence gathering and news-feed process. Who would want to assassinate a member of the Noanoagan high council who was a proponent for not only peaceful relations between Noa and Human but the discontinuation of development of the Aethra Gateway? *To deliberately divide the two species and get the Vultus stirring again for good reason*, Nachman thought.

The Orimer, one of the six positions of the Noanoagan high council, believed the gateway could only bring anguish for both species. Another species said it's a bad idea—yet another reason Nachman ventured to stay in his part of the

Celestial. Nachman could already rule out the Liber Vultus; the Noanoagans and the rebels always had good standings between one another. The GIA couldn't risk a breakdown in commerce, political influences, or interspecies relations for the sake of the Aethra Gateway, and therefore the Gaian Alliance, mainly the mainstream Elitists, those who supported the construction of the thing anyway, could be eliminated as well. Who would benefit from this in the slightest? *Seems kind of odd that the prison break was a week before the assassination —a little too coincidental*, Nachman thought. Besides, none of these prisoners even remotely fit an assassin's profile.

Sadie sensed Nachman's mind opening, making the connection between the murder and the prison break, looking at the puzzle piece that seemed out of place to her deductions. Sadie looked up from stack of Vis-generated papers, wearing a pair of bright-blue neon reading glasses from the 1950s just for the fun of it, and smiled. Her aura's luminescence brightened as she knew Nachman would pick up on the subtle connection she saw between the timing of the breakout and the assassination. Sadie had always been a bit prideful in the fact she was a tiny bit faster than Nachman at solving puzzles. *He has always been the most quick-witted when his mind is stirred a bit*, Sadie thought softly so Nachman didn't overhear.

With that incentum, Sadie had another. Without looking up, Sadie slid her finger down, cutting open the air beside her as if she were tearing the fabric of space-time and reached in, pulling a stack of Vis-rendered files from nowhere. Sadie wanted to take a quick moment and search through a bit of historical data on Human and Noanoagan relations. And being a history aficionado, Sadie kept detailed records of both species' collective histories.

The Tracaelus Solaris began as the final tenet in the grand design the Morsus Mihi had for the Human race. Although Tracaelus would represent the last tenet of the guide to the Auctius, Humans were not going to cease their colonization of the Celestial. The Morsus Mihi proclaimed the

Cordrego, lord in command, of Tracaelus to be the herald of the tenet of stellar travel and exploration. The spiritual and scientific communities saw this Solaris as a stepping-stone to a great crusade of everlasting discovery and broader horizons for Humanity. Even before the historic meeting between the Noanoaga and the flagship intergalactic vessel *Gaian Alpha* eighty-one years ago, the system was twenty years into all terraforma and lunar construction operations.

Gaian Alpha was two weeks into a six-week mission, one of the last training exercises before final departure into the uncharted territory of deep-space. Engine and flight testing as well as personnel training operations when radar pinged a massive, dormant spacecraft that, at first, appeared to be a derelict vessel. Boarding parties were sent, finding tens of thousands of viable ilaita, a Noanoagan word meaning "breath pod," the Noanoagan version of a hypersleep chamber. The crew of the *Gaian Alpha* attached Vis generated towing lines, stronger than the densest titiconium alloy, to the massive vessel and towed it back to Tracaelus. GIA scientists utilized the Gnanimus, with the assistance from the Caiets, and began their exhaustive effort in deciphering the alien technology to awaken the dormant species. Within fourteen months, with a few unforeseen casualties, Noanoagan and Human, the majority of the species had been awakened. Humans could now learn the story of the Noanoaga.

The Noanoagans had been traversing the cosmos for fourteen generations searching for a new home, as theirs was destroyed by a global geothermal catastrophe similar to Gaia. The species survived in space, as Humanity had but without the advancement of terraforma. As the Noanoagans went from galaxy to galaxy, their whole species inhabiting one massive stellar cruiser, they say they had never come across any source of life or a planet capable of supporting their biology, so they kept to the stars, hoping to find something—anything—to settle. Their vessel finally stumbled upon the Human race at the edge of the Milky Way galaxy. Humanity welcomed their Celestial neighbors as the Morsus Mihi proclaimed an everlasting peace with the Noanoagans.

The Noanoagans were adamant believers in an ideal they called shared species evolution. When they departed their home planet just before its demise, they made a mandate to share their technology and culture with any species they would come into contact with in the Fayaía. The Noanoagans shared numerous technological advances, including various engine and stellar vessel upgrades, hypersleep technology, medicines, biotech enhancements, with collaborative advancements in cellular biology and genetic manipulation for the donation of the terraluna, Tasóa. When Tasóa completed terraformation, the Noanoagans shared their culture, ideals, and society with Humanity. But to the GIA elite, it was nothing compared to what would be the ultimate gift from the alien species.

The Noanoagans had designed a gateway that could not only manipulate the interdimensional energy Vis but use that energy to propel a stellar cruiser into another galaxy, but they lacked the means to manipulate the materials to utilize the technology. The Morsus Mihi were more than obliged for the sake of the Auctius, of course.

The Aethra Gateway was a gargantuan megalith; some said it was as big as Gaia's moon, and it was a revolutionary leap forward constructed with megatons of titiconium and other precious metals, many not of this end of the Celestial and donated by the Noas, with the intention of propelling the willing across the unknown. The Aethra was held in a sustained position by gravity attenuators and had been forged, bolted, and laser-fused together by numerous Human and Noanoagan engineers over the course of twenty-six years. It was now mere months from full operation to allow Humanity to leave that part of the Celestial and travel to another in the time it took to flip a switch and jettison a sump unit into space. For these formidable years, a common goal, among the mounting respect and appreciation between two species, had been waiting to be attained by the whole, the ability to travel to another Celestial faster than the speed of light. As Sadie further read the history of this interspecies collaboration, she could sense Nachman's unyielding discomfort toward the thought of the Aethra Gateway being fully operational.

Nachman was eleven and still with his mother, Delylah, living on the seventh luna orbiting the Sapiétas Command Orbis Malus Navis, Terraluna Diiu, doing their best to stay as far off the GIA's radar until the fateful day they would come for her child when the Aethra Gateway began construction. He had known then what Tasóa's atmosphere had done to him before he was born and what his mother sacrificed to keep him alive. When he was a boy, he held a strong sense of discontent toward the new species, as though what had happened to his genes was their fault. A slight twinge of that feeling had never gone away, much like a chronic rash. Nachman always felt uneasy at the fact that the Noanoagans were so willing to not only share all of their technology but help the Human race travel to another Celestial by building the Aethra Gateway.

Nachman could never get over the fact that while the Noanoagans were extremely technologically advanced, they just seemed to know but could never fully explain the inner workings of their type of quantum fusion generators, theories of virtual photon manipulation, and the delicacy of the forging of precious xenometals to make the gateway possible. To Nachman, it didn't seem like they developed anything; rather, it was just downloaded to their species like a piece of literature was downloaded to his nanophage. He had Noanoagan friends, and they had never shown any indications of bad intentions, but Nachman had always been not suspicious so much as curious as to the Noanoagans' true intentions. *Eighty years to plan an invasion. Just get it over with,* Nachman thought.

Nachman, I have said this to you time and again: these particular creatures do not intend us harm and will help the Human race. Have faith, my friend. Sadie projected the incentum, as Nachman would become increasingly defensive when the topic was spoken aloud. Psi-speak: Nachman was still getting used to it.

Scoffing, Nachman turned his attention to the captive in his cargo bay. He looked up and to the right at the screen with his prisoner. Four camera angles levitated inside the border as if they were floating on water. Nachman's pupils dilated; the image that was angled down in the right corner of the hold zoomed in on Prisoner 674. Nachman's pupils dilated again; the image augmented to see 674's face fill the screen. Nachman squinted at the image, noticing the prisoner's eyes were closed and his head slightly tilted back. *Cute. Mr. Vulgar finally wore himself out. Things are peaceful when people just shut up once in a while,* Nachman thought. Sadie glared at him from across the *Satyr,* knowing toward whom the comment was directed.

Nachman zoomed out once more to be sure he was still bound to the cargo chair that was bolted to the middle of the bay. The prisoner's feet were bound to the chair, and his torso was looped with a pliable synthetic titiconium rope connected on either side to a titiconium brace attached to the hull. The titiconium ties were virtually unbreakable, even if the prisoner had nano-enhancements embedded into his soft tissue. *Lessons learned the hard way,* Nachman thought. He slowly enhanced and enlarged the image again. The prisoner's neon-blue lips were tattooed with various geometric shapes, slightly parted, his Adam's apple slowly bobbing up and down.

"What the alvum is he doing? Talking in his sleep?" Nachman said aloud. Nachman had a sense about him. Some of Nachman's friends, the ones that were few and far between and could truly call Nachman a friend for a variety of reasons, called it a pessimistic view on vitae, or "life," as some of the elders from Sapietás traditionally called it. But Nachman had always felt an innate reaction to people or situations that were not showing the best interest of his or those he cared for vitae. The lies, the deceit, the general discontent across the

Celestial—for some reason, Nachman had always been able to see past the facades that people put in front of themselves.

Being good for the sake of being good was always the best laid plan, but when you have mice attempting to be men, then the naivety of the good message gets thrown into the Celestial, and all you have left is the sting of deceit left in the wake of the true intention. Nachman had known he had a good heart once when he was younger. Hell, he even thought there could even be some left. Who said he was the pessimist?

Nachman looked at the monitor again, and when he did, the image magnified to bring the blue-neon lips into full view. They were moving. "Aw, hell!" Nachman felt the cybernetic arm lunge at him before the damned thing had even moved. He threw his arms up in a defensive position, elbows bent, fingers curled, wrists loose, ready for the attack. Nachman grabbed the wrist of the advancing arm, fighting to keep the fingers from crushing his throat like a vise. The microboosters at the elbow and bicep flared; the amputated limb accelerated, slipping Nachman's grip momentarily. Nachman could feel the cold metallic sting of the fingertips barely nick his throat just before his hand clasped over the cybernetic arm. Nachman pinched the nanocluster where the radial nerve should have been, paralyzing the fingers. The fingers might have been limp, but that didn't prevent the microboosters from flaring again and trying to put another hole in Nachman's face. With his variety of enhancements, including a completely cybernetic left arm, Nachman's strength was two times the average. As Nachman applied more pressure, the circuitry of the robotic arm sparked and fizzled. A warm, viscous sludge oozed out of the holes Nachman's fingers made. The arm went limp. Nachman threw it away; it hit the deck with a loud clang. Nachman saw the right arm crawling to the cargo bay release switch; 674 was going to space himself. Without warning, Nachman was floating; that crafty prisoner used the arm's wiring to worm out of the joint and shut off the gravity manipulators. Nachman couldn't reach the arm as he floated in the opposite direction.

"Sadie, shut down his phage! Now!" yelled Nachman.

Even before the arm launched itself at Nachman, Sadie had already teleported herself one deck below into the cargo bay to assess the prisoner. Prisoner 674 had been chanting in a soft, rhythmic tone, almost the way a father would coo to his child, while the geometric tattoos on his lips had a soft-purple glow gleaming off them. Sadie admired the sophistication of the design, nanotransmitters ebbed into the soft tissue of the prisoner's lip, inquisitive. Sadie tilted her head as if an unknown sound had caught her ear; she didn't need to hear Nachman to know what to do. Her image whisked away, leaving a subtle neon-green trail in her wake. Sadie disappeared into the ether of the Gnanimus.

Darkness enveloped Sadie, the aura of neon green around her the only light to show the way as she plummeted into nothing. But the void held no fear for Sadie; she knew where the abyss would take her. No Human would ever see the depths of the Gnanimus as a Caiet could. The Gnanimus was an interdimensional segue of pure Celestial quantum energy, Vis. Through the darkness Sadie saw an infinite number of wonders. What Humans have yet to set an eye on, only theorize and ponder, the Caiets have felt more than once. Sadie had spoken in length to Nachman about the finite imbrication of the Gnanimus and the opening into her realm. What Nachman understood was that the Gnanimus acted as an intricate web of connection, with the core being the Gnanimus mainframe inside the thick ore of Olympus Mons on Mars. Nachman saw a machine, cold and calculated, but Sadie saw an amusement of color waiting to behold. The bright, silken threads inside the mainframe made up the web, which represented individual pathways into a Human being's nanophage. Caiets glided along these pathways to reach the nanophage they sought.

Sadie felt so comfortable here in between realms; the almost pure sensation of the Gnanimus mainframe filled her senses as the darkness faded away. The threaded nanophage pathways opened up in front of her felt like a flower blooming in her soul. Sadie had always been enthralled with the millions upon millions of intertwined techno-organic filaments, each leading to an individual Human user somewhere in the Celestial. Sadie admired the soft glow of each filament; she could always swear the glow smelled like vanilla beans when it pinged her aura. In the equivalent of less than a millisecond, Sadie had traveled the ethereal essence of the Gnanimus to the intergalactic superhighway of neural connection to 674's nanophage. Sadie, with some innate sense, easily found 674's filament, which Caiets saw as a string of an instrument like a guitar or violin. Caiets called this an acrofibra, whereas Humans, having no concept of the inside of the Gnanimus, just call the neural connection a Gnan-string. Because Nachman's nanophage, psyche, and all-around essence was familiar to Sadie, she always was elated to enter another nanophage as it was like sneaking a peek into the window of another's essence. The soul, to Sadie, was something more than a set of neural connections but a wondrous opportunity for expanding knowledge of the Human condition that could easily unravel into an eternal and most unrelenting break from reality. *Tread lightly*, Nachman had told her.

Sadie stepped into the permeable membrane of the acrofibra; the sensation of rolling water smoothly flowed around her aura. Sadie was still unable to create a gravity field beneath her, so she let the wind of energy take her, twisting and twirling her body and legs, straight arms extended like a bird all with a childlike smile as she flew through the acrofibra. She was surrounded by the soft, white light like a warm blanket wrapped around her, and the smell of jasvinder, a sweet, hybrid flower engineered in Crescat, filled her nares. *The flower must have been important to 674*, thought Sadie.

Sadie knew she was coming to the end of the acrofibra as the color of the filament changed, but it was nothing like she expected. Sadie has seen acrofibra change color to reflect the user's current state of mind, but this was curious. Instead of anxious or angry colors such as reds or oranges, 674's neural pathway was a calming lavender. Sadie disregarded the curiosity, as she had a mission at hand. She was always eager to interface with another mind, even if it was a less-than-desirable psychological makeup and maybe the opportunity to interface with another Caiet. Sadie craved variety when it came to social contacts; on a case or transport, Sadie would do the talking, always interacting with another consciousness from an outer perspective. To experience a psyche internally was like being whisked into a spectacular palette of color that flows in and out of your very being. The spark of any mind was enough to fuel Sadie's curiosity for universal knowledge and the Human psyche. Sadie, with a breadth of hesitation, came to the end of the acrofibra and entered the prisoner's mind.

Her smile faded; utter despair seemed to wash over her as the cold veil of darkness overcame the light. It immediately became apparent that something was overtaking the prisoner's mind, with a relentless force that seemed oddly familiar. The current of living electricity that was meant to be firing through the bundles of gyri and sulci was being engulfed by an oily, abysmal sludge. It dripped and oozed down the organic walls; at times, large globules would slowly hang down from the ceiling, eventually splashing into a puddle beneath. Sadie floated to the organic wall and slid a finger down the sludge. The sludge felt similar to asteroid tar but with granules moored in. Sadie knew she had seen this before—but where?

An excruciating pain like a searing-hot coal shot through her finger. Sadie almost screamed as the slime started to visibly erode her aura, which also acted as a protective shielding, but she could feel everything. She temporarily flared her aura, causing the goo to fall off. The bit of ooze slithered purposefully back to the ooze on the brain wall. *The slime felt like it was trying to root itself inside my aura*, Sadie thought. It was a substance that could injure and possibly kill a Caiet. This did not bode well.

Sadie saw the ooze closing the way into the brainstem. A small hole, Sadie's body folded in on itself like folding a piece of paper and vanished. Sadie materialized more than twenty times smaller than her previous size inside 674's brainstem, the housing core of prisoner 674's nanophage. The cavity was large and cavernous by proportion, the walls flush with organic microchips alive with a dark voltage firing through a series of tendrils ending at one point in the center of the chamber where the phage sat. Prisoner's 674's Caiet, if one could call it that anymore, was a wide, bulky, almost-gorilla-featured form that stood in the middle of the chamber, unmoving. The Vis inside the dark neon indigo aura was pulsating, as the attached tendrils seemed to feed the massive monstrosity.

Sadie noticed the form was faceless and smooth with absolutely no features at all. *Oh no*, thought Sadie, *this isn't a Caiet; this is an Automaton*. A blank slate programmed to do the bidding of the programmer, only—and not a Caiet in the least. A synthetic, barren creature made by mad GIA scientists who thought brainwashing people to the ways of the Gaian Alliance was the way to unite the populace. Sadie recalled from Tenebrae's records that Prisoner 674 never activated the algorithm to accept a Caiet. How this monstrosity was implanted, Sadie didn't know right away, but whoever was behind the latent implant probably had something to do with the breakout, she concluded. Sadie put aside her suspicion; Nachman was going to scream conspiracy when she told him.

Sadie continued to survey the creature, her senses heightened as fear crept up her aura. The Automaton's arms and legs seem twisted and coiled like a child's candy with multiple tendrils protruding from its torso. These tendrils appeared to be embedded into the techno-organic interface between the cerebellum and the nanophage, the Ignivalo. The nanophage itself was still where it should be, melded into the brainstem. Small enough as to not cause any damage to the user as well as sending a genetic transmission to the immune

What was next to the scope struck Nachman as odd but eerily familiar. A rifle barrel, slip and lock, lengthened to promote further range. All that seemed normal for a rifle barrel but the shape. The triangular shape is for a very specific type of armin, or in older words, ammunition. *It couldn't be*, thought Nachman, *that's not possible*. To be sure what he was seeing in front of him, Nachman needed to break down the barrel and look at the rifling. Nachman shook his head and looked up at Sadie. Sadie could see Nachman was pale, like he had been fully exsanguinated, his eyes holding the edge of panic and despair that she had only seen a handful of times. Sadie was the one of the only beings besides one other to see a look of perpetual sadness wash over Nachman's face.

Nachman zoomed in on the rifle barrel. He took the image in between his thumb and forefinger on his left hand and pulled it out of the phavix. The barrel seemed to be still attached to the Vis inside the phavix like a piece of rubber being stretched. The original image remained in the phavix portal but latent Vis, LV, stored in the phavix allowed for 3-D analysis and gave the rifle barrel palpability. Nachman was able to manipulate the rifle barrel in any matter, but only for a limited amount of time. Sadie had downloaded a sufficient amount of information from the Ignivalo of 674's nanophage for visual analysis in the phavix, but unfortunately there was an insufficient amount of LV stored in the *Satyr*'s mainframe for prolonged manipulate of the memory. Nachman had been running on a skeletal number of supplies and rations; trekking the Celestial with the idea of a paying job has been foreboding as of late. Rising political tensions between rebels and the GIA would do that to a sympathizer. The construction of the Aethra Gateway in conjunction with current state of political relations with the Noanoaga didn't sit well with the Vultus leadership.

The time constraints forced Nachman to use a part of him he kept buried, a part of him that made him feel less than Human. There were nano-enhancements Nachman did not mind using: the ocular tech in his left eye allowing for increase distance and magnification analysis, the stamina and strength given by the muscular and tissue mods, and other alterations. Nachman could control those aspects of the tech, the mods, but never the neurotic realization that he cannot live without them. But these nanites made him a bit fearful of himself.

The nanites in his cerebral cortex enhanced his higher brain function even when they lay dormant in the recesses of his brain. Problem solving, critical thinking, mathematical equations, to physiological responses and psionic communication were all already high-functioning, given Nachman's existing genetic makeup. These cerebral nanites could unlock levels of cognitive functioning and sensory input; so many sensations would pour into Nachman that it became overwhelming. Nachman's entire brain was opened to the universe on some level equivalent to the quantum computing of the Gnanimus that both he and the GIA were never capable of understanding. This higher level of brain function in conjunction with the microscopic robots gave way to an insidious envelopment of Nachman's personality. Nachman would lose himself in his own mind, a deep chasm of thought, a whirlpool of universal concepts and understanding of things yet to be fathomed into existence. Nachman could swim in this sea of contemplation and never return for the blanketed comfort that the entire universe is whole and with him on a level of true Celestial understanding. Nachman felt the control of self vital to survival in the ever-growing unknown of the Celestial. Sadie had been helping Nachman keep his sanity as well as teaching him how not to control the nanites but coexist with them.

The cerebral nanites had been specially designed to lay in remission, dormant until Nachman activated them, in microscopic, self-contained capsules. These particular nanites could not evacuate themselves from his body without damaging his brain. Nachman had explored many avenues to rid himself of what he saw as pests. Nachman's brain held five of these capsules with just over one hundred nanites apiece.

Nachman hated this part. It often made him feel trapped in his own psyche, caged like the exotic cats he used to see at the Celestial circus when he was young. Nachman's body froze, unable to induce SuiMori until the nanites had completed the analysis. At least with SuiMori, the nanites were still dormant, and Nachman had control; he felt safe with SuiMori. Sadie took over control of the *Satyr*'s flight plan and all other function of the ship while Nachman was stuck in the cavea of his consciousness.

Sadie's aura softened a shade, a forest green much like a fern fresh from a morning dew. Concern shown on her face as the corners of her lips curved downward. Sadie continued to feed the data from the spike ready to cut the feed if stimulus became unbearable for Nachman. Sadie had seen Nachman perform this ability many times before in the service of the GIA, and every time she felt what Nachman felt: always an unspoken terror in the moment he felt he was losing his sense of self.

Nachman's fingers became a flurry, barely visible as they dance in the air with faint, ever so faint, streaks of red Vis stemming from the tips of his nails to the faux barrel. The LV representation of the weapon's barrel was glowing a bright red but slowly fading as Nachman examined it from all possible angles. The way the barrel rotated on its axis, tilting and rolling was like liquid in a glass contained but ready to pour over. No Human who wasn't augmented to the extent of Nachman could manipulate Vis or any other tech to this magnitude. Nachman knew of only a handful of people who could do this, and no one else in the Celestial had as many mods as he had— to his knowledge anyway.

Nachman could only stay in the background, trapped behind an invisible force inside the cavea of his consciousness, watching the nanites control his body from the various lobes of his cerebellum. The microrobots were feeding algorithmic data to his sensory organs and fine motor functions at rates almost equivalent to the Gnanimus itself. He always felt as if they were taking over his body, controlling him. Nachman wanted to scream. He began pacing in the cavea, a small enclosure inside his cerebellar chamber that looked like a translucent bubble. The program the nanites ran would never allow interference from Nachman's waking consciousness; thus, Sadie had created the cavea for him, a place where he could see everything. "I still can control the pieces of alvum," Nachman would say.

A console resembling the main flight console of the *Satyr* sat in the middle of the cavea. Sadie could never get Nachman to calm down enough to keep the shape of anything in the cavea, as the console appeared distorted, as if it had passed through a fun-house mirror and never regained its original shape. Nervously, Nachman wrapped his hands around themselves; his hand rubbed the crest of his head, pushed his wavy hair back, then brought his hands down the side of his face around to his beard. Alvum, he hated these feelings —doubt, angst, rabid paranoia. The damned machines were making him lose his sense of self. *Not again, dammit, not again.* Nachman felt paranoid, like they wanted to take over, push his sanity over the edge, and tip him into a pit with no hope of return.

Everything is the way it should be, Nachman. Sadie appeared beside him like a soothing reminder of stability, calming Nachman, reassuring him the nanites were doing as they were programmed and nothing more. Nachman glared at Sadie, his face hardened by a fearful, frustration a mask for the terror. Sadie smiled and took his hand, so gently, so softly. Nachman fought Sadie's loose grip but let his hand stay within hers. Nachman calmed and let the work continue forward. "I hate this," Nachman said. Sadie smiled.

With a clockwise twist of his index and middle fingers, Nachman turned the gun barrel upright. Sadie could barely interpret his movements, as they appeared to be on fast-forward. The bright red hue was fading quickly; small beads fell off the LV barrel like sand falling from an hourglass. Time was running out; the memory was beginning to disintegrate. Nachman's finger ran down the center of the barrel like a zipper, and with both hands, he opened the barrel like a book. Again, with a motion of his fingers, the LV zoomed into the inner surface of the barrel. The nanites moved like liquid fire along his cerebrum, attempting to send as many algorithmic messages through the nervous system to obtain the information from the fading memory.

Nachman cocked his head as if he heard something, the rifling. "No, it can't be!" shouted Nachman as he rushed to the apex of the cavea. He struck the barrier with a clenched fist; the vibrations reverberated across the invisible membrane like a rock being thrown into calm waters. This membrane kept his personality separated from the machines until he could develop a symbiotic relationship with the nanites.

A bundle of nanites, no more than fifty and operating under strict guidance from Sadie while Nachman was still learning symbiosis, accelerated their microboosters, propelling themselves to the occipital portion of Nachman's cerebrum where they enhanced the optic nerve, giving the lens ten times the magnification power it had with even the augmentations in place. Nachman saw the grooves and curvatures, even the subtle spheroid divots in the rifling to give the armin the specific twist it needed to penetrate the target. This barrel was fabricated for a unique type of armin—he only knew because he had designed it while in the Naibus. Nachman bowed his head and laid his hands against the invisible barrier of the cavea; his fists pounded against it with a deep, muted thud. With that notion Sadie knew it to be true. She sent the incentum, and the nanites went back into dormancy.

Nachman's entrapped persona was surrounded by a light as blinding as a starburst. Nachman squeezed his eyes shut, and when they opened, he was in his ship, his home. His consciousness was restored and under his control. Nachman felt whole in his body again. With the exception of some dehydration and fatigue, Nachman felt—for lack of a better word—safe. What felt like a lifetime couldn't have lasted for more than a few seconds but drained Nachman substantially physiologically with a hefty detriment to the psyche.

He sat hunched, not from the cold of the sweat on his skin but from the weight of what he had come to realize: the realization of his faults and the impact of past actions both known and unknown had had not only on him but also those he cared for most. Before he passed out, Nachman turned to Sadie. "Dammit, Sadie, what did I do?"

Sadie discontinued the data spike, and the phavix folded into itself to the size of a pocket transmitter and docked back into its compartment. She smiled down at Nachman, closed her eyes, and faded into Nachman's nanophage. The *Satyr*'s systems went into hibernation mode, while the head of Nachman's chair reclined and simultaneously protruded a cable that inserted into the base of Nachman's skull, not only connecting him to the ship but also inducing Qusom, Quisthium somnolence, directly into his nanophage. Sadie and Nachman discovered this method of direct interface with the nanophage not only utilized less of the acidic element Quisthium (or, as the mainstream public called it, Qu), but allowed for more efficient regen sequences after Nachman sustained traumas to his body.

The viscous, chalky, pink, liquefied Qu flowed from the catheter attached to the chair directly into the dimple-like port at the base of Nachman's skull—one of the many retrofits, to himself and the *Satyr*, Nachman and Sadie had augmented for their new infusion system. She was proud of the upgrade for one simple fact: it was the first real advancement into making Qu safer for the Human body. The Human body required Qu to endure space travel for extended treks, to save both body and mind from shattering in the deep, deep Celestial. But with Sadie's design, the Qu could be directly fed into the phage, reducing the adverse effects Qu had on any Human who traveled the Celestial. The part that made her shy away from the advancement was that it is exclusive to Nachman. Nachman would always have a distrust of the GIA and therefore never uploaded the schematics to the Gnanimus. He was right that they would end up using it for some nefarious purpose in the future, whether they meant to or not, but Sadie still felt guilt about the fact it wouldn't benefit anyone else. Sadie appeared next to Nachman's Ignivalo, a twinge of sadness for one of the few arguments left unsettled in their years together. Sadie saw Nachman's brain send a neural signal across the gyrus. He had just set the coordinates for Tasóa, the Noanoagan outpost, a terraformed moon or terraluna, orbiting Oatou, the third terraorbis in the Tracaelus Solaris. *Under Qusom and still working the case*, mused Sadie.

Sadie knew that Nachman would have refused the Qusom for the short jump to the terraluna. Nachman always had the want to push himself to the brink, not only to subvert his innate curiosity but to prolong the inevitable painful recall of the past. Rest was needed, however, as the past Nachman had buried was about to break through to the surface.

CHAPTER 3

Tracaelus Solaris, Intraorbis, Direct Trajectory
1 AU outside Terraluna Tasóa, Noanoagan Outpost

Deep, deep into the Celestial past the nebulae, starbursts, and black holes into precipice of another dimension, a place where consciousness and reality meet, stood Nachman on a gray-and-lavender jagged cliff, the texture strange, almost digital in a sense. Blockish, with an almost doughy buoyancy, no edges anywhere—was this real or daydream? Nachman didn't know, never really cared, to be truthful. He wasn't floating, but his feet did not touch the surface as if he was suspended on a cable but able to articulate movement. Nachman would have never been here if he would have thought someone was controlling him. Nachman was comfortable here; he always had been. Known to the few as an Adyta, a realm of imagination where cohesion, centering within self and all can occur. At least that's what the Sitanimi monks from the Celestial monasteries in Sapietás called it. The same monasteries where Nachman first communed with Sadie. The Adyta was a place where Nachman could collect his incentum while he was in Qusom. Not many could call upon this realm of thought. It was known among the theologians as a place reserved for those with a keen insight into the Celestial. Nachman was still trying to figure out how he could get there, but the monks said the answer would come in time. Nachman slowly walked along the edge of the cliff, each footfall striking the invisible path; a soft glow of blue light circulated from his sole. *Sadie, you know me too well*, Nachman mused, staring down into the void beneath his feet. She was right to think he wouldn't want to recoup the wasted energy before reaching Tasóa.

Nachman stared out into the dimly lit, starry void, his aqua blue eyes reflecting the sea of stars in front of him. A random rupture of a supernova or dazzling flash of a comet's tail became a barrage of color folding and bursting would brighten the void from time to time. This is a place—no, a sanctuary —where dreamscapes and nightmares coexisted with reality. A palpable but controlled environment because of the point of origin in his subconscious, some vicinity in the Celestial where Nachman went to be alone. He needed to be away.

Nachman bowed his head. It felt heavy, as heavy as those damn rucksacks he hoofed up Mons Arbellica during boot camp on Rixa. He loathed himself for what he did to people, the random and those who cared for him, or used to. Nachman could lay claim to be an overzealous youth with too much intelligence and not enough responsibility or restraint at the time, but it was still no excuse for the harm caused. He only wanted to invent everything and damn near anything that would help Humanity, naive in his youth to think that the GIA had his or even another species best interests at heart. The present resembled the past in that moment; the invention of the tech led to heartbreak, and the repercussion came full circle.

Nachman wished he could change what had happened to the Orimer, but he did invent the tech capable of her murder. *Of course, I feel responsible; any sane person would.* Nachman's voice echoed out into the starry vastness.

Now, Nachman felt the anchor of penance, not only to those close to him but an entire other species as well. Sadie has always said he had a martyr complex. Nachman chuckled at the thought but was more cynical than jovial. Damn these memories.

An insectal buzzing from no particular place in the Adyta sounded, high pitched and annoying. Nachman cringed and grumbled; looking to his right, he slid his finger down into the empty air. A display screen appeared as if it was unzipped from nothing. The display had a black background with neon-green lettering showing a list of lexes that were received while he had been under. Only a few, but the one blinking was flagged simply because of the name. A name that was as curious as it was coincidental. And a coincidence was almost always a clue.

With that incentum, Nachman awoke in his chair. Nachman's eyes and mouth felt dry, like he hadn't had a drink of water in a few days. He felt the infusion catheter pop out of the buttonhole in his skull. The damned thing felt like a crevice, always itched for a minute or two and gave him a headache but it is something Nachman could tolerate to get the job done.

Nachman leaned back in his chair as the alarm continued to buzz. His left hand came to his brow, and he wiped away the sweat; his skin felt clammy and cold. He thought of the chair warming his body, and he started to warm up, nice and toasty. Nachman smiled. Out of the corner of his eye, he saw the incoming call alert flashing a subtle green and blue on the lower corner of starboard display of Nachman's navigation and communications array. Nachman groaned and slid his finger downward against the air toward the window. The action brought to life a black display with neon-green text with the list of missed lex. Nachman eyed the lex, and the display scrolled down. He glanced at the forward display: two hours until destination. A tingle went down his spine; his anxiety had heightened a degree or two. Nachman turned his attention to the lex. Only six were missed. Four ads all for travel agencies for intergalactic travel bookings—they had been big since the announcement that the gateway was near completion. *A lex from Ma. I have to remember to call her back; I already missed her birthday*, Nachman thought. And that one name, the reason for the annoying buzzing, a name he hadn't seen since his departure from the Naibus.

Natu Sergeant Tyrav Kaadu, Nachman's superior in the

Naibus Alpha squad, but more importantly, his mentor and best friend. Honorable, trustworthy—a man you would follow to hell twice just because you knew you would come out the other side a better man. When Nachman and Tyrav found out that they had both attended the same schools on Diiu and flirted with the same xenolinguistics teacher—a cute brunette with a smile that would light up the darkest pit and a sway that would melt even the most hardened man—they were inseparable.

Nachman felt they had literally been to hell and back serving a few tours during the two-and-a-half-year conflict with the Liber Vultus the GIA called the Caloctus Rebellio, which took place on Hatu, the volcanic mining planet in the Ipsum Solaris. A bloody and often debated-about conflict. Nachman didn't much care for the reasons he had been deployed there. Can't force a person into a way of life they don't want, but back then orders were orders, and Nachman followed them like a good soldier. Nachman smirked, remembering the deployments to Mars to detain and deter rebel and union unrest, goofball antics by union workers mostly. And then there were the skirmishes between two of the five Locus of the Quintus that took place on the twin planets Priun and Pridu in the Ducovímus Solaris. The philosophers these days could never keep the logic in their heads. *Always had to use their fists*, Ty used to say. There were many other missions, most still classified, that Nachman and Tyrav had been a party to, and through all of them, this glorious Human, whom Nachman actually called brother rather than friend, had his back.

For Tyrav to lex Nachman, not only at this time, so many years after the incident in the Vitachlora Solaris, was just—for lack of a better word—odd. Tyrav knew Nachman was not to blame, but the GIA had a way of covering their tracks to save face in the wake of tragedy. They both made a pact not to contact each other for the sake of Tyrav's family, so he knew Tyrav would never risk contact, especially to grab a casual libation and catch up on old times. Nachman shrugged his shoulders. *Let's find out where this leads*, he thought. He swiped his finger over Tyrav's name, and a return lex was sent. Nachman felt Sadie begin to stir from what he interpreted was a nap.

A couple of minutes later, a caramel face that had managed to keep a subtle look of youth while among the dogs of war appeared on the forward display. Tyrav was descended from a long lineage of Indian heritage dating back to pre-Gaia days, long in the jowl and portly, not only from time but from a lack of doing. Nachman mentally laughed at Ty for letting himself go in deep space when he always said to keep a battle shape and stay under the gun, but his smile was genuine for his old friend.

"Under normal circumstances I would say it is damn fine to see you, my boy," said Natu Sergeant Tyrav Kaadu with his most warm, welcoming smile, and Nachman admitted to himself he had missed that glow from the man. "But there is never a normal circumstance with you, Nach, so damn fine to see you!"

Wait. Nachman's brow twitched; something was off. Nothing was apparent, mind you, just something, that gut feeling, that noda in the pit that just tells you something is not right, and not even the circumstance is to blame. It had been years and only a couple of seconds since seeing his old friend again, but there was something off. Not the situation but Ty. For some reason, Nachman already knew—no, felt—that he was just not his brother in arms. Nachman played possum and put on his best "Hello there" smile. Sadie's aura brightened the cerebellar chamber. She made herself known to Nachman, knowing right away to stay in the background and not to make her presence known to Ty.

"It is good to see you, Ty, my old friend," Nachman said, and he was truly happy to see Tyrav. Still, something was off. Nachman kept his guard up but showed no sign of physical tension to give away his position.

"What kind of no good have you been up to, besides

throwing escapees out of airlocks?" asked Tyrav.

"Word travels like a comet in the Celestial, doesn't it?"

"Yeah, well, alvum, Nach," cursed Tyrav. That was about the extent of his curse words; anything more than that, his wife and his mother would have him shipped to a monastery in Sapietás. "When you throw people into the remnants of purusha, do you even try to find out what they're worth?"

Nachman had a feeling Ty was talking about the fact that Prisoner 674 was a part of the assassination attempt, but then what did he know that Nachman didn't? At least Nachman's suspicion of an inside job at Tenebrae was just confirmed, he could surmise that someone within the GIA, maybe even an Elitist, could have been involved. The details Nachman still lacked, and he knew there was still more to come. Nachman knew the GIA or whoever was behind the budding conspiracy was using typical psychological manipulation to derail him in a vain attempt to gain information, but Nachman knew better. Nachman used to teach this kind of stuff in his midyears at the Institutum. He would play along because the *why* in all of this was sure to present itself in time. Whoever was using Ty was lower than space scum; Nachman hated when his friends became involved, it toyed with his emotions. Emotions were something Nachman was not very fond of, and messing with them was never a good idea.

Not only was Tyrav Kaadu Nachman's Natu sergeant of arms—the highest-ranking noncommissioned officer (noncom)—of the Naibus Alpha Squad, but he was one of the only friends true enough to be called a friend in Nachman's book. Ty was only eight years older than Nachman, but the experience, passion, integrity, and love that Ty showed to a young, eager, and angry cadet was enough to cement a bond that was more than Nachman ever had besides his mother. Tyrav had saved Nachman's life, and Nachman did the same for Tyrav, both in more ways than one. Nachman knew this man better than his own mother—hell, they had been stranded in the Celestial together for a still-yet-to-be-recalled number of days on the edge of sanity, and they were able to maintain because of each other. The dinners, the laughs with Ty's wife and three kids—Sadie felt it now. Nachman was positive. That damn noda Nachman felt when he couldn't automatically put his finger on the problem. Ty was not Ty, and Nachman knew that for a fact.

Somewhere inside Nachman's right ophthalmic nerve tract, Sadie was sitting on a green-suede high-back bar stool, right leg crossed over the left at the knee, arms crossed at the abdomen. Sadie sat needle straight, her keen eyes focused on what Nachman was seeing at that moment through a digital display fabricated from one of the billions of nanomachines in Nachman's body. Sadie was slowly teaching Nachman not to be afraid of the little machines and to take full symbiosis with his being, biological, mechanical, and metaphysical. It was a challenge.

Sadie had been observing Tyrav. She liked the man and always felt that he had Nachman's best interests at heart, but she had that same noda that Nachman had. Something was not quite right with Nachman's friend. But what?

Sadie felt a ping, like a ripple across her matrices; Nachman was contacting her via their psi-link, and Sadie shuddered as Nachman felt as if he was ready to jump out of both of their skins.

Sadie? SADIE! I don't know, my best...how did they get to him? But who is they? *This thing is big, Sadie. Why the why is the key to the opening of the doubt? Damn this thing, can't get it centered. The GIA, maybe them or not them but someone, already has knowledge of 674. They are using my tech. Bastards. Pieces of alvum! I should have never gone there. Those people died on my watch. Why Ty? Why would he let them use me? They're going to burn us again. Can't go there, not now. He is not sending any warning signs like he taught me; he should be, but he's not. Something is wrong. Ty is not Ty. Sadie, people have died because of me. It's starting again. She will never forgive me.*

Nachman's mind was near panic, but his body was calm,

collected in his SuiMori state, listening to Tyrav scold him about tossing the prisoner out of the airlock, albeit unintentionally. Nachman's body automatically smiled as Tyrav raved about how he missed sitting on the bridge of the *Achilles* warship—"The finest vessel the GIA has built since your grandfather I'm sure. Sure, she is banged up from stem to stern. Oh, Nach..." Tyrav laughed. "Do you remember that pain-in-the-butt, wet-behind-the-ears lieutenant who pissed himself when the Vorcalus attempted to board and..."—Ty chuckled and snorted, turning his nose to the ceiling as if being offended by a putrid smell—"those damned outlaws are almost as bad as some of the Praetors. Legislation can be a joke my boy even more crooked than the crooks..."

He was saying all the right things. He smiled his half-crooked smile, as the left side of his face had sustained nerve damage from an engine explosion on a transport frigate that required rescuing; the scar above his right brow was still there, an old childhood injury given to him by his brother after a game of cricket. Even the way he stabbed the air with his finger when he laughed. All of his mannerisms and tics that were signature to Ty were there. Whoever this was, was playing Ty even better than Ty himself, but this was not Tyrav Kaadu. Nachman had no doubt in his mind that his friend was not here.

But all the while, Nachman simply sat in his chair on the bridge of the *Satyr* in front of the digital display with a vague, almost bored, expressionless face, and not-Tyrav would be none the wiser that, in a way, Nachman was not even home.

Nachman, Nachman, you're rambling. Collect your incentum, then project inward. You have to settle your mind when psi-linking. You give me a dreadful headache when you burst in like that. But I see what you're implying. Tyrav, to great misfortune, isn't himself. Your assumption about the GIA is intriguing; they are sniffing about this awfully quick and not being very subtle with you of all people, Sadie said.

Alvum! Dammit! Into the star of thought I grow fond. What

the hell was that? Dammit! Get it straight, Nachman. You're right, you're right, Sadie, I got this. Dammit, this psi-whatever makes my brain hurt, literally and figuratively. Sadie, since our nanophage upgrade, and again I thank you, it has made the caseloads more efficient. It seems we are unlocking all sorts of new goodies. Here's what we know so far. Ty is not who he appears to be; there is a definite connection between the breakout and the assassination, and to top off the layer cake, there is some spook inside the GIA that may have connects higher up.

Spook?

Bad guys...I don't know...GIA definitely...someone elite, maybe even Naibus.

Ah. I...see, Sadie said, frowning; the term eluded her for the moment. She would research the history later.

Yeah, yeah, you think I'm paranoid, but there's more, Sadie. Why send Tyrav? Of all people in the Celestial to lex me, it had to be him. Especially the timing of the contact. Come on, right after a political assassination, and I had one of the perps in my cargo hold? Besides I haven't seen Ty since the alvum on—

I know. I know. You don't have to talk about it, even in here.

Thanks, Sadie.

Nachman, I was thinking as I was observing Tyrav. The Automaton I had dealings with seems to be programmed to mimic the user entirely. A direct link into the Ignivalo was established with the black substance. Do you think Tyrav has been compromised? And if so, how many more of those atrocities are among the populace?

That incentum had just crossed my mind, Sadie.

Oh, one other incentum for you to ponder on top of all the others, Nachman, and it might seem a bit far-fetched, but the question I am posing now is not why Tyrav? But why you, Nachman?

The psi-link ended. Nachman was back in full cognizance with body and mind. Nachman was still trying to get used to the feel of SuiMori during a psi-link, another new toy for Sadie to play with.

"I'm telling you, Nachman, the GIA will still pay you

handsomely to recover the rest of the prisoners," said Ty. His smile turned to a fatherly scowl. "Just don't throw them into the abyss until we can get what we need from them."

"And I'm telling you, Ty, the last one was not my fault." Nachman said it with a smile because he had no qualms with the guy floating in the Celestial now that he knew what he knew.

Ty shrugged. "We have you pinged less than a six AU out from Tasóa. Does this mean you were already on your way to collect the rest of the escapees?"

"Yeah, I heard there were more spotted around the outer rim planets and the Aethra," lied Nachman. "Figured I would scout the space around the point of last contact and scrape up a little scratch to keep the lights on." Nachman didn't like lying to one of his oldest friends, but he could very well be working for whoever was behind the assassination. He wouldn't take that chance, not with how big this case was beginning to seem.

Nachman leaned back into his chair and kicked his right foot up so it lay on the console, looking as relaxed as he would with his old friend on any other day. Nachman was used to undercover ops; many tours were spent behind enemy lines, blending in, trying to survive. *Hopefully after all this is over, I can get to know his friend once more; here's hoping I get the chance*, thought Nachman.

"You know, with these jobs, standard ops is to trace your ship during all GIA-sanctioned retributios," said Tyrav. "And do try to leave the *Satyr*'s beacon on as a favor to me."

"Sure, sure," agreed Nachman, knowing Sadie would input fake flight plans and scrub any unsanctioned action from the *Satyr*'s mainframe.

Ty activated the trace code from his end of Tracaelus. Vis ping on the radar indicated Tyrav was one light-year out, orbiting the last orbis in the system to be terraformed, Tizanuu. Nachman looked down at one of the main screens of the console, three physical screens total across the maestro's board, and saw the GIA code input into the *Satyr*. Nachman did his best not to show the contempt all over his face at the moment; he always loathed being under the thumb of somebody with unwelcomed authority over him.

"There ya go, son, all set here. Regardless of all the politics, it is good seeing you again, my friend. Mother and Gyanda would be overjoyed to see you and, most of all, cook for you. I hope you still have the illustrious appetite you were known for," mused Ty.

Nachman's heart fluttered at the memories of the grand dinners with Ty and his family. Once a month, Ty and his wife, Gyanda, would throw elaborate dinner parties for those closest to them. Nachman, as far as he knew, was one of the few invited. Nachman would always be invited; after all, he was godfather to two of three of his daughters, and he enjoyed every bit of their attention. Good kids. Tyrav's Mother's irrcuma curry—some of the older folks said it tasted like the now-extinct chicken—was one of the most delicious dishes in the Celestial in his mind. *Damn them*, Nachman thought about whoever was controlling his friend. Nachman's smile was genuine from the memory. "I look forward to it. Just let me know when. Oh, give Gyanda a squeeze from dear ol'—"

Before Tyrav could get one last joke out of the situation, Sadie appeared as if plucked from nowhere, standing behind Nachman's chair. "Hello, Tyrav. It has been too long, but I'm afraid the intrusion is appropriate. As we prepared for our initial orbit around Tasóa, I detected two phage signals closing on our current position."

Nachman glared at the screen with Tyrav's image. "Following me this closely is going to cause me to doing something not so nice, Ty."

Ty frowned, shook his head, and then smiled, not offended in the least. "None of mine, brother. I know better."

"Well, in that case, I'll lex you soon, my friend," Nachman said to the man behind the mind control. Nachman blinked off the com station before Tyrav could respond and turned his chair 180 degrees to face Sadie. "What do we got?"

"Two vessels, pressing speed, port quarter," said Sadie, her words coming quick and to the point, combat ready as always. "Corpix and Spherix class. Customized—and not too badly, I might add—but black market, most likely. GIA sub-codings, but I can't seem to penetrate through the firewalls of their phages. They're coming in fast, and it doesn't seem like they want to talk."

Nachman looked at the forward-view screen; an image of the port quarter of the *Satyr* appeared so he could assess what he was up against.

Corpix-class fighters were made for air-to-air, air-to-atmosphere, and antigravity combat. Being that this was the fastest production stellar fighter in the Alliance, everybody and their grandmother had one. So, in turn, there were always continual quantum engine and software upgrades making this fighter compact, quick, and accurate on the stick. Made for one pilot for short spurts across a solaris but could be upgraded for the long haul to cross the Celestial if the pilot doesn't mind the cramped quarters. The fighter had short- and medium-range armament and usually could only sustain combat with another fighter within its class. Nachman had never liked the Corpix class, even the Chimera model from his time in the Naibus—not only for the compounding technical issues because of the constant upgrades, but it felt like a flying coffin. He had an incentum that this ship could pack a few surprises since it had plenty of off-grid upgrades, so he had to take him first and catch him off guard.

The spacecrafts remained, trailing half an AU behind the *Satyr*, neither making a move. Nachman took another second to take a quick study of the other craft.

The Spherix class fighter was more or less a planetary bomber; why the GIA had classified this as a fighter was confusing to Nachman, but in the end, the Spherix class could stand on its own in a head-on battle for a limited amount of time, if necessary. A huge advantage over the Spherix fighter-bomber was that it was significantly slower than the *Satyr*. Normally, that wouldn't be the case, but Nachman had customized this normally heavily outfitted Parixia bomber with a lightweight titiconium alloy and the various engine upgrades, compliments of Sadie, to outmaneuver most stellar fighters. The trailing Spherix registered no armament and one pilot; typically Spherix class vessels could only be piloted by a crew of two, and all GIA-initiated vessels were required to be at least half loaded when conducting planetary orbital runs (PORs). Obviously not GIA; the only reason for the empty craft would be for smuggling. *This could be the craft that brought the assassins to the luna in the first place*, Nachman thought. *This isn't going to stay kosher.*

Sadie obviously tuned into his incentum. "Nachman, your noda is correct about our tail. I managed to break the security in their phages; both pilots are prisoners from Tenebrae. Designate 677 in the Corpix and 533 in the Spherix. Neither have any association with GIA or rebel factions. They appear to be mere small-time hoodlums with no official flight logs, Celestial or atmospheric," said Sadie as she sat at the weapons array, next to her navigation controls. She didn't need to sit; she could just phase into the network and control the entire ship, but she liked the "feel," as did Nachman. "Should I link in and—"

"No, Sadie, I got this." Nachman put his arms on the armrest of his chair, leaned his head against the headrest, and closed his eyes. He gave a grin that was teeming with a sinister edge but held a hint of giddiness. Nachman's nanophage fully integrated with the *Satyr*'s mainframe. Through the connection, not only did Nachman control the movement of his ship, but he could also feel the bitter cold of space pressing against the *Satyr*'s hull and sense every macrobit of data incoming through the sensor arrays as they pulsated into his cortex. Even the connection with Sadie was heightened, for she was always wired into the *Satyr* and Nachman. The sensations were glorious.

Feeling the raw data swarming into her physical form felt like a hive of wasps. Sadie stepped away from the console like she was jolted with charged Vis and disconnected from the *Satyr*. Nachman had, at times, overwhelmed Sadie with his emotions, especially in times of high intensity that increased Nachman's stressors. The violence that could sometimes be behind what Humans call Humanity in this species often overwhelmed a Caiet, and Sadie was no stranger to the emotional state of violence. Sadie understood her emotions, but Human emotions were complex—specifically Nachman's. Sadie didn't hold it against him; she never did and never would. Sadie knew Nachman's true intentions behind his actions. Besides, Nachman always enjoyed a good dogfight. Sadie shook her head and smiled at Nachman, as he looked like a kid who had just opened the best present he'd ever received.

The Corpix accelerated and banked downward. Nachman figured the pilot was going to try coming from underneath in an attempt to hit the thin underside of the *Satyr*. The Spherix increased thrust slightly but held back—probably to see if his friend could take Nachman out first.

The fighter's triple quantum engines ignited as the ship descended beneath the *Satyr*. The *Satyr*'s sensor picked up the secretion of quantum dust leaking from the starboard engine as it accelerated. Nachman smiled again as his nanophage gathered the information from the *Satyr*'s sensor arrays throughout the hull. He had just found his advantage over both of his pursuers: maneuverability.

Nachman let the Corpix come within meters of the *Satyr*. Without warning Nachman banked the *Satyr* straight upward, keeping line of sight on his opponent, barrel-rolling just for fun. Sadie shook her head without turning to him, as Nachman burst out laughing. When Nachman felt enough distance had been put between the Corpix and the *Satyr*, Nachman made a sharp U-turn to bring himself into a dive directly on top of the formerly pursuing fighter.

"Nachman, I know this is one of your favorite maneuvers, but can you please not wait until the last minute to fire? I don't have a digestive system, but it is quite nauseating to come within meters of being vacuumed into the Celestial," said Sadie, "and it is rather cruel to let the opposition think they will get away."

The Corpix pilot attempted to correct course to gain some distance. Nachman had already calculated almost every predicted flight path, laying each one out behind his eyelids, and staying tight on his line, not letting the Corpix gain any momentum. Nachman thought of Sadie just as his incentum led him to the rail cannons. A viciously giddy smile was still present on the corner of his lip, teasing Sadie, as he kept accelerating toward the enemy fighter. Sadie cursed under her breath and brought her hand to her mouth. Nachman still couldn't understand how a ball of energy made physical could be nauseous. *No end to the mystery of this one*, he thought. Sadie scowled at Nachman; she had always regretted helping him create this maneuver for his finals in flight school.

Nachman fired the custom dual rail cannons extending from hidden compartments beneath the *Satyr*. Nachman liked his toys, and the rail cannons were among the first upgrades he and Sadie had made after purchasing the junker. The rail shot was 50 mm phase-piercing armin, illegal by GIA standards but not by Nachman's when it came to the deep Celestial retributios. Sadie, who was still disconnected from the *Satyr*, watched out of the forward porthole as the rail shot sliced through the forward hull of the Corpix like a laser knife through a wedding cake. The Corpix imploded into a self-contained miniature black hole created from the disruption in the quantum containment. Sadie admired Nachman's skill as a pilot. When he linked with a vessel, especially the *Satyr*, he could put on a ballet that would make the ancient Gaians weep for sheer joy.

The *Satyr* flew within meters of the Corpix's dissipating black hole. In his mind Nachman felt the starboard port hull warp as if it were made of the quicksand of the desert planet Osyrtis in Crescat. The metal twisted and turned, almost like a woven basket pulling the metal into a different reality, overlapping it with his and then making it solid in his reality once more. *Damn, that's going to be expensive*, Nachman thought. Sadie had no words because it was she who would do the brunt of the overhaul. This minute damage didn't deter Nachman from continuing his favorite tactical maneuver. He put full thrust into the *Satyr*'s quantum engines. Nachman felt the gravity press against his physical body; he would have screamed if he could, partly from the pain of his organs compressing against his spinal column, but mostly from the sheer joy of the fight.

Nachman pulled thrust back abruptly, bringing the *Satyr* into a sharp, inverted turn that would have thrown Sadie around the cabin if she needed gravity, and came directly beneath the enemy vessel. With the nose up, Nachman cut thrust and stayed in line with the Spherix; accuracy was key with the next shot. Nachman retracted one rail cannon to avoid misfiring; with the other cannon, he loaded a half shot, a 25 mm rail, directly at the base of the quantum engine. One precision shot to the outer casing of any quantum engine, no matter the class, would disable the engines and leave the vessel at a dead stick.

The Spherix pilot never saw the finale of Nachman's Finite Loop coming. The pilot tried to shake Nachman, but without a visual and a blocked sensor array, the Spherix was blind. Nachman had been successful in disabling hundreds of enemy fighters, frigates, and corvettes and was point man in gathering intelligence for his Naibus squadron with not just the Finite Loop but many other tactical space combat maneuvers. With that incentum in mind, Nachman remembered he had completed those missions while in his GIA Chimera fighter back when he was enlisted. This was the first time he'd had the incentum to try this move in the *Satyr*.

No time like the present to give it a go. Nachman fired the rail cannon with a blink of his eye. The rail shot sliced through space, lacerating the titiconium casing like a scythe carving a crop of wheat. The Spherix engine's outer casing made a series of miniexplosions along the seam; metal shrapnel began floating off into the Celestial. The fire and smoke dissipated quickly—no oxygen, no life. The inner shielding of the Spherix's damaged quantum engine appeared intact, but— no, wait—it looked as if the shielding was warping, bubbling, almost ready to boil. It could be shrapnel bouncing off the inner shielding. Nachman was sure he had the rail gun set for minimal damage; there was no way he overcompensated this time. Nachman zoomed in with one of the *Satyr*'s hull cams to keep an eye on the enemy's engine as he glided the *Satyr* into position parallel with Spherix for immediate boarding and extraction. Nachman was determined to gather this intel and find out what was going on in his Celestial.

"Is it safe?" asked Sadie with a bite of sarcasm as she reconnected with the *Satyr* and ran a full system diagnostic.

Nachman let out a breath and grinned nervously; he was glad it worked. At least, he thought it had.

The *Satyr*'s sensors would have never picked it up if Sadie hadn't bonded with the mainframe when she did. A moment, only a macrosecond of a moment, after Sadie connected with the *Satyr*, she projected the incentum to Nachman, and he saw two bits of data fed into his eyes from the ship's port hull cam just before the entire matrix went dark from the electric null wave of the explosion. One, the bubbling on the outer casing of the starboard engine was no longer bubbling but detonating as if it was a plasma firework exploding on a Cordrego's coronation, and two, it seemed Prisoner 533 activated the lexcom antenna array and sent off a wave the infrared picked up. What was curious about the latter was that very few people in the Celestial use infrared lex communication; among those who did were spies and assassins.

As Nachman was making these observations, he was simultaneously projecting another part of his incentum into rearing the *Satyr* to a halt, much like you would a purebred stallion when it's ready to jump violently. The thrusters fired, and Nachman pulled the *Satyr* into a looped barrel roll away from the imploding Spherix. The Spherix crumbled like an aluminum can and was sent off to who knows where after the black hole engulfed them. The *Satyr* came to rest well enough away from the implosion–no residual damage to the ship. But the combination of reversing g-force that abruptly and the rapidity of the incentum projection gave Nachman a migraine that would last an entire orbit around Jupiter.

Nachman had to crack a half grin when he glanced at Sadie. Her aura had turned from the somber light-neon green to an aura of a lava flow, pulsating in visible waves throughout her opaque form. Sadie seldom swore, but when she did, she utilized her eclectic language gallery to make cursing seem like silky poetry in any Celestial spoken language. And about the only time Sadie lost her concrete composure was when Nachman overcompensated his shots or questions logic. Sadie knew Nachman was a phenomenal pilot but was alvum as a gunner. Nachman knew he was absolute in his calculations—this time.

"Sadie, Sadie." Nachman's voice was a monotone because he knew Sadie had to finish her subtle yet verbally piercing vocation. "Check them, Sadie, check every single calc. They're on point. From what I'm seeing here this was, plain and simple, the bad guy didn't want to get caught."

Nachman blinked. Two pink dots of light flickered on the cockpit window. They stood still for but a moment and then bounced off one another, and both seemed to pop like a balloon when two view screens appeared. Nachman pulled the memory of the explosion from his nanophage onto one screen and pulled the hull camera feed from the *Satyr*'s mainframe. With a maestro-like gesture, he synced the feeds together. Nachman spread his arms as if he were ready to receive a grand hug; the image expanded into a panoramic view of not only the Spherix exploding but also a parsec or two around the vessel.

The hull camera captured the shot from the *Satyr*, the subsequent impact of the rail shot, and explosion of the quantum engine. Even in the time of the Celestial, the Human eye, biological or otherwise, was still faster than a machine most times. Nachman swiped his finger across the invisible surface, and the image panned to the right. Nachman brought his right thumb and index digit together to form a pinching gesture, and the image zoomed in on the Spherix's antenna array.

Sadie looked at the screen and bowed her head slightly. All the images showed Nachman's shot was accurate. Her aura dimmed and softened back to her natural color, the serendipitous neon green. Sadie felt embarrassed; there were not many people in the Celestial who believed that Caiets could feel. Nachman was among the few.

"It appears the array sent and received a lex. My apologies, Nachman; it seems you are getting better as a gunner after all." They smiled at each other. "Your Human emotions are still...being processed, as it were," Sadie said.

"Sadie, trust me, I get it," replied Nachman. "Of all people, I get it."

"Well, my dear Nachman," Sadie said, quoting her favorite detective, "it would appear we have a mystery afoot. And I would ascertain the primary questions proposed to us now is why the conspiracy and whom the conspirator?"

"Whoever the conspirator is sent a signal to the prisoner, presumably to commit suicide, just after he sent his lex. Besides using such an obsolete tech, whoever our ring leader is didn't want to leave any witnesses. Leaving us at a dead end here. They don't want us to find out what they're up too, but I say we find out," said Nachman. He set the landing coordinates for a quiet landing site outside of Tasóa's capital —the one place, these past five years, he had chosen to stay away from. But now that someone had tried to blow up his friend and ship, he had to put the past in the back seat and get the job done.

CHAPTER 4

Crescat Solaris, Stellar Station R1 Beta, North Polar Orbit of TerraOrbis Resalo
Stellar Station R1 Beta, Sanctioned for Demolition and Redistribution

This GIA Elitist would rather stand in solitude among the cavernous remains of a soon-to-be demolished stellar station than maintain close proximity to the aristocratic simpletons he was usually around. He stood at his window—not so much brooding but contemplating the next move and the move thereafter. The man was foreboding tall, slender but with the hints of athleticism of what remains of the aging flesh, and dressed in the drab color of the elite. Specifically, the greens and tans of the Crescat Solaris, home to the Tenet of Terraforma & Xegriculture. The Crescat Elitist, who assuredly represented the higher echelon of the GIA, elected to take his personal transport as opposed to the drab journey to Tracaelus with the rest of the Elitists on a GIA vessel he interpreted as a grandiose intersolari crypt.

The man stood, straight backed, much like an overlord admiring his conquests, staring out the window of his temporary quarters, with the bitter taste of contriteness in his incentum while contemplating the profound depths of this chasm of what everyone else called the Celestial. *Celestial.* He laughed at the euphemism; there was nothing peaceful or serene about this great beyond. He had experienced this blessed abyss's tentacle grip, and it left his body scarred, robotic, and mutilated. All at once, the void could be a torturous vacuum, tearing and ripping flesh and spirit or a vast nothingness without want, waiting to be manipulated for his gain. He knew in his synthesized bone structure that all of the planetary bodies in this Celestial were waiting to be terraformed, colonized, and cultured by Humanity. He wanted—no, needed—to stretch his species into the cosmos, he thought as he scraped a robotic finger across the tempered glass, tracing a nearby constellation. He brushed his fingertips lightly on the glass again, the tempered metal of the fingertips screeching across. The palpability of the window was real but not. He knew the surface felt smooth with a moderate temperature through the nanotransmitters ebbed into the synthetic alloys of his faux, transparent skin. The mechanized parts within him could sense the nanoregulators embedded in the thickly layered reinforced glass and metals of the stellar station he was soon to depart. The Elitist's right eye, yet another biological component claimed by this great beyond, whirred with a mechanical hiss as it focused on the hand. Without his mechanical assistants, he would not be of this realm any longer. The man scoffed at this thought.

The man blinked. The time, in standard Crescat rotation, appeared behind the lens of his ocumechs. *My transport is overdue. Incompetents*, he thought. The Elitist continued to muster patience as he waited for departure. He continued his contemplation of self; his arm from scapula to fingertip was sleek and smooth, like the ice of the glacier lakes among Venus's south poles. Both arms mirrored each other, made of several layers of lightweight but extremely dense transparent polymers enhancing strength, dexterity, and tactile stimuli, as well as allowing an interface with most modern technology. The miniature celluloid gears and struts in the forearm shifted in silence as he articulated not *his* fingers, he thought, but *the* fingers. *But they are mine to control*, he thought. The algorithms, fabricators, and neural network connections were designed by the pinnacle of nanorobotic engineers in the Ipsum robotics labs. Although the arms were older models, they had proved worthy among the man's standards, which he considered to be well above the average man's. The man believed technology could improve the Human cause, but it could weaken the sensible if given too much prowess. The Elitist stared at the hand not with hate but with the contempt of a brother looking down on a younger sibling after taking the praise from their father. He wanted the flesh but had the machine; he was forced to succumb, to adapt to the machine. For that, he abhorred the machine, and in that vein, he felt he must control the machine in him.

This Celestial claimed not only parts of his physiological being but of the metaphysical as well. His sense of self had been in the midst of an internal war for many years, a war between mind and body, flesh and machine. They competed, the flesh and machine, but he was determined to make them whole. After the last thirty years under the guidance of the Suviira (dedicated rogue holy analysts from Sapietás, empowered to conquer the domain of mind and machine), he had worked to make the man and machine one entity, one mind to maintain absolute control of the machine inside. The man had grown tired of the mundane dribble of the so-called acceptance and symbiosis within himself, as the other tiresome monks preached.

The early years, the painstaking years. Traveling to and from Vitachlora for physical healing and the Sapietás for the spiritual was a waste. No growth, no control—there was only pity from the monks and healers. Sapietás. He scowled at the thought of the Solaris. That Solaris should be shunned from funding or support. *Humanity is about expansion outward, hardly inward*, thought the man. These so-called priests treated him so tenderly and childlike, he loathed them for their pity. If not for the Suviira, he would think there was no logical reason to keep the Solaris around. The man insisted that all was needed was to teach him how to use the new tools that he must be chained to for life for not only quality and quantity, but also so that he could continue to maintain control. The Suviira monks provided him with what he needed. The man cared not for the emotional aspects of living but the logical and practical uses of what was presented to him.

The GIA insisted, however, for him to participate and complete each training presented to him for the fortuitous future of the Human race and for the legacy of his family. He did feel a twinge of obligation to honor the ties to the system, as his family before him had for so many years. As a young man in recovery and coming into his own, he had suffered through the daily lectures of duty and service, however arduous they seemed. He read the Vis scrolls and scribes on how to maintain a sense of self while in transition to higher status, all the while begrudgingly showing those fools how he could adapt to his new mechanized self. The man had adapted very early, but he also was determined to command and overcome.

With the combined efforts of scientists and engineers representing Vitachlora and Ipsum, the man is now mostly mechanized from the nanotech-enhanced liquid metals of the Fusiles River chain on Lortaris, a Non-TerraOrbis in Vitachlora, that were crystallized and shaped to form a new skeleton to the tiny capsule no bigger than a grain of rice, a microrespirator, seated under his nose with microtendrils inserting themselves into his nasal cavity and down into the bronchi, keeping his remaining lung inflated. The other burst when the airlock repressurized. He remembered gasping for recycled air when he was rescued by his father after his first and only deep space walk. It was an inane attempt in the man's mind, as his father had nothing to do with him after the accident and died only two years later along with the rest of his family.

The memory of his family haunted him, much like a poltergeist in the attic of his incentum. The man disregarded the forming memory of his family; there was no time to waste on grief when he and his species had so much at stake.

There must be a perseverance over these insipid frailties in all Humans, the man thought, staring into his reflection.

He admired the remaining cutaneous areas on his face. His cheekbone was high, prominent with a light-caramel complexion like coffee after one dollop of cream. His sharp, angular jawline made him handsome and slightly feminine; what remained was not showing the signs of aging in his midyears but accentuated his Spanish—more specifically, Galician—descent. The left side of his face from temporal skull to lower jaw, including the very prominent ocumech, an artificial eye capable of viewing a microbe .01 AU away, was a silver-and-copper sheen of titiconium interlaced with precious metals the Noanoagans bestowed on the Elitist. The Gnanimus kept the man appraised of all mods, upgrades, and enhancements throughout the Celestial to remain on the forefront of advancement.

A chime at the door. *It must be time to be underway*, the man notioned.

"Enter," the man said, his voice stern, somber, and quiet, yet commanding all in one word. A well-spoken man but more of the tacit type, only speaking when there was something to be said. When he did speak, the audience was enchanted by the man's bass, thick, and silken Spanish accent, articulated with perfect phonation in any of the GIA spoken languages. His synthetic vocal cords allowed him to keep his original accent and phonetics.

The famul, *servant* in the old grammar, entered with his head slightly bowed so as to not make eye contact and addressed the man with his proper title. "Magnus Xon, your transport awaits your arrival and order for departure. Is there anything you desire for comfort or need?"

"Not at this time." Xon did not thank the manservant and asked for nothing, for he was a man who expected everyone to know their duties and perform them without fail. Incompetence was not tolerated in Magnus Xon's camp.

Xon never looked at the famul directly, merely a glance in the reflection off the window. The famul seemed to tremor like a leaf about to fall from the autumn breeze. A small smile bent at the corner of Xon's scarred lip. His glands slowly secreted saliva, Xon swallowed; he felt as if he literally fed on the power he had over those he deemed lesser than himself. Xon had an underlying desire for power. Whether he acknowledged it or not was only for him to know, but most people he came across felt the command authority exude from Xon. Did they fear him for his scarred, monstrous appearance? Or did they simply respect the position? No, neither. *A combination of both*, Xon supposed. Magnus Julius Xon has felt the lust for power, like a quiver behind his ear, for as long as he could remember.

"Thank you for your time, Magnus Xon." The famul departed as quickly as he entered. Those in the lower service, a step above slavery in the rebellion's mind, did not and should not stay longer than necessary when addressing GIA elite. Others were less formal and less frightening than Xon, but all believed in the hierarchy.

Xon looked at his reflection one last time before turning to depart his quarters. His grin disappeared, and the adhesions tightened again to form his lips into a permanent crooked half frown. *How different things would be*, Xon thought. He turned from his reflection sharply on his heel hard enough to scuff the floor. The Magnus sometimes forgets the strength of his augmented musculoskeletal structure. The door slid to the right, and he began his walk down the aged titanium corridors of the private housing suites of station. Xon touched the wall with his right hand, two fingertips left with organic tactile sensation. The wall felt buoyant as a smooth, gelatinous substance was oozing down the side. The clear-blue gel coated his fingertip and began to turn into white foam. Xon rubbed the gel in between his forefinger and thumb as the foam began to sizzle on his skin. Goose pimples slid over his tissue, raising the few dark hairs on the patchwork of skin on his forearm. He missed many sensations as a result of the augmentations, of anything that touched his skin even the acidic burn of the corrosive gel that now eroded his fingerprints. He wiped the gel on his mechanized arm; the corrosive gel had no effect on the celluloid.

Xon knew this stellar station was under orders from Ipsum to be demolished and recycled to make way for a more state-of-the-art stellar station—*or so we told the underlings*, Xon thought—but that did not stop him from staying in his suite that overlooked his home Resalo. With all the associates he was acquainted with throughout the Alliance, Xon knew the stellar station was being demolished and used for scrap metal for the intergalactic cruisers that were to be launched in less than a year through the Aethra Gateway. Being that Julius Xon was the last remaining member of the Xon family to carry on the terraforming legacy, and that his ancestors were some of the founding members of the established way of life, he was shown the respect he knew he deserved. That respect —or fear, if one was to classify—came with the privilege of secrets.

As he walked through the corridor, Xon began to reflect on the past. Xon loathed reflection on meaningless drivel, and that included his memories of the incident. He thought about the famul he had just seen and remembered his hands, the amputation of the fingers of his right hand fresh with nanographs present for adhesion of the biomech. There was a time he was weak and powerless, but Xon vowed the day he received his first nanograph to never let anything stand in the way of the legacy he would leave for Humanity.

The man had been but a boy of twelve when the pain began in the metacarpals of his dominant left hand just after the morning meal intake in the concession hall of the Apollo Traestrum, an intergalactic colony vessel constructed especially for this inaugural deep space exploratory mission. State-of-the-art, as the GIA boasted.

Xon remembered the sharp burn, like barbed wire tearing his nerve endings as it slowly crawled through his thumb and forefinger. His fork dropped to the plate with a loud clang. His father glanced at him without regard; he had always seen

Xon as clumsy. Xon picked up his fork and continued break-fast, only mildly concerned about the pain. He was warned some pressure changes might occur within the joints with such a long deep space mission. But they had departed port only a week ago, young Julius wondered.

The Xon family—father, mother, son, and twin daughters, along with the father's mother and father, three generations of Xon—along with five thousand colonists, set off into the void to create better worlds. The Xon family were known throughout the Alliance as the premier terraforma family were to personally oversee the expansion of Humanity out into the great abyss. The giant stellacruiser *Apollo* had departed from the first intergalactic port, Lactea Alpha, a week prior with all systems nominal, but they had already encountered a minor structural abnormality. The abnormality was minor enough that an apprentice could handle the repair, and according to the captain, he required someone of short stature and certified in untethered EVW, an extravehicular space walk controlled by a propulsion system mounted on the astronaut's back. Young Julius volunteered almost immediately. Julius was forever seeking the approval of his father, and he was excited to perform his first official EVW outside of the classroom.

It was to be the beginning of a new era for the Human species, as his father had put it so effervescently as he was helping Julius put on the spacesuit. His fingers felt numb but pressured, as if a vise were getting tighter and tighter around the joint. Julius thought about telling his father about his pains at that moment, but as he looked at his father as he buckled the gravboots in place, Julius noticed his father smiling up at him. Julius smiled back and felt like nothing could go wrong in the Celestial.

Just before putting on Julius's helmet, his father looked into his son's eyes. At first he just stared, but after a minute, he said, "Julius, my boy, make the family proud." His father, Magnus Thiago Xon, smiled at his son once more with watery eyes and strapped the helmet into place. The suit was made to fit Julius, articulated at the joints and fabricated with a lightweight polymer that made the suit durable and able to withstand most deep space hazards.

Xon remembered his father pushing the button to open the first door to the airlock. The door closed behind him, and he turned to see his father looking at him, a gleam of pride in his eyes. Julius felt closer to his father at this moment than throughout his childhood thus far. Julius pushed a series of buttons on the control panel, beginning the sequence of depressurization of the airlock chamber. With a soft hiss, the gravity escaped from the chamber, and Xon was slowly lifted off his feet. At the same moment, young Julius felt something inside him twist, tear, and ravage his body, as if someone began to stab him inside with millions of needles all at once. Julius screamed a bloodcurdling scream that would have been heard throughout the Celestial. His father's pride turned to anguish as he watched his son's helmet he had just locked into place for his own well-being, fill with the liquid dark of his son's own blood.

If Xon could have seen inside himself in that moment, he would have seen a horror beyond his imagining. The pressurized radioactive particles from the vacuum of space began to pulverize Julius's skeletal structure as if it was a geode under a grinder. His bone marrow began to liquefy, becoming a viscous gelatin oozing into his bloodstream, his bones shattered as if they were glass struck by a hammer; his muscles, sinew, and dermis began to bubble and boil under his suit. The outer door to the airlock opened, and the broken young man began to float into the abyss. The screaming never stopped from both father and son.

As his son floated further into the abyss, Thiago Xon scrambled to put on the extra EVW suit. In less than two minutes, the suit was on, and Thiago hurried to the controls as fast as the suit would let him and initiated an emergency override to the chamber that would suck him into space propelling him toward Julius. The sweat drenched his forehead; panic had set in, but Thiago was determined to save his only son. Thiago braced himself, feet slightly apart, right foot in front, knees bent and ready to launch. Thiago smashed the button and was whipped into the Celestial. He could hear his son's screams through the com system; a tear rolled down Thiago's cheek as he reached for his son. Julius was one hundred feet away from the *Apollo*, turning head over heels. The screaming stopped, and Thiago feared the worst as he opened his arms to grab his son. What Thiago feared could not compare with what Julius would endure, for he had not saved his son from the sweet envelopment of the cold abyss but had only given him to the fear of self-loathing and misery of recovery.

The recovery was more agonizing than the initial injury, the pressure like a gravity well on his skull during the surgeries. He was supposed to be under deep anesthesia, but he swore he felt most of the agony. Xon's right hand went to the nape of his neck as he rounded a corner. He rubbed the scar where the nanophage was rebuilt, and the cervical portion of his spinal column was now a bundle of nanites wrapped around a flexible titiconium spinal rod. The corridor opened up into a cavernous docking bay where his private, unregistered intersolari transport yacht, the *Cultivador*, was waiting to depart, prepped and ready for a multisolari flight pattern. The vessel was state-of-the-art, with many off-grid modifications from Qusom manipulators to armin, allowing Xon to remain in between Solari and not have to dock at the interim stellar stations. Xon could not stomach the lack of efficiency at those backwater stations. He made his way to the docking ramp and boarded his vessel; Xon had very few staff on hand, just enough to man the vessel and provide a way of sustenance. He often had a right hand who accompanied him on almost every mission and knew just about everything of importance for Xon. This man reported to Xon and only Xon. But his primary confidant was away on an errand of great importance for his future plans, and it certainly was not trust that lent this confidant as Xon's extension. So many of those past and current plans have been in motion since the day he began to recover from the tortuous and arduous reconstruction.

The top physicians and geneticists discovered that a rare genetic mutation caused Julius's molecular structure to literally fall apart when exposed to deep space radiation. The Alliance banded together for the Xon family to rebuild their son—but at a cost, of course. While their son was undergoing his extensive anatomical and physiological reconstruction, the entire Xon family was to continue their one-thousand-year mission to extend the Auctius to the Milky Way's neighboring galaxy, even with the final plans to build the Aethra Gateway with an alien species, the Noanoagans, in place. Xon was fully recovered in fewer than five years, and within that five years, great misfortune and in turn opportunistic fortuity presented themselves.

Two years into the intergalactic voyage the entire crew and all aboard the *Apollo* had vanished off all radar and communication arrays. The Tracaelus galactic stations outlying the galaxy's outer rim had lost communication with the vessel shortly after receiving their weekly briefing; Thiago Xon had been the narrator of the brief with his family in attendance. Not only had it been the Magnus's rotation for brief duty, but he also wanted to congratulate his son on a glorious recovery and hoped to see him when the Aethra Gateway was completed. Magnus Thiago had been in awe when he had heard he would be able to see his son again and much sooner than he had anticipated. Magnus Julius Xon replayed the lex in his head as he prepared for his Qusom for the first stop on his agenda, a trip to Vitachlora. This lex was one that he kept, regardless of his lack of attachment to what he viewed as trivial life pursuits; after all, it was the last time he had seen his family alive. Xon saw both his family's elation at his recovery and the fear of their impending demise all in one moment.

Julius's father and mother, Magnus Thiago and Sahyba

Xon, along with his twin sisters, Aracella and Adora, sent tides of joy and good fortune from across the deep Celestial. His mother and father talked of deep dreamscape Qusoms that lasted a full year. They were awoken for a twenty-four-hour period to prevent psychological degradation. Julius could see the twins were playing with their dolls and a Vis-simulated dollhouse in the background. The pale-yellow temporary privacy quarters reflected a soft yellow glow from the ceiling lights throughout the room. The laughter and pure joy coming from his nine-year-old sisters and the look of relief and contentment on his parents' faces always brought a welling of sorrow from deep within Xon, a part of himself that he attempted to completely disregard and would without a doubt pluck out of his system like a festering abscess.

As they spoke of recovery and the future, Xon's grandmother burst into the room, her screams incoherent still to the present day. But from what Xon could make out, it was something about the crew, which included Xon's grandfather, having all gone mad, releasing all gravity attenuators and causing loss of artificial gravity throughout the entire vessel and systematically executing everyone on the ship. Julius Xon had conducted hours of exhausting research into the phenomena that could have caused the entire crew to suddenly become insane murderers. But the only conclusion the Vitachloran scientists could surmise with such limited data was a parasitic organism or a complete breakdown in mental faculties that caused a gross schizophrenic break.

The girls laughed at first until their grandfather casually opened the door to temporary quarters and began aiming a rail pistol at each of them, and with one rail apiece, ended all of their lives with a precise shot between the brainstem and nanophage. The connection to the Gnanimus and the nervous system wiped out in one fell swoop. The last image he saw of his father was a look a pure terror and confusion as the rail shot pierced through his forehead, bringing brain matter and the rail shot through the video feed, making that the last lex Julius Xon and the GIA would receive from the *Apollo*. The ceremonial farewells had been conducted without haste, and with the tragic loss of the entire Xon family, a teenage Julius inherited the family title of Magnus of Resalo, head of Resalo planetary commerce and mediator of galactic terraforma operations.

On the anniversary of their deaths, which happened to be tonight, Xon would replay the lex and weep for them, but over the years Magnus Xon had not felt the need to be reminded of the past but only to strive toward his future. The disease may have ravaged his body and prevented Xon from committing to any voyage beyond the Milky Way, but it had also, in a perverted sense, saved him from the grim fate that befell his family. But now, he had found a way to envision his own personal Auctius.

Xon sat in a cushioned, velvety-smooth chair, rotating it so it faced out the port-side window, with a view of the Crescat sun dipping over the horizon of Resalo, a brilliant cascade of golds and whites pinging off the planet's atmosphere like pebbles skipping over water. A soothing image of his home before drifting into Qusom. The infusion catheter pierces the fistula in Xon's right forearm, the sting lessened by the dulled nerve endings in the patch of skin. As the warm, viscous Quisthium flowed into the catheter, Xon could see his plans coming to fruition. The *Cultivador* was set on autopilot with the coordinates set for his first destination, the planet Medvios in Vitachlora. Xon sent the incentum to bring the quad quantum fusion drive online. With the engine upgrades and the intermingling of Noanoagan engine drive technology into the *Cultivador*, the Magnus was able to travel just under light speed, an accomplishment he had kept out of the Gnanimus and away from the GIA. He would be able to quickly quell a few dimly lit fires in that Solaris before moving to the final transition. Magnus Julius Xon knew the Aethra Gateway was the way to fulfill his dreams, earn his conquests, and terraform a new galaxy, whether it be for the Human race, his legacy, his family, or perhaps...his destiny.

CHAPTER 5

**Tracaelus Solaris, Terraluna Tasóa, Noanoagan Outpost
Eighty-four kilometers outside of Aaila, Capital of Tasóa**

Much to Sadie's protest, as accountability was one of the items on her long list of "species improvement" she likes to provide Humans, Nachman decided to forgo the usual docking procedures at the port stations, instead landing in a secluded valley on the outskirts of Aaila, the capital city of Tasóa. Over the years the capital of the terraluna had become a hub of commerce and political intrigue for the entire Alliance. Tasóa's docking ports alone had been importing and exporting substantially more goods over the last ten years, more than Human exporters, much of it being Noanoagan technology—new otherworldly metals and exotic foods, and, for some reason, the Noanoagans had a knack for fashion. The Noanoagan entertainment and cultural scene was gaining much popularity among the younger Human generation in the galaxy. This time of day, the entire city would be crawling with so many Human and alien eyes that the *Satyr* would be spotted almost instantly; it wasn't exactly an inconspicuous vessel. Sadie had a thing about adding fluorescent accents to the ship's hull that would change periodically, a special crustacean substance from the Non-TerraOrbis Lortaris mixed in with the paint that activated with certain Celestial and atmospheric radiations. Nachman never minded, but Sadie still didn't quite grasp the concept of covert operations and that some eccentricities must be waived in order to get to the truth.

Nachman pressed a button on his chair to release the T-shaped light-blue Vis restraint that was attached to his back. The strands of Vis uncoiled like a snake around the quarter-inch attachment modules embedded into his titiconium-lined scapulae, then receded into a slot in the back of the pilot's chair. Nachman had found from his years as a Deep Celestial fighter pilot with the Naibus that because he was more broad-shouldered than most, the zero-G dogfights always caused microfractures in his clavicles and scapulae with the sharp turns in most of his maneuvers. Nachman decided to get one of the few elective modifications, Elmods, he had in order to eliminate the incidence of fractures.

Nachman walked down the stairs from the console, skipping stairs as he descended, always "leggy," as his mother called him when he was a toddler. Nachman was just over six feet tall, not so much muscular but toned and slender, much like a seasoned runner. Nachman always did like to run especially zero gravity runs, but lately, since the recent residency off orbis surviving in the Celestial on the *Satyr*, he had to rely on the nanomachines to regulate his metabolism and nutrient distribution more closely to keep the slender form.

As Nachman walked he was thankful for his recent upgrades to his bioprosthetic right leg. No more limp like a damn pirate; no more subtle *tink, tink, tink* when he walked. He didn't hate the mods and upgrades, but he wasn't a huge fan of them either, just as long as they served their purpose and didn't take away from the general appreciation of being flesh and blood.

"Sadie, I'm taking the ZGV out for a spin," said Nachman. "See if the old moon has changed its color since the last time I was here."

"Nachman, you haven't brought that floating contraption into service for the better part of a year. Are you sure that is wise?" Sadie responded.

"Sadie, please…I need some time. Stay with the ship; I'm going to look into some of my old contacts in the city."

Nachman said this knowing that Sadie could be with him in an incentum, no matter how far away from the *Satyr* he came to be.

"But, Nachman, I will be able to help you..."

Nachman turned and walked to the spiral staircase that led into the cargo hold. He knew Sadie would be a great asset in the field, but he really needed a few moments to collect his incentum. He felt as if a black hole had sucked his insides out through his ear with all the new information that had just come to light. It wasn't often Nachman became emotionally involved in a case, but this one was stirring up memories that he would have preferred to keep in the deep recesses of his mind.

Sadie let Nachman go, knowing that to argue with him would be a futile effort. In these moments Nachman needed time to process, and Sadie would give him as much space she could safely allow. Even though her logistical thought processes had the capability of processing emotional expansion, she was still attempting to understand and appreciate the complexity of Human emotion. Sadie realized some time ago that to understand Nachman on this emotional level, she truly needed to give him space and time apart. In turn, Sadie developed an algorithm that created a mirage of Sadie's Vis signature, temporarily disconnecting Sadie from Nachman. If Nachman and Sadie were disconnected in this manner for more than four hours, then Sadie would fade back into her dimension. That didn't worry Sadie; what worried her was that she was unsure if she would be able to return or if Nachman would survive without her. Sadie's aura shifted to an icy blue as she activated the algorithm.

As Nachman stepped off the last stair to the cargo bay, the hairs on the back of his neck stood on end as goose pimples formed on the nape, a bitter arctic shudder went through his nerves, and he suddenly felt as if a part of his being had been abruptly culled. Nachman knew that sensation the moment Sadie disconnected; he silently thanked her for the solitude but always was happy to have her back in his head when the time came.

Nachman went to the weapon rack mounted on the port wall. He reached up and grabbed the black titiconium-laced gun belt hanging on the side of the metal rack, strapped it to his waist, and wrapped the thigh holster strap around his right thigh. Two jackets hung on the hooks next to the weapons rack. Nachman selected the worn brown-leather jacket, perfect for the tepid environment of Tasóa. He glanced at the other—a torn, faded-red pilot's jacket he received from someone he tried not to think of these days, someone who was slowly crawling back to the forefront of his incentum. *It hasn't moved from that hook for five years*, Nachman thought as a twinge of guilt struck his gut. He shied away from the jacket and the forming memory.

Nachman placed his eye in front of a retinal scanner attached to the open-faced weapon rack that was programmed to detect only Nachman's unique nanite signature. The four side-mounted Vis-laced titiconium locks buzzed and clicked open. The Vis faded into the tiny storage capsules attached to the lock. Nachman never had a grand selection of weapons but enough to pack a punch when the occasion called for them. Nachman preferred hand-to-hand or knife combat; he always felt there was a little more personality to those kinds of fights. Nachman hadn't worried about going to his personal lockbox in his quarters to select a knife from a budding collection. His favorite was already tucked in a quick draw, reverse-angle knife holster attached to the hilt of his spine, another Elmod he was thankful to have.

On the top rack, there were four rail pistols of all different calibers. Nachman selected his favorite, a 45 mm rail-shot pistol with a titiconium grip, and a mounted Vis sighting that slid it into his thigh holster. Below the pistols on a rack of its own an NXS subspace sniper rifle with a 1/3 AU Celestial Vis scope and various barrels for different occasions, from armored-vehicle penetrations to zero gravity deep-space sniping. The latter always gave Nachman vertigo viewing; the deep Celestial through a Vis filtered lenses reminded him of the lava flows on Hatu. Nauseating.

Next to the sniper rifle standing vertically, two semi-automatic rail rifles—short stock with combat grips, extended clips, and Vis holo-sighting—made for close or open combat. Nachman selected the 7.62 mm rail rifle, snapping on a short barrel he used for urban combat situations, then grabbed a couple of extended clips that held 150 armin a piece. On the bottom of the rack sat two incendiary grenades and three light grenades, collecting dust like timeworn novels. Nachman stared at them for an iota or two, then, plucking them like eggs from a carton one by one, stuffed them into the satchel hanging from the hook on the bottom of the rack. He took the satchel and slung it begrudgingly on his shoulder. Sadie said she didn't anticipate much trouble, but the way this day started, it never hurt to have a bit of firepower when you're out on your own.

Nachman reached for a shelf next to the rack, grabbing a handful of nutrient capsules, supplements that provided enough nutrition for an average adult for twenty-four hours, and stuffed them into the breast pocket of his jacket. He turned, weapons in tow, toward the vehicle mounted on docking clamps in front of the cargo bay door. The zero gravity vehicle (ZGV) was a one-man, open-canvas hovercraft. The ZGV hadn't seen the light of any orbis or luna in a little over a year and hadn't had a proper tuning in that time as well. The elongated shaft showed the signs of wear a six-year-old vehicle would when it is used and abused with minimal touch-ups, many harsh weather dents, armin fire, and various scratches throughout the body. In the direct center of the shaft, an open-canvas cockpit, a Vis-fabricated canopy can cover the cockpit when the pilot permits. A leather high-back chair had a built-in headrest and portable Quisthium cerebral input—an addition by Sadie. Just in case a field op went sideways, Nachman had a place to recover until help arrived.

Nachman placed the rail rifle into a side mount in the cockpit and placed the grenade satchel in a small compartment next to the mount. As Nachman climbed into the cockpit, the system recognized his DNA signature, and the Vis-generated pilot's console turned on, purples and reds blooming to life. Navigation controls, temperature sensors, zero gravity pad fluctuation, speed sensors, and manual pilot control came fully online by the time Nachman sat down. Nachman was waiting for the friendly reminder on the intercom as he pushed the button to open the *Satyr*'s bay doors. The door opened, the slit of light growing like an eyelid opening; the light seemed to have an orange tint to it much like citrus, a trick of light reflecting off the fabricated alien atmosphere of the terraluna.

The announcement Nachman expected came over the speakers mounted in the corners of the cargo bay, the echo reflected off the walls: "Nachman, T-minus three hours and twenty-two minutes before required reconnect. Report back, sync at three hours and fifteen minutes." Sadie hesitated, then said, "*Amicus iter tutum.*"

"Always try. See you soon," Nachman said. Sadie had used the Latin phrase "Safe travels, friend" as a mantra since the first time they disconnected, meaning to both Nachman and Sadie a farewell for the moment and the possibility of an everlasting estrangement.

He powered up the zero gravity pads lining the bottom of the shaft and the dual-layered wings protruding out from the middle of the shaft; Sadie had always thought they resembled dragonfly wings. There was a sputter in the front two pads, and the ZGV tilted forward momentarily; Nachman pushed a button and bypassed power from the middle pads, diverting them to the front pads. The ZGV corrected and stabilized. Nachman slid his index finger upward. Tiny horizontal bars followed Nachman's fingertip, and the accelerator coil sent the ZGV lurching forward. *This thing really needs a week's worth of overhaul*, thought Nachman. The silence was deafening, a muted truss. No snappy accented feminine retort inside his head. Nachman hadn't been fully disconnected from Sadie in some time; he already missed the banter.

Nachman hadn't missed the smell and glare of terra-luna Tasóa though. To him it always smelled musty, as if wet clothes had sat in a washing basin for too long, and the glare off the atmosphere forced Nachman to wear a special tint on his goggles that made the terrain appear shades of aqua and maroon. Nachman literally hadn't set foot on this moon for at least six years, give or take, and he sure hadn't regretted that decision. The ZGV sped toward the silhouette of the moon's capital city, sputtering a bit from the zero-g pads on the right wings. Even though the smell was unpleasant to him, Nachman chose to leave the cockpit open; he preferred the feel of the brisk, chilled winds in his beard and atop his shaved head. The last time he was on Tasóa felt like it was ages ago as his mind sifted through various memories, remembering through a mirror of time. A time when he felt younger, fuller, with the touch and love of a strong, intelligent, beautiful woman. That woman was the only reason he ever saw the delicate artistry of the Celestial. He looked to his left and admired the purple shrubbery and the pink crystalline flowers that were native to Noanoaga shimmering off the dusky light from the horizon. Nachman scowled as he accelerated the ZGV. *Focus on the case, you flustered sap*, he thought.

Nachman knew he needed further information about the victim—or rather, *victims*—of the assassination, the Noanoagan Orimer Buhai and Tejwenn. He didn't know much except that they, specifically the female Buhai, were all-around proponents of peace and prosperity between the two species. The male, Tejwenn, was more or less the face and support of his *Nafusma*. And Tejwenn was still in the wind; no one from either species knew his whereabouts since the assassination. If that were the case, if Nachman remembered correctly, there was something about the bond between the Noanoagans being severed traumatically...Nachman wished he had paid more attention when the science was being explained to him. Nachman recalled conversations about the meaning of the bond. The bond was as sacred to the Noas as the cross was to some ancient Humans. The two Noanoagans essentially become one, becoming tethered by some metaphysical connection that Nachman never did fully understand. But Nachman also remembered that if the bond was abruptly severed, then whichever Noa was left alive suffered some pretty severe consequences and eventually death. All the processes sent Nachman treading into foreign territory, territory he would leave for someone else to interpret and work with it from there, but that was a while ago now, past regrets as it were. *Besides that, how can someone miss a giant, fuzzy, blue Humanoid teddy bear—unless they had some kind of camo-tech that I hadn't heard of?* Nachman thought.

Nachman set his coordinates for the Noanoagan Cultural Center, or as the Noanoagans call it, *Fu Temu Miga*, loosely translated, "The Genesis to the Journey of Peace." Nachman frequented this hub of intergalactic socialization often when the days shined a little brighter on his social life or when information was needed on a budding case in this sector; sources in all Solari came in handy when you were an Arquis. But the last few years, he had chosen to stay away from this sector entirely. Hopefully his contacts at the Miga were still as reliable as they were six years ago. Nachman shook his head, and a grin formed at the crook of his lip. *Survival before ego*, he thought. Nachman glanced down at the guidance system, sixty-five kilometers outside of Aaila. Plenty of time to pick at the unfolding events.

Nachman leaned back and looked up at the stars. Because of the thin but breathable atmosphere, they shimmered brightly like jewels in a faraway ocean, even during the day. He tilted his head from side to side in an attempt to loosen some of the budding tension and looked down at the ZGV control panel. Nachman blinked once, and a private file that Nachman stored in the Ignivalo of his nanophage levitated above the control console. Nachman almost wanted to wipe the figurative dust off the file, as he hadn't accessed it since his last days in the Naibus. This file contained information on sources, military combat tactics, past case files he felt were worth keeping, and beyond containing top-secret GIA informatics, they Nachman kept off radar, as well as any other info Nachman thought worthy of filing away. Nachman sent the incentum pertaining to the specific file he needed; the bright-green lettering on the file tab read Intercerebral Warfare.

Nachman had never participated in the program—it was forty years before his time—but what he had read and researched made him both angry at the GIA for even thinking this was remotely moral and more fearful that this could be the tech Sadie encountered in the late prisoner. *Damn, it might be in Ty as well.* Nachman felt the anger bubble over the fear like a lava flow.

The IW program was introduced during the escalating skirmishes between the Liber Vultus and GIA, a ten-year period after the Noanoagans were discovered, where the rebellion would do almost anything to prevent the Aethra Gateway from coming to fruition.

According to the files, obtained from various reliable sources and Nachman's own meticulous research, Ipsum, Vitachlora, Bellatorius, and Ducovímus Solaris collaborated on the techno-organic marvel, as the elite called it. *More like "twisted abomination,"* thought Nachman. Nachman pushed the disgust aside quickly and read on. The GIA thought that by creating the Automatons and introducing them into the primary leadership of the Liber Vultus, they could dissolve the movement from the inside. The Morsus Mihi did not consider, when giving the authorization to use the tech, the devastating effects the Automaton had on the host.

The GIA strengthened the fervency of the Liber Vultus, not only by failing the infiltration but also murdering six of the eight prominent leaders in the movement. All eight of the Vultus high commanders had been implanted with the Automatons. Four were discovered after full implantation had occurred; all were subsequently euthanized. The other four were discovered just after the implantation sequencing had begun. Two of those four were known to have survived the expulsion of the Automaton. The survivors were considered lucky, but each suffered their own kind of hell before they died many years later.

Nachman glanced to his left; the red numerical display read 33 kilometers outside of Aaila. Nachman glanced at the speedometer, and the numbers began to decrease. *I'm not in that much of a hurry, and this is getting interesting*, Nachman thought as the ZGV went from a steady hurried pace to a brisk saunter.

The first survivor Enlynx for the Bellatorius front, Arnon Wazhley—the Liber Vultus equivalent of high commander and battalion general rolled into one—became a tetraplegic and was clinically brain dead, kept alive by means of various medical apparatus and a direct tethering to the Gnanimus. Wazhley's family eventually pulled the connection. As for the second survivor Enlynx for the Ipsum front, Uyao Qinyo, she did not endure any noticeable physical harm from the expulsion, but the damage to the brain tissue was irreversible, as well as the resulting psychological deficits that followed. Enlynx Qinyo spent the rest of her days under strict supervision in a Liber Vultus run safehouse in an undisclosed location in Vitachlora Solaris.

No one in the private sector or GIA could reason why she survived in such a manner, except that after she died, it was discovered that she had secretly kept her Caiet activated after leaving the GIA. It was a curious turn of events for the movement because all Liber Vultus members were required to severe their Gnanimus connections upon acceptance into the movement, which meant losing their Caiets. Some would reluctantly give up their, at times, lifelong connection, while others would forgo the movement and live in solace among the Alliance. Enlynx Qinyo was one who couldn't be without either; somehow Qinyo's Caiet was able to hide from Vis scanners upon her initiation and kept a soft, untraceable connection to the Gnanimus. But it had appeared as if Qinyo's nanophage had been severely damaged during the expulsion process, mostly from the inside, leaving the nanophage unable to connect with the Gnanimus as well as to discover the whereabouts of her former Caiet. The only way the GIA found out about this information was due to the movement's use of the Gnanimus to perform the nanophage autopsy. Nachman and Sadie acquired the information from supposedly scrubbed Gnanimus files deep inside the matrix of the Gnanimus. Nachman wanted to make sure when he left the GIA that he took some vulnerable secrets with him.

Nachman wondered if what happened in Qinyo's head was anything similar to the skirmish Sadie had with the Automaton she encountered inside the prisoner's head or if the Caiet had anything to do with Qinyo surviving the expulsion process. *Sadie is going to love this research*, Nachman thought.

Nachman felt a ringing in his ear and looked up from the file, scowling, breaking the direct, invisible feed of information from the file. The proximity warning was flashing and chirping for a few seconds at least. Sixteen kilometers; he was coming up to the Noanoagan capital city. *Well isn't this all becoming a load of heavy alvum to shovel up*, Nachman thought. Nachman nervously brought his hand to his beard. This whole mess screamed of conspiracy. Nachman sent the incentum to the ZGV to slow speed for pedestrian awareness, as the outer limits of the city began to become alive with commuters both Noanoagan and Human.

We have a trifecta, Nachman thought, *assassinations, government involvement, and inter-species entanglements*. Nachman let out a low, barely audible chuckle. He was sure anyone he brought this to would chalk this line of thinking up to paranoia—he sure would, from the way this all sounded. Nachman shook his head. If the civilian populace only knew what other secrets the GIA kept in their deep, deep vaults. Hell, the alvum he had on this file alone could bring many of the elite echelons of the GIA down to his doorstep, and not in a friendly way.

Nachman always knew there were many among the higher echelons of the GIA and possibly some members of the Morsus Mihi that conducted not-so-savory activities behind the public eye. It has been ongoing throughout Human history; Sadie would attest to that fact. And, yes, Nachman knew, given the fact that this was one of the biggest reasons he was glad to accept walking papers from the Naibus; there were always the gullible and naive adulator blindly following orders they should at least question as morally ambiguous. The paranoid part of his psyche could never let go of the fact that if anybody gets that much power, government or otherwise, bad things were bound to be attached to the people, or aliens, involved. Nachman knew with every fiber in his body that he would try to break down every firewall the GIA has to expose them for every dirty thing in the Celestial they have been a part of if his best friend, since the day he joined the Naibus, was infected, possessed, brainwashed—whatever the appropriate verbiage was—by one of these damned Automatons. Not only was this a tech supposed to be snuffed by the GIA, but the hard truth was that Nachman's very tight-knit family was being dealt a bad hand by this whole situation. *And I'll be damned if this doesn't all somehow link together*, Nachman thought. Nachman could see why the Liber Vultus was still fighting so hard: it was all personal.

Nachman took another side glance at the guidance system, seven kilometers out. Time to put on the best "hello there." He looked up from his private file, sending the incentum to seal it, and locked it under several layers of code that cycled algorithmic density in his Ignivalo periodically. Only the best network security inside Nachman's head. The file funneled like a small sandstorm above the console, then faded into the recesses of Nachman's nanophage as the dull light of the bustling city came into view.

There were four entrances to the city, as there were in

all six major cities on the terraluna. Nachman always wondered why the cities were so symmetrical and angular, almost a perfect square from the air, but when you got into the thick of the cities, they become lively with vibrant asymmetry. All the personality the Noanoagans were known for seemed to be contained within the city limits; Nachman always thought that was odd design and behavior. Nachman thought he remembered Esas, the East Entrance, as being the least crowded; luckily Nachman never had trouble blending into a crowd.

The ZGV slowed. Nachman looked around the crowd, Noanoagan and Human, walking across the streets, at one of the first busy intersections in the capital city of Tasóa, Aaila. The hustle and bustle of commerce and socialization was a promotion of interspecies progress. *Such progress*, Nachman thought with an edge of cynicism. Down the street, Nachman saw a Noanoagan festival, twangy, bass music, kids' games and carnival rides, and lots of Human and Noanoagan food, Nachman did love the food, and he was hungry; as he floated by a food stand, a Human handed him some meat on a stick. Nachman felt his retina scanned as credits were taken from his public account. The aliens were always celebrating something; Nachman never knew what they were celebrating, and he sure didn't know now. It appeared to be their spring solstice celebration; fresh flowers and other colorful arrays of plant life were strewn around the fairgrounds. Banners and streamers flowing in the soft breeze, lights and lasers flashing, the colors skittering off the buildings as they reflected off the glass. Many Noanoagan families strolled about the festival, the prismatic aliens laughing and enjoying the music and food. There were not as many Human families, though; the atmosphere was breathable but toxic to prepubescent Human life and pregnant women. If you were able to acquire the proper permissions, one could gain access to respirator tech that would allow children to visit Tasóa, and as far as Nachman could see, the only children here were still the children of the GIA elites. *Not much has changed*, Nachman thought. As a matter of fact, everything looked as it always did, like nothing ever occurred. The first assassination of a Noanoagan since they had been here, and everything looked so normal. No heightened security measures or extra GIA personnel on site— not necessarily following the protocols, Nachman knew, but then again, he wasn't a soldier anymore. From the looks of everything, it was almost the same as it was six years ago. *That feeling hasn't changed either*, Nachman thought, *I have never felt at ease anywhere on this damn luna.*

Nachman pulled the ZGV into the parking block next to a bright-orange, gregariously gaudy ZGV, one of many in the lot, not helping the conspicuous nature of the beat-up junker he piloted. With the ZGV hovering over four metal squares protruding from the concrete, Nachman remembered something Sadie had said earlier when he was on the lex with Ty. He wished he could clear up the jumbled alvum that came out of his incentum when he psychically connected with Sadie. Nachman shook his head. No time for self-improvement. He looked down at the control panel and sent the incentum to activate the docking clamps, the four squares beneath the ZGV extended upward, the top latching into the four inlets on the underside of the ZGV. An audible clang could be heard when the docking clamps engaged. Nachman powered down the ZGV, collected his rail rifle, and slung it across his back, barrel down, and he couldn't shake a sudden noda in the pit. The rail rifle barrel, his tech stolen (from where he had no clue), an assassination of an alien delegate with his tech, his friend somehow involved, most likely against his will, and a strange sense that someone was trying to deter him from moving forward. *I must be more paranoid than I even thought*, mused Nachman, *but Sadie did say as such.*

"Why you, Nachman?"

CHAPTER 6

Deep Celestial, Inter-Solari, Three Parsecs outside of Vitachlora Solaris
Thirteen Standard Weeks until Aethra Gateway Completion

The family was happy, the happiest they had been in a very long time. They all laughed, played, and feasted among one of Resalo's gloriously green field parks on a crisp autumn day. The picnic table long, shimmering with lacquer, with an oaken frame handmade from the Asopken tree in the mountains of Surculus, the only terraluna orbiting Resalo. The smallest of Resalo's lunas, Nitánthro, could be seen in the dusk sky, silhouetted by the rays of the Crescat sun as they bounced off the thick clouds. Around the table sat the generations of the Xon family. Father on one end and Grandfather on the other. Twin sisters sat to the right of Father, laughing and playing with their holo-dolls. Mother scolded them gleefully, trying and failing to get them to sit and eat their dinner. *Those two never did like potato salad from any planet*, mused the oldest and only son who sat proudly the left of his father.

Julius, birthright to the Xon dynasty, fourteen now, unscarred and unscathed, never voyaging the fateful stellar mission from which he became deformed, sat with a look of adoration upon his family, wondering if this is how it would have been. Julius looked up at his mother, Sahyba Xon; she smiled down on him, the purple and pink tint of the dusk horizon accented his mother, making it appear as if a serine aura formed around her. Julius felt an angelic warmth from his mother, safe and secure, a blanket wrapped around his being, shrouding the discontent and unwelcome from him. How he missed his mother's touch. Julius reached for her hand, but there was only a brush of air between their fingertips before her hand was taken away to part the sisters, another argument about which doll was having tea and which was serving. Julius smiled. His sisters were bothersome, but he had cared for them and loved them in his own way. Father, Thiago, and Grandfather, Mateo, stand and walk a pace to the grill, turning the spit as the smell of wild pig blackening filled the air. They laughed and hugged, a father and son as close now as they were in youth.

Aracella and Adora, the twins, ran around the table laughing and screaming, Adora chasing her "older" twin, yelling that she took the clothes she wanted for her doll. Mother walked after them to make sure the sibling rivalry was not carried too far. Julius took a bite of his salad; purple and orange leaves fresh and crisp from his Grandmother's garden crunch between his teeth. Julius looked up, smiling at his grandmother. He admired her for her horticultural prowess; she could grow anything on any planet. She was legendary among the Alliance for her green thumb. Julius looked off into the distance. The Crescat sun dipped below the horizon, the rays reflecting off the atmosphere sending an array of purples snaking through the sky. Happy, content, euphoric—all sentiments Xon had chosen not to feel since the accident that took everything.

The Quscape allowed the Magnus to indulge in an opportunity, the one and only Xon would allow and only under the solitude of a Qusom, to bring about an emotionally metaphysical connection to the incentum of an ideal past he believed he should have experienced. In this realm of thought, it wasn't so much a dream but a simulated existence within the mind derived from the chemical interaction between brain serums and Quisthium; it allowed Xon to experience a past that never occurred, similar to an Adyta those bothersome Sitanimi monks teach. The Suviira taught him control, but the thoughts Xon kept buried deep in the caverns of his incentum needed to be nourished, they said. The parts he has chosen to switch off, the emotional state of being that makes Humanity exposed to the whimsical manipulations of outside parties, needed to be indulged for the sake of sanity.

In the distance Julius saw the horizon darken, not a fog or mist but black like a shroud, cloaking the skyline like a void of nothingness. There was something there; Julius observed a small, minuscule speck of light in the dark. *This is new*, thought Xon, *not an aesthetic I have programmed into the Quscape.*

The adolescent projection of Julius reached a hand up to the nape of his neck, forcefully massaging the tissue, feeling new hairs pull from the root. There was a humming throb deep in the base of his skull that sent waves of needlelike pain through his head. The pain was becoming more acidic; young Julius swore he could feel his nanophage beginning to bubble in his skull, almost searing parts of his cerebellum. With his head slightly bowed, the pain in the base of his neck pulsating now, Julius looked around the table, a haze clouding his vision, and his eyes stung like they had been dried by a mound of sand. *How can this be? My eyes are perfect here, both organic and both perfect; I'm in control here*, thought Xon. Julius's young face, smooth and seemingly free of blemish, free of apprehension—the ideal face Xon thought he should have had in the life that never would be—was showing an edge of panic.

A noise was muffled but steadily gaining amplitude behind Julius's tympanic membrane, almost as if every bit of sound was being digitized through a funnel.

Xon, and Xon alone, knew what was inside of his head. The only way he would carry out this cumbrous task, Xon required complete control of his facsimiles while under the suggestion of the Quisthium. If it were not another biological necessity, Magnus Xon would not use the abhorrent chemical, but in order to travel such great distances across the Milky Way, the flesh required preservation. He forsook a Caiet when he programmed his nanophage to dilute the excreted limbic chemicals, narrowing his emotional spectrum to feel only that which is logistical and tactical; therefore, no one outside Xon's precisely controlled aspect of incentum would know what he indulged in while in Qusom. Control of self, a finite discipline that could be threaded through the eye of a needle, with no room for error—a set of standards Magnus Xon held to the utmost were not gone here in the Quscape but dampened. The Magnus showed no flaw, no glint of vulnerability when in the corporeal company outside his psyche. He must—no needed—to have the limbic chemicals in his body at some point to keep him from going completely batty, as his confidant had so delicately phrased it. So he indulged this fantasy, partially out of want but mostly out of necessity.

Using the will of his incentum, Xon attempted to negate the digitized buzzing, but as he sent the command across his membranes, the pulsating becomes a steady beat, vibrating from within his skull. The young Julius brought his hands to the back of his neck and arched his back, raising his head to the Resalo sky and let out a scream that sounded too inhuman to categorize, a cross between a howling feline in heat and the high-pitched computerized static of a broken lex box. Julius crumbled to the table, his elbows slamming the wooden surface. Julius strained his head to look toward his mother, but strangely, she was not looking in his direction. Her back was to Julius, and she was pointing at something beyond the park's horizon. Forcing himself to move was like moving through a barrier of wax while it hardened. Julius crawled across the bench toward his mother; looking around, Julius noticed no one was moving at all. Everyone appeared frozen in midmovement, as if someone paused their lex feeds.

An intense heat seared through Julius's skull; his brain felt like it was ready to boil over out of his eye sockets. Julius extended his right arm. It felt warm and tingly, like ants crawling along his arm. He expected to see a young, smooth, lean limb instead of an arm that had slowly, over the course of many years, become a cyberorganic map of disfigurement. The dermis remaining was thin and aged; multiple clear celluloid encasements lined the arm, and through each compartment, you could see the mechanical intertwined with the biological. The metals sewn into the muscle and sinew, the flesh stretching with each articulation of gears, leaving tiny droplets of blood streaking the fibrous metal. Xon even saw the faulty clip connecting the radioulnar ligament with the subtle scrape on the bone each time he flexed his wrist, the linear etch in his radius prominent. Xon could have sworn that defect was solidified years ago. *What is happening; how can this be?*

For what seemed like an eternal crawl through an invisible viscous muck, Julius finally came to his mother's statuesque form. Julius ignored the outstretched limb of his mother pointing to the unknown and forced his tortuously aching body across the last leg of the bench and underneath her arm. Julius bumped her waist; Sahyba wavered but did not move, remaining as still as an ice sculpture.

Julius strained his neck upward and looked to his mother's face, but her face isn't what he had programmed from his memories. The angelic features were replaced with one twisted with terror, as if she was witnessing the impending doom of everything she had known. Her eyes slowly shifted downward and met Julius's eyes. A single tear flowed from the corner of her eye, slowly moving over her cheek, leaving an ember trail in its wake, and she burst into flames. The young Xon couldn't scream, couldn't move, only watch as the fear washed over him.

Fear, thought Xon, *an emotion I haven't felt since the first time my family died in front of me.* Despite the overwhelming sensations barraging his conscious incentum under Qusom, Xon's subconscious fought to maintain control of the Quscape. The more he fought, the worse the nightmare seemed to expand.

The flames sprouted from her skin, pirouetting from

his mother and licking Julius's flawless skin, the Quscape seemingly interchanging aspects of Xon and his surroundings at will now. With each kiss of the flame, the flawless was scorched away, revealing the synthetic, the mechanical, and for what is left of the dermis the scarred and disfigured. All around Julius, one by one, his family spontaneously burst into flames. The twins, grandfather, grandmother, and finally father—as he looked down on young Julius, he smiled as the fire charred him and the Xon family into ash. The wind was suddenly shrieking, the bitter breeze taking the Xon family ashes, whistling through brush as they were carried away. *Almost as if the Quscape itself sees the satirical in my family's demise once more*, thought Xon's subconscious.

As quickly as the subconscious incentum projected, young Julius was suddenly and violently hurled into the atmosphere of Resalo. Turning, twisting, no control over limb or momentum, upended—Julius was among the stars, staring down at his home planet. In the real world, Magnus Xon began to spasm violently, muscles so tight it made his fingers contort under the tension, a thin, foamy mucus forming at the corner of his mouth, leaving a wet trail down his scarred jawline. The digitized buzzing behind his eardrums grew to an octave so high that Xon's subconscious felt like it split in two. Young Julius curled into a floating fetal position as Xon screamed inside his mind. The spasms turned into full body seizures while Xon sat in the Qusom chair on the *Cultivador*.

Everything quieted. Julius looked around, seeing nothing but open Celestial, Resalo, and its lunas, and he noticed he was now naked. As he looked upon himself, he saw that his untainted flesh from youth was being blown away by an unseen wind, revealing his biomechanical form he held in real time. He felt no pain as he witnessed his body slowly decaying, as if rendered in a frame by frame lex feed, flesh to rot and metal to rust, right before his eyes. But the sight that beheld him next was both terrifying and spectacular.

The bright light that had been set in the distance was

instantaneously above the planet with a ray of light trailing behind. As the ray of light caught up with the luminescent beacon above Resalo, the light began to materialize; it spread into a plateau of pure brightness as the tail of the ray hit. Then the Aethra Gateway, in all of its megalithic proportions, came into existence above Xon's home planet. The giant corona of titiconium and alien metals hovered silently; the reflection of the Crescat sun gleamed off the surface, giving the illusion of a sublime halo above the planet. Xon felt a sudden rush of terror and joy at the splendor of the Gateway. It appeared completed, no gravity rigs or short haulers holding bits and pieces in place as it appeared in Tracaelus at this moment. Even the final element was in place, a mysterious organic metal the Noanoagans call Vyrinox. They claim to have procured during their travels in the Deep Celestial before happening upon the Human race. The Vyrinox was laced and twining around the circular frame, a bright interlacing of shimmering metallic blues and greens of equal count, precise cut, and length. Xon had not yet laid his eyes upon the almost completed gateway and was now—even as he sat in the mind-twisting, nightmarish Qusom—a spectacle to behold.

"My legacy fulfilled!" shouted Xon as he spread his arms as if to embrace the technological wonder before him.

Tendrils, thousands of them, formed from the Vyrinox interlaced throughout the structure and began propelling out of every inch of the Aethra Gateway. The planet-encompassing behemoth steadily hovered over Resalo as the tendrils latched themselves to every acre of the planet, penetrating the terrain like a thorn pierces the flesh. Xon could do nothing but watch as he floated, frozen in place with his arms and legs outstretched much like the ancient sketch of Da Vinci's *Vitruvian Man* except that Xon's mouth stood agape in a terrified, silent scream. Xon watched as the Aethra swallowed Resalo's lunas, Surculus and Nitánthro, whole into a blindingly nuclear light at the center of the megalith. As the moons disappeared into the white hole of the Aethra, the tendrils continued to penetrate the planet's surface. Each tendril pulled and ripped at the planet, almost like the Aethra was intent on pulverizing Xon's homeworld. As each piece of the planet was ripped away from the broken atmosphere and thrust into the Aethra's pool of light, it seemed to break apart further, pixelating and then melting into the light.

The consistent reverberation inside Xon's nanophage grew to the point of excruciation. No longer frozen, he began to claw at the back of his head; the flesh slid apart as the dull, rusted tips of metallic fingers, now on both hands as the Qusom realm continued the tortuous jest of Xon's mind, flayed his skin. The index and thumb slid into the serrated wound, and Xon grasped the hard yet spongy miniature quantum computer attached to his cerebral cortex. Xon timidly pulled at the nanophage stretching and ripping at his muscle and cervical vertebrae; then, tired of being tender, he plunged the tips of his robotic digits into his cerebellum, digging the nanophage from the spongy encasement. The pain was agonizing as the microscopic fiber optic cables tore from the walls of his cerebral cortex. Xon looked at his nanophage as brain matter dolloped off and crimson glints of blood pooled in the palm of his hand. The nanophage pulsated like a tiny heart in Xon's rusting metal hand, but the buzzing didn't stop. It grew to the high whine, a digital sound bite, of a crystallized ember shattering on the surface of an ice asteroid. A sound that cannot be heard in the depths of the Celestial but loud enough to deafen a world. Louder it echoed in Xon's skull, louder, louder.

Xon screamed as he was jolted from Qusom; a cold, acrid sweat dripped from every pore he had left. He looked around. Xon was back on the *Cultivador* sitting in the cushioned Qusom chair. Xon glanced to the upper left corner of his left eye, where a constant Vis-rendered heads-up display was showing the control console of the *Cultivador*, a little over forty-eight hours out from Vitachlora Solaris. Xon wiped the sweat from his brow, examining the aged flesh and metal; both were tremulous and spastic. He cursed the limbic necessity his remaining organic faculties required. Magnus Xon let the autopilot guide the rest of the journey to the Terraorbis Medvios while he ushered in the sense of precise control he required to complete the coming tasks.

CHAPTER 7

Noanoagan Capital City Aaila, Terraluna Tasóa, Tracaelus Solaris
Noanoagan Cultural Center, *Fu Temu Miga*

As Nachman walked the last fifty yards, he couldn't help but admire the eerily natural architecture of the *Fu Temu Miga,* or the Miga, as most Humans called the cultural center/nightclub. It was as if the luna intently formed this structure during terraforma. The foundation of the structure itself looked melded to the earth, one with the terraluna. The siding was dry, like it was cured, and oddly spongy but at the same time, surprisingly, as solid as the titiconium lining the hull of the *Satyr*. The structure was wide like an industrial warehouse and about four stories tall. Windowless, metallic gray with rounded borders and corners, and five dull-white wiry but solid spires with toadstool-like tops jutting from the roof into the creamy yellow evening sky. Even though he admired the oddity of the structure, Nachman was slightly put off at the thought of living or even going inside of a fungus. He has heard of some species of fungi with small ganglia in their cap that adhered to the flesh and melted it away before your eyes. Nachman shuddered at the thought. *Nasty way to go.*

To better know the new residents of the Milky Way, as his instructors had phrased, Nachman had been assigned to study Noanoagan history as an elective at the Naibus Institutum in his early years. Now, Nachman wished he would have continued those studies further into later academia now that the Noanoagans were so deeply involved in one of his cases.

There were portions he could recall; however, the rest he accessed from the Gnanimus. After all, it had been quite a while since an incentum has crossed his mind about Tasóa or anything related to it.

On their homeworld Noanoagans were able to cultivate a vast variety of native species of moss and fungi among the various tropical and swampy regions that encompassed a majority of the planet. With these virulent species, especially a genus of fungi called U'agi (Oo-ahn-gee) translated (again loosely) to "tenacious fungi," the Noanoagans were able to construct a variety of structures from small dwellings to sky-sweeping multiplexes, vehicles, tools, intergalactic stellarcraft—and yes, weaponry. The pliability and durability of the fungi was astounding; the fact that the original Noanoagan intergalactic colossal cruiser was able to withstand the pulverizing pressures, unknown foreign debris, and various quasi-radiations out in the Deep Celestial was an instant selling point for the GIA. The Elitists could not pass up the opportunity to "help" the Noanoagans synthesize an adequate substitute for the alien mushroom. The GIA attempted to break down the genomic structures of the original alien craft, but once the U'agi's essential properties were extracted and smelted, it was almost impossible to mold the final product, Apitia (Ah-pee-shee-a, Noanoagan for "fortified fungi"), into anything else.

Fortunately for Human scientists, no synthesized mushroom extract was needed as the Noanoagans managed to save some unused spores and kept them in a type of cryogenic hibernation for the duration of their journey across the stars. The Morsus Mihi selected GIA scientists from all over the Celestial, with emphasis on Crescat, Ipsum, and Vitachlora, as well as a small contingent of Bellatorius. Scientists perusing military applications went to work on attempting to meld the fungi with Human technology. So far, after fifty-one years, only a select few, Human and Noa, have come close to cracking the fungi's code.

There had been attempts to launch Human-crafted vessels with applications of the U'agi fungi integrated in both its natural state and in the smolten Apitia form out of Tasóa's atmosphere, but they only lasted a few minutes before a full system failure, and the pilot must be rescued before toxic chemicals were released throughout the vessel from the breakdown of the organic material when met with the radiation of the Celestial. Something with the way the Apitia was forged or the erroneous nature of the U'agi from the cultivation process with the terraluna's soil. Nachman didn't care enough to scan this information, as it wasn't relevant to the case. Nachman shook his head as if to clear the fuzz from inside his head, consciously noting that any incentum about the mushrooms had no bearing on the current direction of the case. Why was his mind drifting? Had to be the stress from the last few days. Nachman decided to finish the line of incentum and record it for later. Maybe Sadie could run some psycho-mechanical (psy-mech) analysis; maybe he had a screw loose, like some thought.

Nachman was far from a xenomycologist, but the theory that sounded plausible wasn't from an elite GIA brainiac but his own sweet, whimsical mother, who happened to be a seasoned Magrii or in the traditional English a biomechanical herbalist. Delylah had told him the primary reason could be due to the mushroom's origin. One, the alien fungi is just that—alien—and since originating on an alien world with the blanket of their sun's radiation combined with the planet's atmosphere and certain elements in the native soil, the fungus was able to be cultivated without fail. And two, Tasóa was a terraluna, elements from the previous state of the planet were still present in the petrous core of the moon, thus negating some of the essential properties needed for proper primordia formation of the U'agi.

Nachman cracked a grin, shaking his head again. *This is stuff Sadie's is interested in. Focus*, Nachman he said to himself. As he walked the last few steps, he couldn't help but stop and peer at the five spires as they rose into the sky taller than any structure on the terraluna. At the top of the spire was a wide, spherical cap that made the spires look like towering mushrooms. The five spires were made to represent the five ideals, paianuga (pā-ee-ā-noo-gā), of the Noanoagans. Ducovímus scholars believe, with much uncertainty (as the Noas do not have a written language), the ideals are peace, purpose, wisdom, strength of being, and shared unity in all. These paianuga represented the shared belief system of the entire species. The Miga was built to represent the temples of Old Noanoaga and very much reminded Nachman of the ancient cathedrals from pre-Gaian history. Much like the concept behind the Miga now, the old temples were places of gathering, acquiring knowledge, and meditation during daylight, and at night, it became more or less a dance club. So the ancients could dance to the moon's delight, as the Noanoagans say.

Nachman always thought "colorful" and "glamorous" were never the most accurate descriptions for anything related to the Noanoagans. As he opened the tall, rounded, fluorescent, claylike double doors, Nachman's biomech eye flickered a bit as he was met with what he could only describe as color that was kaleidoscopic mixed with a metallic-neon opalescence. Although he had enjoyed coming here in the past, the constant mods to his ocular mech caused the brilliant color schemes to give him a headache. Luckily the flickering meant the lens filter Sadie and his mother had installed dropped into place to refract the light for adequate visual acuity and less headaches. *I'll have to thank them both later for the adjustment*, Nachman thought.

A multicolored laser light show was bouncing off the bright-white ceiling, the lines of light intertwining with one another, creating a neon brilliance of a solar flare bouncing off the atmosphere. The vaulted ceiling gave the illusion of viewing the spectacle while residing at the bottom of a cave. The laser show began to flicker on and off as a lanky, magenta-furred Noanoagan tinkered with a rounded techno-organic light fixture on the floor in the corner. Directly in front of him on a huge empty space, a couple of Human and Noanoagan technicians were assembling the famed alien dance floor, called the Skimmer by the Human population. But to the Noanoagans, it was known as Símatau (Cee-mā-tā-ow), a moss that allowed anyone, no matter the weight, to skim across the surface. Before the destruction of Noanoaga, the aliens had used the moss in dance rituals, one of many for various occasions, to welcome the new trimoons of Noanoaga, Fai'ma, Lai'ma, and Pai'ma. From what the Noanoagan elders and the Ducovímus scroll-keepers have translated (the cultural practice is to pass on all history through oral communication; Noanoagan body art was the only form of written linguistics to be found and had yet to be fully translated), the moons would come into a perfect alignment twice a year to welcome the changing of the seasons among the planet. Nachman had skimmed in the past and did enjoy it, but he never liked to skim alone.

It appeared to Nachman that he had caught the Miga in transition from daytime family-oriented learning and meditation of the Noanoagan cultural center to a haven of regalement people often describe as not just a nightclub but a metaphysical interspecies experience. Nachman thought this was advantageous for his current case because if he still knew the owners of the Miga, a *Nafusma* of Noanoagans, they would want to get him out quickly to get their nightclub hopping with Human tourists without busybodies asking questions. Nachman just hoped they would still talk to him.

Nachman took another step and was greeted with a thud on his chest by the mammoth four-fingered hand of an eight-foot behemoth of a Noanoagan, likely one of the Miga's enforcers. "Muscular" was an understatement; his right arm was wider than Nachman's entire chest, and Nachman did his fair share of zero-g presses. Now, every Noanoagan Nachman had encountered, including the giant in front of him, had relatively similar features. Whether tall or short, their arms and legs are proportioned, furry from head to toe with the exception of bald hands, feet, chest, and abdomen, and Humanoid facial features with a slightly protruding maxilla at the alveolar process. What really distinguished one from another were their body art and fur coats.

Many Ducovímus xenolinguistic experts were still hard at work deciphering the intricate tattooing called talafau'sia (tā-lā-fā-oo-cee-ā), or tala for short used by the Noanoagans to pass on their individual, familial, and *Nafusma* histories. The scholars always boast how the tala are culturally significant because it is the only form of written language that was known among the species and would be lost once the Noanoagan die, as there were no other forms of written records among the original Noanoagan vessel. Each piece of tala told the story of that particular Noanoagan: their life, work, and accomplishments. No one set of tala was similar to another, and once the Noa became a *Nafusma*, their tala and fur blended to tell the story of the *Nafusma.* Essentially a fingerprint unique to the Noanoagan who bore the tala, as Nachman understood.

While Ducovímus scholars deciphered the various tala, pretty much every other scientific mind in the Alliance had been fascinated with the hollow, silky follicles that covered all Noanoagans since the aliens had arrived. So much so that even though they don't know the full extent of the follicles abilities the GIA decided to dub it "functionally integrated hollow roots"—fihr pronounced "fur" by the general public. To Nachman, this was by far the most impressive survival tool the Noanoagans possessed. The lufuga'o (loo-foo-gā-ow), or hollow follicle, had been known to adjust the body temperature to keep the Noas thermodynamically stable in any environment, can harden like titiconium as a defensive mechanism and had been known to change color in correlation with moods, especially fear and anger. Nachman did envy the rumor that the filaments could refract light to blend in with the environment and create a kind of camouflage. When they first arrived, Nachman always thought they all just looked like giant furry bears, but if one looked closer at their details, a Human could tell an awful lot about their alien neighbors.

There were two important observations Nachman made by first glance at the behemoth before him. One, the Noanoagan was male; he knew because of the ears. Males had pointed ears, whereas the females had rounded, tipped ears. This was the only way Nachman wanted to tell the difference between genders. There was the universal way, by viewing the genitalia, but that was only accomplished during mating rituals, and from what Sadie had graphically described in the most nauseating of detail, it was a very messy process from beginning to end. Nachman was more than happy to stay away from that particular ritual.

When the Noanoagan spoke, he sounded deep, echoing like an opera singer underwater. Something with the vocal cord being much wider than a Human's, which is why Humans cannot speak Noa, if Nachman remembered correctly. A metallic, button-sized transmod, translator module, at the anterior crest of the Noa's slightly more elongated neck emitted a short burst of static. Then a low male voice with a British accent, subtly growled, "We don't open for another hour. What do you want"—there was a small pause—"*sir*?" The "sir" was obviously forced.

The other thing Nachman noticed was the neon-red tattoos of various straight lines and triangular shapes encompassing most of the Noa's chest and face, with five large red hoops in a row lining his bottom lip and red gauges in his ear lobes big enough to fit a Human infant's arm through. The piercings and tala all shouted to Nachman that he had been a warrior for a very long time. His red fihr was fading, and the bare skin a dull gray instead of a creamy pink—both signs of advanced aging in a Noanoagan that had no *Nafusma*. If Nachman had to guess, this fellow was pushing 350 years old. A warrior that was male, unbonded, and pushing geriatric status was probably here because he was no longer fit for service in the Fale'aloa. Regardless, he was still not a Noanoagan you would want to fight for sport.

Nachman put on his most friendly smile and said, "Just here to see the owner about some escaped prisoners from Tenebrae that were seen in the sector a few hours ago." Nachman flashed a green Vis-rendered projection of his Arquis credentials from a bracelet on his wrist, a portable control mod for the *Satyr*. Nachman could easily access the *Satyr* from his nanophage, but he preferred to keep an access point to his ship off the grid. Paranoid? Never.

Nachman didn't like what he saw next. Not only did the warrior Noa ball up his anvil-like fists and let out a low guttural growl that would make the seasoned Naibus trooper tremble, but there was something Nachman hadn't seen before today. The fihr all over his body vibrated and seemed to erect straight out like the needles of a porcupine. The behemoth was tense, angry, and up for something bad; Nachman was sure he didn't do anything to piss him off. *Strange behavior. I've heard of the fihr hardening to create a kind of shell-like shield but never an offensive weaponized form. Absolutely wild,* Nachman thought. *I guess I was wrong about them not being up in arms about the assassination, but still I never seen any Noa act so outwardly aggressive, even among the warriors.* Nachman moved his right foot back and shifted his weight ever so slightly, put his right hand on his thigh holster, and made sure to send the incentum to his left arm to crank up the PSI behind his punch, ready for the pending attack. *This was going to hurt*, Nachman thought.

"Well, if isn't the old dog himself. Nach Rose, get your stinky alvum-chewing ass over here, and give me a hug, bro!" The voice was eerily familiar to Nachman.

As if hearing the command of a higher-ranking officer, the warrior eased back. The barbs that covering his body went limp, as if all the tension had been released, and settled back to the fihr Nachman had been accustomed too. The Noa stood aside as his fihr faded from the bright-neon red of what Nachman knew was the coming fury to the dull red he had seen when he first entered the Miga.

Walking past the elder warrior, Nachman looked into the Noanoagan's golden eyes, and Nachman could have sworn it look as if he was coming out of some sort of daze. The Noanoagan looked at Nachman, and for a moment, a look of confusion cast upon his face, his eyes darting back and forth. Then, as if nothing had happened, the red warrior turned and wandered back to the main door to maintain his given post. Nachman wondered if in the five years he was away from this terraluna, the Noanoagans really had changed that much.

Nachman turned back to where the voice had come from and saw to whom the not-so-much-a-command belonged—not a Noanoagan but a Human, and exactly the Human he expected. Standing behind the Ga'a'ula "Emotional Experience" Bar was a man as tall as a Noa, skinny as a rail shot, and louder than a four-horned Lortarisian mud beetle during mating season: the ex-Naibus Beta Squadron, Recon Specialist Rodan "Ro" Grantes Human, attaché to the *Fu Temu Miga.* Rodan had also been Nachman's Human contact on Tasóa since he was dishonorably discharged from the Naibus on the account that he was caught sleeping with not only the Naibus Institutum Dean of Academia's daughter and niece, at the same time, but also causing a complete shutdown of all Gnanimus activity in the Institutum's sector for over twelve hours just so he would not be interrupted during his shore leave with said daughter and niece. Annoying, undisciplined scalawag, but Rodan was useful when the time came. Nachman did always find himself on the verge of putting a rail shot in his leg just to shut him up about 80 percent of the time.

"Nach Rose, Nach Rose," Rodan said as he strode pompously half the length of the one-hundred-yard Ga'a'ula Bar, "leave it to you to stroll into a place and pick a fight with one of the biggest damn Noas we got here!"

Rodan swung around the end of the bar, his elongated frame towering over Nachman, and took his orangutan-like arms and wrapped them around Nachman. Because of a genetic mishap in utero, Rodan had acquired a cured genetic mutation called Marfan syndrome, where his appendages were abnormally lengthened so it looked like Rodan was hugging himself at the same time. Nachman cringed, not at Rodan, but that he always hated being touched; however, this was the only way to get a loudmouth like Rodan to talk—be friendly and somewhat receptive of the antics.

"Hey, Rodan, long time! Just have a couple questions if you got a sec," Nachman said as he patted Rodan's midback, trying to let go of the viselike hug.

"Rodan, Rodan! Call me Ro, bro. How many times have I told you that? Man, out with the pleasantries and straight to business. Same ol' Nach, straight as an arrow out of the uni as well. Haven't seen you since the last time you were here, what four or five years now? With that fine little bird—what was her name? Ah, I can't remember anyway, but it's great to see ya! How things out in the wide wide?" Rodan rambled on for another few minutes, and Nachman stood in front of him and endured, his patience already worn thin with the day's events. "Boy, oh boy, don't know what you did to piss off Toatua, but he was about to kill you!"

"It must be my way with people, I guess."

"You, a way with people? And my grandma owns the casinos on Venus," bellowed Rodan. "So tell me, my old pal, what brings you all the way back to my neck of the Celestial after all this time?"

Nachman contemplated how much to divulge to Rodan. He didn't get that same noda in the pit he did with Ty, but he had to tread lightly. Nachman still wasn't sure how far into Tracaelus, or for that matter the Celestial, this Automaton epidemic has spread, so he decided to keep the facts thin enough that they were believable. And on a personal note, Nachman refused to call the man "Ro." Call it personal conviction, but he couldn't call someone a nickname if he had no respect for them.

"Just out and about, lookin' for some cons that jumped luna back on Tenebrae, missing two weeks, seen in this sector about a day ago. I had one in binds, but he had a mishap with the *Satyr*'s cargo bay." Nachman made sure to imply that it was an active case and that he was a few feet deep in it. "Have you heard of any of them poking around your way...pal?"

"Mishap? Come on, Nach, you can tell ol' Ro the truth, buddy. He pissed you off, huh?" whispered Rodan. He then got insistently louder once again. "The *Satyr*? Are you kidding? You still have that piece of alvum? Boy do you need an up-grade. How's Crazy Sadie? Still driving people batty with her aspects of Human improvement? She is something. You know, you could sit down and have a drink and pass me a little of those pleasantries since it's been so damn long, Nach. *Damn!*" Rodan clapped Nachman on the back, hard enough that Nach-man lurched forward a bit, and sat him down at a high-backed, velvety barstool at the end of the bar.

The bar itself was designed to look like an ancient speakeasy from the early twentieth century, one hundred yards long, a surface so sheen you can see your reflection as if it was a mirror. It had red-leather cushioned rails, and even a brass footrest lined the bottom of the bar. Rodan had al-ways been obsessed with ancient Earth history, especially the periods where debauchery and festivities were the key to life, as Rodan had so delicately said. The *Nafusma* that ran the es-tablishment allowed Rodan to add "Human elements" to the Miga to allow it to be more appealing.

"So you haven't seen anything then?" asked Nachman as he sat, trying his best to keep the annoyance out of his voice.

Rodan walked behind the bar and began an elaborate air display of mixing drinks. "Besides Buhai getting bloodied, nothing, bro. Alvum, Nach, it's been pretty hush-hush around here for a while, even before Buhai's demise. Since that, well, it's like all the Noas just disregarded what happened and moved on like they don't know how to react or they just call it another day. Weird, huh?"

"Yeah, Mr. Red over there wanted to rip my ocumech out just for looking at him," said Nachman, intrigued that other Noanoagans had been acting strange, but he needed to steer the conversation back to the prisoners in order to get out of here and keep on the case. "Anything actionable?"

"Only tactical intel out there is that it was a planet-side snipe and not an atmo-snipe, which, in my expert opinion, is just easier to get away with, you know."

Nachman did know an atmospheric sniper's nest would have been more tactical, given the multiple avenues of escape and the precision of the shot; however, Nachman also knew for a fact that when he left the Naibus, he took all of the preliminary blueprints for the atmospheric version of the rifle barrel with him, and he had Sadie wipe any trace of it from the Gnanimus mainframe. Whoever was behind the assassination had to have a hold of the barrel he had fabricated prior to leaving the Naibus. Those thieving bastards took it when they raided his private, now abandoned, lab on luna Arca—the one (as there were still a few hideaways the GIA hasn't seized yet) orbiting Hatu in Ipsum—while he was on that fateful mission in Vitachlora those final weeks with the GIA. In addition to the phavix intel he had received from 674's nanophage earlier, it seemed as if Rodan didn't have too much to offer in the way of information. Nachman was just about to excuse himself to investigate the crime scene when a familiar face, one Nachman was always happy to see, stepped out from behind one of the Ga'a'ula Stalks, "G-stalks" for short, behind the bar.

One half of the *Nafusma,* a *Nafusma* spanning a little more than six hundred years, that operated the Miga strode across the bar smooth as a skimmer, and as soon as she saw Nachman, a toothy smile adorned her face. Ines was of short stature for a Noanoagan but was sleek and curvy, pure socialite by nature, expressed in the effervescent neon-lime talafau'sia. Smooth lines curled outward from the crest of her cheek along her face and ran parallel down her chest. *Always beautiful every time I see her tala*, thought Nachman. Her fihr was a dull forest green with flecks of yellow, her part-ner's color, speckled throughout her coat. When she spoke, her transmod voice output represented that of a female New Yorker during the early twenty-first century.

"Oh my, oh my, look what I have found after all these moons. Nachman, my dear, come here and give your girl Ines a squeeze."

Nachman was happy to see Ines, genuinely. When he did frequent the Miga, he enjoyed a few drinks and a laugh with her on those nights when the fun ran into the dawn. Ines could brighten Nachman's mood even on his worst days. Nach-man found that she was one of the few Noanoagans he actually felt he could trust. Her *Nafusma*, Seni, was a different story. Seni came around the corner of the G-stalk just after Ines. She was tall and slender; her fihr was a luminous canary yellow with forest-green tips, but to Nachman, she had the personal-ity of the wood in the bar, and she had been like that since Nachman first had met her ten years ago. Seni glared at Nach-man, her pure-white pupils glinting in the yellow light of the G-stalks. He still had that feeling she didn't like him too much. *At least some things stay the same*, Nachman thought.

Seni and Ines had met when they were in their twen-tieth year during the journey across the Fayaía; they were bonded later in that year and had been *Nafusma* ever since. Nachman had always wondered how two people so different could stay together, let alone keep each other interested in one another for six centuries. But they did know how to run an efficient cultural center/nightclub. During the long jour-ney across the Celestial, Seni was known to run the cruiser's temple's day-to-day operations for the monks, and Ines man-aged the dance and entertainment for the moon celebrations and various other occasions. Seni never fully left the temple behind when the moon came out—antisocial by nature, Ines always said, one reason she stays behind to operate the five G-stalks.

Nachman made an effort to turn away from the five

Ga'a'ula Stalks that protruded to the roof forming the spires that rose from the top of the *Fu Temu Miga.* No matter when he was here, the spires always gave him that feeling of being watched, always a little twinge of apprehension around them. The latest craze over the last ten years had been the Ga'a'ula pill and the immersive stalk chamber at the base of the spire that made the pill's psychedelic properties come to life. G, AA, La, OoLaLa, GooGoo—the fanatics call it all sorts of names, but Nachman knew—no, felt—that this drug got inside your head and probably stayed there. The G-pill allowed Humans with a nanophage to experience a neuronal connection to an emotional experience not their own. Nachman didn't understand the fascination, but from what others had said, the pill in combination with the stalk brought about a psychedelic metaphysical mind trip, letting you feel and experience a variety of emotions in a variety of different immersive environments. *Alvum*, thought Nachman, *I have enough trouble with my emotional state of mind; I don't need other emotions swimming around this incentum.*

"Hiya, Ines. I see Seni still hasn't warmed up to my rustic charms," Nachman said.

"You know to pay her no mind, dear." Ines leaned closer, whispering, "She has a secret crush on you; she just doesn't want to admit it." From the background, Seni let out a low growl that was just a notch below threatening. Both Ines and Nachman smiled. Nachman had missed the old jabbing and jawing. In the background Rodan couldn't keep the spotlight off himself for more than two seconds.

"Yo, Nach! Ines was there when it happened. She saw the whole bloody mess!"

Nachman turned to Ines. "Sorry. My man here is so insensitive."

"We keep him around merely for the customers." Ines smiled. But she only smiled for a second, her full pouting lips turned upside down, frowning, quivering slightly, making her twin hoops in the middle of her lip jangle lightly.

Nachman was about to put his hand atop of Ines, merely in a gesture of sympathy, but he stopped, hovering slightly, as he looked up to see Seni staring daggers directly at him. Nachman might have been away awhile, but he hadn't forgotten the custom among Noanoagans when they are *Nafusma.* Before any kind of contact is made to either Noanoagan in a *Nafusma,* regardless of gender, it was customary to make eye contact with their bond as a sign of respect and acknowledgment of their commitment. Seni gave the most subtle of nods but did not take off the weight behind her stare. When Nachman touched Ines's hand, she smiled. "If I missed you this much, I wonder what others might be thinking about right now."

Nachman disregarded the last comment with a nervous smile. The thought of that one was still a time long ago he did not want to utter an incentum about her—not right now, anyway. With his hand still resting on Ines's, Nachman asked, "Ines, darlin', would you mind telling me what you remember about the shooting? No need to remember the gruesome. Just a general picture so I can get an incentum about what went down."

Ines shrugged; her shoulders seemed as wide as most doorways by comparison. "Sure, I think so." Seni put a hand on Ines's shoulder. Before Ines responded, she put her hand on top of Seni's, and the *Nafusma* fluttered their fihr, a gesture of mourning and respect for the beloved deceased. It sounded like crystal chiming. "I was in the crowd, maybe seventy-five meters from the steps of Parliament watching Tejwenn escort Buhai to center stage. Oh my goodness, they were both so beautiful. Tejwenn's neon blue and Buhai's metallic purple make such a beautiful palette of color. Their royal robes were so brilliant—just a full rainbow of *wow!*" Nachman's chuckle brought a smile to Ines; girl was a fashionista after all. Ines got back on track. "Where was I? Oh, Tejwenn led Buhai to the podium and placed his forehead to hers before he stepped to her left, I think. He looked so happy for his *Nafusma.* Buhai pressed a button on the podium, and a purple Vis display popped up from the top. She waved to the crowd; the cheers were as loud as, oh, how do you say? Oh, yeah, thunder. And that's when it happened, at the cheers. I didn't hear anything at first; then there was a crack like wood being broken in two. I didn't think anything happened to Buhai because she, the poor dear, just… just stood there." Ines began to shed a few tears. Seni kept her hand on Ines's shoulder; it looked as if she would cry as well. "But the strangest thing, Nach darling. Buhai didn't look scared, no not at all, but she didn't look so much happy either. I guess the right word for a Human would be free."

"I'm so sorry for the Orimer and that you had to see such a tragedy, Ines. Two more questions, Ines, is that kosher?" Nachman waited for Ines to nod and continued. "Thank you, sweetheart, I know this is hard for you. First did you see a trail of light, or—excuse me for saying—any blood spatter in any direction?" asked Nachman, trying to be as sensitive as possible with Seni still trying to tear apart his insides with her eyes.

"No trail of anything, but there was an ear-piercing ring, like a knife had sliced through the air. I think all the Noas heard it. We all were almost on our knees for a few seconds; it was pretty painful," Ines said. She rubbed her ear. "There was no blood that I saw, but I think my eyes were closed when the piercing sound started. When I opened them, Buhai was on the ground, Tejwenn was kneeling over her, and I think there was blood underneath her."

"That's fantastic, Ines," praised Nachman. "Final question, and I promise I'm done making you recall the horrifics. Did you see Buhai or Tejwenn look anywhere, off into the distance, for example?"

Nachman always appreciated how much the two species were similar. There were similarities among spiritual rituals, routines, family tradition, even in the common gestures no one would pay any incentum to. Ines crooked her head upward; accessing a memory or even a glimpse of a memory can look the same among any species. Then she looked at Seni. "I wonder if this matters, but I did tell Seni that just before it happened, it looked like Tejwenn wanted to touch Buhai. Tejwenn was reaching for her just as I closed my eyes when that horrible noise started."

"Ines, Seni, I have missed you both—yes, Seni, even you." Nachman gave Seni his best charmed smile, and for a moment, it looked like Seni was about to blush just before she turned to the bar to continue setting the barrels for the first pour. Nachman gave Ines a small hug and turned to walk away when he remembered. "Oh, Ines, rumor is Tejwenn is still kicking and on the lam. Any clue where he would be?"

"Rumor has it that Humans—or wait, no—it was said the Vultus are helping him. I've heard, and Ro would be jealous that I found this one out before he did..." Ines let out a low chuckle. Then, her face twitched ever so subtly. *That is odd*, Nachman thought, but Ines continued. "He somehow made it off-luna to an abandoned outpost on a tropical planet in, oh what is the name, you Humans and your languages, many names for many things, so complicated at times. I have never been to this one, but my people say—" Ines turned off her transmod. She was noticeably sweating. *Do Noas sweat?* Nachman couldn't remember. *What is wrong with her?* With her transmod off, Ines spoke her native tongue; her voice sounded like tinging glass reverberating through water, but there was a faint quiver to it, like she was suddenly afraid. "Fasui'fi'taa." Nachman knew the word—or words, rather. Fasui'fi'ta (Fā-sū-ee-fee-tā) translated to "fire that rotates land," or a Solaris.

Nachman did like the sound of a Noanoagan singer's voice, especially Ines's. When she sang she sounded like soft pitched flute whistling; her tone mixed well with the house beats. But why the fear? *What was she afraid of?* he wondered. Then Nachman saw the weirdest thing, something he would never expect from Ines, whom he considered a friend: she snarled at him. Ines's mouth stretched, baring pearl-white fangs beneath the blue-painted lips. Nachman stood up quickly, his barstool falling backward crashing to the ground, his gun hand automatically going to his thigh holster. Just as Ines's fihr began to shudder, Seni turned, her eyes wide with surprise, and grabbed Ines by her wide shoulders.

"Come, Ines, you must rest before curtain call," Seni said as she led Ines behind the G-stalks. Nachman guessed Ines's dressing room was still in the back of the G-stalks, which led to the stage in front of the Miga where she performed nightly. Nachman always liked skimming when she sang; it always felt like he was ice-skating the rings of Jupiter—in the right company, that is. The company now seemed a little more tense than Nachman expected. As Ines walked away, she turned and looked at Nachman. He saw two things in her eyes from that one look: regret, probably for the sudden outburst (at which Nachman was surprised but took no offense), and there was something else—that fear, almost shuddering terror.

"Nach, bro, what the alvum? You come back, and you just pissing in everyone's edibles," laughed Rodan, who sounded more nervous then Nachman could remember, even during a couple of missions that went south. Rodan was always cool under pressure. Nachman might not respect the man, but he was good at what he did. Nachman once saw Rodan become the target of strafing fire from Vultus rebels while calling in an atmospheric rail missile strike on an ammo compound and walk away with a smile on his face. It was one of Rodan's favorite stories to tell, so for him to nervously walk away from a Noanoagan, let alone one he had known for years, was just downright peculiar. Something about the way Rodan's body movement—he was withdrawn from the Noas, timid, maybe even a little frightened—and he did not make eye contact at all while around the *Nafusma.* All this told Nachman that Rodan hadn't been comfortable here, not in a while. Nachman excused himself from the G-bar, concerned for his friend but mostly confused. Confused by everyone's actions. He had been away for a while, but had things changed so much? As Nachman walked past the less-confused retired Fale warrior and out of the Miga, Nachman wondered why this case felt like it just got even more complicated.

CHAPTER 8

Tracaelus Solaris, Terraluna Tasóa, Noanoagan Capital City Aaila
Scene of Assassination of the Orimer Buhai; whereabouts of *Nafusma* Tejwenn Unknown

Nachman climbed the earthen steps to the orange blood-stained death theater of Buhai, Orimer of Noanoaga. A heinous and what Nachman considered a nonsensical killing poignantly committed, whether intentional or not, right in front of what Humans call the Noanoagan Sacred Parliament. The building was designed in a way that mimicked the look of the ancient congressional buildings that had been lost to the oceans of Gaia. Nachman heard it was an homage to the old world for giving them a new world.

The fungal structure's name was synonymous with what the Noas had adopted as their holy meeting ground of the Noanoagan High Council, Lauma'file'u (Lā-oo-mā-fee-ley-oo). Nachman grew up in Sapietás the Holy Solaris; now he might not be practicing the old ways anymore, but he still had a certain respect for the philosophers and peacekeepers of the Celestial. Like Sadie had said, it was sad to see her taken at such an important time for interspecies and intraspecies communications. Nachman still thought the word "conspiracy" was a convenient line of incentum.

Nachman knelt on his right knee using his left hand, specifically his left index finger, to feel the blood stain. The blood had congealed and crusted when absorbed into the fungal foundation. Using the analytical tech embedded into his mechanized left arm, Nachman was able to analyze the blood for pathogens and poisons specific to Noanoagan physiology. The blood came back free of pathogens or poisons; Nachman didn't think the assassination was a coverup. It appeared as if it was exactly what it was meant to be: an execution. Nachman stared at the blood longer than he intended. He was recalling a memory of a geneticist he once knew. Ines subtly mentioned her back at the Miga. It felt like a lifetime since he had thought of her. She would always throw around facts and quirks about the Noas that he couldn't help but overhear; in fact, he rather missed those times every now and then.

Noanoagan blood turned from blue to orange once it came in contact with the nitrogen in the atmosphere. In the same way Humans synthesize oxygen to keep the organs physiologically functionable, the Noanoagans do this with nitrogen. Nachman was always fascinated not by the science behind the Noas but the person who was telling him about them, such passion and intrigue about all life. Nachman smiled at the thought, but now was not the time. Nachman couldn't get past how distracted he was; not thinking about the past has hindered his current state of mind. Nachman furrowed his brow. *I need to maintain my focus. This case is becoming complicated, in more ways than one. Not only does Tyrav need my help, but I think there is a definite connection between the Automatons, Tyrav, the prisoners, and the assassination. But the why is still escaping me. Let's find the sniper's nest and see what was left behind. Now focus, fool, and figure it out.*

Nachman focused his incentum on the different filters inside his ocumech. Nachman stepped up one flight and turned to face the rest of the city. The sun was setting in the west, silhouetting the city, capturing the shadows in a still frame, beautifully eerie. Nachman admired Aaila; it looked quite serene in the dusk. The purple hues from the dusk sunrays began to change colors as the microfilters dropped in front of his lens and became like a shade over his retina. Nachman began to scan for trace radiations left behind by armin used in the GIA, private sector, Vorcalus, legal or other-wise. All the armin produced leave behind trails of radiation, dissipating to microscopic levels and detectable to only very specific tech, Nachman's included. Plutonium, negative. Ur-anium, negative. Kronidium, negative. Nachman didn't get frustrated or perturbed like Sadie said from time to time, but instead smirked because this was one area that he knew a lot about. Nachman switched the filter in his ocumech to detect trace amounts of quantum disruption in the surround-ing area. The area in front of the podium down to where the body landed showed dissipating quantum disruptions. Just as Nachman suspected: with no radiations present and the remaining trace amounts of quantum disruptions, the only armin that could cause such readings was near untraceable, known in the Naibus as solvo, an armin Nachman had used on countless ghost missions while with the Naibus. Heavily clas-sified (as in "will never exist on the Gnanimus mainframe").

Nachman recalled the specs from memory; no need for the Gnanimus here. The specialized rail shot's outcasing was lined with nonsentient Vis energy and embedded with a few hundred microscopic nanites programmed to work in tandem with the Vis. Once the armin had penetrated the target, the nanites made a direct connection to the nervous system to essentially short out the heart and the brain from anywhere in the body. Then the scant amount of Vis dissolved any trace metals, including the nanites. The Vis then fades, leav-ing barely a trace of a quantum disruption behind. Nachman did like his mods at times, especially when they were useful. When Nachman used this armin, not one of his targets knew what hit them. Nachman had a suspicion this is what killed Buhai. When Ines mentioned the blank look on her face after the shot, the high-pitched sound was something new, but then again Nachman never had a Noanoagan target before. Must have been some adjustment the assassins made after they got a hold of the barrel.

That twinge of guilt struck him. *Because of that barrel,*

I created a Noa for a target. Nachman placed the thought in the back of his head; he would have to talk to someone later get this off his chest. Of all things Nachman couldn't stand, it was guilt for a torrid action he knew he was guilty of. There weren't many, but what were there, well...talking helped, mostly.

Nachman looked up and scanned the horizon. His ocu-mech highlighted a trail, Sadie and her neons, of a faint Vis quantum disruption. The trail appeared as a white-and-pink-translucent speckled vapor that angled just slightly upward to an eight-story fungal building approximately 1.3 km directly west of the Parliament building. Not that far. Nachman decided to hoof it; he could use the walk to think momentarily.

Nachman walked through the streets of Aaila, feeling a bit more than casual, more like a cat ready to pounce, but all around him, it seemed as though it was business as usual. As dusk settled upon the city, the local shops made up of exotic Noanoagan food stores and restaurants, tailors, and touristy-type shops began to close for the day. All the lights and colored arrays of décor seemed to illuminate a direct pathway to the Miga, as if the center of the universe awaited those who followed. The Human tourists that remained looked like they were heading for the Miga for the night festivities. Most of the families would either bunk down for the night at a local hotel or make way to the nearest GIA outpost on the luna or in orbit; most Humans preferred the latter. For some reason, mothers and fathers were still skittish to have their children sleep near what they interpreted as monsters. Human beings still afraid of the new and different, even when Noanoagans have lived among them for nearly seventy years. *No matter the generation, prejudice will remain*, Nachman thought, as he knew he was guilty of his own prejudices.

Nachman was, roughly, one hundred yards away from what appeared to be an abandoned hotel. The foundation and siding looked cracked and dried like the fungus was dehydrated. The quantum disruption looked as if it ended at the top floor, east corner of the building. *Great, a nice tall leap into a fungus that's falling apart*, thought Nachman. Nachman couldn't help but notice again, as he finished the last leg of the saunter, even in a rundown part of town, the casual nature of things, the lack of security from both Fale and Naibus given recent events, and the blank looks on both Human and Noa faces. Nachman could remember when Vultus guerrilla squads would threaten even the lowest of Elitists and Naibus security would triple just from the incentum. Nachman's ear tickled slightly; he got the strangest sensation that he was being tailed. Nachman continued pace, remembering not to look behind him or give any notion that he knew of the leech on his back. Nachman rounded the next corner; he didn't need to since the building was directly ahead, but as there were no reflective surfaces available and Sadie was back at the *Satyr*, it was the only way to lay eyes on his tail without giving away his subtle advantage.

Just as Nachman crossed the smooth line of the corner of the building, his right peripheral caught a quick but keen glance at two male stalkers about thirty yards behind him. Nachman accessed his Gnanimus files and easily identified his tails as Prisoners 745 and 856, two more escapees from the Tenebrae prison break. And, oddly enough, the spotter and shooter from the phavix feed. He wondered where Prisoner 332 could be hiding; maybe he was one of the prois, thugs, from the space fight above Tasóa earlier.

Prisoner 745 had a record an AU long stemming back from his early twenties: grand larceny, extortion, credit manipulation, Gnanimus hacks, nanophage/organ harvesting, multiple assault and battery charges, and to top it all off, a few colorful néco, or murders. Prisoner 745 never appeared to have any kind of honor, most likely steered clear of anything GIA related, and was a just a genuinely nasty fellow. He was tall and built solid enough that he could hold his own in a scrap, so Nachman understood sending him, but a pudgy short stack like 856 who looks like he hadn't seen the inside of a gym since birth was just downright simple. Prisoner 856, ex-GIA loadmaster, had a relatively small rap sheet in comparison but still was not someone you would want to bring home to Mom: breaking and entering, grand theft, Gnanimus hacks, nano-drug trafficking, extortion, and kidnapping. Nachman knew these two escapees were never qualified to perform any kind of tactical operations and was almost positive that they were infested with those Automatons. Nachman wasn't sure if he was supposed to be insulted or not by whoever was sending two brainwashed thugs to keep the behind-the-scenes hush-hush. *Either way*, Nachman thought, *looks like I'm on the right trail if I have company.*

Nachman crossed the mud-sloshed street; Aaila was in the midst of a rainy spring season, no tactical advantage. Nachman knew he had to bring the fight inside. Nachman knew the prisoners were following the programming of the Automaton, and like any other programmed mechanism that he knew of, it would follow the program to the letter. So Nachman kept it predictable, pretending he had no knowledge of the tail. Making himself visible again, pretending he made a wrong turn, he walked a pace slower, a straight line toward the abandoned building, and as predicted, the prisoners follow his path. When Nachman reached the door and pushed, he couldn't help but take a glance over his shoulder and look at his coming companions. Through the x-ray of the ocumech, he saw they both carried 6-mm rail shot pistols on their waists. Both prisoners were right-handed, but both pistols stayed holstered. Nachman could only take an educated guess that they were both programmed to detain, but again he couldn't be sure. He smirked. *It will be fun to see them try.*

Nachman was the type that preferred a heads-on approach rather than sneaking around and setting elaborate traps to ambush the enemy. When the situation warranted, Nachman could be the epitome of stealth, but for now, he was quite in the mood to knock some heads.

Nachman wasn't coy about where he stood in regard to his position in the main lobby of the derelict fungal structure. The lobby was open, wide, and an oblong oval shape with a vaulted ceiling and seven wide circular pillars outlying the lobby. Nachman stood dead center with his left flank to the door, left foot pointed to the door as if it knew where to greet the enemy. Eager yet weary. One did not know what power the enemy truly possesses until engaged in battle, as his masters used to say. One of his favorite combat styles was not one mastered while in the Naibus but one mastered in his home Solaris before and after his time with the GIA. Both grace and ferocity entitle Taga Na, a Celestial martial art derived from a variety of ancient Gaian martial arts by the Sitanimi. Grace, peace, and beauty to tend a ferocious heart; Nachman did like the scrolls as well as the combat.

Prisoner 745 stepped sideways through the door, his width matching the door, with 856 trudging behind. Both began to match step, raising their arms with clenched fists and simultaneously sidestepping to both sides of Nachman, 745 on the right and 856 on the left. Prisoner 856 mirrored 745's movements almost exactly; the Automatons had taken the best of the two's abilities in the given scenario and made the Humans in sync. Crafty, but Nachman did notice the millisecond delay in 845's movements, and 745's Automaton seemed to need line of sight to transmit combat tactics. Nachman already had a tactical advantage over his opponents. Nachman simply stood in the center eagerly awaiting his opponents, left arm pointed down, palm up. A stance to let his opponent think him defenseless and inviting them into the fray.

Prisoner 856 advanced first. *Surprisingly quick footwork and agility for being so short and pudgy*, Nachman thought, but he was prepared. Prisoner 856 reared his right arm back, arching upward in an attempt to beat Nachman's left flank; the prisoner's face was expressionless, devoid of thought, his motions fully autonomous with no soul behind his movements, entirely predictable. Without considering the oncoming fist,

Nachman swiftly sliced his hand, palm down, through the air directly onto the left temple of 856. As if the lights were suddenly switched off, 856 crumbled to the ground, his face bouncing off the floor like a child's ball. Out of the corner of his eye, Nachman saw 745 advance with the same blank quickness.

His movements came in a supernatural swiftness, almost as if Nachman could see his opponent move before the incentum fired across the neurons. Nachman used his momentum from the knife hand to spin left, lifting his right leg, blocking 745's incoming front kick. Nachman continued to spin left as 745 staggered drunkenly from the blocked kick. Like a dancer greeting his partner after a pirouette, Nachman connected with the bridge of 745's nose with his left elbow; the bone-crunching pop echoed in the lobby as Nachman's blow shattered the prisoner's cartilage. Miniature goblets of blood spattered chaotically as 745's neck craned backward. Prisoner 745 staggered, bringing his hands to his nose, cradling his fractured septum, and landed with a loud crash into a row of chairs behind him. Nachman centered again back in his original position, left foot pointed forward, left hand down, palm up, and right arm resting at the small of his back; it was as if Nachman never moved an inch from his original position. Nachman let out a breath; a barely perceptible bead of sweat had formed atop his forehead. He had missed the thrill of a fight, even a mediocre one.

Prisoner 856 sprang to his feet. For a moment he stood in place, the blank stare present, and looked over at his partner scrambling to his feet, wavering about, trying to gain footing while blinded by the blood spatter from his shattered nose. Then 856 charged, faster than his doughy legs should have been able to move. It seemed that there was no attempt at a skilled fight now that the needed skill set had been cut off from the source. As 856 barreled down, ready to tackle Nachman, Nachman pivoted slightly on his left foot and with incredible swiftness drove his right knee into whatever part of 856's face he connected with. There was no sound from 856, but the structures of his face crunched and crumbled like autumn leaves underfoot. Nachman wasn't sure what was damaged, but he knew the end result as 856 went limp, thudded to the floor, and lay eerily still. *Alvum, don't tell me that killed him.* Nachman let out the incentum loudly enough that any psi-sensitive within meters would be able to hear it. *It has been a while since my last hand to hand. Gotta dial it back if I want intel. I kill this other one, Sadie will never let me hear the end of it.*

At that incentum, 745 was sprinting across the lobby, Nachman snapped into a ready position, arms bent at the elbow parallel to his face, partially open fists, feet apart, and his body loose and ready for an impact or a stand-up fight. Prisoner 745 proceeded with the latter; Nachman bobbed from side to side, slipping the lightning-fast jabs 745 was throwing at him. Nachman timed his next move with 745's seventh jab. Nachman slipped to the right, simultaneously grabbing 745's arm with his left hand and cutting his right elbow into the humerus of his opponent. The snap of the bone gave a slight grimace across his face, but still no sound came from 745; his face remained dormant as if the searing pain of the fracture was meaningless.

The ferocity in Nachman finally won over. Was it the frustration at the case or that he was seeing exactly what he did not want to happen to him, losing himself inside the machine? Nachman wrapped his right arm around 745's neck, pivoting so they were standing side by side and with one grand show of force, he lifted 745 off the ground, releasing him at the peak of the lift. Prisoner 745 slammed into a pillar face-first. Nachman thought it comical as he slid to the floor head-first, landing spread-eagle on his back.

As Nachman collected himself, the adrenaline still coursing through his veins, he walked over to 745 and pulled a set of Vis stretch restraints from his cargo pocket. As Nachman bent down to restrain 745, he began to convulse like he was short-circuiting. Nachman stood up quickly, making sure not to touch him, and as he did, he looked over at 856, who was convulsing as well. The convulsions lasted seconds, but it was the blood oozing like a clogged faucet from their eyes, nose, and mouth that gave Nachman the clue that there would be no need for an interrogation. Nachman looks closer. Both of the prisoners' eyes had melted like gelatin in their sockets, and their mouths and nasal cavities looked as if they had sunken into their skulls. *The Automaton has a kill switch; that's probably why that fighter detonated above Tasóa.* Nachman shook his head. *Yep, Sadie is not going to let me live this one down—and it's not even my fault they're dead.*

Nachman turned to leave but stopped in midstride. Whether enemy or friend, he believed one should always have compassion for those one kills or has been party to killing in the heat of battle. He bowed his head; he didn't say the mantras his mother had taught him before the GIA changed his path, but the thought was there. Nachman recorded the altercation and the aftereffects for analysis by Sadie and himself when he got back to the *Satyr*. Nachman, sadly, had known death wasn't done following him just yet; he needed all the information he could get on these Automatons if he was going to find a way to stop them. Regardless of current events, he went to see what other surprises awaited him on the eightieth floor of this abandoned fungal fun house.

Nachman overlapped an x-ray filter over his quantum filter to peer through the walls to find where the quantum disturbance trail ended. Nachman came to the end of a long hall, the walls peeling and crumbling from lack of care. The door to the room was already ajar, so Nachman let himself in. The room was a small studio apartment made for a single occupant, Noa or Human. No furniture that Nachman could see; it seemed void of any occupants. Nachman accessed Gnanimus records that indicated no one had occupied this domicile in quite some time, but there was a purchase made with an obvious false name and phage tag linked with GIA credits for a lease on the top fifteen floors for R & D labs for a six month-period—conveniently expiring one week before the assassination. Nachman scowled. *If I find one more thing connecting the GIA to this, then I'm going to start gearing the investigation toward an Elitist or someone close to one. Nobody would be able to pull this off so close to the chest than someone with close access to the Gnanimus mainframe and only the Elitists in positions of power, the big three being a Magnus of Orbis, a Cordrego of Solari, or a member of the Morsus Mihi themselves. Alvum, Nachman, this is big.* He chuckled to himself. *Go big, or go home.*

Nachman sent an incentum to the control mod on his wrist to project a Vis-rendered mapping of a sniper's nest he had recorded from a similar, nonfungal building layout on a GIA-sanctioned ghost mission on Mercury a long while back. The Vis-rendered layout became superimposed over the domicile, slight imperfections here and there. A light-green hue from the Vis outlined the room like Nachman was standing in the middle of an emerald. Within the layout Vis renderings of Humanoid forms took position around the room in the same places as in the phavix memory engram, one being Nachman in the sniper position. With an incentum, five oval-shaped Vis displays hovered in the air. Nachman brought up five separate lex feeds from the Naibus troopers' ocumechs; all were posted behind Buhai and Tejwenn. Their feeds showed the outermost perimeter of the assembly area, and they were the only feeds that showed the building Nachman was currently standing in.

As Nachman viewed all of the footage simultaneously, he could see a very subtle speck of light shine from a window of the building. He changed the filter on the displays to the same quantum reader that traced the trail of the armin. The window on the video feed lit up like an old-time Christmas tree. With a brisk nod, Nachman then applied the filter to the superimposed sniper's nest. Not to Nachman's surprise, the window frame was the exact dimensions of the window from the feed and the same where the trail of quantum disruption ended. Nachman smiled, but it faded quickly. He had found the nest, but this was about the only bit of evidence that linked the sniper party to this spot. There were no DNA signatures, trace nanophage signals, or even a hair stuck on the wet paint. The prisoners were obviously linked. Even though Nachman had already dispatched five, accidentally or otherwise, the rest were on the lam—no trace, no trail.

Nachman had hit a dead end. *Might as well lex Sadie and figure out where to go from here.* Just as he was reestablishing the link between him and Sadie, everything went dark; he felt as if he had faded into the nothingness of the deep Celestial. It felt strange, but he wasn't fearful of the deep void. The comfort of a slumber that would bring the peace he was so desiring these last few years—he almost welcomed it. Nachman had two feelings that he hadn't brought to the surface in that instant: anger at the fact he would succumb to the dark and worried that it didn't frighten him in the least. From this moment on, Nachman knew his body and mind were unwilling passengers in the blind onslaught that followed.

As soon as Nachman's head bounced off the wall, the man's wide palms were there to catch it. Nachman could hear the whisper of the seques, flex metal, lining this bestial man's muscles as they rippled and curled lifting Nachman into the air like he was just a mere sack of dirt.

A drop of serene ruby liquid dripped from the laceration above his victim's brow. The globule graced his cheek; the man smiled and shuddered as he licked his lips. The brutality of this mystery assailant was imbued into his cells, literally. Genetic modification made him the perfect killer; even so, he was always in the mood to maim and murder. Beyond the genetic implantation, the man welcomed the blood and death. It wasn't joy from the kill, the thrill of the hunt, but the feeling he got when that first drop of warm sanguine fluid fluttered like butterfly wings upon his skin. It just simply excited him. The man shouted as he hurled Nachman across the room, slamming him into the solid U'agi wall. He admired the splattered pattern of the blood upon the wall where his victim's head had now hit twice. Oh, how he wanted to unleash the artistry of anguish and bloodletting upon Nachman. But fortunately for the little piece of alvum, his murderous messenger was under orders to impair not execute.

Back at the *Satyr*, Sadie was watching one of her favorite mysteries, *Rear Window*, on a Vis holo-display and beginning to initiate a series of diagnostic checks on the engine and hull when she got a ping across her aura. It sounded like a crystal chiming, the alert she received when Nachman was finishing up his private time. Sadie accessed the time and considered initiating contact, but with thirty minutes to go, Sadie decided to let Nachman have fifteen more minutes. He would check in. Sadie was suddenly unsure. *He will check in again shortly; he always does.* Sadie gave the fifteen minutes but began prepping the *Satyr* for takeoff.

Nachman knew he hit the wall again; he knew it was hard. Did he actually dent an Apatia reinforced wall? *Alvum*, Nachman thought, *this guy is a monster*. Nachman made his best effort to crawl in some direction, but his head was spinning, and he couldn't get his bearings. Before he could pass another incentum, he was lifted into the air again, but this time it felt like a clamp had been placed around his neck, and it was slowly getting tighter. Then there was a series of jaunting burns across the left side of his face. He felt as if solid block of titiconium was being beaten across. Nachman fought to breathe more than he fought his assailant, but the will to endure was still there. Nachman's biomech arm lay limp at his side, but with the last ounce of resolve he could muster, he slapped away the arm of his attacker on his next punch. Nachman's one organic eardrum ruptured from the loud crack off of the U'agi wall from the wild punch. Nachman tried to knee him in the gut, but the vise grip tightened around his trachea. Nachman felt the battle being lost; the black began to settle in again, a warm comforter around his dura mater.

Nachman's eye fluttered open, the other swollen shut, seeping blood from a cavernous cut on his brow, and Nachman felt new pains blossom in his chest. The bestial assailant released Nachman's biomech arm, and from what Nachman saw through the swelling, it looked as if his arm was snapped and hanging loosely by exposed seques and organic sinew. Nachman could feel the grayish biofilm that lubricated his arm gushing out of the craterous wound. Then there was his skull. Nachman didn't think he was supposed to feel his skull indented, but then again, *I'm not a medic*, Nachman chuckled deliriously inside his head. He wasn't on the wall anymore but across the room where he watched blurry feet stalk toward him as lay on his side on the cold, damp U'agi floor. The floor seemed softer than Nachman remembered. *I should just shut my eyes for a minute, get some strength back. No! Stay awake! Fight!* Nachman screamed at himself. Nachman refused to believe that someone was able to sneak up on him, not like this. Something had to be blocking his proximity sensors. But, regardless of the sensor mods, Nachman felt he had been well trained while with the Naibus and in the private sector. How could someone get the drop on him? Nachman reached his shaking, fractured, blood-soaked hand toward the feet that were now circling him like a vulture, waiting to pick Nachman clean. Whoever this is, is going to get the beating of a lifetime. *If I survive*, he thought.

Sadie giddily sat in Nachman's captain's chair kicking her feet back and forth. He was so particular about his space at times. She glanced out of the forward window and saw the last tip of Tracaelus's sun set behind Aaila; the purple and green wavy shimmers reminded Sadie of her dimension. The fluidity struck her as serene. With six minutes left before re-connect, Sadie decided it was well beyond time to contact Nachman through their psionic connection to gently remind Nachman that time was almost up. No response. "That's odd," Sadie said aloud, "where is he?" Sadie tried the connection again, but again she was met with something that sounded like a cross between static and boiling water. Psionic scrambling. Sadie stood up immediately, set the security measures on the *Satyr*, and vanished into a swirl of incandescent color.

With the tracer on Nachman's wrist-control mod activated, Sadie had no issue finding Nachman's precise position, but the psionic scramble did make a little difficult to get to him. Sadie appeared two feet from Nachman's bludgeoned body. Sadie didn't panic, but the situation put her to the edge almost instantly. As she lurched to Nachman's side, she glinted a shadow from her peripheral. Sadie looked from Nachman's face toward the entrance of the room, where she swore she saw evil incarnate. The broad, Cheshire Cat–like smile from the boyishly handsome face spoke of more agony to come from the beast. Although the horrid image would haunt her metaphorical dreams, Sadie managed to record his image before the madman disappeared, storing it aside for later analysis. Now there was a far more important matter to attend to. Sadie hadn't worried about turning their connection back on because as soon as she touched Nachman, with a solid minute to spare before permanent disconnect, her aura changed back to the neon green of norm, indicating the bond between them was fully initiated.

"Oh, my dear Nachman, what did we stumble upon this time?" Sadie said as she picked him up and proceeded to carry him the distance to the ZGV. Luckily Nachman's mass meant nothing to Sadie; strength was meaningless to her as her corporeal form could bend the gravity around her to her will.

Sadie linked with Nachman's Ignivalo and got up to speed with the current state of events. Sadie was always impressed with Nachman's martial arts abilities. Sadie was proud to call him master in that aspect; Nachman had taught her everything she knows regarding the art of war. Sadie always preferred the fine art of knowledge process rather than direct download. Some of her species had still been slightly turned away from intermingling Human traits with Caiet. This was a majority of the reason the worry she felt for Nachman was fully distracting her from the present situation. It was still a very new sensation, as Caiets and Humans had similar but equally different emotional spectrums. Sadie knew analysis would have to be saved for later, so she pushed the worry aside but let the thought of it drive her focus into Nachman's well-being and the pursuit of the truth behind the mystery figure who wounded her comrade.

For now, Sadie knew there was nothing she could do for him but keep him stable under Qusom while they journeyed to the only person in the Celestial who knew more about Nachman than Sadie. She sent an automated emergent lex to Nachman's mother, Delylah. Nachman would be furious, but it was for his own physical well-being this time, not the mental. She strapped him into his favorite chair, sending the incentum to initiate a deep Qusom with a direct connect to his nanophage. Sadie was intent on maximizing healing for the journey. She increased the dosage of Quisthium, putting Nachman deeper into Qusom, and sent the incentum to allow the dormant nanites to pursue rapid individualized anatomical healing. Sadie could feel Nachman's Ignivalo growing weaker, the connection to his phage fading. Knowing Nachman's intellectual capacity, he would not interpret this trip as a deep Quscape. *But according to these readings and the massive swelling to his techno-organic brain matrices, I have no other option but to send him there again, or he won't survive,* Sadie thought.

Sadie whisked away to the navigation control station where there was already a neon-yellow oval Vis display with a green highlighted map plotting the fastest course for Sapietás Solaris, Terraluna Diiu at the fastest speed the *Satyr's* archaic engine cores could put out. Sadie sent an incentum acknowledging all preflight checks, and then an emergent override was sent to light up quantum engines and break atmo as soon as feasible. She whisked away again and sat at her faux oaken desk she had constructed from the Vis earlier; there she monitored Nachman's vital signs on an oval Vis display hovering over her shoulder like a news anchor's screenshot. She could easily sense them, but right now she needed the security of sight. Finally Sadie connected with the Gnanimus and downloaded all information she deemed pertinent to the investigation with the new information she just received from Nachman's encounter. Sadie would much rather sift through the Vis stacks of Naibus media and Fale sound bites at her leisure, but Nachman would want to know Sadie's game plan the moment he woke up. Besides, Sadie knew the day would come where she would have to disclose to Nachman the fact that she had sent him to another dimension, Sadie's specifically, a time or two.

CHAPTER 9

Vitachlora Solaris, Terraorbis Medvios, Coordinates Classified Zeta Level
Abandoned GIA Genealogical and Biochemical Research and Development Complex

The remainder of the journey was uneventful for Magnus Xon, no further tricks of the mind to take focus away from the goal. With the insipid emotional spectrum discontinued from his organic neural network Xon's nanophage and the rest of his artificial neural mapping, he could continue to process the calculations needed for this next endeavor.

The research facility he was descending upon had a sorted history, but none of this was important to the reason Xon needed this particular facility. Even though they had been publicly outlawed by the Morsus Mihi, and the major reason for the Liber Vultus's movement, the genetic engraft and mitochondrion manipulators were the reasons Xon had to keep this facility both open and functioning but so far off the GIA radar that he could not be associated with it even if it were discovered. The risk was great, but it was a risk the Magnus was willing to make.

The stellarcraft landed with a jolt, and a balanced Xon walked down the extending ramp of the *Cultivador*. The stellarcraft, an Impes class cruiser, appeared small, sleek, with a nonconfrontational angular exterior appearance. Inside there was a grand comfortable interior for the deep Celestial treks plus a sizable armament to match, much to the standard of a Magnus such as Xon. But with all its modifications, the vessel had the swiftness of a premium Spherix fighter.

Xon stopped at the bottom of the ramp and surveyed a vast charred, wasteland. Where once lush forestry and fluorescent plant life sprouted now stood an ashen, irradiated graveyard. A battle was fought here with neither side the victor. Xon was assured secrecy here. This site and twenty others around the planet each having a blast radius of fifty to seventy-five kilometers in diameter made these areas uninhabitable for at least thirty more years while Ipsum's automated hazardous materials units (AHMUs), cleansed the areas. The Magnus needn't worry about the radiations that would ravage the physiology of normal Human; the U'agi tech infused into his techno-organic structure rendered them harmless. The Suivira never did quite explain how they attained the tech, but no matter. They had taught him the methods, and it gave him the abilities needed for what he had planned.

Xon stared off into the distance as if he were seeking something from the nothing. Part of the horizon appeared as if it was caught in a bubble, wavy and opaque. Xon's pupils dilated, and the shielding that covered the research laboratories, abscondum camotech acquired from his contacts in Ipsum and modified by Xon's own designs using Noanoagan U'agi tech, shimmered like a starburst and then faded into a dull, blackened, oblong rectangular building. Charred scars laced the windowless building, and part of the roof looked as if it imploded on itself. None of that mattered to Xon because the site served its purpose. Xon's nanophage connected to the security mechs hidden around the facility and shut them down; all were nanosensed and programmed to attack any DNA not Xon's or any DNA Xon has not authorized access. That list was infinitesimal. With all security measures deactivated, the Magnus stepped through the doorway; compressed gases from the sterile sealants hissed as the outer doors open, the metals creaking softly. Not too far inside was another door, this one reinforced titiconium with an outer layer of Vis shielding. A small port above the door opened, and Xon's nanophage was scanned by the sensor. Four rail cannons in each corner of the antechamber disengaged with an audible click, all slacking downward as the abscondum camotech disengaged. The door slid open with a soft hiss of hydraulics, and the Vis shielding disengaged, fizzling out of sight. The luminescent white surface caused Magnus Xon's ocumechs to momentarily flicker, but he readjusted quickly. The main floor of this facility was a massive clean room; sterile processing was required when splicing genomic structures.

As Xon stepped into the decontamination antechamber, he noticed the silence among the blinding light; it was foreboding but to be expected. With events pressing Magnus Xon's patience was wearing thin, and there was simply no reason to remain sterile in this environment, for the work here was already complete. Xon merely needed confirmation of information in person. Xon sent the incentum to bypass the infection control measures to the facility's private mainframe. The decontamination process ceased, and the clear-plastic doors crinkled silently open.

Xon steps echoed in the processing room. There were only ten Vistations, waist high, slender poles topped with a small smooth orb, lining the walls awaiting users for interface. Geneticists and biochemists could analyze, manipulate, code, and render genetic material at their whim with one of the Vistations. As Xon approached the main terminal, he had not wondered why the standard lex per week had not come on his coded private line, for he knew the facility was already abandoned. Xon had planned for the facility to be a crater by this point but delayed the destruction for the informatics and confirmation of his subordinate's failure. *Delays, delays.* Xon could not tolerate any further delays. Xon had also not pondered the incentum that the geneticist he had had in his employ would still be breathing. The prisoner Xon acquired years ago from the death dungeons deep within the bowels of Ordom Mor in Bellatorius had succeeded with the other two loose ends hidden in separate Solaris, a biomechanical engineer on the domed Orbis Navvre in Ducovímus and a cellular biologist on the uninhabited industrial Orbis Olria in Tracaelus. His confidant had dispatched those famul a month prior, but the one in question was not to be handled quite so easily, it had seemed. One way or another, all in his employ would betray him, even his loyal confidant, but to figure out when was the key. Then, he could use it to exploit as much of their raw talent as he could before their deception could take fruition. The weaker ones, like these scientists, would run at the first incentum of blood on their delicate hands. Xon scoffed; the fact that they could not see no further than their own Solaris was laughable to him. no ambition, no grand design. "The—my—Auctius will not be stopped," Xon said.

There was no sound other than the faint metallic rubbing of techno-organic fibers of Xon's musculoskeletal structure as he stopped in front of the lone slender cylindrical waist-height stand at the end of the room. The orb, smooth and crystalline, levitated atop, waiting for a connection to an authorized nanophage. Of the Vistations lining the walls around the vast clean room, there was only one the geneticist had used in her time here. Xon had monitored every zenobyte worth of data that had been input into these Vistations since the inception of this endeavor. He was leaving nothing to chance; all of the geneticist's daily activities were monitored, her research was recorded, and even the occasions she stepped outside of the facility to take a walk in the moonlight in full hazmat gear were strictly monitored. Xon knew he granted this particular geneticist a little too much freedom by his own standard, but it was not in vain, as she had the key to Noanoagan gene code. Xon allowed some comforts as to make the mind of the meek, his instrument, seem at ease to in order to fulfill his plan. *No matter*, Xon thought, *the work has been done, and the deed can move forward unabated the loose end shall be put to rest soon enough.*

Xon stepped onto a small platform that held the primary Vistation. The platform illuminated underneath him; a soft white light blossomed at his feet. The light seemed to create a halo effect underneath Xon. Then the color changed to a moonlight blue, indicating the linking to a nearby nanophage. Xon prepared himself for the annoyance of the scan. He felt a slight pinch at the nape of his neck as his nanophage was scanned once again. The facility mainframe recognized Xon as the progenitor. A bright-neon-red pentagonal Vis display fizzled into existence, and the platform changed colors again to a forest green, indicating the mainframe was in safe mode. The mainframe had confirmed Xon was not a threat. Xon saw no physical evidence that the clean room hadn't been used in some time because of the timed sterilizations of the facility, but the static-like nature of the Vis indicated the Vis charge cells hadn't been recharged in a month or so. This one knew Xon was coming to tie up loose ends. *She is a clever one.* Xon sneered at the idea of someone anticipating his plans.

Xon blinked, and a series of Vis-rendered file folders shuffled symmetrically inside the Vis border. Xon kept his incentum in a precise, functional order, and the system recognized the personality trait when Xon's phage was scanned and kept it as such in Vis formalities. The files continued to flutter by. Then Xon stopped on the last file, the current genomic project coded in the system as ACTGY. The Noanoagan genetic matrix, the life code of the alien species that now supposedly shared the galaxy. Xon right hand lay on his hip; he flexed his index finger to open the file. There was nothing inside the file, nothing at all.

The Magnus knew he needed the entire genetic makeup of the alien species broken down and decoded to combine with the works of the biomechanical engineer and cellular biologist. The scientist hidden at this location had been tasked with breaking the Noanoagan genetic code in order to bond their technology with existing Human tech. At least, this is what he had told the geneticist. Xon never trusted anyone, let alone a famul, with the full aspects of his plan. As such, Xon and an Ipsum Gnanimus engineer had embedded an algorithm inside each of complexes to collect and compile keyword data to Xon's precise specifications. Each scientist knew just enough to complete their assigned task, allowing the Magnus to put the pieces in place to make his grand vision of the Auctius a reality. *But now this particularly useful speck seemed to figure out what I had been doing. But how?* Xon wondered.

As Xon backtracked to the main screen, the red Vis border emanating from the orb flickered. Xon looked at the orb and platform; they still shone the forest green, so the Vistation was still operating within normal parameters. Within the border a pixelated murkiness seemed to pour inside, and a single bright-neon-green line of code, indiscernible number and letter combinations even to the trained eye, flashed in front of Xon. Nothing else—just the singular line of code floating in the black surrounded by static red Vis energy. Xon quickly attempted to access the rest of the files. As expected, each file opened was blank of all data. Xon accessed the internal memory storage of the mainframe. The mainframe fed the time coding of the file deletion directly to Xon's phage. The file Xon needed, along with all files in the system, had been wiped clean by a time-delayed nanovirus, erasing all data just before his arrival.

Xon had anticipated some kind of resistance from all of the scientists if they happened to discover his true intentions for this venture—hence the need for close-ended employment. Xon didn't let this minor turn of events affect his stability. He knew he had the complete file along with all of the data he needed to further his deed. The algorithm Xon had implanted accounted for such actions so that all data was backed up and sent to the *Cultivador* mainframe directly after each incentum cast into the facility's mainframe. But this green line of code continued to flicker, nagging at something in Xon. The code appeared harmless per the mainframe's security system, and Xon's analysis of the code brought zero results. The code was absolutely useless. Regardless Xon ignored the nag to investigate further and attempted to terminate the Vistation functions. Xon turned away, but the hardware did not power down; Xon could not exit the facility until all Vistations were powered down or there would be a trace attached to this facility when his deed here terminated. *Alvum*, thought the Magnus. With slight hesitation Xon clicked on the code; for a moment nothing happened. Xon heard a click, and the sterile bright-ivory clean room was plunged into darkness like a black hole released its core into the very station the Magnus was standing atop. A deafening silence surrounded Xon; he tensed prepared to defend himself if needed. The lights flickered to life once more. The Vis display remained dim around the edges, still appearing to lose connection. Xon looked around the room: no proximity alerts, none of the automatic security measures activated at a sudden power outage, no GIA or Vultus troopers storming the building. *Odd*, thought Xon, the half of the organic brow furrowing in not only frustration but curiosity. Xon accessed the *Cultivador*'s mainframe with an incentum. The Magnus's internal neuronal sensors, psionically connected to the *Cultivador*, pinged to acknowledge all data had been received from this undisclosed complex from the inception of the project to the last second Xon had been connected to the mainframe before the minor blackout. No trace viruses, nano, ether, or otherwise.

Xon attempted to access any file in the compound's mainframe; the mainframe had now been wiped clean. Xon sent the incentum to locate the source of the power surge and whether it connected with the seemingly volatile line of code when a lex from the *Cultivador* came through over his private channel. Xon acknowledged the lex and a man in his mid-thirties, with a large acid scar that made his face appear as if it were melting like wax on his left side, automatically appeared in his ocumech. The image of the man seemed to be hovering right in front of the Magnus; the clarity of sound made it seem as if the man was standing next to Xon.

"Magnus Xon," the man said, slightly bowing his head

with a deviously childlike smirk in mock acknowledgment of the Magnus's position, "reporting as scheduled. I must say, the time table you gave me struck me as quite frankly asinine, but here you are. I wanted to make sure you heard from me first." Xon's associate was cut off before he could finish.

"Hold. Your. Tongue." Xon spat the words at what he deemed to be his lackey with an acidic edge to each word.

The man was stunned. No one spoke to him with such disrespect and lived another day. "Who the alvum do you think you're talking to?"

Xon ignored his protest. "Attikus, did I not say to eliminate all scientists? All were to be dispatched prior to my arrival on this particular compound!" Xon fought to maintain an eased composure despite the situation. "There were three, only three to contend with, and yet I receive no word about the third's death. Now two months after I gave you the order, the geneticist is gone, probably still alive somewhere in the cosmos, and the compound's mainframe appears to have been nanohacked!"

"Don't know about any hacking job. Not my forte. But the geneticist I have been tracking for some time. When I had arrived at the facility, I found it had been abandoned for some time. I found her hiding with some Vultus members on that backwater luna Tasóa, but she slipped me. By fortune I happened to take care of her amator a little earlier than you requested. The Arquis was investigating on Tasóa, pretty thoroughly. He took out the low-level prisoners easily. I trailed him to the sniper's nest after he took them down. He is injured and incapacitated as ordered, should take him at least a few weeks to recover, given the variety of nano-enhancements he was born with. Now I do have a lead on the geneticist, smuggled off luna, unknown carrier, but that's no matter to me; I find my prey. Which is why, Magnus, I'm on my way to Sapietás Solaris to claim her head."

The man named Attikus lowered his voice as if he didn't want to be overheard. "Now that I'm done with business. I'm going to give you the benefit of being an Elitist and let you get away with taking that tone with me." Attikus paused for but a moment and smiled, making sure to stretch the thin flesh of his scarred side. "But then again, I really don't give a damn who you are, Magnus, or what you have on me, so there is no way in hell you get to talk to me like I'm one of your little famuls running around granting you your wishes. I have no huge stakes in this current course of action you are on, so piss on your plans. It would be a pleasure to see to it personally that my hands are wrapped around that robotic throat of yours until the life is sweetly depleted from your shell. And you can bet I will be on the first barge out of Tracaelus, and no one will never find me."

Xon glared at his subordinate via the lextech embedded behind the lens of his ocumech, the latest premium mod added to his private collection. Attikus looked confident, so sure of himself, truly convicted to wrapping his hands around the Magnus's throat. Xon remembered his volcanic temperament in his youth after the death of his family while in training among the Suivira. While Xon did respect the man's methods and ideologies, he was still a tool to be used to further his Auctius into the next galaxy the way he saw fit. No matter; this tool had almost run its course and would be discarded soon.

Xon was pleased with this new tech, as it gave him a perfect rendering of Attikus's face. His hair was a dull brown, wavy and folding to the right with a square, sharply proportioned jaw and smooth mocha complexion. His piercing aqua-blue eyes made him handsome even with the rotted appearance of the flesh adorning the left side of his face like potholes from old asphalt roads from chin to ear—well, half an ear, as it appeared to Xon. Attikus didn't appear ashamed of it; as a matter of fact, he preferred to show that side as if it were a badge of honor earned from a brutal battle. It pleased Xon to know he could crush this man with the speed of his incentum.

"Now I will put the idle threats to the wayside for the time being, and I will let you think you will be able to accomplish what you say," Xon said, the scar tissue stretching thin as a silk veil to reveal the mechanized musculature underneath, mirroring the sneer Attikus gave Xon a moment ago, "but know this. With a single fleeting incentum even from where I stand across our known galaxy, I can set off a nanovirus that is programmed to insidiously burrow through your phage and brain matter, rendering you a shallow husk of the proud man that you think you are." Xon's demeanor changed to that of a politician running for reelection. "Now I will be sending a tactical team made up of four of your brethren from T-Block 9 where I scraped you from the guards' boots. They are all enhanced with basic nanotech, not as capable as yourself, but I am sure you will find the proper use for all of them. Take them to Sapietás, and terminate the geneticist, but leave the Arquis to be dealt with at my discretion; he must not be excessively harmed. You will follow my orders to the letter without further delay. Do I make myself amply understandable, Prisoner 999?"

Xon had no need for expression; his words were enough, but the added emphasis satiated Xon's ego. Attikus might have been a hardened, coldblooded cutthroat, but when you put anyone's life on the breadth of annihilation, it would change a composure rather quickly.

"Yeah, sure, we understand each other," Attikus said, but there was a slight a quiver to his voice. Attikus turned away as the lex discontinued, and Xon no longer saw the face of his minion but the blank Vis screen in front of him. Xon knew he had not broken the man's spirit entirely. *This one's will is strong*, thought Xon, *and without the hint of a genuine compass of guidance, then there is no qualm about what he would do to get his vengeance upon me or anyone who crossed him.* Xon knew he would have to eliminate that threat as soon as the opportune moment presented itself.

With the entirety of the mainframe wiped clean, this facility was no longer of use to Xon. As he turned away, the Vis screen fluttered and disappeared as if never existed. Xon walked with a more hurried pace now that his plans had been minutely altered. Xon activated the *Cultivador* and booted up the mainframe to chart course for Tracaelus, specifically the Aethra Gateway launching platform. Xon cursed himself for not following up sooner with this geneticist. He should have known better than to leave business like this to a subordinate, even one as capable as Prisoner 999.

Xon climbed the platform into the cargo bay of the *Cultivador*, stopping as if he heard a voice on the wind. Xon had turned toward the compound when he felt overpowered by an electric jolt that shot through his leg as if his neurons just laid upon hot coals. Xon grimaced; his knees became gelatinous beneath him, and he faltered backward but did not scream. Even in the presence of none, Xon refused to show any form of weakness. Xon rubbed his right thigh. *Strange*, he thought, *even with the few organic components of my body still intact, the nanites and small fusions of experimental U'agi tech should make any type of pain imperceptible to my nervous system.* Xon had noticed an inescapable feeling since the Quscape incident, a lack of control.

The pain subsided. Xon shrugged off the cursory feelings turning again to face the compound. "There is still work to be done," Xon said, staring at the research facility. Xon's pupils dilated, and two monstrous swarms of mosquito-sized nanites, too many to count, flew silently out of small openings on the *Cultivador*'s wings. The two clouds of black flew in sync toward the compound. When they closed within a hundred meters, the nanites spread like a net, enveloping the building in a sea of buzzing blackness. Each nanite clicked into place, covering every inch of the concrete and metal. The miniature robotic insects began to hum almost like children during play. The melody was smooth like silk entwining the eardrum. Xon smiled as he always appreciated a well-orchestrated symphonic display. With each note the melody soured, octave by octave, the tone increased until it was a high-pitched whine slicing into air. Xon did not move; the sound had no effect on him, for it was now encased inside the nanite net being conducted straight into the building's molecular structure. Xon watched in silence as the building began to convulse violently and then stopped. Xon felt the ground subtly vibrate underneath him. Xon's attention was drawn back to the building as the nanites began to increase speed. Faster, faster—and then, too quick for even the most advanced ocumech to see, it was gone, into nothing. No sound emanated when the building was vibrated into its basic molecular structure and then dispersed into the air as if it never existed. Satisfied that no quantifiable piece of evidence was left intact, as everything the nanites were touching including the nanites themselves were vaporized, Xon turned and limped up the platform while it rose steadily, sealing the *Cultivador*'s bulkhead for space travel.

Xon made his way to the bridge down the one long corridor of the vessel; white walls and floors gave the appearance similar to the clean room at the now demolished compound. Xon prepared the stellarcraft for takeoff and set up his illustrious Qusom chair, high-backed and bucketed with ports lining all points of pressure, a modification to care for biomechanical aspects of Xon while under Qusom. The Magnus refused to go into the Quscape for the short three-week journey to the Aethra. He could recover just as well under a dreamless, silent Qusom. He did not believe he could endure another psionic assault; to feel his emotional spectrum so intensely after the many years of dormancy was quite overwhelming. It was like all the emotion coiled around him, smothering the life out of him. Xon still couldn't determine how anyone could break down his phage's firewalls and invade his incentum; perhaps recent events allowed his Gnanimus connection to be tracked and hacked. *I have to be more careful for the remainder of this venture. I am beginning to get the feeling I am close to being exposed. To be expected, I suppose,* Xon thought. The Magnus sat in the chair and initiated the Quisthium infusion into his forearm infusion port, while the chair connected to the bionic ports throughout his body. Xon's entire body felt aged, as if everything was catching up to him like some slow, arthritic infestation. Even the nanotechnology from the sequaes musculature to the hardened metallic marrow in his bones seemed to ache. Xon sends the incentum to break atmosphere and make way to Tracaelus at maximum velocity. Xon induced Qusom without the dream realm of the Quscape, allowing the drug to take the full sedative effect, dangerous for a normal Human psyche but with the modifications to Xon's brain and nanophage, he could withstand a Qusom without the Quscape for a still as-yet-undetermined amount of time.

Xon allowed the Qu to take him under, his eyes fluttering as his final thoughts drifted to the journey through a new galaxy, a dream he'd had since boyhood. It wasn't often he was willing to let the drug overtake him, but lately the with stresses of his Auctius coming to head, the strengths he held so close to the chest seemed to be evading him. And that strength, that sacred control, was what Xon required for the fruition of the Aethra, the culmination of a lifetime of work, and the journey beyond to expand the Auctius with or without the backing of the council. Xon was assured by his interventions that his plan had remained intact, and despite the potential exposure and the fallibility of his agents, the final phase was about to begin with the alien terraluna Tasóa being the beginning of the end.

CHAPTER 10

Location Unknown, Time and Space Unknown

Alvum, what the hell just happened? Nachman awoke, his vision clouded like a cataract had covered his eye. Looking around, he felt as if he were blinking away a long slumber from his eyes, but he couldn't feel his eyelids. Nachman's head didn't quite feel right, almost detached, floating maybe, and warm—he was so warm. *What a weird sensation.* He heard his thoughts so clearly, but Nachman could not feel the vibration of sound off his tongue. *Where am I...whoa!* Nachman's vision cleared, and what he saw was like nothing he had ever encountered on any world he had visited in the Celestial.

Everything around him seemed to be shimmering, as if the dawn sun were glinting through a waterfall. A beautiful aqua blue was seamless all around him, like everything was one and the same. Nachman felt like he had no depth perception, like he was in a box, but the box had no end, making Nachman feel just a bit claustrophobic.

Nachman thought he was alone but soon found that not to be true. Small, shining orbs, hundreds of them, either lavender or bluish green but pearlescent and viscous, gathered around Nachman, clustering together but none touching him as if touching him was acidic. Six orbs remained behind while the rest just seemed to float away. All around him there were millions upon millions of orbs some swimming, floating, or rhythmically bouncing through and about one another. *So many blobs. They seem purposeful with their movements,* Nachman thought, realizing every thought was loud like chimes echoing all around him. Nachman looked around. At least, he felt like he was looking around. So many of them, some in rows others in columns, or some just clustered together like a social grouping. The orbs were no bigger than an oyster's pearl, smooth and fluid like a drop of water shaped into a perfect circle. The six began to flow back and forth seemingly erratic at first, but the more Nachman watched them, he saw purposeful patterns emerge as if the movements were a way of communication with one another.

Did I die and get reincarnated as a dewdrop? Where am I? This is definitely not my adyta. I've got to be dead, no question. Recall, Nachman, recall. What's the last thing I can remember? Oh, right, that behemoth blindsiding me, I can't wait to see that one again...wait...why can't I feel anything? Where's my body, and why don't I care if I have one?

Nachman could feel his mind intact, sharp, ready for whatever was coming at him. Well, he thought so anyway, but the rest of him was just simply not there. Nachman saw— no, wrong sentiment, more like he *felt* the vision that allowed him to see—that he was made of the same fluidity as the rest of the orbs that surrounded him, except his coloring was different, and he was less cohesive. A tiny globule here and there would break off and then coagulate back to the main glob as if he wasn't fully put together. The orbs all had different shades of blue green or lavender, but Nachman didn't appear as the rest of the orbs. He felt like he was orange highlighted with some kind of red. Nachman looked not with eyes but more of his feeling of vision, a sense of touching something that exists but not on the same level of existence as everything he was accustomed to, and a sense of a vibrant energy around him nipping at his current form. It didn't hurt—more like a recurring static shock. Nachman chuckled as he remembered shocking himself as a kid and watching Sadie jump to the ceiling like a startled feline. The pure energy surrounding him and the orbs was warm, not painful or disheartening but a spirit of harmony that felt like a soft cushion of contentment and peace.

Nachman knew he had felt this before, this same exact feeling, but the memory was distant as if it were covered in a layer of metaphysical fog. Nachman had never felt this sensation in the real world or his realm of reality, if this was some kind of reality. But to feel like this, he wondered if—Nachman felt like he shrugged his shoulders—maybe he wasn't dead after all.

The group of orbs, Nachman thought he counted six, four blue green and two lavender, that stayed behind began moving with such grace appearing to meld into and around each other like a fluid ballet of color. The movements were mesmerizing. Nachman knew he was watching, but *watching* was the wrong sentiment. He felt like he was feeling everything they were doing, almost, but something was missing. Nachman had a strong sense that this is how they communicated, but Nachman had no idea what they were saying, or rather projecting, to him. The "conversation" appeared to be one of mutual understanding as the orbs' movements were smooth and almost calming as Nachman watched. As the orbs swam into each other, the colors changed frequently: blue, green, lavender, turquoise. Nachman, even though he couldn't understand them, could feel a few of the orbs discontent that he was here. It felt like a fingernail scraping softly across the skin; it wasn't painful, but he knew the animosity was there. *Why be angry at me? I didn't ask to be here.* Nachman sensed that the orbs held nothing back. Everything the orbs projected Nachman felt; some of the projections felt smooth and warm, while others bit at Nachman's incentum. But he just couldn't quite make sense of the projections.

The orbs sped up; then two broke off, a blue green and lavender, waiting a yard away from the others. But Nachman felt like the lavender one was watching him. The other four flurried, swimming faster and faster like they were arguing. The lavender orb that broke off from the group jolted toward Nachman and tried to intermix with his orb. The lavender fluid flowed into Nachman's orange orb, making the mixture appear a rusty reddish brown for only a moment, when the lavender orb was thrust away from Nachman's orb like some invisible hand had shoved it away. The orb paled for a moment —it didn't appear injured—then shone to the highlighted lavender coloring, gliding to the side of the blue-green orb that had left the grouping. Nachman had no stomach at the moment, but he started to feel a bit queasy.

Oh, alvum, please don't do that again. Felt like I was being churned into goat butter for a sec. Huh? That's strange. Why am I not nervous, even terrified? Well, a bit fearful anyway. I should be ready to fight it out to the end with you dewdrops, but I feel, just feel to my core, that none of you mean me any harm. I feel almost at peace here. The one that tried to...merge with me (hope you're OK, by the way) couldn't for some reason. Is it because I'm not in control of the Quscape? Or am I even in the Quscape? So if I'm wrong, tell me. Talk to me, guys.

The orb let it be known to Nachman he was correct, sending the sense across the liquid essence surrounding them, but other than that sense, there was no further elaboration. *It seems through your traditional methods, we are unable to communicate. But what you're sending to me is almost a sense of an emotion, or rather feeling, of a situation, which is why what you're saying comes in kind of like static. It sure is a weird sensation to almost feel your intentions like a vibration across this form, a tickle sometimes and others a slight pin prick, which I think I'll steer clear of those, but I know there is more you want to tell me, isn't there? You're straining to project anything, almost like you have a story to tell me.*

Nachman knew they weren't trying to hurt him, but what did they want? *I know, for some reason, I just know, you all are peaceful, none of you know violence inherently, and none of you hold anger against anything. It feels as if you only want to spread vast knowledge that brings peaceful intent, but there is a struggle.*

Nachman strained to sense what they were trying to convey by stretching his essence like fingers, reaching for anything to touch, reaching but just not far enough. *I feel like I've been here already, and I know, just know, what you are but my mind is...*

A blue-green orb blew out of the commingling like a bullet, then flattened and elongated in front of Nachman's ill-formed orb. Nachman's orb shuddered; he would always be suspicious of anyone's or anything intention's until he was sure he could put his trust into them even if these sentient beings were projecting nothing but peaceful intentions. *Everyone says I'm paranoid; might as well own it.* Those kinds of thoughts Nachman had once, only to himself, and buried those kinds of distractions deep in his memory files. *Why are they so loud for these orbs to hear?* Nachman wondered. Distraction will always get you killed; it was an ideal that had kept Nachman alive in this unforgiving Celestial all this time. It felt like wherever he was was seeping into him like he was becoming whole with the realm around him and by that, becoming whole within himself. His mind was opening up to memories he had kept buried, concepts from technical specifications for nanophage upgrades that he had theorized while at the Naibus academy, and lines of thought he hadn't even considered until this moment. *Wild,* Nachman thought, *the Sitanimi, those cheeky monks were right.*

And that was all he could think of when the orb started to flash images on the flattened surface. *The display kinda looks like the Vis holo-screens on the* Satyr—*in fact, almost exactly.* The images were seemingly random at first. Humans throughout the ages from the dawn of mankind surviving the harsh deadly terrains of an infantile Earth to the dawn of the space age of man as their Mother becomes a toxic mausoleum of Humanity's past. Random shots of what Nachman thought were nightmarish monsters, but the images flashed by him at blinding speed so fast he couldn't quite make out what he was seeing. *Slow it down a bit; can't make out what you're trying to show me.* Nachman realized that the orbs could understand him when the images slowed, and Nachman saw that the Noanoagans weren't the only alien species in the Celestial.

The image gained clarity, and Nachman was introduced to a species that seemed to have lived on a lush, brightly multicolored forest planet. *No, the atmosphere is too thin for a planet.* The orb—Nachman was sure they understood him now—zoomed out to give an atmospheric view of a moon orbiting a gas giant twice the size of Jupiter. The planet didn't look like anything Nachman had seen in on this side of the Celestial, no recognizable constellation patterns. *Another galaxy?* The gas giant showed multiple gigantic storms in the stratosphere with swirling purples and yellows throughout the planet. *Beautiful.* The orb's surface shimmered and zoomed back onto the moon's surface, twisting and turning through a rainforest that was eerily similar to the Amazons of ancient Gaia, except with an array of color that would leave a painter busy for a month, directly to a village of alien creatures Nachman could have sworn look similar to the genetically engineered giraffes he had seen at the Martian zoos when he was a child.

The giraffe aliens stood on two lanky, almost rubbery-looking legs with three toes the size of a Human fists towering over Nachman, in Human form, standing at least two and a half meters tall with their necks making up half of that height. The arms of the creatures extended down to their knees, as if they were hanging vines from their lush surroundings. Their eyes were on the sides of their heads, oval and black like two grand agate gemstones. Long snouts protruded from their faces with mouths that seemed to be in permanent grins and small humps like dulled horns on the tops of their heads. The orb then sent flashes of the village and the subsequent evolution of the species throughout what seemed like a co-habitation between the giraffe aliens and the orbs from what Nachman interpreted as roughly seventy-five years. The species had evolved, it seemed, culturally and technologically, from a village in appearance of ancient Chinese civilizations to an infrastructure reminiscent of early twentieth-century Earth, except more organic in nature with some advanced technologies, such as self-sustaining farming equipment and electricity that seemed to operate on some kind of solar-powered apparatus. The orb sent the feeling to Nachman that they helped the species advance in such a manner, the orb directly communicating that he (for some reason, Nachman knew the orb was a *he*) felt a sense of pride in helping the species grow and evolve. The image of the giraffe-like aliens faded, and while it transitioned to another series of images, Nachman felt a sense of mourning and sadness form the orbs. *I'm not quite following. I see you helped these creatures advance technologically and gave them advanced knowledge, mathematics, linguistics, and such, but did you know these creatures personally? The way you feel right now is how I felt when I lost friends in the Celestial Wars and among other skirmishes. Comrades in arms? Friends?*

Nachman sensed, from the flattened orb, a bit of frustration directed at Nachman as the next set of images slowed so Nachman could comprehend what he was viewing. *Hey, I'm trying, give me a break.* The flattened orb's color faded a shade or two, Nachman felt that he usually was calm and collected, but there was a feeling of urgency emanating from the orb. *What's going on? Why so nervous?* The orb ignored the question and continued with the history lesson. The images presented almost seemed similar with relatively the same evolution of the giraffe-like species. This species looked Humanoid, two arms and two legs with five elongated fingers and toes. All had spindly torsos that seemed stretched unnaturally like they were just taken off a torture rack with long legs to match. Their faces were similar throughout the species; flat noses with wide nostrils, small, thin-lipped mouths, and furry pointed ears. The aliens' eyes were a piercing diamond shape and completely green like a pasture on a sunny day. Nachman laughed. Nachman sensed the confusion from the orb at his laughter. The aliens looked as if the species had stepped out of an ancient Mardi Gras parade, their brightly hued clothes and hair screamed eccentricity that would make a peacock jealous. *I've only seen people from where I'm from dress like this when they are celebrating or just trying to stick out in the crowd.* The orb communicating with him gave Nachman the sense of playfulness and joy when thinking of this species. The orbs had grown to care a great deal for this species. The images played out to project a span of 250 Gaian years, but to Nachman, the images only took a minute or two to siphon through. The last image showed a desolate planet that had been overtaken by natural phenomena that had wiped out the entire species, the orbs unable to assist the species save the planet along with themselves. The flattened orb as well as the rest of the orbs observing the conversation became silent again, mourning the passing of another species. Nachman also felt a sting of sadness by the final image. This struck a chord in Nachman. *You all live quite a long time. I would probably end up talking to the little nanorobots in my head if I lived that long. Um, question. What's going on with this place? It's like I have no filter anymore.*

The emotional sensations were a bit overwhelming but nothing Nachman wasn't familiar with; he was just used to separating them in himself and others and using them to his advantage. Nachman did his best to keep his emotions inside, never letting an overexposure of familiarity with anyone lest it be used against him. Emotions weren't so much foreign language, just something he preferred to stay away from; they tended to do more harm than good in Nachman's experience. Sadie and his mother, Delylah, had seen Nachman's true emotional self on few occasions, and Sadie was downright incorrigible when understanding the complexities of social interactions and hindering emotions. Nachman's big question was this: Why had he been made so vulnerable to these orbs?

Have you done something to me, or is it this dewdrop state I'm in? Maybe this isn't real, or maybe I'm in a coma, and this is the way my brain is protecting my conscious mind—by putting me into this dreamscape. That's it. A dream, not a nightmare, but a pleasant out-of-body dreamland. But this...just...feels so...real? The sensation Nachman felt next assured him that this realm was in the realm of the real and not a fabrication of a broken mind.

Fear, even the most remote feel of the sensation, was palpable and universal among any species, and it was something Nachman battled and continued to overcome. But the intensity of this dread he felt now was like thorns boring into his epithelium. Nachman had always felt when someone was afraid, when someone reached that level where reason and logic became waypoints in the back of the mind and the fear overwhelmed even the most sensible. Hell, he had made plenty feel that way himself, and Nachman always knew how to use it to manipulate the situation to his favor.

The orb had a sudden glance of apprehension toward Nachman with the feeling Nachman was projecting. *The manipulation is only a tool. A tool I use to get the job done.* The orb wasn't convinced and was beginning to transform back to the spherical shape it was before.

Come on, don't leave. I'm not going to hurt you or even manipulate you. I really don't want a miscommunication here. What's strange is for some reason, I trust you, and I think you trust me. I'm not a prideful man—well, not all the time—but one high item I do pride myself on is my word, and believe me when I say I'm not the bad guy here. Might have been close to being one a spell ago but not anymore. I don't know how I got here, but I'm here, and I get the feeling I'm supposed to be here because you wouldn't be showing me these alien species if I wasn't meant to see them. This means something. You can't tell me directly, but I'm getting the feeling this is connected to what I've been working on. And I'll be damned, but I can somehow feel your intentions, and now I'm starting to understand, I think. You all had some sort of bond with these species but, wait, you're not—regardless if I have an idea of what you all are or what exactly I am right now, fear shouldn't exist between us; you can trust me. I have a good incentum that what you're showing me is going to help. What it's going to help with in the grand scheme of things, I haven't figured out quite yet, but I'm sure a lot of people are going to need it, so please let me help.

The orb's blue-green surface reflected back what

looked like orange mud from the bottom of a dirty river. Nachman could safely assume the misshapen globule was the form Nachman took in this realm. *I know I'm not one of you, but couldn't I look a bit shinier like the rest of you? Instead I look like spittle on the mouth of a sleeping hog.* Nachman didn't think the orb got the joke, or he did but just didn't care. The orb floated in place, unflinching. Nachman knew if the orb had a face, there would be a pondering look written all over it.

As if he had let out a breath he had been holding, the blue-green orb flattened again into the oval-view screen. The hesitation was still noticeable as the image slowly (even more slowly than Nachman needed) flickered into reality with an atmospheric view of a planet approximately the size of Mars. The atmosphere was thickly clouded, no sun rays able to penetrate, as if pollution overtook the planet hundreds of years ago. The image zoomed to the surface, revealing a colony of technological wonder. Towering glass buildings, paved roads, lush greenery from trees and brush, and Nachman could not even begin to identify the oddly shaped, apparently techo-organic mechanical structures throughout the compound. The entire structure was almost perfectly centered on the otherwise barren planet. A dome covered the entire compound; Nachman assumed it was for protection from the harsh environmental conditions. Attached to the dome was a reinforced wall that encompassed the entire circumference of the compound with many large indentations, as if the wall had been ravaged by centuries of furious sand storms and other elemental hazards. There was absolutely nothing surrounding the compound, the entire planet had the look of an uncultivated wasteland, dry and cracked as if a dust bowl was forbidding the growth of any harvest. *What the hell happened here?* The orb ignored Nachman's incentum and continued with the slideshow.

This species had the closest look to Human that Nachman had seen, yet the way they made the orbs all around him feel told him they were the most alien race of them all. The image wavered to reveal a large group of Humanoid aliens of differing heights, weights, genders, and ages, but strangely every single one of the aliens gave the other orbs that same uneasy feeling; it felt like an arctic breeze stinging off his skin. Still hesitant to show the images, the flattened blue-green orb pressed on. Nachman had a feeling they didn't talk about this part of history too much.

All the aliens were varying shades of lavender, some solid in color, others a blend of different shades. Their bodies were very similar to Humans: two arms and legs equally proportioned to their torsos, five fingers and five toes to match although there was no discernible way to tell gender apart from first glance as all were completely bald with elephant-like skin, thick almost like an armor. The faces all varied with the individual, but the same generalities were present. Eyes the shape of inverted teardrops with the tip touching at the septum of the nose, the eyes a hair larger than that of a Human. Each alien had a marking over the left eye. The markings looked geometric, similar to the angular shapes he was taught in grade school. Most of the aliens had what appeared to be triangles, others pentagons, hexagons, and octagons. Some of the young ones didn't have any such markings. *Ranking structure maybe? A militaristic culture? And if so, who's the leader of this colony? There is always a leader; an alpha is always present with these sorts of groups.*

The orb didn't answer, but Nachman got the feeling he was pleased with Nachman's deduction. The orb seemed to want to focus on these aliens' features, as if he wanted Nachman to get the best picture possible of the creatures. So Nachman continued to study and made sure he remembered every detail. The ears were on the side of their head, much like a Human, but wider with a lowercase *t* shape for the ear canal. The ears curved to the back of their heads, the tips of the ear connecting to the base of the alien's skull—for what purpose, Nachman wasn't sure—and Nachman was sure the orb didn't know either, but Nachman thought it looked like some kind of antennae. The aliens' noses were mostly flat, with wide nostrils leading to sharply angled cheekbones, giving the appearance of a razor blade protruding from either side. Finally, their mouths were lined with full lips that were actually somewhat appealing, but when their mouths opened four rows of teeth on both upper and lower jaws gleamed inside that would make even the largest shark both envious and afraid. The aliens weren't horrendous—hardly the most terrifying creature that Nachman had seen in the Celestial thus far —but that same feeling was still being projected from the all six orbs just the same, for lack of a better word: terror. The orbs truly were terrified of these creatures, and Nachman was eager to see why.

The flattened orb showed the next image with an amount of guilt the equivalent of a boulder sitting upon Nachman's shoulders. *Yeah, buddy, I know exactly how that feels; it's hard to put behind you. But what did you do to hold so much on your back?* The orb let the image tell the tale of the guilt. The orb had fast forwarded the timeline 163 years, and from what Nachman could tell when the image faded into view, the aliens were dying. Throughout their techno-organic city, dire straits and chaos were abundant. The once-glorious metropolis was now dwindling to a husk. The buildings of towering glass were now cracked and teetering like a playground toy; the many techno-organic structures appeared without power and now appeared more like a fungal growth than an interfacing apparatus. Bodies, vehicles, and sewage lined the scarred streets. And the dome that protected the aliens from the harsh outside environment was shattered, a gaping hole atop as if a vessel had tried to explode outward.

Nachman couldn't make out an individual figure in the giant mass of bodies piled on either side of a large ship, presumably the one that failed to escape the dome as it was directly below the gaping breach. The purpose of the piled bodies Nachman could only determine was lack of a disposal site. The aliens that remained scrambled about, avoiding the dead and generally the living as well. The survivors were much like ants in disarray, scurrying lost from their colony and eventually trailing to a crowd around a crashed vessel. One by one they walked, crawled, or articulated their bodies however they could to reach the vessel. The sight made Nachman want to turn away, but he couldn't; he had to watch, had to know. The bodies were dropping where they stood, crawled, or walked whether from starvation, thirst, or for some, existing injury. Every single alien looked as if death had joined them at the hip. Nachman found it odd that none were trying to help each other; even as young ones and elderly were falling in heaps around them, everyone just kept to themselves. Each alien just simply meandered toward the downed ship as if it was the last refuge in the ravaged city. The radioactive dust seeped into the city, covering everything in a thick film like a suffocating blanket; the winds bit at every surface, and the temperature dropped to levels that no Human could endure. *It looks like these poor souls don't have much of a life left ahead of them.* As the orb flashed the next set of images, Nachman could sense shame and disgust in the orb. Nachman didn't ask him to elaborate; he was getting the sense from this orb that he blamed himself for what transpired between him and these aliens. Nachman knew all too well what self-loathing could feel like. What happened next was something Nachman never expected to see then again; he still couldn't believe he was talking to dewdrops and was, in fact, one of said dewdrops.

A bright, blinding light entered through the crevice in the dome. The light was shaped much like the orbs surrounding Nachman, but this one was much larger. The ball of light glistened in the dust and grime; then the surface became smooth like a fresh layer of ice covering a frozen pond. The pure white orb now hovered over the wrecked ship, unmoving. Many of the aliens reached for the glistening sphere as if it were their last salvation, but the rest simply stared in not so much awe but curiosity. Not a curiosity that Nachman thought was innocent—the orb projected the feeling that

Nachman was correct. *What kind of creatures are these?*

The giant orb opened a slit much like iris in the center of the sphere. A dense fog and dull light shone through the iris. A vast ray of light shone through, and as if someone opened a floodgate, thousands of balls of light poured out of the sphere. Each separate ball of light seemed to have a purpose, as all the balls of light chose an alien and hovered above each of them. Once all the balls of light had taken their positions above each alien, the giant sphere let out a sound, more like a vibration, like someone humming. The lights hovering over the aliens shimmered and seemed to solidify but with a gelatinous consistency, much like the orbs in front of Nachman now. The sphere seemed to tremor, then vaporized leaving nothing in its wake as if it was never there. *That's your species, isn't it? But what are you—*

Before Nachman could finish his question, the blue-green orb let out a feeling that punched Nachman in the proverbial gut. The images flashed quickly in front of Nachman, almost too quickly, as though the orb did not or was not supposed to show Nachman what had happened.

The gelatinous orbs floated to the nape of each of the aliens' necks, just barely touching their leathery skin. The image zoomed in on a blue-green orb sprouting ten tendril-like appendages adhering to the alien's flesh. The alien did not look in pain but euphoric, as if it had been given exactly not what it needed but wanted. The orb fused into the skin of the alien. Once the orb was entirely melded within the alien, it was as if a light had been clicked on inside the head of each alien life form. Nachman felt fear from the orbs that surrounded him, but from the image, he felt a sense of liveliness, something that the species had not felt in hundreds of years. It was like a current of electricity running a wire full of spark and vigor for the first time, or so it seemed.

The flattened orb flashed a series of images that showed a marked progression in the species over the next month. Starships were rebuilt, techno-organic functions restored to their various adapted technologies, life and vibrancy had been essentially restored. The species appeared to be vibrant with meaning and purpose, rebuilding their technology like it was the only meaningful thing to do in their desolate world. The orbs in the images of the past thought this curious, as they were only focused on the technological aspect of their culture. The orbs found it curious but did not seem to mind as they gladly helped, giving knowledge to assist the alien species rebuild. Then one day, from out of seemingly nowhere, the work ceased, as if the alien species completed the exact job they were intended to perform. The orbs lived in symbiosis with the species, allowing them to maintain independent function and thought. The flattened orb projected the thought of control. They must have the ability to inhabit a host fully if the situation demanded; considering the intent of the orbs, it seemed they did not use this ability unless absolutely necessary. Nachman had the strangest noda that the orbs should have taken over right away.

A sudden electric jolt struck Nachman, sending a ripple of what he could only interpret as pain through his gelatinous form; it felt as if an invisible force was pulling at him, as if trying to rip him from this plane of existence. Although he felt the pain, Nachman ignored it for the time being. For some reason unknown to Nachman, these orbs and their information seemed relevant to was happening in his part of the Celestial and could probably help the current investigation when he got back. *If he could get back*, Nachman thought to himself.

Nachman's focus went back to the images with a feeling of utter loss and sadness. The image seemed serene enough. So where was all the anguish coming from? Every alien in the now reinforced city was surrounding the newly rebuilt transport vessel at the center of the city, the same one that had failed to break through the dome. Every single alien, young and old, stood perfectly still, their eyes closed, arms extended by their sides palms up, and feet slightly parted in a kind of meditative state. Then, for the first time, the ship opened. A door that also functioned as a ramp, lowered and from the inside a figure appeared. Nachman didn't recognize this one, but the orb sent the perception that this one was the leader. *Why is this the first time we are seeing this one?* The orb didn't answer. The lead alien was larger than the rest, built much like a gorilla, a subtle lavender shading to its skin, and had a large diamond shape etched or burned over its left eye but the rest of the features were roughly the same as the other aliens. For the first time Nachman heard the alien, any of them, speak. It sounded like a series of clicks, like a tongue snapping off the roof of a mouth, but after a second, the orb had translated the "words" into English for Nachman to understand. It was only four words, and the power of those words weighed heavily on every single orb. "Now is the time." The alien's voice was gruff, coarse, like he hadn't spoken in years, but those words were enough for Nachman to know that this was a turning point for both species.

Nachman felt the pull again. *What the hell? What's happening? It feels like something is trying to pull me out of here. Are you doing this?* Nachman interpreted the orb's response as roughly the shrugging of proverbial shoulders. *Great, well, better speed things up. Doesn't seem like I have much time left with you.*

Chaos, absolute chaos, is what came next. Not in the sense of chaotic imagery but chaotic feelings and intentions. The aliens projected what felt like contentment, intrigue, and power, but the orbs felt nothing but betrayal and terror as they were held captive inside the aliens. The images were coming at Nachman so fast that if he had a head at this moment, it would feel like it was imploding into itself. What Nachman could sense, as the images were just too fast and the orb didn't seem like he was going to slow them down, was an absolute loss of freedom and willpower, not by the aliens but from the orbs. Every single orb embedded inside these aliens became a hostage in an instant. It was as if with one cohesive, collective thought the aliens had absolute and total control over each and every orb that was bonded inside their minds. Some of the free-floating orbs looked as if they escaped, but most were suspended where they levitated, unable to move or communicate. The next series of images showed the conquering aliens in a lab experimenting on the orbs, rebuilding their ship, and then the ship breaking orbit with the planet imploding, like it was being absorbed through a black hole. An absolute certainty had struck Nachman at the moment the planet was blinked from existence. If he were to ever encounter this species, he would strike first—no questions asked, no quarter given.

Well, that was an interesting feeling. Hell, everything about this seems implausible. From what I can interpret—and stop me if I'm wrong—but it seems like your species was able to bond with these aliens, much like the Noas bond with each other. It is some kind of genetic ability that's beyond me, if I'm understanding you correctly. The orb projected nothing but kept the image of the leader in full view like he, she, it was the key behind the subterfuge that enslaved the orbs. Nachman continued with his assessment. *The other aliens your species bonded with seemed to live symbiotically with you learning, building, and adapting, but this species was something you never expected to encounter...it seems they deceived you somehow and gave the sense of peace. But once the big bad leader came into the fray, these aliens just...it felt like their true selves came out and they were instantly projecting volatility, loathing, and power with the truth of their ultimate goal always being enslavement. Somehow, I think through that alien from the ship, their leader apparently, they were able to take away your free will and ability to disconnect from these beings. They seem psychically powerful, and all of you became their slaves in an instant, and from what I feel now, it seems like a lot of you still are.*

Nachman wanted to help; he could never leave someone in dire straits, but this felt like it needed more than just his investigative background, it felt like he needed an army but to what end he wondered. *Look, I am truly sorry this happened to you and yours, but how is this supposed to help back—*

Heat, searing heat throughout every inch of his perceived form, is the best way Nachman could describe what he was feeling at that moment. *Ah, damn, what the alvum is that? Ah! What are you doing?* The orb reformed into its former spherical shape and floated right in front of Nachman's form. The orb gave the impression that their time together was at an end. *Wait, you haven't told me everything; what am I supposed to do?* Another jolt sent Nachman's orb reeling backward, as if a tether was pulling him away from whatever plane of existence he was on. Nachman did not know what was transpiring at this moment, but it was over just as quickly as it began. An envelope of nothing swarmed over Nachman, leaving him feeling utterly alone. He could no longer feel the orbs, his gelatinous form—he couldn't feel anything at all.

CHAPTER 11

**Sapietás Solaris, Terraluna Diiu, Community Kinship Beta,
Home of Delylah Rosenblatt
Eleven Standard Weeks until Aethra Gateway Activation**

Well, that was fun. Nachman knew he was lying flat, a bit disoriented and dizzy but definitely flat on his back. The surface was soft, cushioned, and warm, like a fresh blanket from the laundry. Nachman could feel his body again, thankfully, and he didn't mind that it felt like insects were crawling inside his skin or that he felt like he was rundown by a rogue ZGV; at least he could feel himself again. Nachman knew he wasn't in any kind of restraint, but still waking up from the dream, out-of-body experience, or whatever had happened to him made him a little on edge. He didn't want whoever was in the room —one person, maybe two people—to realize he was awake. Taking a series of short, rapid breaths, just enough to calm himself but not enough to show more chest rise, he listened to the apprehensive voice directly above him.

"How is it? And I am sure I already know the answer, from the injuries I'm seeing to both the organic and cybernetic components, even with the Vis tubules flowing through him, that my son has healed more than three times the speed he normally would in less than three weeks?"

Nachman knew his mother's voice, but to hear it so stern, almost on the verge of anger, was highly unusual. She was always so calm in voice and demeanor, even when performing the most complex techno-organic micro-surgeries. He could only surmise the other person in the room was Sadie, but what was happening? Nachman listened, remaining as still as before he had awakened, hopefully he could gain some insight into what his mother was so upset about.

"Delylah, I, I..." Sadie stammered to the only person that can make her doubt herself.

"Don't say it. You said you didn't know the danger it presented on Nachman or yourself, yet you sent him there again. Sadie, you promised me you would never send him there again, even under the most dire circumstances," Delylah said, turning her attention back to removing shrapnel from Nachman's ocumech, her salt-and-pepper hair falling over her creased but young eyes as her head moved in almost mechanical articulation.

"I know, but he was dying. If I hadn't sent his Vis into my realm, he would have been—" Sadie stopped, turning away from her surrogate mother. If a Caiet could cry, she would have at that moment.

He heard the voices, Mother and Sadie, but they sounded distorted, like the signal wasn't strong enough to hear. Were they real or fake? *I know those voices*, Nachman thought, *but is it a trick? Gotta be some kind of subterfuge to acquire information.* The rise of panic stung at Nachman's brain like chaos thundering inside his gyri. "Permanently paranoid" is what his mother, and others, always told him. He always fought these sensations when out of his comfort of control. The only thought crashing against his incentum was to fight his way out then run, but he had to stay calm. He knew so strongly he was home, but the panic was still ever present. Nothing like almost dying to disjoint his training and his senses. Nachman tried to relax before he let them know he was awake. Keeping his eyes closed and his body still, he felt his muscles relax and loosen as if they were weightless; the anxiety faded back into the recesses of his incentum. He silently thanked the rigorous training he had received in counterintelligence and interrogation techniques that had paid off many times in the past and now was nothing different. His senses were coming back to him slower than usual, but Nachman had staved off the edge of panic and the need for a weapon in his hand. Now he had to concentrate and find out what the hell was going on; there was a lot piling up in the Celestial, and Nachman had a feeling he had only scratched the surface. *Wait a minute. Did Sadie just say she sent me to her realm?*

What was that? thought Sadie, looking up from the surgical table. A sound, almost like a soft whisper in the corner of her mind, but it sounded like...she looked down at Nachman, who was still sound asleep in a chemically induced coma to reduce the swelling to both the organic and cybernetic components of his brain. Sadie concentrated but heard silence, physically and psychically, Delylah seemingly unconcerned by any distractions. Sadie turned back to her task at hand, re-knitting the Vis tubules lining Nachman's left hand, silently thinking to herself, *How am I going to tell Nachman what I did— not once, but three times now?*

Nachman knew he must be where he thought he was, but there was a nagging doubt in his mind that something was off, like his Vis being sent to another dimension, for example. *Stop it, Nachman, you paranoid schmuck. You're here, you're with family, they are helping. Let them, for once*, Nachman thought softly. But that noda, the one he knew would never go away even with time and training, was still there, so he continued to lie still. Nachman heard the annoying beeps of medical devices, a subtle buzzing of electricity from the archaic fiber optic wiring throughout the room, the wisp of clothing rubbing together as whoever—*most likely your mother, Nachman*— was working on him moved about in very precise, corrugated movements. Nachman felt his left hand again, a little tingling, but it was there. Nachman said a silent thank-you to Sadie. Then, to Nachman's surprise and without the usual ringing dinner-bell sound that accompanied the initiation of his aurimod, audio modification, all the static in his head cleared, and he heard the muffled whispers of familiarity tickling his ears, bringing a figurative smile to his incentum. *They are real*, Nachman thought, *I'm home.*

One voice, now that he could hear it clearly, he hadn't heard in almost a year, but it was one that he would never easily forget. The other was his trusted ally and confidant. Sadie and his mother's voices were argumentative, much like a doctor and her assistant, but more familial as the tones held nothing but care and love. He was home.

They were no longer arguing over where Nachman's Vis was sent but over how to repair Nachman's cybernetic arm that was nearly torn off by the madman he had met at the sniper's nest on Tasóa. *At least I'm somewhere I know.* He laughed to himself. Nachman could feel the tinkering to his left arm as Delylah cauterized some internal wiring, removing near-microscopic damaged components and replacing them appropriately with the swiftness of a longtime, skilled surgeon. Nachman had always admired his mother's finesse. She had never caused him any pain and never used synthetic pain suppressants after his battle with a highly addictive and volatile nano-drug. The surgery did have a slight burning sensation, but Nachman ignored it; Sitanimi meditative techniques help immensely in these situations. His incentum drifted. He couldn't help but think about Sadie's comment. He had so many questions for her. Did he travel to a different dimension, or was it a different plane of existence? Were those dewdrops really Sadie's people? He and Sadie were definitely going to have a nice long chat later.

"But, Delylah, I have found that if you interlock the coupling to the radius and the metacarpals, then Nachman will have a quicker reaction time and a higher PSI," Sadie said with Vis teeth clenched in frustration.

Delylah Rosenblatt hunched above Nachman on a circular metallic stool attached, by the underside, to an articulating arm suspended from the ceiling. The arm was attached to a rail system embedded in the ceiling that was linked directly to Delylah's nanophage, just like the rest of the equipment in the room. She could have upgraded to the zero-gravity tech, but she preferred the "feel" of the mechanical across her incentum, not the aloofness of zero-gravity; it always made her feel disjointed. There was only one terminal in her clinic that she kept connected to the Gnanimus simply for patient information and medical-record access. All other equipment, Vistation or otherwise, was off grid. Delylah never liked prying eyes; as she would always say, "Like mother, like son." As such, having a direct connect to her nanophage allowed Delylah to shadow her entire living facility from the Gnanimus without utilizing illegal means by GIA standards when the pressing need came. Delylah had always been careful of others, even before the incident on Tasóa; she always said his father taught her well. Besides, Sadie had been more than happy to help Delylah upgrade her security measures throughout the years.

Nachman began to open his eyes, and through the small parting of his eyelids, he saw a very familiar setting. The clinical suite was a semisterile environment made for quick interventions and repair of various biomechanical apparatuses set up in the back of Delylah's home. The walls were tiled for easy cleanup as well as the floors, but the décor was that of home rather than a work environment. With the exception of the medical equipment, telemetry monitors, surgical instruments lining the walls as if they were kitchen cutlery, the medical gurney in the center of the room, the bright surgical lamps above the table, and a singular Vis console in the corner of the room that seemed as if it has been sitting there unused for a century, he felt the room had a certain warmth to it. Nachman always knew that warmth didn't come from the room, but who was in it. And to Nachman, that warmth meant he was home. Nachman's mind eased a bit, the tension falling away from his muscles slowly like melting wax. Nachman often wondered if everybody felt this comfortable when they were operated on by his mother.

"No, Sadie, if you recall, the coupling should only be linked to both the ulna and the radius. I'm sure you have noticed the coupling wearing down in a matter of weeks because of the lack of sufficient stability and lubrication of the joint itself if linked as is, but if you add a buffer to the distal carpal mechanism, it will provide sufficient support, as well as the desired psi," Delylah responded, smiling, letting her expertise in biomech healing shine but not too much, to avoid discouraging Sadie. "Now, on a motherly note, yes, the old lady is going to start lecturing now. I still don't agree with you two gallivanting around the Celestial like some private detective force, solving people's problems like from those silly ancient films you two watch." Delylah sighed heavily, looking at Nachman's face. Then she turned back to Sadie. "Look what happened this time. Next time could be even worse. Besides that, you both make me worry when you go off on your adventures. I really don't want either of you hurt." Delylah looked solemnly at Sadie and gave her another smile, prominent dimples showing on each side of her lips.

"We know that, Ma; why do you think we don't tell you half of our stories?" Nachman said hoarsely as he attempted to sit up on the table. He quickly realized that his head was still feeling detached and had the sudden urge to vomit.

"Nachman! Mind yourself. Lie back. Let Sadie and I fix your arm," scolded Delylah.

Nachman, head spinning, laid back looking woefully at his mother. He had missed her, and being home felt right at this moment. Nachman knew the lecture would continue later; it always did, and no matter how old or experienced he was, she would always treat him like her baby boy. Nachman didn't mind; in fact, he welcomed it—to a certain point. *I should visit more often*, Nachman thought.

Delylah looked piercingly at Nachman, almost as if she heard the consideration. Perceptually, Delylah was deceptive, as she was much shorter than Nachman, but always had an intimidating air about her. In her early sixties with salt-and-pepper hair, she didn't look a day older than forty in face and body, and the innocence that surrounded her was that of a grandmother that has baked fresh chocolate chip and oatmeal cookies served with a glass of warm milk on a Sunday afternoon. That fooled most who came across her.

Delylah had been well-renowned in Sapietás as the premier Magrii, a biomechanical healer, of the Solaris for the better part of Nachman's life, nearly thirty-five years. Nachman remembered traveling to the moons of Malus Navis as a child watching his mother work. Ever since the first time he saw Delylah rewire a severed SKY-200 titiconium alloyed leg back together with only a laser saw and spare parts—most medics and docs he knew in the Naibus didn't have his mother's skills—the look on her face hadn't changed while she worked. Tongue protruding from the right corner of her mouth, brow furrowed in concentration...young Nachman could have sworn he saw Delylah's earlobes twitch when the challenge tried to best her skill set. It seldom did. The intricacy of combining robotic engineering with biological medicinal healing was an art only few could master. She was so fluid, precise, and compassionate about her work that she had become a master Magrii faster than traditional and exceeded the skill set of most known master Magrii in the Celestial. But most of all, she was helping, and it would always benefit Humanity and progress the Auctius forward; to Delylah, that was what mattered. That ideal stuck with Nachman, whether he showed it or not.

"Nachman, it's a good thing you're awake," Sadie interjected, "there is much to discuss."

"Sadie, I believe the all-important private eye work can wait until I'm finished with Nachman's repairs and he has something in his belly," Delylah said with an edge of irritation to her tone. "My boy looks like he hasn't eaten a morsel in a Gaian year. Besides, it's not like the Celestial is at stake." Delylah did not look up as she put on the final touches of an assiduously arduous microsurgery. Realigning a complex biomechanical appendage, and one as unique as Nachman's, required Vis magnifying filters, which were lined on the lens of Delylah's eyes as to align the filaments in the tubules that allow millimicrons of Vis energy to flow through the cybernetic and organic components of Nachman's arm, keeping them functional and symbiotic within Nachman. Sadie would put on her special touches outside of Delylah's sight. Delylah was as sensitive about her work, as Nachman was, but Delylah had taught Sadie everything she knew, so Nachman knew he was always in good hands. The Naibus and the rest of the Alliance had been trying to coax the specs from Delylah for years. The tech she created for her son to live symbiotically with both the man and machine would never be given to anyone, lest it be used against Nachman.

"Yeah, that's a good idea, Ma," Nachman replied. "I could eat a Venetian horse right now." Nachman smiled, which prompted looks of utter bewilderment from his Mother and Sadie.

"You did hit your head hard," laughed Delylah. "Since when do you smile? Never seen you squirm during any of my surgeries, but smiling—that's a whole different story!" Delylah continued to laugh and joke while keeping a skillful hand microlayering the last set of caro-servos, cybernetic lubrication joints, connecting the arm's system.

Sadie could contain the sound of laughter, but the color change of her aura she could not; subtle hues of bright pink began to creep into her normally forestry green. She adored Humans' rousing humor. Her species didn't have much sense of humor or a concept of laughter but felt what other species interpreted as emotion. Sadie turned away, knowing she was attempting to hide the obvious. Even though she had been with Nachman almost his entire life, Sadie hid her snickering. Sadie knew the line she towed with Nachman, but very few, Sadie included, could get away with poking fun at Nachman. The list of people was finite, and the ones not on that list almost never walked away without a fist to the face.

Nachman felt a ping like a static charge across his gray matter as the connection made its way across the Vis-enhanced nerve tract of his left arm to the neurons of his brain. Nachman brought his hand into the bright surgical spotlight; using the Vis enhancements in his ocumech, he zoomed in to a microscopic level, watching the nanites crawl over his prosthetic limb. Since Nachman was a child he was fascinated, not overly excited mind you, how each tiny robot linked together like a grafted mesh around the prosthetic forming a synthetic skin that looked, felt, and acted like Human dermis. The nanites covered the cybernetic skeletal structure completely like a glove, even forming pores and synthetic hair filaments to allow full physiologic feedback.

"You have always been fascinated, albeit discontented, with those little things," Delylah observed, standing away from the surgical table. "I just hope you have remembered your teachings. Anyway, I'll fix you something to satisfy that never-ending belly of yours." Delylah smiled as she lay a comforting hand on her son's shoulder before walking toward the kitchen.

Nachman smiled back at his mother; she had always known that the meditations were still a struggle for him. Even now, Nachman would attempt to force his will instead of allowing his will to be heard. Both Delylah and Sadie said there must be mutual respect between man and machine for symbiosis to occur. Delylah had been studying a variety of medicinal arts, as well as spiritual and philosophical techniques with the Sitanimi monks for years before Nachman was born to enhance her skill as a Magrii. The Sitanimi did their best to train a headstrong young Nachman to prepare him for a life in the GIA. A life that separated mother and child for a torrid amount of time that would challenge every aspect of his well-being biologically and mentally as well as cybernetically. Nachman appreciated the Sitanimi now and would dabble in their teachings and meditative techniques, without Sadie's knowledge (or so he thought), but he had always preferred to have his own mind and logical deduction of facts to guide his actions.

As Nachman watched his mother walk into the kitchen, he couldn't help but reflect on the lower times of his life. Nachman knew his mother was aware of the synthetic avenues he took after the incident in Vitachlora, a story that only a few know about, and while the substance did give the illusion of alleviation for a time, the nanite-driven synthetic drug Nanoyn brought much darker thoughts into his incentum. Thoughts, actions, and omissions too abysmal for Nachman to stomach as such for those he loved and subsequently lost. The rehabilitation was intense, and while recovery from the synthetic diversion was ongoing, Nachman would still learn, gradually, to live in symbiosis with the machine. "Always learning, always teaching," Delylah said quite often, as if it were a catchphrase or family motto. Nachman loathed when his mother made sense literally and figuratively, which is why he didn't want to admit that Sadie was helping him combine the logical with the spiritual, a challenge all in itself.

As soon as Nachman saw his mother cross the wall of the surgical suite, he turned to Sadie with a look in his eyes that meant nothing but business. "Sitrep."

Sadie needed no more prompting; her aura quickly changed to a soft winter-green, and she began her briefing. "The man who attacked you is an anomaly. Any information is sparse at best. In my search, extensive as it was, almost the entirety of this man's Gnanimus ceragscio has been eliminated from the mainframe. This presented a clue in itself, as the oddity could have only been accomplished by the Mihi and a very select few among the Elitists." Sadie paused momentarily, catching a glance at Nachman's face and noticing the uncertainty behind his blue eyes. *But uncertainty for what?* she wondered. *Had he overheard?* Sadie continued, her attention now skewed slightly by Nachman's curious demeanor. "Using the recordings from your ocumech as well as my data stream collection, as I was able to catch a quick glimpse of your assailant. With a Vis rendering I was able to extrapolate his likeness." Sadie looked at the dusty Vis console in the corner of the room. With a flicker, like a candle wanting to burn out, a magenta rectangular Vis display hovered over the skinny console, revealing the man who assaulted, nearly killing, Nachman. The name Attikus floated in bright-blue letters underneath the face of his assailant. Nachman said nothing, simply staring, studying every feature of the one person he was willing to kill in a long time.

The face of a madman is not what it looks like, thought Nachman. Instead of the broken, beaten, and scarred look he was expecting, Nachman saw a flawless face like a porcelain doll. The Naibus credentials were at least forty-five years old, so Nachman was sure he didn't look this anymore. Tight square jaw, bright-yellow eyes like stars set in perfect symmetry above a sharp, angled nose, high-and-tight-cut hair with a wavy lock through the middle of a perfectly round head, and skin so smooth it was as if there wasn't a pore out of place. Sadie, as if she were reading Nachman's mind, zoomed in on his assailant's eyes. Nachman saw exactly what he had been thinking when he was being flung around like a rag doll —the look of the emotionless glassiness of a manufactured killer.

"Near perfection, but those neon-yellow ocumechs are a dead giveaway. I have a feeling someone circumvented the pact between the Vultus and GIA and allowed some genetic experimentation after the fact for military application," observed Nachman.

"Your powers of deduction are impeccable as always, Nachman." Sadie paused but saw Nachman was not amused with her reference. "From the genetic information I was able to absorb from DNA left on your damaged tissues, I can conclude that he was modified and genetically engineered in utero. Donor and surrogate unknown, regenerative nanotech and DNA knitting genetically engineered into every cell in his body, and later on in his limited Naibus files, I found he was further modded with titiconium laced cybernetics and Vis enhancements, both GIA-sanctioned and off grid. The rest of the information I was able to gather is, like I said, sparse but meaningful," said Sadie. "From classified Naibus files that were almost completely scrubbed from the Gnanimus, I found that he and others were tasked to the Apscon division of the Naibus. From the fragmented files, I was able to piece together there were many black ops missions engaging the Vultus and other targets designated as rebellious in various Solaris. All actions dating back to EG 1367, during peacetime or otherwise, were sanctioned by the GIA for approximately 75 years. Apparently, it was kept so far off the grid that no one in the Naibus, save a few higher-ranking Dux, knew he was a cryptogenically engineered, or as you and so many other Humans so colorfully call them, cryptos."

"Well, regardless, if it was Excelsior Dux, Vashra herself that knew about the cryptos or created these things right under everyone's noses. I never did like the idea of a Human cryptogenically engineered exactly the way someone wants them made; it's just unnatural and unfair. I for one am glad they were outlawed given the present situation," Nachman commented, knowing the same argument could be made for the cybernetic augmentations he received in utero. "These cryptos can live a very long time, really unknown at this point, but I'm guessing our boy Attikus was among some of the first."

Sadie continued. "I presume the same as well. After it was made common knowledge by a variety of Gnanimus hacks that Attikus and others were engineered in clear violation of the Aperio Pact most of the Gnanimus files, both biotech and quantum digitized, are just gone, no trace left behind. When I was able to fully reintegrate with you and your phage on our trip here, I managed to find very fine threads, among other information, that the man was subsequently dishonorably discharged for reasons blacklisted. Like other engineered Humans from his era, he suffered from severe psychological deficits. Some specifically developed enhanced biotech knowledge that allowed him to circumvent the safety mods installed within their gene code allowing for psychic feedback, enhanced tracking skills via sensory mods, and simulated ZG tech, giving him enhanced agility and strength. This also made all of this generation of cryptogenics highly unstable. And given that your assailant was modified to the superior level, the man designated Attikus was slated for sterilization by the GIA, as mandated in Section XN.234 of the Aperio Pact of EG 1329.

"After the Mortales movement dissolved and the splinter factions began to form roughly EG 1332, the GIA kept much of the military and personnel ceragscio off the Gnanimus entirely, being that the Gnanimus was still in its infancy and easily tampered with. Instead the GIA began storing personnel and tactical information in various Ducovímus controlled Cirvo Mainframes throughout the Celestial, which have been abandoned for some time. Again, this is where information was quite obviously tampered with again, but Designate Attikus, supposedly sterilized, resurfaced in EG 1455. He was seen on footage from security mechs breaking into and subsequently liberating five maximum security inmates from a covert Bellatorius instillation in the Ipsum Solaris. The men who escaped appear to be augmented as well but not engineered as Attikus. After that the Gnanimus is void of information, ceragscio or otherwise, on Attikus until your confrontation on Tasóa." Sadie concluded her briefing.

"The crypto is older than I thought. Sadie, there is something huge at play if someone that high up completely wipes someone's entire Gnanimus rag off the grid. As in a member of the Morsus Mihi." Nachman didn't mind being blunt about this preconception. He always had notions that the corruption inside the Gaian way of life went as high as the almighty founders themselves.

"Nachman, are you going on about one of your many conspiracy theories again? You're always so paranoid, even as a child, always questioning..." Delylah trailed off as if having her own conversation as she continued to prepare a quick but hearty meal for her recovering patient.

Clattering pots and pans, rushing water splashing around the recyk-sink, and AI appliances almost running amok in the kitchen, but I'll be damned if she didn't hear our entire conversation; the woman has ears like a blind Occan bat, Nachman thought silently. He smirked to himself. That's all he needed—for his mother to psychically overhear his mental bantering.

Nachman's attention turned back to Sadie. The frustration was starting to inch up his spine; he had to find out what part of the puzzle was missing. That piece was here—he knew it. And how do the new revelations he discovered on his side trip to the Caiet realm, if that is indeed where he was, fit in to all of this convolution? "Sadie, did you find out any other useful information on the five now-deceased prisoners from Tenebrae or their rags while I was taking a nap?"

Sadie accessed the Tenebrae mainframe and the prisoners' ceragscios, memory files, instantaneously. "Other than they are all career felons with multiple retributios tied to them from multiple Solaris and they all hail from the same detention block where four other prisoners are still unaccounted for. But there is nothing overtly heinous about them." Sadie paused, a thought occurring to her. "By the way, Nachman, I was able to trace the infrared lex used by Prisoner 533 just before the vessel imploded."

"Really? Good work, Sadie," Nachman said. "Wait a minute. Aren't those untraceable?"

"Yes, well, by Human standards," said Sadie, a touch proud that she was able to impress Nachman.

"Where did the lex end up?"

"The signal dissipated to mere trace elements relatively quickly, so I wasn't able to ping an exact Solaris but from the line of star-sight algorithm I created while we were still with Naibus tech and intel, my specific Vis signature can pick up trace lex signals of almost every frequency or spectrum within this realm and others," Sadie said, seeing the look on Nachman that meant the specifics of the algorithmic design could wait until another time. "The signal dissipated Intersolaris between Ipsum and Crescat with the trajectory toward the latter."

"Wait, wait. You're telling me a bunch of farmers have been messing around with archaic military frequencies all tying into the brainwashing of barely memorable inmates in a conspiracy to assassinate an alien delegate?" Nachman queried. "I'm not buying it; it just seems too far-fetched."

"I didn't buy it either, as you say, so I furthered my research and as the great detective Sherlock Holmes has said, 'I have made point of never having prejudices and docilely following where fact may lead,'" Sadie said proudly and continuing on with her myriad of revealing information while ignoring Nachman's upturned face at her reverie. "There is only one connection that I was able to make with the limited data on the cryptogenics in the Gnanimus mainframe. After stretching my essence to slip under the firewalls, I was able to extrapolate two bits of data that seemed too coincidental to overlook." Sadie again looked at the dusty console in the corner of the room, and the crypto named Attikus whisked away like a sea of fireflies in the night. The magenta hue of the Vis screen changed color to a midnight blue, and the Vis became dense, almost heavy to the eye.

"Extrapolation was tedious. I had to manufacture dormant Vis that was not a part of this particular Vis signature, as it was severely fragmented, and overlay it on top of an encoded frequency made to systematically disintegrate any associated Gnanimus footprints. My apologies for the weight on your phage, Nachman. I've encrypted the Vis signatures, psychic resonances, and all outgoing comm signals with our encoded cryptoglyphs so you're free to view at your leisure," Sadie said as the image appeared and is instantly familiar to Nachman. The inside of Tenebrae's Containment Block DD, the former home of prisoner 674. The corridor appeared deserted and dark, the immense aquamarine silhouette of the Bellatorius Command Terraorbis, Manixis, shining through the window providing the only light into the cell block. The camera angles modulated every sixty seconds to a different angle of the cell block. All the prisoners were sleeping, nothing out of the ordinary. Nachman, already connected with the Vis feed, blinked, and an opaque time stamp appeared over the video feed.

"Good eyes, my dear Nachman," commented Sadie.

"I thought the scenery looked familiar," Nachman observed. "From what the time stamp says, this is about an hour before 674 appeared to be in the midst of the implantation process. What do you think this—" Before Nachman finished his incentum, he got his answer in the form of a shadowy figure stepping into the frame directly in front of 674's containment unit.

With barely any light, Nachman and Sadie could not make out who the individual was. Before Nachman could ask, Sadie said, "I have already attempted to isolate and enhance the Vis pattern in the feed, but there is some kind of interference coming from the individual himself. And that is the only parameter I can establish that the person is a Human male. Well, mostly."

Nachman nodded without taking his eyes off the screen. Nachman wanted to make sure he absorbed every iota of detail with what little was offered at the moment. The man was tall, maybe a hair taller than Nachman, and walked with a limp, a familiar limp that Nachman knew all too well. Nachman's former limp on his left leg, among other alterations, was a harsh reminder that he would never be fully physiologically Human. Until he received the upgraded cybernetics and Vis filtering in the Naibus, the limp was a mainstay for the better half of Nachman's childhood. From what Nachman could see, the man had an archaic cybernetic design more than fifty years old but still in pristine condition. The frame looked skeletal, like the hollowed machinery of an abandoned factory most likely not combat ready with synthetic dermis covering only his right arm. Either he couldn't upgrade for lack of GIA support or refused to upgrade; Nachman did know a few Elitists who preferred to keep with the older technology for fear of hacking or kidnapping by pirates to acquire parts for black market sales. The cloak draped over the man's shoulders was unnaturally black. Nachman remembered hearing about this kind of nanotech with the Naibus tech boys. Fiberspar tech allowed the user to disseminate the light around them, making them imperceptible to most modern sensor technology. *That explains the interference in his Vis signature*, Nachman thought. When the cloaked figure approached 674's containment unit, he turned to face the triple-layered interlaced titiconium door, revealing his face to the camera, but all that appeared was a swirl of distortion inside the hood of the cloak.

"Sadie, I'm not going to bother with a facial reconstruction because I'm going to say it's safe to assume you already tried with every modality we and Ma have available, right?" Nachman asked scowling at the display.

"I'm afraid so, Nachman," Sadie responded as she walked to his side.

From under his cloak, a sleek but obviously robotic right hand appeared, this one a little more modern, a dull black titiconium alloy with rounded fingertips, small cylindrical phalangeal joints, and a rounded palmar surface. Nachman squinted and the display zoomed in on the palm. In the middle of the smooth, robotic surface, a small oblong capsule lay, the surface of the capsule shimmered and began to swirl, flattening and sliding off the robotic hand into a microcrease on the containment door. The image rippled outward and then faded away.

"That's the end of the file," Sadie said. "All other data has been deleted or corrupted."

Nachman leaned back on his heels and stroked his beard. "Well, we now know our theory of a physical implantation is proven. Whoever is behind this is an Elitist because no one can bypass security mechs on Tenebrae unless you

213

have the proper clearance or the available tech to circumvent said security. I don't even know anyone with that kind of tech available but someone does. The question is who...who?" Nachman asked himself. He then suddenly turned to Sadie. "Sadie, he had to have a vehicle. Were there any unregistered craft, ZGV, or otherwise anywhere in your scans?"

"Negative."

"OK. Outside-the-box thinking here, but were you able to scan the perimeter for any Vis resonance?" Nachman asked.

"I did scan the perimeter of Tenebrae's main compound where the prisoners were held," Sadie said, "and found the usual Vis interlocking conduits, and there was a large concentration of Vis in the surrounding geological formations, but there was some type of shielding I have not encountered. I could not find an algorithmic sequence to override the shielding."

Nachman smiled. "Try the one I showed you when we went to Ampluus and found that schmuck trying to thieve the solar fibers from the communication cluster. Gave him that little shock, remember."

"Yes, it was a bit morbid," Sadie said as she accessed the appropriate file and entered the algorithm.

"Ah." Nachman dismissed the morbidity with a wave of his hand. "It makes a nice deterrent to would-be thieves and hackers; besides, the guy recovered. I used it in the Naibus when we were under those deep stealth ops to modify the Vis dampeners of all kinds of vehicles and tech, not only to drop receiver shielding but to give me all of the vital stats of the systems including registration tags. Never needed the algorithm again until now."

"Regardless of need or morbidity, Nachman, I have found what we are looking for," Sadie said. "Impes class stellarcraft. Registered under the name *Cultivador* with GIA Elite subcodings. The owner is shadowed, but I can easily bypass it with a simple vermis tunneling encoding and there. Xon, Julius Quentin, Magnus of Orbis, TerraOrbis Resalo."

"Xon, Julius Xon," Delylah called from the kitchen. "I knew a young boy by that name a long while ago. When I met him, I was just beginning Magrii training. If I remember he was injured as a young man very severely on one of the first voyages launched into the Outer Celestial past Tracaelus." Delylah continued clanging around the kitchen, drowning her voice slightly. "Poor thing had a rare genetic disorder that disfigured him from head to toe when exposed to a deep Celestial radiation. Mostly cybernetic when I was brought in on his case, nothing modern except Vis nano-cells that preserved the age of the organic components; he preferred the older model cybernetics. Wasn't the nicest boy either, very bitter..." Delylah trailed off. Nachman fought the urge to question his Mother further, for the anxiety in her voice was a little curious. *I'll ask her about that later*, Nachman thought turning his incentum back to Sadie.

"First of all why does a relatively low-key farm boy Magnus from Crescat want to infect prisoners on a Tholus Detention Luna in Bellatorius, of all places, with an Automaton that isn't even supposed to exist anymore? And the second most obvious question is how does this Xon character fit into the assassination of Buhai—what's his endgame?"

Delylah stepped out from the kitchen with a tray full of morsels and drinks and a pale look on her face as if a long-dead relative had just walked through the front door. "Nachman, oh my dear Nachman, I have so much to tell you."

CHAPTER 12

Sapietás Solaris, Terraluna Diiu, Home of Delylah Rosenblatt Hidden Underground Bunker, Negative Gnanimus Connection

How long had his own mother kept this from him? He couldn't believe what he was seeing right now. Nachman knew Delylah had loose ties with sects of the Liber Vultus Movement, but to know that she had this built while he was away marching through the Celestial was simply astounding. The walls of the labyrinthine cavern were moist with stale condensation; moss and various fungi lined the creases of the dirt wall stabilized by large, smooth-edged rock. As far as Nachman could tell, there were no tech or Vis connections present, however deep he was now. He was glad Sadie was still with him; he still trusted her after all, even after the dimension hopping.

"You might notice that your connection to the Gnanimus has been temporarily disconnected. We are totally isolated from any technology GIA and Vultus alike," Delylah said. "But I am glad to see my theory about your connection with Sadie is still intact, Nachman. Your enhancements have allowed you two to maintain a physical connection without the use of the Gnanimus. Absolutely amazing!"

"Yeah, that's great and all, Ma," Nachman replied, "but, excuse my bluntness, but what the alvum is going on here?"

"Language." Delylah sighed. "I have been waiting a long time to tell you everything, Son. The Vultus can be even more strict than the GIA at times with protocol, but to hell with the bureaucracy now. We have known something has been happening among the GIA but never knew what until…oh, Nachman, I couldn't." Delylah stopped and took Nachman's hand gently into hers. "But now so many I care about are mixed up in this, and if you get hurt again…" Delylah turned toward the wall directly in front of the group, lowering her head, half turning back to Nachman. She opened her mouth to speak but instead choked back a lump her throat, tears welling in her magenta ocumechs. Instead she waved her hand in front of the damp wall. The mossy rock face vanished in a blink, and a small flat counter slid from a hidden alcove. At the same time, a mini-Vis console rose from the surface of the counter. Old-school holographic camo-tech that was completely off the mainframe of the Gnanimus. *Mom always was good at covering her tracks*, Nachman thought.

Delylah blinked. A turquoise light waved over her left eye, emanating from a small eyelet on the top of the rounded tip of the Vis console. The wall shimmered like a disturbed puddle and vanished, revealing a long, dark corridor. A series of lights on the ceiling flickered on like they hadn't been used for years. Down the unusually long corridor, a large solid-titiconium door silently opened at the end of the hall, as if waiting for the group to approach. As the trio walked down the hallway, Nachman noticed to the right and left were more large, solid doorways with similar mini-Vis consoles next to each door. As they reached their door, the corridor split parallel with their doorway. Two hallways each led down darkened corridors; Nachman could only imagine what secrets they held. What was his mother into these days?

Nachman noticed Sadie had been quiet the entire trek down the tunnel system. She was either maintaining a high state of alertness or incredibly terrified; Nachman thought it was a healthy mixture of both. He would ask her later during their debrief. For now Nachman had to focus on the door in front of him and what lay beyond. They walked into yet another cavernous room, this one large and rectangular with an oblong table and four cushioned, high-backed chairs ready for the party to sit in. But despite all of his composure, intellect, and years of experience and training, when Nachman stepped through the door, he wanted to turn and run with his proverbial tail between his legs. When he saw her, Nachman felt the heat rise up his neck, as he knew his emotions were about to get the better of him.

"Novia." Nachman said her name, and it left his mouth as dry as a desert. "What the hell do you have to do with all of this?"

"It's nice to see you too, Nachman," said the woman who had cordially vexed his incentum for the last five years.

Although his incentum was often tormented by her, Nachman would always be pleased to hear Novia's voice, as it was like the coo of a songbird in the midst of a shiny spring season. His heart palpitated in his chest when he thought of the betrayal she had felt by his actions and the years it had taken him to get past his machismo and admit that what he had done to her and in those following years to himself was wrong. He had admitted that to himself a while back but never did work up the fortitude to tell the one person who needed to hear his confession. This strong, stunning, massively intelligent woman hadn't graced his presence in five Gaian years because of his shortcomings, and now that he found out she was somehow tied to all of this, the least Nachman could have done was to say hi and try not to be an ass. Yet Nachman's temper continued to flare, his taut sense of self-control dwindling by the nanosecond; he couldn't hate himself more for acting the way he was right this moment.

"Well, let's see here. Since I took the damn case, I've been shot at by mind-controlled assholes, my best friend might be one of those mind-controlled assholes now, I've been assaulted by Human and Noa alike, damn near blinked out of existence by some crypto madman...my mother has been keeping secrets from me for who knows how Celestial long in an underground hideout with my ex-fiancée, who is standing in front of me looking absolutely fantastic despite the fact the

I have no clue how in the alvum she or you fit into all this damn shit!"

"Nachman, watch your mouth, and listen to me. There was no way I could tell you without causing more trouble than what is already going on in the Celestial."

"You could have said something! If Novia of all people is tied up in this mess, I have a right to know!" Nachman shouted.

"Wait a minute," Novia interjected. "I'm not one of Sadie's stories; no need for the third person routine."

"Nachman, maintain your composure." Sadie lay a hand on Nachman's shoulder in an attempt to calm him. Nachman slapped it away. Sadie's aura darkened a hue with a hint of red around the edges. Nachman's anger was seeping into her; Sadie didn't mind the emotions, but anger was her least preferable. Sadie stepped back, continuing her silent observations.

"Nachman Ashli Rosenblatt, I will not be spoken too in that tone of voice, and I will not let you treat Sadie or anyone in this house with such disrespect!" Delylah said sternly. "If you are finished with your tirade, maybe you could be so courteous as to let Novia and myself explain the situation."

Nachman didn't loathe his middle name but never did like hearing it aloud for two reasons. One, Ashli was his deceased father's maiden name. Mom had given it to him partly as an homage to, as she said, one of the only men to truly understand their place in the Celestial. Nachman had never known the man, so how could he understand him? It frustrated Nachman that he was still trying to figure that one out. And two, Nachman knew he was in deep alvum when Delylah used his full given name.

"Ah, Ma, I'm sorry." Nachman turned sheepishly to Novia, who took a place by Sadie's side, comforting her from Nachman's temper tantrum. "Hey, you two, listen, I didn't mean anything..."

"You better be sorry, Nachman. You and your rash bullheadedness is one reason I didn't come to you sooner." Novia's mousy voice was gaining in octaves. "With everything that's happened and is happening, your first reaction is still—"

"Novia, please," Delylah interrupted, "let's start from the beginning. Please sit if you want."

Nachman looked down at his feet. *I need new boots*, he thought. Nachman could only feel embarrassed; it was rare that he was caught in heated personal situations, and when he was, it usually involved the women in his life. He hated when cases got personal.

A steaming hexagonal silver metallic teapot sat steaming on a serving tray with three teacups already waiting on the table. Delylah never liked to discuss serious matters without a cup of tea; it calmed everyone's nerves, she said. It was almost as if Delylah were expecting tempers to be flared in the initial meeting.

Delylah sat at the head of the table, pouring herself a cup of the liquid calm, motioning for the others to do the same, as well as Sadie who smiled and generated a cup of Vis tea for herself. Nothing real, just a formality, as she says. They sat in silence for a moment, Delylah the only one looking at everyone in the room. She was the first to break the heavy silence. "Now that we have all that out of our systems, let me first say that, Nachman, you have known about my involvement with the movement for quite some time. Local gatherings, organizing meetings between Solari, and general day-to-day relations with GIA officials, but in recent years, I have extended my role deeper as their local Magrii, as you can see from the surroundings." Delylah held up her arms like she was presenting the room for show.

The room didn't feel like it was tunneled beneath the soil, but one could clearly see it was. The entire berth of the room appeared lined with rock and dried mire in more or less a checkered pattern like the rest of the underground cavern, but inlaid into the walls were shelves lined with medicine bottles of varying shapes and sizes, plants and other herbs under simulated ultraviolet lights on small shelves on the back wall, two small cots behind where Delylah sat, and at the other end behind Nachman's seat was a long table with field diagnostic and lab equipment lining the top. Nachman was impressed; Delylah had built an underground field hospital.

With a look of pride, Delylah continued, "With the Vis dampeners and the ingenious internal security monitoring Sadie installed for me, I have been able to maintain a relatively inconspicuous existence on my little luna for quite some time. With my position as Chief Magrii, the Vultus leadership has been adamantly pursuing me to take a chair with the Conclave Excelsum for some time. But of course, as you all know, all of that is just nonsense to me. I prefer to keep my nose clean, thank you. Anyway, for the past few months I have had young, eager Vultus members coming to me with headaches, hallucinations of varying nature, vertigo, and various other neurological symptoms. With the first few patients, I treated it as stress and fatigue prescribed rest and relaxation with some herbal calming agents and sent them on their way. All of the patients I had treated seemed to make a complete physical recovery within a few days of visiting me." Delylah paused, her brow furrowing with concern. "The patient flow was steady for about two weeks. Then there was a total cessation of patient activity. At first I was pleased with the recoveries, but I started to notice personality changes on my follow-up visits and among others who had not come to seek my aid. Not for the worse, mind you, but just no change at all. It's as if everyone I treated seemed aloof of the fact that they had saw me. Everyone disregarded my concern, as if I were the mad one. Others I hadn't treated but interacted with seemed flat and disengaged from normal day-to-day activities, just going through the motions as it were. I did extensive noninvasive scans: bio, techno, and Vis. All came back inconclusive. All seemed physiologically healthy from neuron to nanophage." Delylah paused and sipped her tea. "I began to research the signs and symptoms that related to my patients and others around the Vultus. I found connections between my patients and early experimentation with mind control and psychic interrogation techniques. I almost laughed at the possibility when a day later, I was contacted."

"Who, Ma? Who contacted you? The GIA or your buddies in the Vultus?" questioned Nachman.

"I don't know," replied Delylah. "Whoever it was told me, in a pretty threatening tone, not to further investigate my line of research. Every time I tried to back trace the lex, I would end up being blocked or diverted to some random Gnanimus hub clear on the other side of Malus Navis. About two days after I was contacted by the mystery man, I noticed my hub that is, or was, connected to the Gnanimus had been nanohacked; all information on the patients I had treated along with my research into commonalities had been scrubbed. No further communications from the Vultus Conclave, any of my patients, even my friendly contacts within the Vultus have come my way. I have essentially been blacklisted by the Vultus, but why and who, I don't know."

Sadie interjected. "With your permission, Delylah, I would like to access your backup servers and Vis conduits to obtain all information pertaining to your mind-altered patients and incoming lex logs?"

"Of course, dear." Delylah blinked, sending all the information to Nachman's nanophage and, in turn, directly to Sadie.

"Thank you, Delylah. Fascinating. You have some intriguing research, especially on the Automaton assimilation processes that I would love to discuss further, given a more opportune time," Sadie replied as her aura lightened to a soft lime green as she compiled the information she just received. "I am also enhancing all firewalls and security measures in and around the complex."

"Thanks for that, Sadie. You and Ma can have your tech talk later," Nachman said. He then turned to Delylah. "Now, Ma, are you telling me that no one from the Vultus has contacted you?"

Delylah shook her head while pouring herself and Novia another cup of still steaming hot tea.

"For how long?"

"The last Vultus member that made contact with me was a young recruit, male, early twenties, about four weeks ago. I treated him for a fractured right ulna after a training accident, pretty standard fare from a Magrii standpoint. He seemed as normal as we are now and didn't report any symptoms relating to my previous patients."

"The timing seems too coincidental, doesn't it?" Nachman began stroking his beard, putting the puzzle pieces together mentally.

From across the table, Novia sank down in her chair, much like an embarrassed teenager caught ogling the new kid at school. She always did have a thing for Nachman's beard stroking, as she always thought it denoted a genuine intelligence and essential curiosity for life's quizzical nature. And to top it all off, she still felt like a giddy little schoolgirl around him, and that made her furious. Novia sulked and listened to Nachman, doing her best to keep the look of contempt for her emotions off her face.

"I mean, alvum, Vultus members not contacting their Chief Magrii for anything, even a Vis burn? Complete silence from the Vultus Conclave right before the assassination of Buhai screams outright suspicion, and that would no doubt lead the Naibus and rest of the GIA to connect the Vultus to the killing. Then I notice most of the Noas on Tasóa are either oblivious to the assassination of one of their most prestigious high council members, or they are trying to rip my head off for saying hello," Nachman said.

"Nachman, I have answers that will only beget more questions, but then again things are already far from simple," interjected Novia.

Nachman couldn't help but stare at her. He looked for a mere nanosecond, but that was just enough time for everything around him to slow to a crawl. Nachman felt emotions he had tucked away for years crash over him like towering oceanic waves; it was almost overwhelming. Nachman wasn't quite nauseated, but he did have that butterfly-in-the-stomach kind of feeling. Damn, he missed her; there was no other way Nachman could see it. The ferocity behind the intelligence is what had shaken Nachman to the core from the second he laid eyes on her at the Rixa training grounds. Nachman was surprised by her from the start, her athleticism to her courage in the war sims, both mech and nonmech combat. Nachman never forgot that even scientists needed field training. The beauty was a bonus, and as Nachman took in the woman he had never forgotten, it almost felt like he was taking a snapshot of Novia, as if he would lose her again. Novia. No surname as far as Nachman knew. She had a flowing mane of golden-brown locks extending to the crest of her buttocks, almost always in a loose ponytail, eyes that shimmered like opal stones, pulling Nachman into a blissful trance almost every time he gazed into them, and the fullest lips Nachman ever had the pleasure of touching. Stature and a bantam frame were certainly a deceptive combination, as her right hook —her mother insisted she train in Celestial martial arts and Noanoagan boxing—could put you on your ass faster than you could perform a slingshot orbital maneuver around an asteroid. Nachman knew that he couldn't have been happier than when they were together. It excited Nachman to know that he could be touched, even moved, by someone like Novia, but in a way he was frightened by that because he felt like he would lose himself entirely. If only he could have seen past his demons of anguish and obsession. But regardless of doubt or circumstance, in that briefest of moments, all the other problems in the Celestial were forgotten.

"Yeah, how much more complicated we talking here, Novia? 'Cause it sounds like whoever is behind the Automatons I have encountered has infested people within the Vultus ranks as well as Naibus and GIA Elitists," Nachman said, leaving out his suspicions about Tyrav. The news would have distracted Novia too much; she'd always had a special place in her incentum for Ty. "And there have been many aspects of this case I have witnessed firsthand so far, on a variety of differing levels." Nachman glanced at Sadie, whose eyes widened, as she knew all too well that Nachman did, in fact, know where he was on his side trip to her realm. "That has made it a hell of an adventure so far."

Novia ignored the jab intended for Sadie. "I think it would be best if I start at the beginning and preface this conversation by saying I know for a fact Xon is at the forefront of this whole conspiracy, from the assassination to the strange behavior from Noanoagans and Humans Delylah has treated. The former I can prove. The latter, however, not quite yet." Novia paused, looking down. Nachman could see the guilt pour down her face, suddenly aging her far beyond her years. *What did Novia do?* Nachman wondered. Novia looked up, her eyes moist but with no tears flowing, and said, "I am thoroughly ashamed for the actions perpetrated by myself and for the events that have led to this moment. I assure you all, I thought I was creating something for the betterment of Human and Noanoagan alike, but it turns out that I was deceived and became aware of the deception way too far into my R & D. When I attempted to rectify my actions and sabotage the research, I found I was too late to stop the process of what we are now all trying to stop."

"Novia, what does all the cryptic remorse have to do with—" Nachman didn't get a chance to finish his thought when Novia shot him a look that would have turned the Gorgon Medusa into stone.

"Do not interrupt me, Nachman," said Novia, her voice as cold as the Venetian mountaintops. Nachman smiled innocently, knowing he had better not overstep. He leaned back in his chair and gestured with his hand that the table was all hers. Novia suppressed a smile, but a small smirk crept to the corner of her lip. *He's still cute when he's an asshole,* Novia thought.

She continued, "Julius Xon is not only the Magnus of Orbis for Terraluna Resalo, but he is the Elitist behind the whole conspiracy, and I have proof. But the only thing is, I don't know who to trust with all this brainwashing nonsense going on."

"You knew about that." This was from Sadie, who came to Nachman's side and generated her favorite chair, the high-back riveted old-leather style, and joined the table.

"Yes, longer than all of you, but I will come to that." Novia let out a sigh. "Xon hired me for what I thought was a covert combined Solaris operation to enhance Human technology by breaking the gene code of our Noanoagan visitors. Much like the pre-Convergence Human Genome project of the late twentieth century that every first-year Naibus geneticist reads about in the history books. Anyway, it was a project that consisted of three components in particular: the engineering, the biochemical, and the genetic, which was my role as the lead geneticist. I didn't think anything of the key components being separated as they were. I've been privy to many top-secret projects that have organized the workload in this manner before. My main goal, or so I thought, was to finally figure out a way to bond the U'agi fungi with our Vis tech to prepare stellarcraft for transport through the Aethra. For almost a half a Gaian year, I worked on the project at an abandoned research facility on Medvios."

Nachman wanted to ask but said nothing as he felt his blood run ice cold.

"Yes, the same location," said Novia looking at Nachman. "I knew the history behind the facility and that region of the planet. I didn't find out until later when I broke the encoded files on the lab's mainframe that I found out your involvement."

"You know I had nothing to do with what happened there." Nachman felt the anger boiling behind his eyes, waiting to explode like a volcano. "All of you here know I was set up to take the fall for those people's deaths. It took me years after the Naibus to clear my damn name; it started the spiral that ruined us, and that alvum still follows me."

"For that I am sorry, Nachman, but I do think that even those events from years ago tie into all of this and lead back to Xon." Novia looked solemnly at Nachman, who looked away to his fingertips, which were doing nothing but strumming on the table. Novia, familiar with Nachman's anxious tic, continued. "The facility had originally been used as a bioweapon testing facility, so I had most of the equipment I already needed to begin my research in an underground bunker that had survived the catastrophe. Xon assured me complete autonomy and privacy from the Gnanimus mainframe. I failed to asked any questions, as I was purely excited about advancing the breakthroughs I had already made into the discovery of the genetic markers of the Nafusma phenomena. I was blinded by my childish nihilism." Novia clenched her fist, her knuckles turning white. "The research breakthroughs I made are legendary, to say the least, and with the help of Xon's research from the other parties involved, I broke down and resequenced the entire Noanoagan genetic code in less than six months! Now adapting it to existing Human technology was going to be the challenge, when I started to receive less and less information daily until three days after my breakthrough, I stopped receiving lexes altogether." Novia paused, visibly shaken by what she was going to say next.

Nachman leaned forward, intent on hearing every detail of Novia's turn of events.

"I tried for days to make an outgoing connection, lex anyone I knew in the Celestial. But no signal would penetrate, even with every trick taught to me by the comm techs in Ducovímus. I decided to turn the investigation inward and broke down the entire mainframe of that lab. What I found disturbed me beyond words."

Delylah reached her hand, encircling Novia's and squeezing tenderly. Nachman figured Ma had already heard the story. They had been close since the first day he brought her home for dinner. Nachman couldn't help the temptation to reach for Novia; even after all these years, he still wanted to hold her, to be her rock when things became unstable. Instead he sat there and watch the love of his life be tormented by memories he could not take away.

I believe she understands now, Nachman.

Nachman wasn't shaken by the sudden echo of psionic communication from Sadie, nor did he respond. Maybe he was finally getting used to the psi-comm after all these years. Nachman thought that Sadie might just be right for once, reading a Human emotion dead-on. Regardless of whether Novia understood, Nachman still had to live with it day by day. Even now he relived past tragedy and discovered new ones weeks ago, because the tech he had built in good faith for the Naibus for the "security and defense" of Humankind was deliberately used to murder an innocent civilian. He wanted to crush Xon for what he had done to his family, to the Celestial, and for what this damned Elitist has done to Novia, but what Nachman heard next literally had him teetering the edge of maddening rage.

"Before I go further, I want everyone to meet someone who has been literally at the front line since everything began," said Novia.

A creak of old wood came from behind the wall behind his mother's seat. Nachman almost jumped from his chair, gun in hand, if it hadn't been for the soft, subtle touch of Novia's fingertips barely brushing the tips of his. Nachman's skin tingled with goosebumps. *She can still anticipate me.* Nachman, again, shook off the boyish urges to focus on the task at hand.

The Noa almost touched the ceiling, towering over Nachman by at least sixty centimeters. Nachman still wanted to reach for his sidearm, regardless of the state of the person in front of him. This Noanoagan seemed familiar to Nachman. *But it can't be him.* Nachman almost didn't recognize Tejwenn, Nafusma to Buhai Orimer of Noanoaga. Tejwenn still remained the proud Noanoagan, attempting to stand tall in the face of death, as he looked like he was going to join his

Nafusma in the Noanoagan holy realm, Molapaia, any minute.

Nachman remembered the Naibus lexvids of a Noanoagan rapidly decaying after a Nafusma meets a violent demise. *All parts of the training simulations brought to you by the Naibus Institutum.* Nachman had refused to watch death and decay if he had a choice. Nachman averted his eyes slightly downward but not enough to notice, so as to not offend Tejwenn. Sadie, however, blatantly stared, forever fascinated with all things in the Celestial. Sadie saw the lexvids as well, but that never deterred her need to study the phenomena up close. Nachman was proud of Sadie for resisting the urge to rush up to poor Tejwenn and start examining him like a lab sample.

As Tejwenn started walking toward the table, he stumbled, his legs giving way beneath him. Novia jumped from her chair, taking Tejwenn's arm in hers, and helped Tejwenn to the table. As Tejwenn's still-hulking frame sat, Nachman took in how serious Tejwenn's condition was and how quickly it was progressing. Nachman could have sworn he saw the decaying changes happen before his eyes. Tejwenn's fihr, once brilliant-neon blue with specks of Buhai's phosphorescent purple melded in the strands, was now ashen, as if all of the color had been sucked right out. His large, imposing muscular frame, while still much larger than Nachman's, looked frail and sunken. Each bony prominence protruded from his skin as if lances were ready to burst through at any moment. Tejwenn's skin looked rough, leathery, making his ornate spherical and octagonal tattoos no longer geometric but like a soup of ink blotted on his skin. Sloughing, patch-like reddened wounds were sticky with dried viscous fluid on his cheeks and forehead, while blisters surrounding his eyes and other mucous membranes on his face looked like miniature geysers ready to spew the purulence forth. Nachman couldn't figure out how Tejwenn was still alive, let alone walking into this room.

Sadie was the first to speak. "On behalf of all of us, my dear Tejwenn, our sincerest condolences for the loss of your Nafusma and the tragedy that has befallen you."

"I thank you, my friend." Tejwenn's voice was hoarse, almost as if his transmod was affected by the deterioration of his body. Tejwenn broke into a harsh coughing fit. Novia grabbed a napkin from the table, and Tejwenn coughed into it. As he set it down, Nachman caught a glance of an orange stain on the napkin. Nachman knew from the quickly congealed Noanoagan blood that Tejwenn didn't have much longer.

"As you can see, Molapaia calls to me on behalf of my dear Nafusma." Tejwenn, a Noanoagan of more than five hundred Gaian years, give or take, was still eloquent, given his dire straits. "As Novia has mentioned, the situation is more sinister than it seems. I will let Novia continue, as I must preserve what strength I have left."

"Thank you." Novia tenderly set Tejwenn's hand on the table and walked to Delylah's side, looking directly at Nachman. "When I infiltrated the compound's mainframe, I found out Xon's true intentions for my gene sequencing." Novia paused again; a tear ran down her cheek, but she never took her eyes off Nachman. "Xon has been utilizing all involved with the project to build a gene bomb specific to the Noanoagans. He plans to wipe them off the face of the Celestial."

Nachman wanted to yell, scream in rage at and for Novia. *How could she be an unbeknownst fool like me?* Nachman thought. Yet he wanted to run to Novia and hold her until the pain he knew had cut her deep to her core went away. Instead he sat and kept his eyes locked with Novia's. He smiled at her, and she smiled back; they understood each other still, the silent bond still remaining between them.

Novia continued. "Once I found out about Xon's true intentions, I dug a little deeper as quickly as I could. I knew that little alvum had me tapped and traced already, so I rewired the Vis synthesizers into the console and routed them to the lexcom paneling to bide my time—a little trick our Arquis Nachman showed me a few years ago." Nachman didn't intend to tone out the conversation, but he couldn't suppress the thoughts coming to the forefront of his incentum. Nachman had taught her the ins and outs of being an Arquis just before they had stopped speaking, but Nachman had no idea she retained so much of what he had taught. She was one of the best pupils Nachman had had—well one of the only pupils, anyway. Nachman continued to listen, trying his best to keep a stoic expression. "I found out where the other scientists were being held through some back-tracing but I couldn't pinpoint an exact orbis or luna. I narrowed it down to one of them located in Ducovímus and the other in Tracaelus. I don't know which scientist is where. I would put the engineer close to the device to maximize security around the asset and allow for quicker deployment of the payload. Best guess is the one in Ducovímus is dead, and the engineer will be soon," concluded Novia.

"You're probably right from a tactical standpoint," Nachman said. He knew Novia never liked field operations but also knew she would never forget her training, and she was a damn fine field operative when she needed to be. "Xon has a massive head start on us, and I can safely guess that he is likely to tie up the loose ends we just mentioned, and quickly."

"I deployed a nanocam just before I escaped in a derelict Devixo Gamma class junk hauler. It took an hour just to get the manual flight controls operational. About eighteen hours after my takeoff, the nanocam captured an unregistered merchant vessel deploying scramble tech." Novia said this to Sadie.

"Most likely our genetically modified pursuer," Sadie commented.

"Most likely," Novia said. "The hired gun has been on me since I left Vitachlora and is probably still tracking me Nachman. And Xon I missed by two days. The people are not taking any chances. Just before the nanocam was destroyed, it was able to lex footage of Xon deploying an experimental nano-netting that broke down the structure and all surrounding inorganic particulates to its atomic elements. No evidence left behind at all."

Delylah, who had been sitting at the head of the table sipping her sweet Martian berry violet tea imported directly from the fields of Olympus Mons (her only indulgence is the tea, she claims), spoke without lifting her eyes from the inside of her warm cup. "Nachman, my contacts have just reported an Erigo construction frigate, Beta class, masking its GIA sub-codings with an undetermined crew count, estimate more than four, was found leaving Intersolaris Stellarport Einstein between Tracaelus and Sapietás approximately forty-eight hours ago Sapietás Solar time on an intercept course with our location. Bellatorius has been notified of the incident, as there were civilian and Naibus casualties at the port when the vessel was stolen."

Nachman didn't ask how she came across the information. The Vultus, it seemed, had some toys Nachman hasn't been privy to quite yet. Pretty high end if it allowed Delylah to get a signal through a dampening screen. Nachman sighed as he realized with the news of impending trouble, he needed a bigger plate, as the alvum was beginning to overflow. "That's probably my crypto buddy coming to intercept us to finish the job. We are going to have a lot more dead 'cause I don't think this psycho cares about getting caught anymore."

"That lunatic that nearly took Nachman from us is the most likely candidate for our scientist's assassin. He is obviously Xon's lackey. I made sure I masked all traces of your ceragscio from any user who has access to the Gnanimus, civilian or otherwise. No one should have been able to hack my defenses. I was supposed to be pinged if anyone looked into your files. Xon must know a substantial amount of information about the lot of us if he knew where to target you, Nachman. I should have masked everyone's ceragscio. Oh, I am so sorry, everyone," Sadie said, distraught.

"Or we were poking the bear and getting too close to figuring out his master plan. You had no way of knowing, Sadie; you are not responsible for any of this in the least, you hear me?" Nachman said. Sadie nodded, her aura brightening a hue.

"I'm not sure how Xon was able to find out info on any of us, but he has an advantage that I can quite frankly say scares the alvum out of me," said Novia who turned to Tejwenn, laying a hand on his weary shoulder. "Are you well enough to speak?"

"Novia, it doesn't sound like we have the time too."

"Nachman, trust me, you are going to want to hear this before we leave," Novia said adamantly.

Nachman nodded and then turned to Tejwenn. "The floor is yours, pal."

Tejwenn nodded back, coughed another orange-tinted globule into the napkin, and said, "I will make this as quick, as I can sense the pressure is mounting. As you all can surmise, my beloved Buhai was not assass..."—cough, cough—"killed for her unity speech. I strongly believe that she was murdered to cover up the—I can never say, forgive me." Tejwenn blinked and quickly but momentarily shut off his trans mod. *"Fa'umai."*

"Awakening?" Sadie said making it a question.

"Yes, thank you." Tejwenn's transmod crackled as he adjusted the device and continued. "Some of my people have been awakened from a dreamless slumber."

The room was quite; then Nachman furrowed his brow. "Mind control?"

"Yes," Tejwenn responded, "For the last few years, many of my people have been freed from this mind control. Awakened to realize the last of our generations have not been ours to live. Buhai and I were among the first to wake. When it first occurred, it was as if we awoke from a thousand-year slumber, but we recalled everything that has happened to us and our people from the time our species began our journey across the black sea. I, for example, remember the day of my birth on the Mother Vessel to the ceremony bonding myself and Buhai to this very moment I speak to you all. However, no one can remember anything before the start of the journey."

"Did Buhai or yourself know who was behind the alvum with your head or why some of your people are overriding the mind control?" asked Nachman.

"I don't know who or what is controlling the minds of my people, Nachman, but I do know this coward Xon is the Human we must seek out, for he has answers for both our species." Tejwenn held up a hand, bringing the other with the napkin to his mouth, breaking into another coughing fit. Novia helped Tejwenn up and began to escort him out of the room. "One moment, Novia," Tejwenn stopped and turned to Nachman. "Nachman, my people have dormant psychic abilities, some more powerful than others. Buhai theorized that our psychic prowess allowed us to be some of the first to awaken. Buhai had also discovered that Humans were being altered as well—for what purpose is unknown to me, I'm afraid."

"Yeah, Sadie and I found that out the hard way," Nachman responded. "The big thing that doesn't make sense is why the Automatons? Why even the brainwashing for either species anyway? Xon doesn't need the population controlled to commit genocide. We either missed something or haven't connected that dot yet. Either way, we can figure it out on our way to Tasóa." Nachman stood and addressed the group. "Tejwenn, do you have your research accessible to the Gnanimus?"

Tejwenn nodded.

"Good. Sadie, get the security nodes from Tejwenn when you get topside, reconnect, and sift through all the info on the Automatons and Noa mind control the honorable Buhai collected. Everyone else, with Xon on his way or already at the detonation site and crypto-psycho after the lot of us, we are pressed for time. Grab the gear and tech you will need for your tasks at hand. Realign your Qu infusion sites because we are going to have to shorten our Qusom to access the Gnanimus for intel gathering before our rendezvous—but do it quickly." Nachman paused, never caring to include what he had to. "I hate to say it, but grab whatever weapons and ammo you deem fit for our journey, preferably small arms and hand-to-hand weapons. Meet Sadie and I at the *Satyr* topside in thirty minutes."

The group departed. Novia and Tejwenn walked to the hidden wall behind Delylah's seat, and Sadie wisped away in a neon-green swirl to preflight the *Satyr*. Nachman walked to his Mother, who he knew would not be joining them for this leg of the so-called adventure.

"Ma," Nachman stammered. "I, I...don't..."

"It's all right, my baby boy." Delylah stood and cupped Nachman's face gingerly in her palms. "You have always been a passionate creature, Nachman, and I will never hold that against you. What I will hold against you is the idea of you not being able to patch up things with that sweet dumpling, Novia. Now that I will hold over you." Delylah smiled and kissed Nachman on his cheek.

"Thanks, Ma," Nachman said as he disappeared out the door, leaving Delylah standing in the field hospital by herself. Nachman didn't look back as his silhouette faded into the dark hallway.

Delylah prayed that she would see her boy again; she had faith she would be seeing him. But happy—now that was something she had been praying for since the day she made a deal with the devil.

CHAPTER 13

Tracaelus Solaris, Terraluna Tasóa, Noanoagan Outpost
Fu Temu Miga, Off-Grid Subbasement, Ten Standard Gaian
Weeks Until Aethra Gateway Completion

Xon stepped off the stair of the *Cultivador*, the limp to his right leg worsening with each step he took. Xon swore he could actually feel the cybernetic components stretching as if they were warping on a molecular level. Pain—another useless sensation to take away focus. Xon dampened that feeling long ago, just after the Celestial ravaged his young body, beginning his transformation into something more. Something Xon couldn't quite understand was how he was feeling this discomfort in his cybernetics when his nanophage was reporting confirmation after confirmation that his internal sensors were registering all systems, organic and cybernetic, operating at nominal function, zero discrepancies. Xon ran another quick diagnostic. Within seconds, it was just like Xon suspected—everything was normal, according to his physiology. Xon's frustration was peaking to the point of boiling over. *Control yourself, old man; break the control, break the mind*, Xon thought.

Xon limped away from the vessel, he thought about the cane in his quarters for a moment but continued away from the craft, as he couldn't afford any signs of weakness at this point. Xon felt, through his nanophage, the *Cultivador*'s systems go dormant, keeping the craft hot and ready to go in case of emergency. He docked the craft at a private Elitist port about two kilometers away from the Fu Temu Miga. A dull-gray ZGV pulled forward to come to a stop directly in front of Xon. A tall, caveman-esque male driver exited and opened the rear hatch for Xon. No words spoken between the two for the entirety of the short trip.

Xon arrived a short time later at the rear entrance of the Miga. The driver saw Xon opening the door and hurried to catch it before the Magnus opened it. Xon waved him off as if he were a pest in his ear.

He approached a large metal door; in the center, a bright-yellow-glass octagonal window stained with blue mildew blocked his reflection. Xon's left hand, a patchwork of flesh and cybernetics from the wrist down, reached for the handle. Xon's hand, then arm, then entire body stopped in midmotion. Xon could hear and feel the grind of metal on metal as it struggled to function. A tremor began to burrow insidiously from fingers to wrist, the feel of acid crawling along his vessels and Vis conduits becoming too much to bear. Xon wanted to scream but could not. Xon wanted to bring his hand closer to his ocumechs to inspect the malfunction further but couldn't. Xon felt panic throughout his mind and couldn't find a way to control the sensation; chaos and anarchy reigned inside his mind. Struggling with all his incentum, his hand seemed forever frozen, unable to move. This was beyond his control. *How could this be?*

As Xon strained to articulate any part of his suspended appendage, he felt that there was something, a force, an entity. Xon did not know, but whatever it was, it was preventing him from doing anything at all.

A whisper spoke from behind Xon's consciousness: *Your strife is my will.*

This phantom incentum seemed to push Xon's control to the background, almost caging it so that Xon was only a witness to what was happening. Xon felt the aged musculature remaining in his hand tighten and twist to the point that Xon was sure it would snap in half. An electrifying spark seemed to jolt through Xon's entire arm. Xon wanted to double over, but the force prevented it, forcing him to endure the anguish. Then just as quickly as they began, the pain and tremors stopped. Xon felt nothing again, not even a residual burning sensation from the torture that had just occurred. Xon sneered in irritation as his internal diagnostics read nominal function.

Xon stepped into the doorway; a musky, almost rancid odor penetrated his inorganic olfactory mechanisms. *Dirty creatures, but their tech will be most useful in the expansion*, thought Xon. He attempted to block the smell, in vain, limping down a hallway adorned in an assortment of colorful paintings leading into a storage area. Boxes, bottles, party decorations, lights, and an assortment of other paraphernalia that a dance club would have were seemingly hoarded into the small room. Xon looked around, curling his lip and brow in disgust. *Such disarray, such disorder, dirty creatures*, Xon thought. For a moment, that voice, the scratch, a gnaw at the corner of his control as he thought in circles. The creatures must be purged for the species to thrive.

Xon came to a wall, the only wall clear of clutter in the claustrophobic storage area. An infrared beam waved over Xon's body. A hidden door sunk into the wall and slid into a compartment inside the wall. It was an archaic technology but mostly untraceable by modern scanners as they lacked the components to trace infrared.

Xon stepped from behind the long Ga'a'ula bar, managing to slip by the annoying elongated man whose attention was solely on the female patron at the bar. The Noas, however, were acting somewhat peculiar, even for the repellent creatures they already were, Xon thought, walking past a pair of brightly colored Noas standing at the end of the bar. The Magnus stole a glance at the Noas. Their faces became blank, their eyes lost all focus, seeming to stare past Xon into some hidden void, and their bodies became slack as if the muscles were gelatinous. Once he cleared the Noanoagans' field of vision, they appeared to awake from a daze and continue their lighthearted conversation with laughter and a clinking of their drinks, as if Xon never walked by them.

Xon ignored the creatures as he always did, paying them no mind as he walked to the far side of the Miga, to the back offices. There were not a lot of patrons around the lunch hour, as the Miga transitioned from grand cathedral to dance club. The few Humans knew the garb of an Elitist, no matter where they hailed from. Humans knew to avert their eyes, seeing Xon's green-and-gold sash coming to a point like a snake's tongue surrounded by sandy tassels around his waist. The coloring signified that Xon hailed from Crescat, and the conjoined double diamond shaped sunburst yellow jewel on the end of the sash showed his rank of Magnus; the shape and color of the jewel signified his planet of origin, Resalo. Noanoagans, regardless of whether they knew his status, had always avoided Xon; he didn't mind in the least.

Xon limped across the ostentatious dance floor disregarding the engineers assembling the contraption, the antigrav mechanism not yet operating, the clink of his bare cybernetic right foot making a soft echo off the canopy of the cathedral-like ceiling. *Dancing—foolish games for foolish minds*, Xon thought. Xon made his way past a series of tables to a far wall cut open with a wide archway. Xon descended the stairs under the arch to a swinging doorway that led beneath the Fu Temu Miga. The stairs descended twelve flights, where Xon reached the bottom and blinked, activating the nanophage scanning device atop the doorway. With a soft click, the solid door opened, and Xon stepped through to an antechamber with a singular opaque door directly in front of him. With the same procedure, Xon's nanophage was scanned, and the opaque titiconium-laced door slid into the wall.

The light, dull as it was, from the hallway beyond the antechamber nearly blinded Xon as the door shut behind him. Every part of his body seemed to be overly sensitive or malfunctioning in some way, and this left Xon with a feeling of trepidation. Continually wondering why all internal systems read nominal when he did not feel nominal in the least. Never-theless, there was a task to accomplish for the whole of his grand design for the Auctius. Xon could afford to push through a few disjointed pains. Xon continued, head slightly bowed, down a small ten-meter hallway that was carved no fewer than six months ago; fresh U'agi dust mixed with moisture from condensation gave it a musty odor. Although this site had been in use for more than half a Gaian year, if the U'agi did not undergo molecular refining routinely, then the regen-eration rate was astounding. Luckily Xon's Ipsum engineer for hire was a clever little man. Keeping the humidity and pres-sure at just the right range, Xon's little helper had managed to keep the site off the grid and under his own guided main-tenance. Another archway at the end of the hall, condensation dripping onto Xon's shoulder as he walked under into a small, circular, almost-barren room. There were no other doors or archways leading to another corridor or secret alcove and no windows giving the room the ambiance of a coffin. This room, like the hallway, had been reconstructed only a short time ago.

A dwarfish, cachectic-looking man with stringy, greasy, shoulder-length black hair and a beard to match (the beard tied at the end with a grime-soaked string) sat on the floor in a fluid-stained jumpsuit in front of a device just about as big as the man himself. The device stood on a tripod stand and appeared as an upside-down teardrop. A panel was open in front of the man with bright-neon-blue-and-green Vis con-duits exposed. The man looked to be in the midst of applying the finishing touches to the Vis interface. The little man was surrounded with small lab tables about waist-high, with vari-ous tools and parts placed aimlessly. The man appeared to be tinkering with the device, blindly reaching for parts, a pen-sized cauterizing torch resting on his lower lip, and muttering what almost seemed like an incantation.

"As this blue attaches to the central site, so-so-so the green sees the flow of Vis." The little man's stutter was a particular trait Xon could do without, but he was efficient and asked very few questions.

"Sku, my boy. How are the preparations coming along?" Xon addressed the lowly engineer much as a seasoned politician would a child along the route for Resalo's annual founders' parade.

The little man jumped slightly, startled at the presence of another in his little hovel but not surprised to see the Magnus.

"Fine, Magnus Xon. Everything is ready as precisely prepped, per your timeline." Sku raised his head from the conduits; his hands never stopped moving, making a point not to look directly into Xon's eyes. "No-no-nothing wrong here, just a few of my little touches of fi-finesse, Magnus."

Sku Higs, the Ipsum biomechanical engineer the Magnus hired more than two standard Gaian years ago for this project, had been hard at work all that time. With no contact with the outside world save for Xon's sporadic visits, Sku had been designing, fabricating, and adapting other scientists' work into a specifically designed device for a Magnus he had worked for many times in the past. Sku had fabricated various terraforma apparatuses, harvesting mechs, and the few under-the-cuff genetically altered crops for the Magnus and his friends. Sku didn't mind being the man at the bottom as long as he got to tinker; it was what he did best, after all. Besides, Sku thought himself smart enough that he knew better than to question this particular Magnus, to his face anyway, not only for his somewhat volatile nature but the fact that Magnus Xon had never steered Sku wrong before.

Xon approached the device, smiling and feeling mildly elated, touching it with a calloused fingertip. The few sensory neurons remaining felt the cool titiconium pulsing with Vis energy as his finger slid across the smooth surface. Xon smiled at the prospects ahead of him. *The future of the Auctius is merely a touch away*, thought Xon, *and I shall lead the way.*

"Very good, boy, very good." Xon admired the engineer's work. He was quite skilled, this one, even for someone as low as he. As that incentum crossed his synapses, a wave of vertigo overtook the Magnus. Xon swayed, his hand leaving the device, grabbing for a handle to stabilize himself, but only air whisked through his fingers. Xon's vision blurred; his head felt like a child's toy spinning furiously on a tabletop, and then he toppled, slamming into the ground. His mostly metal skeletal structure echoed loudly in the tiny room.

Sku wasn't aware the Magnus had toppled over until the impact. The echo hurt his ears. *Everything is so harsh, I've been here the last how many months now...oh, no matter,* thought Sku. However long Sku thought he had been here with this machine has made his tympanic mods a touch sensitive. *I'll adjust them after the Magnus leaves,* Sku thought. He slowly looked up from his work, cautiously standing. He timidly scuttled to Xon, his left foot dragging behind him. An old engineering injury from a terraluna build that never healed quite right. With the credits Sku made from this job, he was sure he could get it fixed properly, maybe even get a nice cybermod like the Magnus. Sku wasn't sure if he should touch the Magnus or not. Sku was frightened of the Magnus but didn't want to see him hurt. *Why is he shaking like that?* thought Sku.

"Uh, M-M-Magnus, are you OK?" asked Sku. "I wonder if your parts are failing; you are very old even for a cyber-net-t-tic. I wonder what kind of mods you have to keep your synaptic functions from failing without compro...compro... messing with your phage's Ignivalo." Sku reached down to touch the fleshy part of Xon's neck to feel for a pulse. The next thing Sku knew, he was falling to the floor; then the searing pain through his limbs began. The Magnus was on top of him, viciously clawing and ripping at Sku, tearing the flesh from his bony forearms. Sku did his best, but it was an almost feeble attempt to protect himself. Sku couldn't feel his arms anymore. Warm liquid sprayed onto both sides of his face. Sku tried to look past the viscous fluid, but it began to clot on his eyelashes. *Smells like copper,* Sku thought, *I've always liked that smell.* Sku finally saw the Magnus's face twisted and gnarled like a feral animal, and that was that last thing he saw. Xon's thumbs thrust into Sku's skull, making gelatinous blobs of his eyes. Sku finally screamed as Xon began to squeeze his skull. The pressure pushed blood into Sku's mouth, his scream turning into undecipherable gurgles, foaming spittle forming at the corners of his mouth. Sku's convulsing body finally stilled when his head caved, popping almost like a ripe cherry, blood and brain matter bursting onto the feral man atop the ravaged engineer.

The Magnus felt like he was waking from a living nightmare. Xon blinked the haze away. *Where am I?* he thought. Xon looked around the room. *Ah, yes, the Noa gene bomb, the little man was just putting the final touches on the Vis flow.* Xon stood his body, organic and cybernetic, felt like he had spent the last few hours in a Palu Pressure Chamber adjusting to pressure gradients for paluorbis, gas planet, operations. Xon looked down to see the carnage that lay before him.

Xon stumbled backward, bringing his hands to his face, his victim's blood fresh and warm dripping between his fingers. The little man lay at his feet, a face no longer but a mass of fractured bone and globs of fetid flesh staring back at Xon. The Magnus tried feverishly to wipe the blood away with his robes but came away with more blood, more flesh, more bits. Xon felt the wetness on his face, his hands—it was everywhere. What had he done? This was not him; he was not in control.

"What? What?" The Magnus stuttered; fear was not a concept Xon had been open to since the day he saw his father murdered by his own grandfather. But experiencing the emotion again in such a short time...*Something is breaking my control*, Xon thought. A sudden flood of emotions, again, like on the *Cultivador*. Xon shook his head. He laughed, cried, and screamed in anguish almost all at the same moment. In the back of Xon's mind, he heard the same something from earlier, a faint whisper into his incentum.

Finish it.

Xon whirled around looking behind him, up, down. Where was that coming from? He frantically searched the small round room. No corners for anyone to hide. Under the device, no one, nothing. A series of clicks and whistles bouncing off the walls of his incentum. The language as it seemed was alien to Xon, but he understood the phantasmic whisper. How?

The vassals must be ended.

"Who dares?" Xon screamed into the room with only the corpse of Sku and the gene bomb to hear him, neither of which produced an answer for the panicked Magnus.

We are close.

Xon grabbed his head with the blood-soaked hands and fell to his knees. The soft echo in the back of his mind became a thudding force on his frontal lobe. The digital hiss sounded as if a serpent was readying for strike to the jugular.

You were mine then, as you are now. You have never had control. All will bow before me. Humanity will fall like all the others. Our servants will bid our will. You...are...all...mine...

The tortuous hiss faded to the soft echo, then was gone entirely. *They are here. They promised me control,* Xon thought. *How could I have been so naive?*

Xon found himself alone with a bloody, deformed corpse and a technological nightmare capable of genocide. For a moment Xon felt nauseous at the thought that he had just brutally murdered someone, albeit not under his own guise. Xon had a more humane demise in process for Sku, but this...

Xon looked at the mass of flesh. It was not something he would have had the stomach for. After all, it was the first time he was to commit the act with his own hands; he wanted to have the decorum a man of his stature should have been privy to. For a moment Xon felt remorse for the broken little engineer. He looked down at the remains, just chunks of meat now, no use, no purpose. The emotional sensation faded quickly. The Magnus's nanophage was beginning to suppress his limbic system once more. Xon knew he should have felt remorse, fear, anguish, but so long without the touch of emotion had made him feel devoid of any, even with the phage suppression. No matter. Xon had work that needed to be accomplished, and there was no need for emotional entanglements now that all was almost complete.

Xon knew in himself that he had no need to fear those who are coming. He would find a way to break their subtle control over his mind. Xon stood grabbing a towel from the dead engineer's table. Wiping his hands and face, Xon discarded the towel without care onto the corpse and contemplated his next move.

I don't even know their names. These creatures that seek to undermine me and control my very being. The Auctius is mine for the taking, not theirs. The Xon name will no longer be known for failure to harvest the cosmos. No, I will be at the forefront of the newly enlightened Auctius. I, Julius Xon, will lead the terraforma of a new Celestial galaxy. These beings know not the control I have. They know not what I am. The Aethra is mine! The Auctius is mine!

Xon let the incentum project loudly. It was careless of the Magnus to do such a thing for any psi-sensitive within a hundred meters to overhear. Xon was feeling as if someone was peering over his shoulder like a taunting, nudging force, but there was no one in the small room except the dead and the bomb.

Xon shook off the sensation, turning to leave. *I am in control*, he thought this time silently, *no being controls me.* Xon repeated this mantra in his mind, bringing comfort and strength to his being, but a part of him still felt disjointed. Xon blinked; the antechamber door hissed open from across the room. Xon believed he possessed the foresight to impress upon himself that he did not need these creatures' devices to bring his vision of the Auctius into fruition. Xon limped to the archway, the pain no longer in his joints, organic and cybernetic, but the weakness persisted. As he reached the archway, he stopped and turned to the gene bomb. An incentum crossed his mind. *The Noas have seen me and could be easily manipulated by anyone, Human or otherwise, to divulge my intentions*, Xon thought. *Might as well dispatch the useless creatures rather than have them stain my plans for the Auctius.* Xon limped back to the device, purposefully avoiding the mangled corpse.

Xon peered into the jumbled multicolored neon Vis conduits inside the device. Sku seemingly finished his finessed touches, as he said. The device began functioning as it emitted a low hum as Xon connected the last Vis conduit and closed the small hatch. The hatch disappeared, leaving no edging to trace. Xon touched the device just above the now nonexistent hatch. An old-fashioned square numeric pad emerged like liquid from the gene bomb's smooth black surface. The keypad lit up with a bright-purple glow. The symbols featured on the keypad were ten letters taken from the ancient Greek alphabet. Xon punched in three symbols: χ o v. *The letters of legacy*, the Magnus thought, *the Xon name shall carry on.* Once the final symbol was punched into the keypad, it melted away, but no residue was left behind as if it simply vanished into the device.

With the gene bomb activated, Xon turned and walked out of the circular chamber. Xon left the scene, confident his task was close to becoming a reality. Xon strangely felt no need to hide what was beneath the Miga now. He didn't activate the camo tech that was keeping the door hidden; he didn't send the incentum to secure all doors, and everything was left illuminated for all to see.

As he walked through the Miga, the crowd on the dance floor steadily growing as the Noa DJ began a new mix, Xon looked around at the mix of Humans and Noas. Xon couldn't help but smile, a very Cheshire Cat smile, the thin flesh on the right side of face stretching so that it was almost translucent. There was no way to stop the sweeping devastation coming to the Noanoagans. *And I will lead the new wave of exploration for Humanity.* Xon departed the doomed disco and made his way back to the *Cultivador* to depart for his final destination: the Aethra Gateway.

As Xon drifted off into his comforting Qusom, he couldn't hear the voice in the deepest recesses of his incentum like a soft echo. The omnipresence that had burrowed deep within his mind, a puppet master from across the black sea of the Celestial smiles as well. After all, she is a king, and a king knows when to reveal their presence at the opportune moment.

CHAPTER 14

The *Satyr*, Intersolaris Transit, Thirty-Seven Parsecs from Tracaelus Solaris Outer Rim
Eight Standard Gaian Weeks Until Aethra Gateway Activation

Nachman paced on the ledge of a crystal-clear cliff. Scatter-brained, emotional, lovestruck once more, there was so much going through his mind. *Focus, Nachman.* He watched his foot-falls change the colors of the rainbow as he stroked his beard deep in contemplation. Nachman's mind worked furiously to understand the whys and the hows of what had been progressing. Why the mind control, and how did Xon infect so many in such a short time? Why murder an entire species? What's Xon's endgame? He needed a plan. *Was it almost time to wake up?* he wondered. Make a plan, and adjust for the inevitable changes —wise words from his mother, as always.

But there was another incentum nagging at his mind. A spectacle of color with waves of neon shot out of random starbursts as they popped in the foreground. Nachman ignored them. The nebula he designed, a proud moment of imagination in his early years while learning to control his Adyta, swirled and spun in the background, changing color so quick that all the color was warped together in a palette of wonder. Normally, Nachman would stare at the nebula, lost in the incandescence, but this was far from the normal Nachman had been used to. Nachman thought about the many events that had occurred since the start of all this hoopla. Nachman's Adyta felt chaotic. There was so much incentum to filter through, so he continued to pace, waiting to wake to continue the mission at hand. His mind had flown to the only person he had never stopped thinking about when an internal alarm screeched inside his mind.

Nachman stretched, yawning like a bear waking from hibernation as the Qu spike disconnected from his port at the nape of his neck. Nachman stood from his favorite chair at the helm of the *Satyr* and stretched again, looking down at the helm with the Vis displays shrunk to conserve power. Nachman sent an incentum, and the displays enlarged. Nachman saw no one on the sensors; they had approximately ten hours until Tracaelus space. Nachman saw a shadow in his peripheral vision that took his gaze to the *Satyr*'s promenade area to see Novia waking from her Qusom. Nachman saw Novia pull her spike from her right hip, the port sealing with flesh, no scar, as smooth as if nothing was there. The majority of people Nachman knew inserted their Qu spikes in an arm or shoulder. Nachman's was pretty much hardwired into his nanophage, as were most Naibus soldiers. Nachman had to smile. *She still doesn't care for Qusom or her port, never has liked deep Celestial travel*, he thought. Nachman smiled at her. It was good to have Novia back on the *Satyr*, but Nachman didn't think she felt the same. The look in her eyes as she looked up at him was ice cold. Novia stood from the thin seated Qusom station as it folded into a wall alcove. Nachman stared at Novia with only mild confusion as she walked to the back of the *Satyr* toward Nachman's lab.

Nachman walked down the steps of the helm. Across from Novia's Qu-station sat Tejwenn in a deep sleep, not attached to Qu-spike but in a type of hibernation the Noanoagans can use when in deep space. Nachman had never truly understood the science of it. Nachman heard rumors that this was the method their ancestors used to make the journey across the galaxy to Ancient Earth over a millennium ago.

Tejwenn was wheezing audibly as he labored to breathe. His fihr was blotchy, shedding in droves, and Nachman could swear he saw his flesh peeling away before his eyes.

The things we do for love, Nachman thought.

"Sadie," Nachman said to the air around him.

Sadie whisked directly in front of Nachman, her nose literally touching Nachman's with a wide childlike grin on her neon-green face.

"Sadie, this is a serious situation," Nachman said. "We don't have time for this." Yet Nachman could not keep the grin off his face. "If you're done, I need you to prep for a hostile landing; I have a feeling we won't be welcome."

"Copy that, but…"

"But what?"

"Don't do what I think you're going to do, Nachman." Sadie stood her ground. "You know she loathes it when you push the issue."

Nachman glared directly into Sadie's eyes, nose to nose, both smiles now gone. "There is no issue to push, Sadie." Nachman walked down the stairs directly through Sadie without saying another word.

A   Sadie didn't turn around; she simply walked up to the maestro's helm and said, "I'm sorry, but you have to hear this, my dear Nachman. You tend to make an issue."

Nachman stopped in midstep, jaw clenched, but he didn't turn around. Nachman took a deep breath and continued to his lab. *She always has to put her opinion in the mix*, Nachman thought. The door to the lab slid open. Novia was sitting at a stainless titiconium lab table with five diamond Vis displays opened in front of her. Various numerical data, Noanoagan gene sequences, and medical data were flowing like lava on the screens. Novia looked distressed as she looked at the data in front of her.

"Dammit! Why can't I find the damn sequence!" Novia yelled.

"Such language from such articulate lips," Nachman said as the door shut behind him with a soft click.

"Cute, Nachman, very cute."

"You know I try. What's got ya rattled? Besides the obvious circumstances," Nachman asked.

"I knew it," Novia said. "I knew you would do this, Nachman."

"Do what exactly?"

"This." Novia turned to him, her hands waving down Nachman's silhouette, tracing his form. "Act so charming and debonair, like we never left each other. Like five years hasn't passed between us. Like you never…"

"What? Never went a bit crazy and destroyed what we had," Nachman felt the anger bubbling, that part of his life was difficult enough, but considering current he put on his best charmed smile. "Well, you know, I really can't help it if I couldn't get you out of my head all these years. Besides, now that you're here, you didn't think I was going to miss the opportunity to have a chat with you, now did you?"

"And there you are, the smug old Nachman."

"Did you miss me?"

"No," Novia said, but inside, so close to the surface, she had. She had missed him dearly.

Nachman stepped close enough to touch Novia, and she abruptly stood from the stool, sending it clattering to the floor. Novia turned her back to Nachman, looking up at the Vis screens. The screens swirled and then blinked to nothingness. Nachman wanted so badly to grab her and hold her closely, tightly, like he used to when they lay in bed staring out into the stars, but Nachman knew that was a bad idea. Things had ended horribly between them in the aftermath of the fateful Vitachlora incident. The deaths, the lies, the heartache—he wouldn't put her through that again. Hell, he would probably wind up with another scar above his eyebrow to match the one she gave him just before they broke it off.

"Why didn't you lex me, Nov?" Nachman asked. "Sadie and I, we could have helped, you know."

Novia turned to Nachman, and for a moment, Nachman was caught off guard by her gleaming violet irides. Novia had spent a majority of her childhood on deep Celestial science vessels with her family exploring the Outer Reaches. One mission entailed hauling a series of volatile synthetic chemicals from an asteroid belt; a resulting accident had left her blind. Her eyes were replaced with highly advanced nanotech ocumechs shortly after the accident. Nachman learned shortly after they got together that when Novia became stressed or highly emotional, a chemical reaction between the organic and cybernetic caused her cybernetic irides to become a fluorescent purple. Nachman almost smiled; he thought it was cute.

"Don't call me that." Novia's voice raised an octave or two. "And you know, Nachman, I don't need your help every time I'm in trouble. You're not my knight in shining armor anymore."

"It has nothing to do with that, and you know it. I could have told you the guy was a crook. I—"

"You could have what?" Novia's eyes felt like weights on Nachman. "Saved me from the same mistake you made?"

Nachman felt his temper rising from his gullet when the *Satyr* shook and lurched forward. Nachman fell onto his back as Novia fell forward into his arms. "You always wind up here, don't you?" Nachman said as he helped her up and ran toward the helm before she could make a protest.

"Sadie, damage report!"

"I believe this is our welcoming party, Nachman. Erigo class construction frigate, same identification tags as the one stolen from Einstein Station. They are utilizing a modified docking clamp with a gianysium geode tipped laser torch, and they are cutting through the hull!" Sadie shouted as she whisked away to the weapons station at the rear base of the helm.

"How did they get past our sensors, dammit?" Nachman ran up the helm's stairs, blinking furiously, bringing up oval Vis displays of multiple outer-hull microcams. "Deploy countermeasures. Get that damned clamp off us now!"

"Countermeasures deployed, Nachman," Sadie responded. Outside the ship, tiny drones, about a hundred, deployed from hidden compartments around the *Satyr*'s hull. Half split off and surrounded the docking clamp at all calculable weak points, while the other half took off toward the freighter. The drones around the clamps detonated. The concussive force rocked both ships. The clamp sustained little damage; it might as well have been shot at by small arms fire. The other drones reached the freighter, exploding just before impact. Sadie could feel Nachman's pulse quicken; she didn't even have to say anything, but she did anyway. "Ineffective. They have some kind of modified shielding that we have not encountered before. The clamp has the same shielding, and it is going nowhere fast!"

Nachman hurled himself away from the console, running down the stairs. Sadie whisked away from the from the *Satyr*'s helm, appearing next to Nachman, gliding by his side, a stream of misty neon green trailing behind. Novia came running out of the lab, stumbling as the *Satyr* rocked back and forth. Nachman looked up at a blazing-hot red section of the hull on the aft starboard section. *Damn that's a powerful cutting jewel.* Nachman had no idea anyone was able to refine gianysium yet; it was the only thing capable of cutting through their hull. Regardless, Nachman knew the cutting clamp was close to tearing through the hull like thin rice paper. He needed a plan.

Nachman's internal cybernetic sensors could already detect the change in pressure as the atmosphere inside the *Satyr* was already depressurizing and adjusting for the clamp's penetration of the hull. Sadie held a hand out to Novia to stabilize her as she stumbled again from the jolt of the ship. Novia looked at Sadie and said, "We can't wake Tejwenn; he's too weak to tolerate this fight. How can we protect him, Sadie?"

"I can create a Vis shield around his Qusom station and camouflage him from our intruders. He will be safe," Sadie said with confidence. Novia never had any reason to doubt Sadie.

She nodded and then turned to Nachman. "What do we do, Captain?"

"They will be on board in about fifteen minutes, give or take. That gives Sadie and I enough time to activate our fortified defenses, and you can stay with Tejwenn behind the shielding. Protect him—"

"Are you serious, Nachman? You actually think I would hide behind some Vis shielding while you and Sadie have all the fun?"

Nachman couldn't help but smile at her. Damn, he loved this woman; his mother was right again. Alvum. Not only was she an actual genius, but Novia had the spirit of a born fighter, and with that combination Nachman could never forget in a woman like her.

"All right. Sadie, Novia, I'm sending the plan through our psionic link," Nachman said. He closed his eyes, paused momentarily, and opened his mind once again to Novia. Like a brisk autumn breeze whisking through his mind, he connected with the familiar scent of jasvinder. "All right, all, you know what to do. Prepare to be boarded."

* * *

"Attikus, we have cut through. Weapons at the ready. Orders, sir?" a low guttural voice said from the port side of the stolen freighter.

Attikus sneered at the pentagonal Vis display in front of him. The *Satyr* sat on the screen latched to the freighter like a fetus to a placenta. He loathed all aboard who escaped him. They should have been trophies rotting in his nanophage long before this moment. He would have his trophy. "Clear this heap; get on with it," Attikus said, a bored monotone touch to his voice.

The inner docking door of the invading freighter opened. Four men, former prisoners of MaxSec Zeta (a maximum-security black site harboring the GIA's hush projects including the cryptogenic Humans that were supposed to be extinguished from the Celestial), identical in every way down to physiological function of their organic parts, burled their way through the door in full combat gear. The outer hull door and door to the clamp's walkway opened in a star-shaped swirl simultaneously with a mechanical hiss. Two of the squared-jaw gorillas led the charge. Prisoners 994 and 995 of MaxSec Zeta terrorists, mass murderers, and close allies to Attikus, simply known to him as Q and C, Quatro and Cinco, respectively. Q and C were dressed in identical black jumpsuits, dual railshot sidearms in thigh holsters on each leg, and titiconium laced cybernetic flex muscled arms extended out each of their short-sleeved tops. Both carried massive two-handed weapons, specially crafted chain rail blastguns. These weapons fire a large buckshot of fine crystallized railshot that spread in a wide arc when shot and then can be detonated by user in-centum slicing through an adversary's combat gear like paper. Cinco, also the communication technician, wore a war helmet with lexcom nanotech that connected the rest of their team onto a singular nanophage channel, the commander's phage, Attikus.

The other two mercenaries, Prisoners 996 and 998, call signs Plague and Famine, respectively, held little significance to Attikus except that their skills became highly valuable during his incarceration, and their reputations had preceded them. The former chief to the warden of the black ops site could attest to said skill set, but he was no longer capable. Plague and Famine fell behind Q and C holding semiautomatic railshot rifles on shoulder slings. Plague carried with him a backpack full of Vis-laced T6 explosive charges, while Famine carried a long tube on his back with a blue-tipped rocket inserted. The rocket had enough explosive in that tip to create a small black hole around the *Satyr*, vaporizing it from the Celestial.

"Breach! Move forward and set charge," ordered Quatro.

Plague stepped forward, pulling a square charge from his pack. The gianysium jewel-tipped torch pulled away from the hull, globules of melted liquid metal dripping from the burnt-out edges. A circular melted laceration lay in the hull of the *Satyr* where the gianysium had cut through the solid titiconium hull. Plague stepped up to the circle, slapping a sticky explosive dead center. He blinked, and a light atop the charge began pulsing, "Six seconds to breach," Plague shouted.

The cryptogenic strike team stepped about five meters back; each of them held up a forearm parallel to their faces. A small slip the size of a pinpoint opened in the middle of each team member's forearm. A green-blue shielding opened from each pore like a digital mist manifested from inside each mercenary. The digitized mist formed a solid construct in front of each team member. Attikus walked up slowly from behind. He did not bother to take cover or bring up his shielding. He hardly cared about the dust when there was so much blood he wanted to release from the meat sacks on this ship.

The explosion was muted by a last-second Vis shield that was blinked into existence by Attikus. The shielding shrank back into Attikus's arm; the idiot Plague used too much T6. Attikus was glad that man was expendable. If he didn't need him as a distraction, he would pull his pistol and put a railshot in Plague's phage himself. Attikus's eyes narrowed as an anticipatory grin etched on his face. He was standing behind his men, not like a general would to command his troops but the way a self-proclaimed god would stand over his minions. Attikus's flex metal musculature rippled as he held his arms behind his back, breathing heavily in anticipation of the coming battle. He carried one railshot sidearm attached to a permanent magnetic port embedded into his right scapula. His body armor, a sleek incandescent metallic blue, was lined with six nanite charges, three on each breast. The charges were enough to blast the ship into oblivion if the situation arose.

The concussive blast sent the newly cut porthole thudding to the metal floor of the ship with a loud clang; shrapnel and melted titiconium followed behind. No ropes were needed as each man dropped into the *Satyr*'s promenade, all landing with the silence of a cat. Q and C fanned to opposite ends of the promenade, standing at the ready as Plague and Famine swept the open room, weapons up and front sweeping left to right. The promenade area was completely open, save for the two closed areas to either side. The two mercenaries split up, Plague to the Captain's quarters and Famine to the lab, while Quatro and Cinco swept the aft section of the ship. From what Attikus could sense, not only through his lexcom phage connection but his psionic sense as well, the schematics were accurate. Attikus felt his mind ping off each man like a radar; he could see every inch of the ship his men could see. It was refreshing to Attikus to know through an earlier realization amid the journey that he did not need his mercs interlinked through phage. Attikus had felt his psionic abilities grow immensely since Xon liberated him. *But to grow so quickly*, Attikus thought, *it had to be the serum the Magnus gave me. Either way, this Elitist Xon has been amply prepared.*

"Clear," both men shouted as they exited the rooms. Q and C came out of the engine room. "Clear," Quatro affirmed. Q and C both moved forward in sync, taking over the former positions of their comrades in front of each room as Plague and Famine moved forward to further inspect the ship. To the forward was a staircase wide enough for two people to walk side by side. Both Plague and Famine moved forward, separating on either side of the stairs. With weapons trained forward, they swept side to side, up and down. Both men saw nothing and continued forward past the stairs. The forward section of the target ship just behind the staircase held an open dining area with an oval table and four skinny-backed dining chairs all hyperbolted to the floor. At the rear base of the towering stairs was a Vistation advanced enough to put the best at Bellatorius and Ipsum to shame. Around the Vistation, a series of titiconium tables and stools hyperbolted the floor, strewn with an assortment of parts for various weapons and tech.

"All clear," shouted Famine.

"Clear, moving forward," confirmed Plague.

Q and C moved to their positions at the entrances to each horn section just as their plan dictated. They both dropped to a knee, continually sweeping the promenade as if they expected an unknown assailant to step from the shadows. Attikus had at least warned Q and C about the capability of the captain. The other two prisoners were, needless to say, expendable to Attikus; they needn't know. Q and C knew better than to disobey the boss's orders and when to keep their mouths shut. Plague followed the plan as it was drawn out by Attikus prior to arrival at the target. The blond-haired (dyed to give himself a sense of identity), manufactured Human frowned, hunched forward, drawing his weapon in closer to his shoulder, and proceeded down the port horn walking past Q. Quatro stood and took a staggered position behind and to the right of Plague; they both continued the search into the shadows of the horn. Famine then turned from the promenade and proceeded into the starboard horn. Cinco stayed to guard the entrance they had made in the *Satyr*'s hull, keeping eyes on the promenade continually vigilant.

Attikus had ordered his men, per Xon's orders, to detain the Arquis, some kind of special plan Xon had for the man. Secondary orders were to eliminate any resistance from civilian population aboard the ship. Frankly, Attikus thought Xon's orders were foolish, and he could not care less if everyone aboard was left a heaping pile of bone, blood, and flesh, whether they resisted or not. However, Attikus would placate his handler and follow orders until Attikus found it suited him to defy those orders.

After a detailed download of the *Satyr*'s schematics from Xon's personal Gnanimus files, Attikus knew his target's ship by heart. He knew the civilian targets were likely in the horn sections of the ship. Attikus stepped down from the newly cut porthole, both feet landing with a soft thud, and his hands remained crossed behind his back. Attikus decided he would send the rookies to fetch the scientist and the dying Noa; he did not need to be bothered with the easy prey. No that was not where the sport was; the sport was the captain. Oh, how Attikus had been looking forward to the kill order. While under Qusom, he had dreamt of holding that lousy Arquis's head in his hands, squeezing the Vis from him nanophage after Attikus had ripped it from the man's cerebrum with his bare hands. It brought the wildest smile to Attikus's face. Attikus was very much considering disregarding that pompous Elitist and bringing the pleasure of the kill back into his incentum.

The horns of the *Satyr* had been custom designed by the Arquis and his pet Caiet, per the schematics they were given at the briefing prior to the takedown. From the intel this had been the only ship in the Celestial with this specific design. Attikus thought it pretty stupid to have such a recognizable ship when the Arquis was intent on keeping a low profile. However, the ingenuity behind the design was a precedent for how his target—or rather, prey—could adapt in any given situation. No doubt there would be some surprises awaiting them as they searched the ship.

Attikus scowled at the techno-organic ambience; it was as if his prey wanted a piece of himself to remain within the safety of home. *Weak, soft, too much sentiment*, thought Attikus. Attikus had to admit even though he had bested his prey, weak man that he was, on their initial meeting, he did have the advantage of surprise over the Arquis. Attikus walked to stand beside Cinco, watching his soldiers proceed down the dark corridors to acquire his targets. There was a part of Attikus that wanted his crew to fail to leave him to capture the Arquis himself. He smiles at the incentum, basking in the pleasure of beating his prey to a bloody pulp. It would be ideal.

Quatro and Plague proceeded silently down the smooth, round-walled hallway. Per the schematics there were four rooms on each horn each with a Vis station about a meter tall directly outside the door. The tips of the horns held an alcove with observation windows. As they rounded the curve of the horn to search the first room, Plague held up his fist; Quatro stopped, weapon at the ready. Plague tilted his head, straining to hear from ears grafted haphazardly in place on their travels after their escape from the MaxSec. The prisoner waved his hand forward and took a step. Quatro heard a soft click and then saw a blinding flash of light from the ceiling. Quatro heard a high-pitched screech in front of him as he shielded his eyes.

Plague looked up to see a pink supernova of light flash into existence in a perfectly symmetrical square grid. Before Plague could activate his countermeasures, the nanite laser grid smoothly sliced through his arm, and Plague screamed for the only moment he was capable. The grid continued moving downward slowly enough that Plague felt every nerve searing touch of crystalline plasma. The grid, indifferent to Plague's agonizing screams, slid through him like a knife through melted butter. As the grid of light reached Plague's feet, it vanished. Plague fell apart like a broken puzzle, chunks of meat falling to the floor with several wet thuds. Quatro opened his eyes, curling his nose as his hand shot to his mouth in an attempt to still back the vomit as the stench of charred meat filled his nostrils. Quatro looked down to see perfectly square cubes of his former comrade in a small meat mound in front of him. Quatro felt a mild wave of nausea in his stomach but pushed it down. He activated the Vis scanning in his ocumech to scan for any further traps down the corridor. The Vis enhancements picked up two crystallized railshot rifles and two railshot blastguns imbedded into the walls of the horn. The scan revealed what appeared to be micron motion sensors. Any false step, and he would be torn down just like Plague. Quatro sent the incentum to Attikus for access to the *Satyr*'s mainframe. Attikus didn't allow access but easily bypassed the traps' simple algorithms, allowing Quatro to proceed. Quatro shook his head. *The boss is always in control,* he thought, stepping over the meat pile of his former colleague, activating a color spectrum that allowed ocumechs to see trails of residual Vis. As soon as his vision went from an array of color to a dull gray, an intense vibration like an earthquake in his head sent him to his knees momentarily. Quatro blinked, his vision returning to a normal spectrum. "Damn that piece of alvum!" Quatro spit curses to the countermeasures implemented by the Arquis. Cautiously, he continued to search through the darkness room by room.

Famine heard the scream of his cellmate echo from the other side of the ship. With his next step he hesitated putting his back to the wall clutching his weapon close to his chest. "This is not the alvum I signed up for," Famine whispered. But he was getting paid a pretty nice chunk of credits, so he swallowed the lump in his throat and proceeded forth. As he walked by the Vis station into the first room, he did not see Sadie's head materialize through the wall.

Sadie watched Famine search the room with his weapon forward and ready to shoot the first shadow he came across. Sadie smiled a devilish grin and sunk back into the wall. Famine exited the first room, paused, peering down the abysmal corridor, uncertain whether or not to continue. *Alvum, Attikus will tear me in half if I turn back*, Famine thought. Famine took a deep breath and proceeded forward. He thought himself lucky as he cleared the first two rooms without any surprises. The third guest quarters held a tripwire that would have detonated a splatter charge filled with microcut gianysium shards. Thanks to his cybernetic enhancements, he was able to detect and disarm the bomb before being torn to shreds by the shrapnel. "Third guest quarters clear," he whispered to the air.

"Copy," replied Q. "Plague confirmed down, KIA. Some kind of laser defense grid sliced him to bits, tripped by motion. Proceeding with caution. Disarm devices as required. Out."

Disarm as required, no alvum, Famine thought. He became presumptuous in his ability to outwit his targets. He continued to the fourth room, no wiser to the fact that the trap had already been sprung.

Sadie signaled Novia through a telepathic link established through Nachman's phage while they were still a couple. Neither had wanted the link terminated when they parted ways. *Number Five is on his way to you in ten seconds.*

Copy. Nachman, how are you?

Nachman replied through the shared link. *Number Four is now tiny bits. Two is heading my way. One and Three have taken standby positions in the promenade, starboard horn entrance. You have fun with Five, Nov. All standby for target acquisition. Sadie, One will send Three your way as soon as Five is out of commission. Take Three alive if possible. Number One is all mine. How copy all?*

Copy. Novia responded as she sat like a lioness ready to pounce from the darkness.

Copy. Sadie responded, legs crossed, sitting inside a divot of the *Satyr's* wall as she was the size of an Old Earth fairyfly watching Intruder Number Five walk by. Nachman smiled; his team was at the ready.

Famine entered the fourth room, weapon sweeping all corners. A twin cot was hyperbolted to the wall in the rear left corner; next to it was a small metal nightstand with a single lantern on top. All hyperbolted to their surfaces. To the right of the bed across the room a small sitting alcove with a bench for viewing out the porthole into the Celestial. Famine scanned the bench—no surprises that his tech could see. He lifted the seat to reveal an empty trunk. The alcove was clear, Famine proceeded to a tall titiconium standing closet between the bed and alcove. He cautiously opened the metal doors and peered inside. All clear. He turned to search the bed, all clear, then proceeded to exit the room.

Novia, silent as a hummingbird stealing nectar from a tubule perennial, slid open the hidden door at the back of the closet. *Now.* Novia psionically projected the incentum to Sadie, and almost immediately Novia shimmered out of sight. Sadie used her ability to manipulate Vis by bending the light and Vis around Novia, cloaking her from sight. Famine stepped to the door; it slid to the left opening to the empty corridor. Famine heard a tiny *ching* from behind. Novia stopped. *Dammit, Nachman, pick up after yourself!* she thought as a small metallic part rested near her cloaked boot.

Famine turned quickly with his rifle pointed directly ahead, but there was nothing there. "What the hell?" Famine said aloud. He walked a meter back into the room and stopped. Novia backed away but was still directly in front of him with her nose nearly touching the tip of his rail rifle barrel. Leave it to Nachman to pair her with someone that was comparable to her height, Novia thought. Novia backed away a centimeter. Famine looked confused for only a moment and then blinked. His ocumech switched from night vision to the VisThermo vision. Novia didn't realize Famine was smart enough to know about Caiets shielding their allies until almost the last second. Fortunately for her, she wasn't just a scientist, as most had made the mistake before. Novia was top of the class in her field training among the Academics, as they called themselves; the rest just called them geeks and bookworms. As Nachman had constantly reminded her, the attention was in the detail. Novia saw Famine's ocumechs change from the hazy green of night vision to a brilliant indigo, indicating the ocumech's change to VisThermo vision. Novia was ready as soon as 998 made his move.

Famine shoved the tip of his rifle into the woman's face, but she was a quick little minx. Right before he could pull the trigger, Novia swatted the weapon away with her left forearm. With the swiftness of a seasoned boxer, Novia jabbed her right knuckles into the intruder's throat. Famine took a stumbling step backward as he clutched his throat, hungering for air; he caught his breath quickly. Baiting his target from a wounded-duck position, he waited for his target to get in closer. Famine spun on his heel and planted a burly left foot into Novia's gut; she fell to her knees, and Famine shattered her nose with a hard knee to the face. Novia fell backward, blood dripping in thick globs from her crooked nose.

"You know, bitch, if it wasn't for my regen cells, any normal Human would be dead from a punch like that," Famine boasted as he gingerly touched his throat as his lip sneered with giddy, vile anticipation. "I'm supposed to take you alive and untouched, but since your boyfriend killed my celly, I'm going to do a whole lot more than just kill his woman."

Famine sauntered to Novia, fumbling with his clothes as he clambered for Novia. As he fell upon her, Novia brought her knee up into his chest, preventing him from falling on top of her. Novia could feel his grimy fingertips scrape across her silky-smooth throat as she tried to push him back. With the pain from her nose burrowing throughout her skull, Novia felt weak and nauseous. Famine laughed. "Struggle all you want. You're mine, little girl." The prisoner began to get a grip on Novia's throat. Out of the corner of her eye, Novia saw Sadie materialize into existence by the entryway into the room. Sadie stood there, hands behind her back, and smiled at Novia, much as friend would who knew she did not have to intervene. Novia smiled back and shoved the prisoner off her with a mustering of strength that took Famine by surprise. Famine stumbled, drew a large curved blade from a chest holster, then lunged downward with a savage yell one last time. Novia slammed the heel of her boot on the floor and then kicked her leg upward. A silver blur swung up to Famine and connected with his chin. Famine tried to say something but was unable as a blade the length of an old-fashioned fountain pen wedged his jaw to his skull.

"I could use a little help now, Sadie," Novia said as she held Famine's body weight with her leg, "He's getting a little heavy now."

Sadie laughed and helped Novia relieve herself of her assailant.

Nachman heard Novia's triumph over Intruder Five. Pieces of alvum have no right to come aboard his ship and threaten his family. *Four will be down momentarily. One is sending Three now. Sadie, stand by for target.*

Copy. Sadie acknowledged pulling the deceased intruder off Novia's boot, whisking away in a murky whirlpool, the dead man dropping like a marionette with the strings cut. Novia pushed herself to her feet, the pain in her face now a memory as adrenaline had taken over moments ago. Novia ran out the door, scooping up the intruder's rail rifle as she went to meet Sadie to take down Intruder Three.

"Sir, I have now lost biographics on Famine as well as Plague. Q is still in the port horn," Cinco reported viewing telemetry readings through his ocumech.

Attikus put a hand on Cinco's shoulder and sniffed the air, much like a predator sniffing out the weaker animal. "Would you be so kind to see what that moron Famine fouled up? I'm going to meet my prey."

Cinco stood, training his weapon forward, moving slowly down the starboard horn. He shook his head and strained not to look behind him. Attikus always sent a chill down Cinco's spine, and cryptogenics are supposed to be made to be fearless. He slowly made his way around the bend, not knowing what awaited.

Nachman sat in the alcove of the port horn staring out into the dark of the Celestial; the stars seemed to be dancing for Nachman with the bright star of Tracaelus Solaris off in the distance.

"Bring your hands up. Interlace your fingers behind your head. Do it now. My orders are to bring you to Attikus alive, but I will kill you if I have to," Quatro said as he pointed his rifle at the base of Nachman's skull, in direct line with his nanophage, seemingly getting the drop on his target.

"All right, buddy, you got me," Nachman said as he puts his hands behind his head, interlacing his fingers. He smiled at his reflection in the mirrored window. The reflection shimmered pearlescent; Quatro raised a scarred eyebrow then the crimson spurt from his nose filled his vision.

Nachman stood, almost casually, knowing the 0.9-second delay he had caused to the intruder's ocumech. Simple yet effective visual wavelength disturbance, VWD, from his contacts in Ipsum. A little toy Nachman used to throw people off balance. The VWD sent faulty signals to an assailant's ocu-mech delaying the neurotransmitter to the brain. Nachman wanted to whistle as he grabbed the rifle's barrel, slamming it into the invader's nose while bringing a solid left hook into his face. Nachman felt the merc's jaw shatter. When the intruder turned back to Nachman, he looked as dazed as a drunkard after a night at the bar. Nachman didn't let the Crypto compose himself. Nachman was laying a series of haymakers across Quatro's face just to vent his current frustrations onto to something palpable when his punching bag exploded all over Nachman's chest.

"I tire of all this cat and mouse. Don't you, Arquis?" Attikus said, holding the smoking rail pistol in the air. Nachman could not believe the dead-eyed smile on the scarred man's face. The crypto somehow overrode the genetic programming. *Sick bastard enjoys the kill.* "Now that we have him out of the way, are you going to come with me quietly, or do I have to use force? Oh, please let me use force; I really don't mind," Attikus taunted as he holstered his sidearm with a click to his magnetic port on his right scapula.

"Yeah, well, I prefer the stand-up fight, too, but damn, man, you won last time. Why so bitter?" asked Nachman as he set the dead man on the ground in front of him.

Attikus didn't think Nachman was funny in the least, but he laughed. A booming laugh that echoed in the corridor. "Oh, oh, my dear Arquis," Attikus said, rubbing his eye with a single finger then bringing his hands to rest behind his back once more. "You have just helped me come to a conclusion to my quandary. You might heal quickly, but to hell with Xon's orders. I'm going to enjoy adding your trophy to my collection."

Nachman felt his heart quicken as he approached probably the most dangerous man he had ever faced. Part anticipation of the coming battle and part unsettling nerves for the fear of what could happen again: defeat.

Attikus didn't charge, didn't yell, just simply swayed toward Nachman as if this were just a game to him. *This guy is nuts; well, no turning back now*, Nachman thought. Nachman's muscles tensed just enough for him to feel it but not enough to show his opponent. He brought his arms up to his face and waited for his opponent to approach.

Nachman didn't see the kick coming until just before it connected with his chest. *Man, this guy is fast*, he thought. Attikus's foot pushed Nachman into the wall, knocking the air from his lungs. Attikus followed with a vicious hammer punch that felt like a rogue luna slammed across Nachman's jaw. Nachman recovered quickly, tightening his jaw pain crawling to his ear, and brought his forearm up to his ear to block a large fist swinging to left temple. Nachman countered with an uppercut to his opponent's jaw. Attikus arched backward, losing his balance momentarily. Nachman followed with a flurry of body punches in an attempt to knock the wind out of Attikus. Nachman didn't let up continuing the flurry alternating his punches, body, body, face, face, body. Nachman wouldn't, couldn't, let up. *This psycho almost broke me before, not again!* Nachman screamed inside his head.

Oh, you will be broken, rest assured. Nachman was thrown off by the sudden psychic flare. "Surprise," smiled Attikus. He began to throw several punches, sending a right hook across Nachman's jaw. Using the momentum from the punch, Nachman changed tactics and spun, landing a solid right foot in Attikus's temple sending him flailing into the bulkhead. Attikus didn't struggle to stand. Attikus stood straight, arching his back, as if unphased by Nachman's barrage and laughed.

"Oh, oh, that was good," laughed Attikus. "I actually felt that a bit." He wiped his lip. "You are the first to make me bleed." Attikus pulled a hypo-syringe from his pocket and jammed it into his neck. With a hiss of the autoinjector, a yellow-orange-flecked chemical was thrust into his augmented bloodstream. "Now, Arquis, let us make this interesting." With a violent roar that echoed through the *Satyr*, Attikus charged his hulking form, intent on pulverizing Nachman. Nachman had braced himself for the impact when the bestial crypto was no longer in front of him but flying sideways into the tip of the horn.

"Great timing, guys," Nachman shouted with a smile to Novia, who held the smoking rail rifle. Sadie whisked into existence beside Novia. She looked down the hall and then to Novia; Sadie couldn't help but smile. *Just like old times*, she thought.

Nachman ran toward the smoldering pile of crypto. Squeamish was one thing Nachman never was, and staring at the charred hunk of man-meat that was Attikus, Nachman couldn't suppress a smile. Bastard got what he deserved. The lower half of the Crypto's jaw had been disintegrated along with his entire left torso and left arm; only a cauterized stump of shoulder flesh remained. Nachman pulled his sidearm, just in case. He held the weapon in his right hand pointing at the gullet of the burned body and then reached to feel what was left of the mercenarie's neck for a pulse. When his hand touched what he thought was a dead man's neck, Nachman saw the Crypto's foot jolt upward from his peripheral vision, aiming for his skull; Nachman open fire. The railshots tore open the gullet of the Crypto; entrails spilled onto the floor in globs from the front and back as the hole widened with each shot. A gorilla-sized right hand ensnared Nachman's throat. Attikus stood, how Nachman would never know, and picked Nachman off his feet and began to squeeze.

As Nachman felt the life literally being squeezed out of him, he thought about how much he hated being psi-sensitive. The psionic shout inside his head bounced off every part of his cerebellum; his mind felt like it was searing as if boiling oil had been poured over his brain. Nachman felt every muscle in his body tense as he began to lose oxygen and synaptic function started to slow. Nachman strained to reach for Attikus's chest. He could feel the pin of the nanite charge on the gorilla's vest brush his fingertip. Attikus screamed inside Nachman's head, *I will tear you limb from limb, synapse from synapse, Arquis. You destroy my body, but I will decimate your mind. Your phage will burn inside your brain while you watch your family suffer. I will kill them all. Everyone,* everyone, *you have ever met will die by my hands in a blood-soaked bath of their own viscous insides, and you, oh you, Arquis, will be alive long enough to see me dine on their entrails before I slowly, painfully end your misery.*

Sadie appeared behind Attikus. Nachman felt his eyes fluttering and the world began swirling into blackness as Attikus crushed his throat with the little sinew he had left in his right arm. Attikus never heard Sadie appear. Sadie brought her hands to what remained of Attikus's temples. Her fingers slid into his skull as if she dipped her fingers through water. Sadie placed her fingertips around his brain, putting only the slightest amount of pressure where her fingertips touched. The link broke; Attikus screamed a wet, garbled noise like a calf being led to slaughter. He started convulsing, dropping Nachman to the ground. Nachman landed on his knees, not too agile after almost having the life choked out of him. Sadie nearly screamed, "Nachman, I can't hold him for long, he...is... a powerful...psychic!" Sadie struggled to maintain the hold on Attikus as he sent psychic pulses into Sadie. The pain through Sadie's aura felt like some stripping thin layers from her essence. Nachman knew he had to act quickly. He reached for the nanite charges on the crypto's chest and activated one charge, then side-kicked him to the tip of the horn. Attikus flew backward, passing through Sadie, slamming into the alcove. "Sadie! Vis net *now*!" Nachman turned and ran toward Novia. "Run, run!" They both ran. Sadie expanded her Humanoid form into a flat, green, clear surface enclosing the entire tip of the horn. Attikus just stood tall, showing no fear from the one eye he had left, one second until detonation; there was nothing he could do but threaten Nachman one last time. *This isn't over, Arquis.* Attikus exploded spreading bloody bits and pieces all over Sadie. Sadie's Vis net form bubbled outward as the blastwave hit her, protecting the rest of the ship. The concussion rocked the ship knocking Nachman and Novia off their feet. The *Satyr*'s hull blew outward, taking whatever trace of the crypto was left out into the Celestial. A titiconium armored wall slammed loudly into place, preventing all aboard from meeting the cold vacuum of the Celestial.

"Well," Nachman said as he stood noticing how sore his ribs were at the abrupt movement, "that was fun."

Sadie wisped in front of the bloodied couple. "I would rather not like to feel a nanite explosion again. It sends an odd sensation through my Vis."

"Yeah, sorry about that, last-minute thing. I'm glad that guy's off my ship," Nachman said as he turned his head. "Thank you," he said, smiling at Novia.

"Anytime." Novia smiled back; she even blushed a little. Nachman noticed.

"Oh, Nachman, I do believe there is still a bit of work to tend to," Sadie said pointing to the prisoner, the crypto Attikus called Cinco, lying Vis-tied in an unconscious heap at the end of the corridor.

"Great work, by the way, Sadie." Nachman pointed to his temple. "The whole the finger-in-the-head trick," Nachman said. Sadie raised her eyebrows and smiled, but it quickly faded. Nachman looked to the lump of alvum unconscious on his deck. "All right, let's get to it."

CHAPTER 15

Tracaelus Solaris, Intrasolaris, Twenty Parsecs from Terra-luna Tasóa
The *Satyr*, First Caiet-Initiated Cryptogenic Cerebral Platform

"Sadie, I want you on comms at all times, no exceptions," Nachman said through his psionic link with Sadie. "You have never been inside a crypto's head, and we don't know what kind of surprises to expect."

"I really wish you wouldn't use such a derogatory term, Nachman," Novia commented through the link. "Such intelligence but such a lack of eloquence." Novia never did like the language Nachman insisted on using at times; Nachman always told her it added to his charm. Novia had insisted on being awake with Nachman for the last leg of the journey to Tasóa. She was like an excited child as she had wanted to bear witness to this event, as this would be the first time in history a Caiet entered a genetically engineered Human's mind. Undiscovered country, as Novia put it. Sadie shot him a disapproving scowl as well; she never cared for vulgarities either.

"Delylah and I have been telling him that for years, Novia. Nachman is a stubborn one though," Sadie said as she and Novia laughed.

"Okay, you two. Cut the chatter. Focus," Nachman interjected, only mildly irritated. "Sadie, tell me everything you see."

"Copy, Nachman." Sadie began her dictation. "I am currently one hundred meters from the cerebellum just passing the hypothalamus. The hypothalamus is massive like it is going to rupture. There is a viscous black substance wrapped around it; it's pulsating, almost as if it is a living material just like the substance present in Prisoner 674."

Nachman interrupted abruptly. "Sadie, don't touch it. Remember what it did last time."

"I remember, Nachman," Sadie said, a bit irritated at the interruption. Sadie was slightly feeding off of Nachman's earlier irritation. "My Vis still hasn't felt right on my shoulder since it touched me last time. However, I do have dual layer shielding in place that I hope will protect me while I am here. Now as I was saying, the substance is oozing out of every cavity in our prisoner's brain. The ooze is coating the gray matter completely in each crevice of the sulci. From what I can see, there are physical changes happening to the cryptogenic Human's brain. The substance seems to be adapting its environment to suit its means of habitation."

"A parasitic relationship instead of symbiotic like with the bond between a Nafusma of Noanoagans or a Human and Caiet," commented Novia.

"Absolutely fascinating!" Sadie reached to touch the goo but stopped, remembering what it could do to her. Nachman always thought her innate curiosity would get her killed. Sadie trudged forward, her aura preventing her feet from touching the black ooze underneath. "I am coming up to the pineal gland. The gland is extremely small, most likely to inhibit the release of melatonin prolonging the waking period."

"Improved combat efficiency," said Nachman, an edge of bitterness to his voice.

"They did the same too you, as well, I remember," commented Sadie, but she didn't press the issue. "It seems the entire anatomy of the brain has been altered to promote increased intelligence, stamina, and aggression judging from the complex alterations and nanocybernetic implants. The substance is beginning to thicken as it did before entering the cerebellum of the other prisoner. I'm getting close to the—"

Sadie fell. It was as if the fleshy ground beneath her opened and swallowed her. Sadie regained control of her aura, slowed herself down, and began to hover.

"Sadie, report!" Nachman shouted. "Sadie, are you there?"

"Nachman, calm down," Novia said before Sadie could respond.

"Yes, Nachman, I'm fine," said Sadie. Novia looked at Nachman breathing a heavy sigh of relief at his partner's status.

Sadie looked around seeing nothing at first in the cavernous dark of the midbrain. With an incentum Sadie brightened, her intense neon green illuminating the entirety of her surroundings. A narrow passage, a vein by the looks of the congealed blood waving sluggishly forward. The vessel was overtaken with the dark muck, slithering and writhing like a thousand snakes moving in synch. She slimmed her form as to not inadvertently touch the vessel wall or the random tendrils protruding from the wall. She looked around, seeing nothing useful, and hovered to the opening that took her into the vessel.

Sadie regained her bearings as soon as she reached the apex of the blood vessel. She gathered that in proportion to her position the midbrain would be. Sadie smiled and floated to the precipice. Although the ooze writhed all over, Sadie knew she was behind the pons and that would mean she should be just in front of the opening Caiets use to enter the cerebellum, the arbor vitae. "I can see the arbor vitae passageway. The ooze has coated the entire midbrain and most of the cerebellum. It appears to be thickening as I speak. I can feel my aura dampen much quicker here than in the other prisoner's brain. Maybe it is the fact that it is a cryptogenic brain, or it could be some other kind of anomaly from the Automaton; I can't be sure without further study. But unfortunately there is no time for that. Stand by. I'm going to reinforce my shielding," Sadie closed her eyes and clenched her fists, her Vis aura brightened like a flare. "OK, I'm heading in. Alvum!"

"Wow, Sadie, language!" Nachman laughed.

"Stow it. I have no choice but to partially come into contact with substance in order to pass through the vitae," Sadie constricted her form as much as she could and passed through the opening, groaning silently under her breath as the slime seared her slimmed form. The acidic burning lasted only a second but Sadie knew her Vis was going to be depleted soon, "I'm inside the cerebellar chamber. Nachman, Novia this is incredible the entire chamber is coated with that viscous substance. The substance seems to ebb and flow from the nucleus, a direct interface with the subject's Ignivalo. This might mean the Automaton is linked with the Gnanimus. Oh, my, such possibilities, both enlightening and sinister. I—"

"Sadie," Nachman cut her off. "You might want to curb your scientific and philosophical curiosities until after the mission."

"Right, right. I get so caught up at times, don't I?" Sadie couldn't help her curious nature. She still was young, even by Caiet standards. "I'm going to have to utilize some resource Vis to float above this muck. It is getting harder to concentrate, Nachman."

"Hang in there, you're doing great." Nachman did his best to be encouraging. If Sadie noticed the slight offbeat of hesitation in his voice, she didn't say anything.

"When I interface I should be able to conduct a salvage download of all relevant information from the Ignivalo if—" Sadie was suddenly caught with her words. She tried floating forward but couldn't move further. Sadie tugged; her felt as if her foot was snared on something. Then came the pain—an intense lightning-hot jolt up her shielding that she should have never felt.

She screamed as she saw what was eating through her essence. An oozing tendril wrapped around her ankle, melting away her shielding as if it was salt in water. Sadie could see millions of cilia lining the tendril, attempting to drill into her shielding. Her shielding was a lining a millimeter above her Vis form; she could feel the tendrils squeeze the barrier. She didn't have enough latent Vis reserves to manage a quick regen of her shielding. The cilia drilled through, slowly, almost as if it as intent on torturing Sadie. She had never felt pain like the acidic melting burn that began to disintegrate her true Vis form. Sadie couldn't help but scream; as she did, she dropped her shield. The millisecond the shield was down was enough for Sadie to slip free of the acrid coil. Sadie twisted her floating form up and away from the muck on the ground, reengaging her shielding. Her fingertips flared a neon yellow, her dao saber sword digitizing brilliantly in her hand. Her Vis flared like embers dancing in a fire as she swung a ferocious downward slice at the tendril, the saber gleaming bright with white Vis fire. The tendril fell into the pool of viscous blackness beneath Sadie, absorbing into itself once more. Sadie felt a drain of energy sudden and violent; through a blur of pain, she saw the ooze pulsating. She could feel the black siphoning her very being. She arched her back as the pain sent tidal waves through her, the Vis that made her fades in and out. A sizzling sensation like bubbles popping along her Vis traveled throughout her mind and body. The intensity dissipated as suddenly as it started, giving Sadie a moment to catch her metaphorical breath. She tried to contact the crew through the link.

"Nachman, come in, Nachman." No response. "Novia, are you there? How copy, Novia?" Nothing not even psi-static, Sadie tried to lex. "Nachman, how copy, please, Novia, anyone?" A beep to acknowledge the end of her comlink, but nothing, no static, psionic or otherwise. Sadie was alone. Her Vis felt congested, sluggish, as if she was in a dense entrapping haze; it was getting hard to concentrate on maintaining her shielding. Sadie had never felt sudden panic or even anxiety for that matter. Human emotions were too complex at times. Sadie pushed the emotions aside; she would analyze the fear state on her psyche after the mission. *Assuming there is an after*, she mused.

Sadie was on her own; how long she could maintain her Vis she did not know, but everyone topside needed the information stored in this cryptogenic Human's nanophage. Besides this was an adventure Sadie had been looking for, just not as frightening as she imagined. Sadie pulled her Vis together; she brightened to a dull, fiery orangish yellow and slowly floated forward. She kept an incentum on her saber; she had a noda she would need it as she neared the cerebellar nucleus, the hub of the Ignivalo.

Sadie could see the nucleus directly in front of her highlighted almost like a halo in the center of the cerebellum. The chamber felt humid as if the cryptogenic's brain was feverish. Sadie, who was able to manipulate the ambient temperature around her aura, felt the fever seeping through. All around her a soft, buzzing hum, much like the flapping of a butterfly's wings, gave an eerie ambience to a normally comfortable environment for Sadie. Sadie did enjoy traveling through other incentums, but after this, Sadie didn't think that a brain other than Nachman's would feel comfortable to visit for a while.

With her shielding and a small part of her aura already penetrated from the previous tendril attack, she had to fight harder than normal to float above the mushy surface of the chamber, the black ooze coating the walls began to seep insidiously to the floor. The muck rose a centimeter or two. Sadie wasn't sure, but she thought the muck was following her. Sadie had no choice but to try to hover, but she continued to weaken as she could feel the almost-palpable drain of her Vis the closer she came to the nanophage. She had to hurry, for she knew her theory about the substance dampening the Vis field inside the brain seemed to be correct. Sadie approached the nucleus cautiously but with great haste.

A large pulsating ball of pustule black ooze sat in front of the nucleus that was the center of the cerebellum. Sadie saw the nanophage completely engulfed in the black ooze; it bubbled slightly on the surface. The giant blob was latched to the nanophage with hundreds of fine tendrils attached to almost every surface of the nucleus and the nanophage. The blob of ooze infested the Ignivalo, the tendrils pulsating as if all had one heartbeat. The nanophage sat atop the nucleus, a small round protrusion from the ground beneath that looked similar to a bean. The nanophage looked as if its diamond shape was beginning to melt like a wax candle onto the circular base; five jagged, decaying leg spikes latched the nanophage to the nucleus. From the base of the nanophage, a small techno-organic mesh fused the nanophage and cerebellar nucleus together, the Ignivalo. Although disgusted by the sight she beheld, Sadie held up her right hand, her index and middle fingers melded together forming a data spike. With her left index finger, she pointed at the Ignivalo, concentrating on the center of the techno-organic mesh. A short burst of thin white-hot Vis shot from her finger where Sadie pointed, and the ooze hardened and crumbled like dust. Sadie had never felt this drained of essence; it was as if shunting the Vis from her surroundings had become a daunting physical task instead of the usual autonomic responses she was used to.

The blob continued to pulsate as Sadie approached the Ignivalo, her finger fabricated as a data spike and poised to insert into the torrid data mesh. The sizzling feeling upon her Vis shielding where a drop of ooze fell gave enough time to brace for the impact of the gorging tendril that wrapped around her waist. Sadie knew it would have never touched her at full strength, but there was no time to dwell. *Focus on the now.* Sadie was hoisted into the air, the oozing tendril slithering around her eating away at her shielding. A vise-grip-like pressure wrenched her neck, her left arm bubbled from the blackened touch, and her legs pinned at the knee. Sadie couldn't move as she felt like she was being eaten alive. Her shielding was failing quickly, Sadie had but one option. *Fight!* Sadie screamed at herself. Sadie writhed against the grip of the Automaton sludge, managing to get her right arm free, raising it above her head. Sadie's saber formed with a blinding light on the downslice. Following through with the swing, Sadie used every ounce of remaining energy to slice through the tentacles. Sadie fell to the floor landing on her knees, Vis pads faintly forming under her preventing her from touching the sludge. Her shielding fizzled; her Vis felt as if it was being funneled into the goo, and the pain from the ooze seared her natural form. The tendrils wrapped around her went limp, sliding off, plopping to the floor, absorbing into the pool of ooze that had taken over the cerebral floor. Sadie could feel the fine hairs among the goo reaching for her, attempting to eat away at her very being. Sadie felt like she couldn't gain her strength; her vision began to blur, and the air felt choked and hot. The black monster jutted from the floor, one giant gaping mouth, a black hole to swallow Sadie into oblivion. Sadie rolled to her side, avoiding the beast just barely. Wave after wave of abysmal sludge crashed toward her. She ran to the opposite side of the cerebellar nucleus. Sadie felt weak, like her essence was being pulled directly from her core. All she could do was sluggishly avoid the monstrosity trying to kill her until it was successful in its pursuit.

"Sadie! Sadie! Come in, Sadie!" Nachman said, an edge of panic to his voice.

Sadie felt the psi-link; it was faint but it was there. Another roll to the left. Her saber sizzled out of her hand just after carving off a series of tentacle whips; then her shielding failed. "Nachman, I need help, shield gone…it hurts," Sadie said, her voice soft, mousy.

"I'm sending a Vis shunt now!" Nachman yelled.

Sadie felt the charge surge through her, a vibrant light of energy swimming through her aura. The pain, the burning sensation was still there, but Sadie knew she could push through and finish the Automaton. With all the power she had left, Sadie increased her mass, growing twice the size of a tick but more than four times the size of the oozing tarry Automaton. Her aura flared an intense crimson; Sadie screamed as she side-kicks the now not-so-intimidating creature. The Automaton fell backward at the same time Sadie leapt into the air, her hands clasped above her head. A javelin with a bright fiery-orange speared tip formed from each side of her clasped hands. The javelin pierced the creature directly between its eyes—or where Sadie assumed the creature's eyes were. The Vis javelin disappeared, reabsorbing into Sadie's shielding. Sadie brought her right arm across her chest, forming the white-hot saber sword. The ooze receded into the floor, revealing the robotic Automaton creature beneath, and with a smooth stroke, she cut off the damned thing's head. Sadie turned to the Ignivalo behind her and inserted the data spike, retrieving all the information the prisoner had on his mind and phage. Sadie turned and looked at the dead thing one last time, smirked and whisked away out of the rotting cerebellum.

Sadie appeared in the promenade of the *Satyr*, instantly falling to her knees, speckles of Vis like crystalline dust falling from her dulling green aura. Bright-blue jagged lacerations covered her body as if she was whipped repeatedly through every centimeter of her body. Her left hand began to fade in and out where the Automaton ooze had coated the hand when she impaled the creature; a craterous gouge was sliced into her right shoulder with her right arm limp at her side, and as she lifted her face she said, "I must look quite a sight." Sadie smiled a half smile.

Novia let out a tiny squeak next to Nachman. Nachman ran to his friend's side. "Oh, Sadie, no no, no, no..."

Sadie looked at Nachman. "I got what we need."

Nachman didn't cringe when he saw Sadie's left eye hollowed out; tiny specks of white and green Vis sparked and flared inside Sadie's head as her essence slowly, much more slowly than usual, regenerated.

"Why don't you take a break, Sadie," Nachman smiled as he knelt by his friend's side and placed a hand on her shoulder. "I think you have more than earned it." Sadie whisked away; a slow swirl of pine green misty Vis hung in the air.

Nachman felt Sadie arrive safely in his cerebellar chamber. She cleaned all viruses, parasites, and hidden cryptocells from the cryptogenic intruder's downloaded nanophage that would be harmful to Nachman, formed a data spike, and inserted it into Nachman's Ignivalo.

"That's everything I could get in such a hurry, I'm afraid," said Sadie.

Nachman felt the information download into his memory files; it felt like a permafrost covering his brain for a moment like a chilly blanket. Nachman could not believe what Sadie found. There was so much. Nachman knew exactly what to do next. "Sadie, you rest; regenerate as quickly as you can. I'm going to get a plan together." Nachman looked as if he was talking to himself in the *Satyr*'s promenade. Novia giggled at him. "Rest up, Sadie. I'll let you know when I need you."

"Copy that, Captain," Sadie said as her Vis vaporized into Nachman's Ignivalo with the hopes of being able to assist her friends when the time came.

Nachman sighed as Sadie melded into his mind. It hurt him deeply to feel, let alone see, one of his best friends in such agony. *Mind on the mission, Nachman.*

"Sadie will be all right, Nachman," Novia said.

Nachman just nodded. "Wake, Tejwenn. We all have a mission to finish."

CHAPTER 16

Tracaelus Solaris, Aethra Gateway, Docking Port Gamma Three
Elitist Vessel *Cultivador* Refueling and Navigation Dump, Three Standard Weeks Until Activation

Xon admired the crowning achievement he offered the Celestial as he walked the gangway from the *Cultivador* docking seat to the entry control hub of the Aethra Gateway. The Magnus had been to the Aethra on multiple occasions, being one of the four overseers, over the course of the construction of the megalith, but each time he saw it, he was caught with wonder and excitement. The possibilities were endless to Xon, but only if he could resolve the current issue inside his mind. This voice, such a familiar voice, the only thing that could postpone those possibilities. Who this was inside his head, he did not know, but they would pay the price for interfering in Xon's Auctius. *But how*, thought Xon, *could this problem be dealt with?*

Xon strained to look up, both organic and augmented parts stiff like frozen rubber, at the protective dome encircling the structure following the arching to the top of the grand gateway. *The Aethra is stunning*, thought Xon.

That it most certainly is. You Human skaav do have a certain, ingenuity, to your design.

Xon stopped. "You will be banished from my incentum," he whispered. A single high-pitched squeal from the back of his mind. Was it laughing? Xon straightened—dignity must be preserved—and continued the walk to the control hub, oblivious to the stares from the skeleton crew. Less splendor in the air now, for it had been sucked into the abyss with this thing inside his mind. A bead of sweat ran down the organic portion of Xon's face. Xon nervously looked up once again to survey this glorious feat, this time without interruption. The sweeping arch of the top of the Aethra was at least a thousand meters high from where he stood. To Xon the arch was picturesque, as if it were a painting extracted directly from the canvas. The Vyrinox alloy gleamed with a purity that only Xon could see—beautiful. The Vis conduits seemed fluid like water smoothly flowing through the tubules as they intertwined through one another like lovers entangled in embrace. Xon couldn't smile, couldn't enjoy the prospect of his Auctius, until the trifling voice inside his head ceased to exist.

Cease to exist, eh?

Xon ignored the voice and walked along the metal catwalk until he came to a dual vacuum-sealed titiconium door. Xon stood in front of the door and let the mechanism above the door scan his nanophage. A digitized woman's voice came overhead. "Magnus Xon, welcome to the Aethra. Protocol dictates you are not to arrive for two standard days. May I inquire as to why the early arrival?"

The Magnus pushed aside his irritation with the woman. At least she was real. "Upon the orders of the Morsus Mihi, I am to supervise the final initiations of programming for suitable orbis and luna profiles for terraforma development. Apparently, there have been complications within the navigational matrices of the Aethra control sequences that require my explicit attention."

There was a moment of hesitation; then the voice came over the intercom once more. "The MM verification has been identified with phage confirmation. You are clear to proceed, Magnus Xon."

Xon nodded and stepped into the circular airlock; the airlock closed behind him with a soft hiss, then multiple blasts of condensed air shot at Xon to decontaminate him before entry. As the Vis scanner flowed over him scanning for any abnormalities to his anatomy, Xon felt a wave of vertigo swim over him.

Vyrinox. Such a sweet smell. The sweet, sweet psionic metal. As if the ash from the molten lakes of my long abandoned homeworld are flowing into your synthetic nostrils. The closer you Humans come to completing our gateway, the more powerful I become. Oh, my dear, unbeknownst the rest of your skaav, you, Julius, have brought upon end of all you know. I don't thank my skaav, but I do thank you, dear Xon, for bringing this, my grand design, the Krytar's vision into the glorious light.

Xon shook his head as if he could rid himself of the smooth, silken, almost endearing feminine voice by rattling it around his head. Xon tried to walk, but the vertigo was getting stronger. He looked down the catwalk and the world in front of him was twisted, contorted as if he were stepping through a looking glass. He couldn't move. He tried to take a step. Move a finger. Open his mouth. No, no, no, no.

Yes. Yes. Yes. Julius you have known since you were a boy in those silly monasteries recovering from that dreadful accident in the spacesuit. Well, accident is such an understated word for happened now, isn't it? Pure agony is more like it. The creature's cackling laugh bounced off the walls of Xon's mind. Xon grabbed his head and screamed to the Aethra. The Aethra did nothing. *They said it was a disease of the genes, a flaw in your Human DNA. But did they ever truly know what it was. Did you, dear Julius, know what it was?*

From a pit deep, deep inside the Magnus's mind, Xon was surrounded by a thick shroud of blackness. The shroud weighed on him but did not crush him; there was no light, no sound, just her, the Krytar. The panic would creep into his incentum, then rush away as if he was supposed to taste just the tip of the fear. Xon couldn't see, couldn't smell, couldn't hear anything except for the voice. Royalty she said she was, prospects for the future would be shared, she claimed. Xon was stricken by her from the beginning, and now he knew there was nothing in his control. Control was a myth; he knew that now. His Auctius was at an end.

"You did this to me?" Xon felt the memories flood over him as the Krytar released them from a pit deeply buried in the back of Xon's mind. From his pit the young boy Xon could have been angered, but he wasn't. He was relieved he finally knew. "You have been here all along, inside my head, guiding my actions to your favor. You are a king, the Krytar; I believe you said when I was a child. A weak and vulnerable child. You possessed me. I remember now. I never had control. You were always there in the back of my mind tilting my incentum in ways to benefit your agenda."

You have always been so insightful, deary. It is finally time for me to make myself known, to conquer your species. To make them mine like the Noanoagan skaav so long ago.

Aethra technicians began to ignore their duties, slowly moving from their Vistations, unplugging themselves from their immersion sets that communicated with the Vis inside the Aethra, and stare at the Magnus. Whispers among the gathering crowd, inquisitive to the current mental state of the Magnus. "Who's he talking to?" "He looks like a statue." "Magnus Xon, do you need help?" "The Magnus has gone insane."

The Magnus could still see through his ocumechs, hear with his audiomechs, but the people around him were of no consequence now that he could have his answers, answers he had been seeking for so long. Ignoring the whispers of mock concern, Xon turned his attention back to the Krytar. But for a brief moment, a thought about his life struck him—the ways things were, the illusion of control he once had—and then, a flash of his family suspended in the zero-gravity environment blood-soaked and dead, forever to rot in the void of the Celestial. He had to know. "Were you responsible for my family's demise?"

But of course, I was, my dear Julius. I was curious as to when you would ponder that question. The Vijsi, members of my royal guard, had tried too early to control the minds of that vessel—oh, the name escapes me.

"The *Odysseus*." Xon's small voice echoed in his mental prison.

There we are, that's it. The Odysseus, *silly name, silly Human legend. Those Vijsi were executed for their presumption of the Krytar's goals. Sadly, with their intentioned fervor, there was an insufficient amount of Vryinox built into the early Human gateway to complete a psionic transfer. In a sense, Julius, the signal was not quite strong enough, and with the complexities of your Human brains, the entire complement of skaav aboard went insane. As Krytar, I can admit I was a bit overzealous as well, you might say.*

Xon had always known. In the back of his mind, he had always known his father and grandfather hadn't gone mad. This entity inside had been responsible for the death of his entire family. And there was nothing Xon could do to seek his vengeance.

But that experiment did grant me a grand insight into you, my dear Julius. Xon could feel nothing from the Krytar—just that cold, calculated mind working within his own. *If not for the demise of your kin, I would have never been able to penetrate this glorious mind of yours. So susceptible to suggestion when Humans are in pain. And the creation of this nanophage of yours has not only been a blessing to us but a curse as well.*

"What do you mean?" Xon asked, cowering in the recesses of his mind. No longer the proud, foreboding Magnus he once was. A man that could have carried the Xon legacy into the Auctius for all of Humanity to have a chance to see the unknown past the Milky Way. He could have been the leader of terraforma for a new generation. Now the man, the once-proud man, sat in the dark, the lonely dark without control, without power, without the will.

That no longer matters to you, Julius. But it does appear as if we are drawing a crowd. I do say we dispense with the history lessons and continue the task at hand. Shall we, my dear?

"What are you going to do to them?"

What any Krytar shall do to a pest in the way of glory: re-

285

move them from the equation. Xon could feel the Krytar smile from half a galaxy away. Xon could only watch as his body was used in ways he would have never thought.

The screams echoed throughout Xon's mind. He watched as his hands tore limbs from torsos. A woman's screams came to gurgling gasps as her jaw was separated from her head. Xon's robotic hand plunged into a man's chest and ripped his still-beating heart out and let the man watch his heart die. He felt his teeth sink into the supple neck of a young man whose terror brought sheer joy to the Krytar's face. All Xon could do was watch, a prisoner in his own mind, as she, the alien voice from across the Celestial, the king of them all manifested the true purpose for Xon's survival.

We are Requenoc. We are here.

The millions of roaring psionic echoes tore through Xon's mind. Xon wept for himself. Xon shrank into the corner, now the boy he was before it all culminated to her control. Alone in the abyss of thought, he wept not only for himself, but for all.

* * *

Ruler, baroness, king—there have been many appellations in the hundreds of millenia of their existence, but above all she is known throughout her horde as Krytar of the Requenoc. She is the Krytar, only to be called Krytar, as her psi-name means no more. This Krytar, the 883rd iteration, sits indulged on a molten throne of the pure psionic metal Vyrinox, satiated by the psychic flares from the crowd she beholds. The Krytar licks her already moist lips as she sways to the lush hum emanating off the unique metal from their homeworld. Millions of Requenoc send psychic surges throughout the entire mother ship like a raging tide crashing forward ready to enslave a new species. Her Vijsi, the elite guard of the Krytar, fifty in all, stood tall to her sides, adorned in gold and purple armor. They needed no weapons, for their minds are their weapons. The smooth, glimmering yet shadowed silver metal capably projected the brainwaves to the Krytar. They tasted sweet with symphonic melancholy dancing off her antennae. The Krytar closed her catlike, jewel-green eyes. Her ears twitched. She let out a vocal moan, so sweet. A tubule attached to the point of each ear, wrapped around her head much like a crown pulsated from the psionic song absorbed through swaying stalks atop the tendril. The Krytar could hear not only her followers but the psychic waveforms of the skaav race and soon to be enslaved across the Zymej, the Forever Black. The Noanoagans, the current skaavs, had been most useful, providing luscious technology for the Krytar to become stronger. The Humans would do as suitable replacements, most suitable for what the Krytar needed for eternal conquest. The Krytar had let the Human skaav build their illusioned empire over the millenia. The Humans continued creating lush planets and moons for the Requenoc to harvest. Now that the pawn skaav Xon had finished the conduit to their side and assimilation of the skaav had commenced, the invasion could begin. She was the ruler of all she can see, has seen, and that which will soon be seen. And she had seen much, much more than any other Krytar before.

Behind the throne a grand, magnificent mural, the Zatoj, adorned the wall, as wide and tall as the ship itself as an homage to the past, but this Krytar paid it no mind for she had been the longest to reign. She knew her reign would be eternal. Still she did not part with it out of an airlock because, well, she liked to have the past at her back to see the future ahead, a future with her as Eternal Krytar ruler and pacifier of all skaav in the Zymej. The Krytar did look upon the past from time to time to see the mistakes of her predecessors and how to avoid them. The Eternal Krytar hardly need seek counsel from the ones not worthy of life. The dead are to be mounted, displayed for all. Each geometric symbol laid upon the Zatoj represented a separate Krytar. Within each shape the Vyrinox-coated head of each leader of the conquered skaav races was mounted to show the victories from the Krytar's reign. Their psionic patterns imbued into the Vyrinox that was smolten to their head. More than eight hundred shapes adorned the mural as trophies of honor to all the past Krytar. Each past Krytar's psionic resonance fed the current Krytar, making them more powerful than their predecessor. Only a handful of shapes sit empty for the failure of that Krytar, shame to those who have disgraced the Requenoc, shame to the Pagim Krytar of past.

The Vijsi and the rest of the Requenoc waited, poised for war across a massive ship built by a multiple slave races that would soon follow tradition, destroyed and replaced by another. Per the reports the Krytar had received since the birth of this skaav race, the Humans showed a resilience she had yet to come across in any other species. No matter. *My horde shall wash over them.* The Krytar let the thought project over to the Vijsi empowering them. Show them no quarter, no mercy, for their Krytar knows no mercy.

All are psionic but none as powerful as the almighty Krytar. The psionic creatures scream a warrior's call, baring seemingly endless rows of razor-sharp teeth as they raise their heads to the Zymej. The lavender-skinned beings stood adorned with golden Vyrinox laced armor, battle ready, tall and proud in the basking glow of their Krytar. The horde, made of lessers but with her purpose, carried a golden staff with a transparent Vyrinox spearhead, the loj. The loj would allow the horde to overpower the skaav and bring them to their knees in front of the Krytar. All Requenoc were at the ready to show yet another skaav race that they were Requenoc, and to the Requenoc, all others were nothing.

CHAPTER 17

Tracaelus Solaris, Terraluna Tasóa, Fu Temu Miga
One Standard Week Until Aethra Gateway Activation

Tejwenn collapsed against the wall of the Fu Temu Miga, hacking, coughing. Bright-orange blood pooled in his hand as he brought it from his mouth. Novia rushed to his side to help. Tejwenn had never felt so weak; he would have pushed Novia away, but he had not the will nor the strength to do so.

"If the Noanoagans had not strived for years of peace within ourselves, I would try to seek vengeance on this Xon for what he has attempted on our people. Genocide of all atrocities!" Tejwenn broke into another fit of coughing and hacking and vomited a copious amount of fluids on the pavement.

"No need to worry. I'll handle that end," Nachman said over the lexcom. "I'm going to take this freighter to the Aethra to stop Xon. The *Satyr*, my poor ship, is in the cargo hold in desperate need of an overhaul. Listen, we don't know what's coming through the Aethra, but I have a noda that it is nothing well intentioned."

"How's Sadie?" Novia asked.

"She's fine now. She sustained some pretty serious injuries, but she is regenerating well inside the phage," replied Nachman.

"Good, glad to hear." Novia hesitated. "Are you sure this is wise for us to split up now? I mean we could…"

"I know; strength in numbers is best," Nachman said. "But we don't have the time for that. We can't be two places at once, and the Aethra will be operational anytime. I will get there and stop whatever comes next. You and Tejwenn need to get to that gene bomb. Remember, find Rodan; he should be able to help."

"Nachman," Novia said softly, "good luck."

"You too. Good hunting." With that, Nachman cut communication. Besides losing psi-coms once he broke orbit, Nachman had learned the hard way about delaying goodbyes. Something Ty taught him long ago. Dull the warrior sense, he used to say, and the sentimentality would get you killed in the heat of a battle. Nachman was still alive, and he wouldn't mind staying that way a little longer now. With the *Satyr* securely in dry dock inside the cargo bay, the blood-owned freighter's massive quantum engines flared to life. Nachman broke orbit of the terraluna and made way to the Aethra.

Novia couldn't help but part with a heavy heart. She left Nachman after the debriefing feeling as if so many things about past, present, and a cloudy future were left unsaid. Something was coming through the Aethra—that much they knew—but what, now that was something that creep Xon kept pretty securely hidden somewhere in the deep in his incentum. Sadie, given all of her sacrifice for the information, was able to attain much data from Xon's minimal trips to the Gnanimus mainframe. Xon's connection to the Tenebrae and MaxSec prison breakouts and the subsequent assassination of Orimer Buhai became quite apparent.

How could a Magnus do such a thing? Novia recalled the debates, as Nachman called them, about the benevolence of the Morsus Mihi and the GIA. Novia knew they weren't saints, but she did believe that those among the Elite were there to protect and guide Humanity into the Celestial on the grand Auctius, as the slogans boasted. She didn't feel any naivety but betrayal to her way of social thought. Nachman wasn't right, but he wasn't entirely wrong either. *But I won't tell him that,* she thought. How could she trust a system and its ideals she had come to hold so dear after learning of an utter betrayal of the system in which Humanity was supposed to stand for?

Novia shook the troublesome incentums, helping the ailing Tejwenn down the hall to the door that came out from behind the grand bar of the Miga. Tejwenn might have been slightly over two meters tall, but with his fihr nearly molted off and his near-skeletal, abscess-ridden frame, he was much lighter than he seemed. Novia might have had a small frame, but she held Tejwenn's wide torso over her shoulders. Tejween bucked into a coughing fit, spraying blood on the floor. Novia stumbled as she heard a familiar drawl from the dark at the end of the bar.

"What the alvum is wrong with this one?"

Novia stopped, looking up and lifting Tejwenn's body with her.

"Novie, that you!" Rodan shouted, his head peering from the shadow.

"Yeah, Ro it's me," Novia answered. "Why don't you grab Orimer Tejwenn a chair?"

Novia walked with Tejwenn to the end of the bar, meeting Rodan, who sat a chair down in front of them. Novia sat Tejwenn down as gently as she could.

"Thank you, my dear." Tejwenn coughed immediately after speaking, his transmod crackling like a broken speaker.

"Rest, Tejwenn. I must speak with Rodan," Novia said.

"Go, go, I will be fine for the time." Tejwenn's transmod skip at the end leaving a painful static in the Orimer's ear, he leaned back into the cushioned chair and closed his eyes. His breathing had become more labored and rasping, as if the air was thick inside his lungs.

Novia gingerly patted Tejwenn's leg, her smile only a mask. Novia knew what was coming for the brave Orimer. Tejwenn tried to smile, but even that took much effort, and he was growing weaker by the second. Novia needed to hurry if they were going to make it to the gene bomb.

"Ro!" Novia—who found Ro just as annoying as Nachman but also found him quite charming when you got to know him, which Nachman refused to do—shouted as she ran behind the bar wall decorated with a large, long mirror and lined with an assortment of colorful beverages. Some of those bottles now lay shattered on the floor. Novia was going to comment on the sticky, wet floor, but as she rounded the corner, she looked to her left to see the titiconium door to Ro's office laser welded shut with loud snarls and grunts coming from behind the door. "Please don't tell me you have one of your infamous"—Novia made a quotation gesture with her fingers —"'Celestial Parties' back there."

"No, no, sugah, I only wish it were one of those days." Ro looked unusually tense, and when tense, the Cajun accent he tried to hide came out. "The Noas man, they—they're acting weird."

"I don't understand." Novia looked up at the tall man puzzled, then looked around. "Wait. Where are Seni and Ines?"

"That's what I'm saying." Ro was growing hysterical as he spoke. "They starting losing their alvum just after Big Red over there attacked me."

Novia looked over to the main entrance. The Noanoagan door guard every patron called Big Red lay dead in a puddle of orange blood with a combat knife sticking straight out of the top of his head. "Oh, Ro, did you have to kill the poor thing?"

"Well, yeah. Alvum, it was him or me, sugah. He started screaming like a damn bear being poked during the long sleep, so I went over to check on my boy, you know. Next thing I know he lifts me in the air and tries to use my head as a chew toy. So I had to fight and buck like a graduation date at a local fair..."

Novia peeked around the corner to check on Tejwenn while Ro proceeded to extravagantly tell her about the moments leading up to Seni and Ines's entrapment in his office. She saw that he was relaxed, his former hulking form raggedly breathing, but he seemed almost at peace for once since the whole situation began.

Tejwenn felt sunken in the cushioned chair, as if he

could wrap the softness around him and be consumed by it. His eyes were heavy; it would be better to keep them shut. He didn't want to move. His body was weary; he would rest. His mind felt as if it was parting from him like a cloud separated from the cumulus; he would let it float away. Then, his eyes opened. He was no longer in the Miga sitting behind the Human's bar—but no, it couldn't be. *Noanoaga, my home. How could this be*? he thought. *It's beautiful.* The pink skies shone bright with the trimoons, larger than he imagined, brushed into the background watching over and protecting the planet as of legend, just like Tejwenn was told during moon masses on the *Journey* ship as a child. The air smelled so clean, as if untouched by the modern Noanoagan. Tejwenn was never able to see, smell, touch the beauty of his homeworld, but the rumors about the extravagance of the planet were true. If this is where he really was.

Tejwenn took a seat on the pad of a wide, flat, blue-and-green mushroom. Tejwenn reached a hand to the pad; he seemed to move at half speed, brushing his fingers across the top. *Fuzzy*, he thought, *a mossy mushroom. Never seen this type before.* He looked to his hands. No more sores, no more pus, his fihr full and lush with the magnificent blue of his birth and the light purple of his beloved *Nafusma* Buhai. The sweet minty smell of a fresh U'agi field filled his nostrils. He was sitting in the middle of a clearing surrounded by fresh stalks of the wonderous fungi. Tejwenn looked up into the red, mute, but sunny daylight sky to see a field of mushroom stalks as tall as him swaying with the wind. The fluorescent purple mushrooms, pulled directly from a fungus painting of the home he had shared with Buhai on the *Journey* ship. In fact, this was so eerily similar. Tejwenn stood abruptly, looking around startled. *This is the painting!* Buhai and he used to stare at this painting for hours upon hours imagining themselves running through the fields, building a house, raising a family, growing old together in this very meadow. Parting together. Peaceful, happy.

A purple mist floated above the mushroom stalks. It

twisted and twirled playfully toward Tejwenn, stopping in front of him. The particles swirled, coming together, gaining more mass; Buhai appeared in front of him like being plucked from air.

"My love, my *Nafusma*," cried Tejwenn. "How are we, you, here?"

Buhai smiled. "My heart, how I have missed your presence." Buhai reached her hands to his head and brought his head to hers. They touched foreheads; their fihr fluttered together vibrating a soft hum, a whistle along the wind. "We don't have much time here in the Mamaú, the Elders call me back with haste. I am not supposed to be interfering with corporeal affairs after death, but I could not watch my *Nafusma* suffer on this great tribulation alone."

"I am weak, my love. I cannot go any further." Tejwenn bowed his head. "I have shamed myself and our family." He reached a hand to Buhai's belly. "Our child would have known a world of peace and joy without whoever was controlling our people."

"The Requenoc," Buhai said. "Now that I am among the ancestors, they have given me the sight to see what they have seen throughout the ribbon of time. These creatures are a vile, powerful race of psychic beings that only seek to spread their reign throughout the Fawaía. They must be stopped."

"But how? I am so weak in the real. Buhai, my love, let me rest. My time has come to an end." Tejwenn bowed his head, ready to weep at his feelings of cowardice.

"Oh, my love"—Buhai lifted Tejwenn's head—"but you must persevere; the fate of our people depends on the actions you take now. Your body might be weak and dying from our parting, but there is still this last task you can perform. To save our people. You are no coward, my heart, as you might be feeling now. I and all the ancestors believe in your fervor and the grace that remains within the mighty soul of the Orimer. We are Orimer, and I am with you always, my *Nafusma*. Now, stand tall and press forth for our people so that we may be together again in the Mamaú. We will be whole very soon, my *Nafusma*. Not much further now. Gather your reserve and go."

Tejwenn felt strength in those words from his love, his heart, his missing link. Forever a *Nafusma,* always a guide. Tejwenn felt the new empowerment and smiled at Buhai and kissed her on her cheek. When he touched her, their tattoos flared like a spiritual fire. Tejwenn knew he could finish his task. The Noanoagan people, a *Nafusma's* people, would be saved and most of all free.

"What's wrong with him. He dead?" asked Rodan.

"No, I believe he is having an Agae'oati," answered Novia.

"A what?"

"In the roughest of translations, a death vision," said Novia, smiling. "He will be fine."

"Um, sure, OK." Rodan slowly put his large knife, that Novia didn't even know he had, into a sheath at the small of his back. "Anyway, the rest of them, the Noas that weren't acting like I poked them with a hot coal like poor old Red over there. I mean all of them, girl, just stopped and looked up at the sky. Like they were waiting for something to fall out of it or something. Like I said, weird." Ro scratched his head as if everything was finally starting to sink into the realm of reality for him.

Novia looked up at the five Ga'a'ula stalks. She needed to tell Ro about the stalks, but how? She could hardly believe it herself.

"Listen, Ro, things are about to get weirder still." Novia took a breath ready, for Ro to lose his calm. "Nachman needs a favor." Novia put up a hand right before Ro opened his mouth to protest. "I know, Nachman doesn't treat you the best, but he knows you're a professional when you need to be, and the most important thing is he knows you're not compromised by the G-stalks."

"Wait. Compromised?"

"The G-stalks are so not what they appear to be." Novia

paused intently just to gauge Rodan's reaction, something that was key from the data Sadie collected. A telltale sign that never could be erased, per the GIA top-secret Gnanimus files the Magnus had attained, was the dilation of the right pupil with the millisecond pause of accommodation of the left pupil when an Automaton knows it is being subverted. And only those equipped with a nano-enhanced biological eye or an ocumech would be able to detect anyone with an Automaton. Luckily, Novia had said nano-enhanced eyes that told her good ol' Ro was good ol' Ro for sure. Novia sure hated when one of Nachman's conspiracies wound up being true. "Nachman knows you can't stand someone in your head just as much as him so that's why he, we, know we can trust you. The G-stalks have infected Humanity with something that could bring our entire way of life down. This is serious, Ro. We need everyone on board who can be on board for this. Will you help us?"

Without hesitation or any other consideration, Rodan Grantes stood tall, taller than most, like a soldier should ready to do his duty for the common good. "Where's the boss need me?"

Novia smiled. "I always knew we could count on you. Now, I don't have much time. Tejwenn and I need to be further into the Miga while he can still make it. The stalks are the reason why we need your help. We cannot be two places at once, so here is what I need. I need you to blow the stalks up."

"He he hahahaha!" Novia let Ro get the laugh out that he so sorely needed. "OK, you need to what and why?"

"Have you ever heard of the Automaton program?"

If Rodan wasn't already pale, then he was now. "What about it? Supposed to be a myth, right?"

"Well, not so much," Novia said. "I'll give you a quick debrief, and I have to get moving. Nachman is going to stop the Aethra from activation to prevent something from coming through."

"Hold on now. Something is coming through that giant ring floating out there?" Ro just paled another shade.

Novia continued. "Yeah, and that's just the half of it. The stalks aren't there just for entertainment and emotional transference. They're also used as implantation nodes for the Automatons. Short version, the Noanoagans are under some kind of mind control themselves by parties unknown and built these crazy stalks to start some insidious process of implanting the Automatons to infiltrate our society. Why, we aren't entirely, sure and there is no time to postulate the reasons. But what you need to know is that this is where the process starts, and this is where you have to end it." Novia reached into a tactical pack on her shoulder, handing Rodan five thermal nanite charges. "Use these on a seven-minute delay; give me enough time to get clear."

Ro took possession of the explosives gingerly as if they were to detonate by breathing on them. "OK, so the Noas are puppets, you stop that, the G-stalks are evil, so I blow 'em, and we save our way of life, got it. Wait a minute, just you?"

"Yeah, just me," answered Novia solemnly.

"Not asking any more questions. Consider the stalks blown Celestial high!"

"Oh, and Ro, do get Seni and Ines out of here before the stalks blow." Novia tossed the tall man a couple of syringes. "That should be enough tranquilizer to knock out the heftiest of Noa."

"Copy that. They will get more sleep than I will all week," Rodan said, turned, and left. That's one thing Nachman could count on with Rodan Grantes—when there was a job that needed done, Ro would get it done.

Novia went to Tejwenn. Tejwenn was awake now and smiling.

"Is everything all right, Orimer?"

"Yes, yes," answered a now-content Tejwenn. "All is well now. Buhai has prepared me for what is to come."

"Even in death, you are not parted," quoted Novia.

"As the tala of *Nafusma* enlighten us, they enlighten you as well."

Novia smiled as she put Tejwenn's arm around her shoulders. As they made their way across the main floor of the Miga, Novia and Tejwenn took notice of Rodan's claims of mesmerized Noanoagans. No matter the age or gender, the Noas that had begun to trickle in for the moonbeam mass to honor the trimoons were standing absolutely still, staring upward with their mouths gaping open. Novia wished she had time to study the phenomena at hand, but that would have to wait because another complication presented itself. How would she get the some forty Noanoagans out of the Miga before it exploded? Hopefully, Ro would see this as well and help the Noas. Hopefully she could clear away in time to help as well.

Novia held the ailing Orimer the best she could, given her height disadvantage, as they came to a wide staircase. They slowly started down the hallway at the bottom of the staircase, down which they both almost tumbled but gained their footing in time. The pair encountered no more entranced Noas or any resistance on the way to the open doorway to a large chamber. Novia anticipated more security than they had encountered. *Wonder how lucky we can get?* Novia thought, *Oh, no. I sound like Nachman.*

"Here, Orimer, sit and rest. I will go secure the chamber and see what's in there," Novia said as she leaned Tejwenn against the wall.

"Thank you, my friend. We all thank you."

Novia smiled at Tejwenn; she felt honored to be considered a friend of not only an Orimer like Tejwenn but to all Noanoagans. As soon as she stepped through the archway into the chamber, her smile was washed away by the grim reality in front of her. The entire front half of the round room was covered in blood, Human blood. *Did I just step into a slaughterhouse?* Novia thought as a wave of acid crept up her throat. Novia was proud of herself for not vomiting everywhere; she never could stomach the sight of blood. Novia took a cloth from her pocket to cover her nose and walked further into the chamber.

The first thing Novia saw was the bloody pile of bone and flesh. "Thing" was appropriate as she could not identify anything corpse with almost all of the midsection carved out and the face of what Novia thought was a man caved inward. There were no tools or blunt objects at the base of the large device or body; someone made this carnage with their bare hands. Novia couldn't hold it in anymore; she turned her head and retched up everything in her stomach. Novia was glad that she didn't deal with the dead or dying that much; death wasn't something she liked to confront.

With the vomiting out of the way, Novia assessed the device in front of her. It appeared to be a modified DNA sequencer with a direct Gnanimus connection capable of linking with a nanophage. A secure link for only one user. *Clever*, Novia thought, but she already knew how to bypass those measures. As she manually accessed the control panel, she noticed that everything was still in active mode. But to her surprise, the timer showed 40:01. Novia wondered why there was so much time left; wouldn't Xon want this deed done as soon as possible? Novia looked down at the mass of flesh and felt nauseated again. *Stop looking, Novia.* Novia wondered again why would someone leave every security measure unlocked for all to see? The only explanation she could fathom is Xon, in some way, wanted to get caught, but why? Novia pushed the incentum aside. No time for irrelevant summations. Since her nanophage was not linked with the device, she continued to manually input codes and algorithms to find the backdoor access into the bomb's mainframe. After about two minutes, she was inside the gene bomb's mainframe. She glanced at Tejwenn, who sat with his eyes closed, his breathing raspy and audibly wheezing. Novia quickened her keystrokes onto the magenta holographic interface. Novia had found the self-destruct sequence through the convoluted security system that was ingeniously created by whoever built this thing. Novia couldn't help but assume the mind behind this instrument of genocide was lying in the mass of flesh in front of his creation. As she accessed the self-destruct algorithm, a port extended out from the machine with a small needle attached at the end. *Well*, she thought, *this is as far as I go*. With an overwhelming ache in her heart, she went to wake Tejwenn.

Tejwenn tried to sleep but couldn't. The coughing, the fever, the itchiness throughout his body, and now the racing nausea through his two stomachs just would not allow him rest. He worried not, however, for he knew he would be in the arms of his beloved soon. Tejwenn knew the end was near, and he couldn't be more grateful for it. Tejwenn wanted the pain to stop ever since his *Nafusma* was taken for him. So weak— he felt so weak. Tejwenn said a small prayer to his departed. "Buhai, my love, give me the strength you gave me in life to complete this task so our deaths are not in vain."

Rodan's voice came over the micro lexcom in Novia's ear. "Charges set. I'll meet you at the rendezvous in six minutes thirty seconds."

"Copy that, Ro; see you shortly. Don't forget the Noas." Novia turned to Tejwenn. "Orimer, it's time."

"Very well." Tejwenn tried to stand on his own but slid back against the wall.

Without a word Novia tenderly took Tejwenn's arm and helped him to his feet. "And to think this week Buhai and I were going to climb those grand mountains of Tasóa," Tejwenn joked.

Novia forced a laugh but knew nothing was funny, but she would indulge the ailing Orimer. Novia led Tejwenn to the device of death in the middle of the chamber. Novia took a wide berth around the corpse to avoid slipping on the entrails. Tejwenn could barely stand. When they reached the machine, Novia leaned Tejwenn against the gene bomb. "From the specs downloaded from the invader's phage, the device has multiple failsafes in place in case someone tampers with any part of the device, but they were all offline. Not sure as to why, but I can't find anything that would stop us now. It appears as if we have twenty minutes until detonation."

"Is it safe for me to disarm the weapon?" asked Tejwenn.

"I've checked and rechecked, and from what I can see, I think we are in the clear."

"You think?"

"If I am wrong, then I will be right here by your side," said Novia. "I will not abandon you."

"Well, then, shall we?" Tejwenn said as he put a hand out. Novia took his hand. With the last amount of strength the brave Orimer could muster, he stood tall, swaying side to side with Novia balancing him as well as she could, but tall and proud in his last moments.

"Apparently, all you have to do is place your finger here." Novia pointed to the small steel hollow tubule protruding from the left of the holographic keypad. "From there, I don't know what will happen, Orimer. I'm sorry."

The Orimer smiled. "No need for apologies. This is what I am meant to do."

Novia didn't know what to say except, "May your *Nafusma* greet you with open arms."

Tejwenn smiled again but said nothing. The Orimer took one last deep, raspy breath and placed his finger above the tubule. Tejwenn felt a tingling sensation at the tip of his finger as if he just had a small electric shock; then a stab of pain went through his hand as the needle punctured his skin. A tiny drop of orange blood fell to the floor, mixing in with the congealed puddle of red leaking from the dead body at his feet. A bright blue line of Vis flowed like ethereal tendrils across the remains of Tejwenn's fihr, igniting the tala etched in his skin. The tala became like a liquid fire flowing in place, purples and blues flowing like sand underwater. *No pain*, thought Tejwenn, *only bliss*. Novia stepped back as the Vis flowed over Tejwenn through his skin, his eyes, his nose. The Orimer seemed to levitate slightly off the floor. The Vis became brighter, almost a pearlescent white flowing faster, churning all over Tejwenn. Tejwenn arched his back and turned his head to Novia, smiling. Then with a blink, Tejwenn was gone. The only thing left behind a singular drop of orange Noanoagan blood on the tip of the metal tubule. The tubule retracted into the death machine. A hum of power slowly shut down from the machine, and the genocidal creation of a madman went dark.

Novia breathed a sigh of relief for the Noanoagan people and wiped a tear from her cheek. She was saddened by the fact that she could not know Orimer Tejwenn a little better, but she knew he had been a great man. Novia turned and jogged out of the chamber. No time to waste; she had to help Rodan finish evacuating the Miga as quickly as possible. Her incentum went to Nachman as she reached the bar where Rodan was loading the sedated Ines and Seni onto a cart. "The rest of the Noas are clear. If they were sheep, I could have led them to slaughter, you know. They just followed me right outside. Three minutes to go. Tick-tock, darling," shouted Rodan. Novia nodded, running for the main entrance with Rodan in tow. *Nachman should be reaching the Aethra by now*, Novia thought. *I hope he's safe.*

CHAPTER 18

Tracaelus Solaris, Aethra Gateway, Docking Port India Four Eleven Standard Days until Scheduled Aethra Gateway Activation

Nachman woke from a short Qusom. He needed a quick regen before he was going to confront whatever force Xon had waiting at the Aethra. "Well, Sadie, I'm still getting a few Noanoagan bioreadings from the Aethra, I guess Novia and Tejwenn were successful; the bomb didn't blow. So, hey, there's an upside to this whole screwed up mess."

"Nachman, please open your Ignivalo. I can regen faster that way," Sadie said begrudgingly. Sadie and Nachman agreed long ago that she would never intrude into Nachman's privacy unless he allowed. Delylah always measured it out to a brother having a diary from his little sister. Nachman hated the term; Sadie adored Delylah for it. Nachman's nanophage allowed full access to Sadie's matrices, which she did not mind. She was an open book to Nachman, but access to the Ignivalo would allow for a much quicker healing cycle. Nachman knew as much as Sadie knew about herself, and Sadie knew much about Nachman, but there was still much more to learn about the man. "You know, I am still trying to understand you. How do you think I am understanding the intricacies of Human cynicism?"

"Sadie, cynicism is essential to being Human," said Nachman as he felt a tingling shock down his neck. Sadie just connected to his Ignivalo.

"Well, regardless of cynicism, I must say Orimer

Tejwenn has made a brave sacrifice, and his people are alive for that choice. Now, regardless of the need for your cynicism, I know you know the pressing need for stealth in this instance, Nachman," Sadie said, wincing as her shoulder knitted itself back together. Sadie always loathed regenerating, especially this quickly; it was as if a field surgeon were stitching her up without anesthetic.

"Yes, Sadie, I got that, but heed your own words sometimes." Sadie could feel the smirk inside Nachman's head. "I've done as much as I can with this boat. Dampened the engines, autopilot the ship, activate some of the mechs on board, and cut all nonessential power including minimal life support. We won't be shadowed—this damn thing is too big—but at least they might think we are an incoming mech hauler here for support drops," said Nachman. He intentionally ignored Sadie's comment about the Orimer. He did appreciate the Orimer's sacrifice, but now was not the time to mourn; there was a mission at hand.

"You will do the best you can, as always."

Nachman smirked. *Nothing but the best always*, he thought. Nachman blinked; an oval viewscreen appeared in front of him. The console sure the hell wasn't the *Satyr*'s, but if it had a panel, he could pilot the ship. The blocklike assembly and the crystalline Vis interface of the seventy-five-year-old ship was something to be desired, but Nachman was linked to the sensor, and all was clear. Unusually clear, not a ship on sensor, no movement but bioreadings abounded. Sounded like a creepy nursery rhyme. *But alvum*, Nachman thought, *this has to be done for everything.* The dock was clear as everything else, and Nachman let the clunky freighter guide itself into the docking clamp. With a loud thud the clamp latched. "Sadie, stay dormant, stay ready, regen as fast as you can," Nachman said.

"Of course. Always on the ready."

Nachman's voice softened. *"Amicus iter tutum."*

"Always, Nachman," Sadie said as she cut connection to

quicken the regeneration process.

Nachman felt the flood almost wash over him, the damned flood of emotions that took him from time to time. Nachman went to his Adyta when these floods happened, but now wasn't the time to falter. Now was the time to push through. *Complete the mission, Nachman.*

Yes, ha, ha, ha, you're here. Do try to complete that task at hand. Stop the Krytar if you can, but it is without a doubt that I will penetrate that luscious mind and open my way into the Other.

"What the hell was that?" Nachman said aloud.

Oh, nothing, just the friendly voice in your head telling you to join me and save you and yours. I want to kill them; oh, please believe me, I do. It excites me at the prospect of tearing their entrails from their throats. But you have my word as the Almighty Krytar, none will come under my hand. Just let me have your essence, and be my gateway to the Other.

"The Krytar, the Other, what the hell? I know this isn't Sadie, who the..." Nachman stood up. The voice, smooth, almost silky, rolled over him. *Mine, you want to be mine.* Nachman pushed away from the console and ran to the exit hatch. He didn't stop to gear up weapons and equipment; he came prepared. "OK, Nachman, get a hold of yourself. Xon's files suggested something along the realm of the psionic, but alvum, man." Nachman let out a long breath. Something waited for him beyond those doors. *Expect the unexpected.* He checked his gear one last time and opened the airlock to the main concourse of the Aethra Gateway.

Desolate surroundings, musty, congested air, and a taste of bittersweetness on the tongue had the makings of an old horror movie from Sadie's archives. The truth of Nachman's assumptions hit him straight in the face. As he made his way down the corridor to the main entryway, he saw where the pungent sensations were coming from. Splashed on the clear door of the former Vis-fortified entryway was the red of what Nachman could only guess were the remains of some unfortunate that got in the almighty Magnus's way. Nachman stopped, bringing his hands to his head. A buzzing like a hive of insects inside his head—quick, painful and gone, quiet, like nothing was there. *Damn,* Nachman thought, *if Sadie was in better shape, I don't think this psi-pain would be happening right now.*

Nachman walked up to the blood-spattered oval door; it hissed open. *Well, they are expecting me; door's wide open,* Nachman thought. There was a glint in the corner of Nachman's eye. He looked up to see a palette of muted colors twisting and churning inside the eye of the Aethra. It looked like Vis, but it seemed denser much, like how Sadie appears inside his phage without shape or form. Nachman didn't think the gateway would be this active. The strange Vyrinox metal that made up the giant ring seemed silhouetted by a tint of silver gleam. Nachman never had been to the Aethra, but he was sure this wasn't how it was supposed to look. How could nobody have seen it—the primary component in the gateway brought by the Noanoagans harboring the mechanisms to let something bad into this side of the Celestial? Nachman kicked himself for not acting on his noda sooner.

Your skaav is a curious one. Your feelings, emotions, they drive you as a species. Skaav with the most amusing psyches. Join me, and you will never feel anything, again.

"Oh, OK, here we go," Nachman said, wincing, dropping to a knee. The feeling in his head was like a seismic jackhammer chipping away his brain. His attention was quickly pulled back to the moment. Damn, his hand was on fire; now why was his hand hurting?

The Krytar can control the nature of flesh and the cybernetic, as you skaav call it. Attached to a mind, anything can be manipulated, controlled to the Krytar's will. You skaav have given me more power. Building my portal, enhancing my power, your will is becoming my will.

Nachman flexed his cybernetic left hand, it was tight like his flex muscle was freezing. Everything from the nanoscopic Vis tubules that ran like blood vessels through the mechanized matrices to the nanodermal skin covering the cybernetic felt like fire flowing through the entire arm. His arm stiffened. *My arm is fine; this thing is in your head, Nachman.* Nachman refused to scream. Counter-psiwarfare was essential in Naibus ops; he could fight this. Nachman's hand began bubbling, then blistered. Nachman couldn't show panic; this would not break his will. This was a hallucination, and hallucinations cannot hurt. Nachman winced. *This pain sure feels real enough.* The blisters began to pop one by one, a viscous blue liquid flowed slowly out of each blister, twining around his hand and fingers. As the blue fluid wrapped around his fingers, they cracked audibly then simply fell off his hand. He needed to find his peace of mind, his focus. Nachman closed his eyes thinking of a point in his life that brought back his focus. He pictured Novia's creamy caramel skin, smooth and delicate, always soft like down feathers. Her eyes, a glacial purple, always made Nachman think of an ice flower in bloom. Her lips full and pouting, the smile so sweet and inviting. They sat on a beach, a Venetian beach, the clearest water Novia had ever seen, her favorite place to have a picnic in all the Celestial. The best moments with her, the most peaceful were here. The crystalline chimes of Venetian dolphins filled the air with a sense of bliss as they sang, gleefully jumping from the emerald waters of the Zragas Ocean. Eight years since the last visit, maybe they could go again sometime. Nachman opened his eyes.

Nachman looked at his hand, slowly rotating it. The pain was gone. He had all his fingers, cybernetic but they were his. Nachman inspected the rest of his left arm. The fleshy part that met with the cybernetic prosthesis looked a little reddened from the lack of regen sequences but otherwise nothing abnormal. *Keep it in my head*, he thought, *the psi-waves shouldn't hurt me, but they could. Whatever this is it is powerful.* Nachman walked down the concourse, seeing the blood smears and spatter patterns along each and every wall, Vis console, and almost every surface he could see. Puddles splashed with every footfall. Nachman had seen his share of carnage from battles fought during the wars, but this was a sadistic mess. His right hand went to his outer thigh holster. Nachman never liked them, but he needed the comfort of his pistol grip right now.

That crude weapon will do you no benefit here. Give yourself to me, give yourself to the Krytar, and the pain will be only what brings you pleasure. Resist from here—the voice softened intensely intimate, sultry, lustful, and Nachman could have sworn he heard her, at least it sounded like a her, whispering in his ear—*and you will know nothing but suffering. Oh, I tremble at the prospect of your glorious torture.*

The corridor opened into the main control room of the Aethra. A slender metal catwalk, wide enough for two, led to an almost perfect sphere that appeared to be floating off the center iris of the Aethra. A clear, titiconium reinforced dome encompassing the room gave a direct upward view of the apex of the Aethra. Nachman had never been to the heart of the Aethra. *People weren't kidding; that's a helluva view.*

Nachman saw someone standing by the main console in the middle of the wide room. Nachman couldn't get a clear view. As he walked, his vision was getting fuzzy; he shook his head trying to get it to clear. *You're mine, skaav, you are all mine.* A ringing in his ears started that made him stop in his tracks. The ringing kept getting louder; it felt like a pick grinding into his audiomechs, Nachman buckled to his knees and brought his hands to ears. The ringing didn't muffle under Nachman's gloved hands. Nachman didn't hear himself scream.

The voice pitched an octave; it was excited. Nachman did his best to ignore the morbid descriptions of his use, but he would be a slave, a skaav, the voice kept saying. The torture would be intimate, but the pain would be sensual, the salivation was audible at thought of Nachman's coming suffering. Nachman tried to focus on Novia, his peace, his stable plane, something to grasp to be rid of the pain. The voice was like an ancient Siren of sailors' mythos, calling Nachman into her deathly embrace. The noise, the noise wouldn't go away. *I will never let you have me; I will kill myself before you take me over,* Nachman shouted inside his mind. Nachman reached out to Sadie. He could feel her but couldn't reach her.

Magnus Xon sauntered into view. Nachman forced his head up, squinting in an attempt to focus, but he felt disconnected from his body like he was a marionette. But Nachman was sure of what he saw in front of him. The physical body of Magnus Xon was here, but the way he moved seemed like how Nachman was feeling, disconnected. Nachman was sure this was not the Magnus he came looking for.

From the pictures Nachman had seen of the Magnus of Resalo, Julius Xon there was a prideful man of Spanish descent, his appearance aging even for a cybernetic but still confident in his position, standing tall, always, and indulgent in his stature as a Magnus, an essential ruler of a planet. His etiquette to those of his stature never faltered, and to those below, they needed perform their duty and then dispense from his presence, but there was never a loss of composure, of grace, of control.

The man in front of him danced and twirled to music Nachman couldn't hear. Nachman was positive the Human he read about was no longer inside that body. As the Magnus danced around Nachman in a circle, Nachman's vision began to clear, and the intense ringing in his ears stopped. He couldn't stand as he felt anchored to the ground, but the pain was gone for now. Nachman almost wished his vision stayed fuzzy; maybe his olfactory had cut off as well. The Magnus stopped in front of Nachman and revealed that he was completely naked and reeking of rotting, rancid meat; the reasons why were far too apparent. Globs of wet flesh clung to the exposed bits of alloy; Xon had not wanted to hide his mechanized form with nanodermal skin like Nachman. The organic skin of his chest and left side of his face caked with dried blood, both Human and Noanoagan, made it look like congealed brown pudding. Xon stood tall, right hip jutted to the side, almost feminine with his hands resting on his hips. There was something in his left hand just behind his thigh, dangling against his leg—a steady stream of brownish fluid flowing down his leg.

"You're wondering what is behind my back. Among so many other questions, I think this one will be the most fun to answer." The voice was deep, the voice of the Magnus, but there was a sultry, playful inflection to his tone. "I know you two were acquainted—oh, not well, mind you, but you did enjoy your interactions when they did occur. A hello there or how's the family? What did your species call it back on your Gaia—chit-chat? But that is precisely the point, my dear Nachman." Nachman looked up with that latter comment. The only other person in the Celestial that had called him that was his mother, Delylah. The Xon character did not wilt from the fury in Nachman's eyes. "If I could do this to someone who is a mere social association, imagine what pleasure it would bring me to impose my will on you and yours."

Xon held up his hand. Held by a braided ponytail with a horrific, distorted look permanently etched into his face, the head of Aethra construction operations, Litiquis Victor Kole. Nachman did know this particular Elitist. The Litiquis was always cordial, jovial, and always a riot. Victor always had a joke for him whenever Nachman visited on cases or missions when he was with the Naibus; he didn't deserve this. Nachman was infinitely sure that this was not a Magnus. Whoever or whatever this mad thing in front of him was that just threatened his family. Nobody threatens family. Nachman had to get out of this psychic hold, but how?

Simultaneously Xon spoke in the real, and the female voice echoed inside Nachman's head: *"Oh, you can try, my dear; just ask the gullible Magnus Xon. There is no way out. You, Nachman, will be the source for my eternal reign, my access to the Other, and together an unlimited power source. There is no escape, no quarter, no freedom. Not for Xon, not for you, not for any of the Human skaav. We are here. We are Requenoc, and I am the Eternal*

Krytar of the Zymej."

The ringing and the pain seared like hot lava through every sulcus in Nachman's brain. Nachman knew he wasn't screaming, but he could hear the psionic screams of the man behind the beginning of this whole crazy mess. Nachman couldn't make out what he was saying, but the screams were of a boy though, an innocent in all of this.

The psychic projection of a young, terrified Julius Xon unscathed from the incident in the deep Celestial, knelt, as if praying to a God in whom he never believed, in a dark, murky hole no wider than an arm's length inside the deepest chasm of his mind. The only thought pressing on his incentum was the horror he unwittingly unleashed upon Humanity. He knew he deserved the heavy psychic chains draped upon his naked, dirty, body. He was alone, forever alone but never so clear. There was nothing he could be now but a prisoner inside his mind with his warden, a psychotic alien hell-bent on ruling the Celestial eternal. How could he have been so blind to it all? Julius wept and wept, his eyes swollen red. No concept of time or any iota of what was being done with his body. Julius screamed, knowing no one could hear; he had to let it out. Julius sunk into the muck and began rocking back and forth, whimpering one phrase over and over: "I'm sorry; I'm so sorry."

CHAPTER 19

Tracaelus Solaris, Aethra Gateway, Main Control Room
Psionic Platform: A Conscience State of Existence Known but
Unresearched by Humans

I am the master of this plane. The Requenoc come and go as we please here. All among my kind can be here, but only a few I deem worthy can manipulate what you call the psionic platform, but what we call the Psik. I, as Eternal Krytar, sit on the brink of interdimensions through the Psik. You skaav barely know what is here. But you, a member of this skaav race, will give me the key to open so, so much in my reign as Krytar. The alien voice echoed inside Nachman's mind. Nachman had no choice but to listen and observe. While the thing cackled away, Nachman took in his surroundings, which weren't much. An arm's-width round ball—no exit, no entry.

Curious. This scenario does not frighten you. And you appear as you do in the Real. Apparently not ashamed of who you are. Prideful, confident but there is, ah, yes, there it is. This will be a challenge indeed, but no doubt you will break. The omnipresent voice hid in the dark like a cat waiting to pounce.

Nachman might have been on uncertain ground, but he stood at ease, hands behind his back. *Show no fear.* "Well, would you look at that? I always like a challenge too."

"You will regret your resistance!" The voice boomed around Nachman; he felt every syllable crawl along his skin.

"Oh, I'm sure I will," Nachman whispered to himself.

Sadie stirred in Nachman's phage; she immediately felt tethered. Her orb shape floated in the dark, unable to take form while still bound to the Ignivalo. Sadie knew she wasn't fully regenerated, but something was amiss. Outside, there was trouble out there, but the danger was in here, in Nachman's mind. It felt like it was being torn apart. Sadie felt there was no other choice; Nachman needed her. Sadie disconnected herself from the Ignivalo. *Half a regen would have to do*, she thought as she appeared in Nachman's cerebral chamber. Sadie physically shuddered, as if sheet of ice instantly covered her aura.

Nachman couldn't see—well not exactly. There was a pink haze, almost gelatinous, in front of him, but no definition to anything. He knew he was suspended in the pink gel. He felt his nanophage like a ZGV had been parked in the base of his skull. Nachman was getting an idea. He looked to his left. No arm, no leg. But he could see the nanites creating the limbs he required. His mother never believed him when he told her he remembered this experience. Nachman knew where he was now, the womb. He had never felt so comfortable and safe as he did here.

Nachman reached a tiny right hand with stubby, semi-formed fingers to the wall of the uterus. *Smooth*, Nachman thought. As Nachman brought his hand away, a jagged white spike pierced straight through. Nachman almost screamed. *As I said, the level of pain depends on you.* The entire uterine wall exploded with spikes different shapes and sizes, but all angled toward baby Nachman. The terror the alien projected washed over him. Nachman couldn't breathe. *Your first source of sustenance will be your first taste of death.* His umbilical cord lanced around his throat; his only hand clawed for the cord but was unable to grip the slippery feeding tube. Nachman opened his mouth to scream, but there was nothing; he was mute. *Think, Nachman, think; there is a way out.* Nachman floated to the wall, careful not to touch the spikes and used a spike to cut the umbilical garrote. The uterine wall began to close in on him, the spikes edging closer. Nachman would not let this thing have him; he swam the best he could until the world went black.

Sadie paced the chamber. A twinge of static, mildly painful, flared across her aura. It changed the blackest, coldest black of space but for a moment. Nachman was in pain. Sadie's aura flared orange, her least favorite emotion, anger. But it didn't make sense. Nachman's nanophage was active, but he wasn't responding to any kind of communication. He was here physically, but his incentum, his mind…his mind. Sadie knew where he was, but how was he there? Their training in psionics was still a work in progress. More importantly, how quickly could Sadie free him from the psionic platform?

Nachman sat at the end of a long table in a chair with a wooden high back. Nachman could move his upper body, but when he tried to stand, his legs felt cemented to the floor. The table was made of a dark-charcoaled wood that reminded him of ash. Nachman looked around the room. Dark. Nothing but dark, but light surrounded the table. Where was the light coming from? A soft rubbing came from the far side of the table. A loud smack of lips slurping. Nachman saw a wet, stringy piece of meat slither into the shadow. From the shadow a bright glinting arc made of jagged, sharp teeth. Sprawled in front of the shadow thing was a platter of bloodied carcasses, but they didn't appear to be any animal Nachman was familiar with. *Yes, an animal, a skaav, a lower life form compared to me. A bit chewy for my taste, but extremely gratifying. Would you care for a platter, Nachman?* In front of Nachman, a large silver platter appeared piled high with Human and Noanoagan entrails. A large Noa chest in the center, Human arms and legs arranged around the torso like a garden of meat, and directly in front of Nachman, the heads of Novia and Delylah, twisted faces of terror etched into permanence of death. Nachman would not scream. His face twisted, his eyes teared, but he would not let this bitch get him.

Nachman, my dear Nachman, I will have you. I know you have seen so much, much more than most of your skaav. You have been privy to such glorious suffering. The civil skirmishes where neighbors tear each other apart for their next meal, the battalion warfare with those crafty rebels, the stealth assassinations. Meh, I prefer more carnage personally, but well executed if I can say. One of your most exciting creations, oh, so much death. Children, women, and men pustulating and dying so slowly in their own blood and bile. So sweet to witness. But only to have you spoil it with fire.

"Enough!" Nachman's yell echoed throughout the empty hall.

The Krytar smiled. *Julius was so much easier to break. Although the poor skaav was barely worthy of a meal, he still was not worthy enough to eliminate those furry beasts. No matter. He was fun to puppet for the time. The memories of his family were the most fun to twist inside his broken mind. Like any challenge, there is frustration, but you are worth the effort, my dear Nachman. You Humans have so many ridiculous phrases we have documented all too well throughout your history. One in particular comes to mind now—oh, how does it phrase? Your paint is chipping, dear Nachman. Now, how about we see what your future holds?*

Sadie, still in Nachman's cerebral chamber, having run every scan she could on Nachman without being detected by what was ravaging his mind, knew she couldn't enter the psionic platform without being attached to Nachman's psionic signature. There had to be something pulling Nachman into the platform, something enhancing the psionic carrier signals. Sadie cursed. If only Humans would delve more into the psionic than the Vis and quantum aspects of thought. *Think, Sadie.* How can she break the connection? Nachman was not infected with an Automaton, he hated the G-stalks, he had not been nanohacked; she would have felt that instantly, there were no chemical or genetic components of compromise anywhere in Nachman's body. Maybe it was not his body at all. Sadie was running on latent Vis, not completing the full regen sequence prevented her from expansively using her Vis manipulation. She had to be precise in her teleporting. She cleared her mind—only one incentum at that moment: the

Satyr's promenade. With that, Sadie was gone, a trail of green Vis mist dissipated in Nachman's brain. Sadie sought her answer at home.

The Krytar's essence sat in the hallows of Nachman's mind, no form, no shape, a psychic projection not near as powerful as she wanted. Soon she would be upon penetrating the skaav's quadrant of the Zymej. For now the limited Vyrinox within the vicinity of this possessed skaav she had inhabited would have to give her the power supplementation she required to break this man. The Krytar tilted her head in the dark as if something caught her ear. *Ah, the other one, the skaav is almost whole. But I can't quite—no, the skaav goes to the satellite, it will surely shut it down and the hold will break.* The Krytar felt as if she could touch the Caiet, but it was just beyond her mental grasp. *No matter; I'll have a bit more fun with this one. That will bring it to me, and my Vijsi will be the first to dine alongside their Krytar.*

Nachman woke staring at a gleaming silver floor. He lifted his head; it felt as heavy as a fresh sandbag. The first thing Nachman realized was that this Krytar was still putting alvum in his psyche. The second he couldn't move, again. He looked to his right arm; it was bent above his head, his hand exposed, but his arm looked like it was melding into whatever metal he was attached to. Panic rose in Nachman. His left hand seemed farther away from his body than it should, but he could still move and feel his hand. Nachman looked down at the rest of his body. Everywhere there were cables and tubules making pathways in and out of his body. His body was melded to the ashen silver metal. A trickle of blood slid down his bare cheek. Nachman tried to look up but caught a reflection of himself in the metal across from him.

Attached to his forehead and winding around his head looked like what he thought was a crown of thorns, the metal jutted into so many parts of Nachman's head he lost count. Coming from the top of his shaven head, a large clear tubule was attached to the—is that what Nachman thought it was?—

the Aethra. The tubule ebbed and flowed with red and blue Vis mixing in a bubble at the crown of his head into an ink-like purple. The Aethra was fully activated. A cyclonic whirlwind of Vis churned at the center of the Aethra and around the Vis cyclone waves of liquid-like tendrils. What were they reaching for? Nachman wasn't sure what it was and didn't care at the moment. *What the hell is this crazy alien doing to me?*

Nachman heard a loud pop above him like a stellar vessel engine firing. It looked like nothing he had seen in any Human or Noanoagan vessel. The angles were sharp, defined, but the vessel had a sleekness, with almost no clefts or ridges. The pop Nachman heard was a GIA fighter exploding. Nachman took in the scene before him, and he saw nothing but a sea of corpses. Human, Noanoagan. Men, women, children all splayed throughout the Aethra control center. Directly in front of him, everyone he had ever known was flayed and displayed on metallic posts. All their arms bound above their heads but suspended in place by some unseen force. Novia, Delylah, Ines, Seni, everyone. Nachman tried to run to them but couldn't; the Aethra flared to life, the eye of Vis churned in the middle and then exploded outward into the liquid and alien vessels. More of the sleek kind began emerging through the Aethra. Nachman felt his life being carved away by the Aethra, every slice serrating his very being. Every ounce of energy needed to power the Aethra was siphoned through him. Nachman felt acid through every cell in his body, and at the same time, he was being twisted and bent as if he was being pulled into someplace else. The Aethra powered down, and Nachman saw why he felt the acidic burn—it seemed as if Nachman was directly integrated into the Aethra itself. And he felt like a piece of himself, a small piece of who he strived to be and who he already was stayed inside the Aethra.

There you go, dear Nachman. Now you understand your purpose.

"Not quite yet. Enlighten me, will ya?" Nachman felt something a twinge like a small shock from his nanophage.

Sadie. He tried not to think of anything, but he needed to let her know.

Sadie appeared in the promenade of the *Satyr*. Not being able to afford to expend anymore Vis, she limped to the lab where she stored the piece of debris that crashed into them months ago. Sadie had been unable to analyze all components of the debris except for one elemental alloy present that was all too familiar: Vyrinox. Both Sadie and Nachman thought it odd that such an old space satellite would have a metal not seen this side of the Celestial until the Noanoagans appeared. But with everything that happened since, she hadn't put the pieces together. Sadie reached the Vis scanner where her continual analysis had been taking place. The piece was there, and as she suspected, had already infested the *Satyr*. *There must have been a cloaking virus or something to hide this from us for so long*, she thought. Sadie felt crushed, as if the biggest mistake of her existence had been made. Sadie had given a back door, an indirect connection to Nachman's nanophage. She had to sever the connection.

Sadie shuddered, a vibration across her aura. Nachman was alive but not for long. Sadie very quickly sent Nachman the most shorthand version of what she was trying to do along the same Vis carrier wave, trying not to alert whatever possessed Nachman to the plan and to conserve energy.

Nachman felt the jumbled code across his brainwaves. *OK, Sadie needs a few minutes. Keep her talking, Nachman.*

You will be the conduit into the Other. The realm of those skaavs you Humans call Caiets, energy beings, ha. They are a mere source of power, as are you, to expand my reign. Infinite power to traverse the Zymej at my will. I excite myself at the prospects.

Nachman was still infused with the Aethra, but the acrid burn in his body was dissipating, and he could think a little more clearly. "Now tell me, how do you suppose you're going to do all this now that the GIA and the Mihi know about Xon and his delusions of grandeur? And spare me the part about the Automatons; my crew already handled that."

If you're referring to the implantation ports at the silly dance club, Xon's idea was quite brilliant actually—the Krytar broke out in hysterical laughter—*and he thought he was going to have his own army. Brings a tear to my eye. If those are what you speak of, then yes, you have stopped the production. But how far into your society have we already integrated? I wonder how much sway the Cordrego of Bellatorius has over the military defense decisions of your populace. Or how about the member of the Morsus Mihi...no, I say too much, but as you see, I am everywhere already.*

"So you send an alien race to integrate into our society to set Humans up to be made a slave race. Great, so, correct me if I'm wrong, but like the Noas when we are of no more use, what? You throw us away as well?"

We will have much use for your species, skaav. You, Nachman, are but a stepping-stone for many. You will cease to function eventually; you are not eternal, but more power conduits can be made in your stead. From you, I and my reign will be eternal.

"Wow, and Novia thought I was full of myself, but you, queen bee, take the crown for narcissism." Nachman felt energized. Sadie was reconnecting, but Nachman wasn't sure that was the right move. But Nachman trusted Sadie; she knew what she was doing. He knew he was being played by this Krytar character, but he needed to keep her gabbing. "Either way though you have been inside my head, and you know damn well that I would rather throw myself into the vacuum of the Celestial rather than be your slave and bring down the rest of the Humanity in the process." Nachman broke his right arm and left leg free of the gateway. The metal crumbled like dust around him as he freed himself from his restraints.

The connection weakens. Congratulations, Nachman, you have regained what little control remains in your grasp. But this is all what needed to be.

Nachman was back in his body, kneeling in the domed Aethra control room. No wires or tubes. He wasn't a fetus and wasn't surrounded by his dead loved ones. Nachman looked up past the dome to the explosion on the far side of the Aethra.

Sadie succeeded. *Damn, I loved that ship*, Nachman thought. He watched as his home for five years became nothing more than specks in the vacuum. Nachman wasn't mad; it would be stupid of him to be. Sadie did it to save his life and maybe everyone else's as well.

Sadie appeared beside him. Nachman felt immense relief to see her in one piece. Sadie was still badly injured but nothing worse for wear. Nachman felt like his head just collided with an asteroid field at full burn. Nachman and Sadie dispensed with pleasantries and exchanged nods, their attention turning to the madman in front of them.

The Xon puppet tossed the head of the Litiquis to the side; it landed with a soft thud at Sadie's feet. In Xon's voice, the Krytar spoke. "Welcome, welcome, I have been waiting for this moment. The link between the two wide open under the Zhyrje. Earlier than expected, but my Visji, as are the rest of my flock, are prepared to take what is yours for the Requenoc, for their Krytar." Xon stood on tiptoes and spread his arms wide spinning like a dancer. "Oh, it is to be a glorious conquest for the Requenoc."

Nachman and Sadie looked up at the Aethra; the intertwined Vis tubules lit up like festival lights, the eye of the Aethra churned with a dense mist of Vis, the liquid waves fluctuated from the eye. The Aethra was powering up. "She said when we are together, the link is stronger, whatever that means. Please tell this isn't what she means," Nachman said, standing and pointing to the Aethra.

"I think she means much more than just the Aethra powering on early," Sadie said, "From what I gather from your incentum, you had quite the adventure in the Psi Platform."

"Sadie, please, not now, shrink my head later," Nachman snapped.

"What do we do, Nachman?"

"Wish I knew."

Xon stopped twirling like a mad dancer. "Now that I have corrected course and set my intention back on the proper path, I no longer have use for the dear Magnus Xon. The Requenoc will begin coming through the Zhyrje in moments, and you, Nachman, will be the beginning of a new era for me as Krytar." Xon floated above the ground, arms spread wide, and head turned to the stars, he shouted, "It will be glorious!" Xon exploded into a million pieces, but the pieces didn't spread out; Nachman wasn't covered in an immense amount of blood, and there weren't wet chunks at his feet. The Xon pieces floated jagged, irregular like a puzzle, hanging in midair. Nachman was still able to make out the shape of the former Magnus. Inside Sadie and Nachman's head, the voice of the Krytar echoed: *"This is but a taste of what I can and will do, skaav. My mere presence would overwhelm your tiny skaav mind. If your race comes quietly, the pain will be minimal. Resist and... well, Nachman, my dear, imagine what I will do to your precious loved ones when I am at full strength. See you soon."*

The Xon puzzle fell from the air. In one giant wet glop, the remains splashed on the floor. Sadie felt a small flutter trace over her aura as the Xon pieces fell to the floor. A small code pinged off her aura. *What, is this Xon?* Sadie thought.

"Now that's disgusting," said Nachman.

Nachman stood, pulling a handkerchief from his pocket, wiping the blood and small bits of Xon from his beard. "OK, then, that wasn't my idea of a resolution of that case, but there you go."

"Are you OK?"

"Oh, I'm golden, but now here's the problem," Nachman said, walking to the main console of the Aethra control grid. "How do we shut down the Aethra and stop queen bee from wiping us all out?"

Sadie limped to Nachman, but she was smiling. "I think the Magnus can help with that."

CHAPTER 20

Tracaelus Solaris, Aethra Gateway, Main Control Center
Aethra Fully Functional, Forty Minutes until Requenoc Invasion

The churning in the Aethra's eye slowly swirled, then stopped abruptly. A brilliant spectacle of light spread through the ring and filled the eye of the megalithic contraption. The translucent liquid in the ring fluttered. Sporadic parts inside the liquid began to become blocky, digitized, making the stars that were seen through the liquid folded upon itself. Through the blocky digitized sections, seven at Nachman's count, sharply angled beaks appeared. *The noses of stellar vessels*, Nachman thought.

"New problem emerging, Sadie. Looks like seven—no, now eight—vessels coming through. Maybe thirty minutes until they are fully reconstructed. But it looks like the process is quickening pace," Nachman shouted in frustration as Sadie searched the Aethra mainframe for whatever she was looking for. "I hope Xon gave you something good after what he has put us through. Sadie, Sadie?"

Sadie was intentionally ignoring Nachman. She couldn't break her concentration—not enough energy. She was expending so much being directly connected to the Aethra's mainframe, and she needed every bit of Vis to find this hidden door Xon's Vis had given her just before he died as quickly as possible, before the first ship made it through the Aethra, or the Krytar would be back in control. She sifted through file after file. *Where was it?*

"Sadie, one of the ships is halfway materialized, and I don't have a big enough gun to stop it right now," Nachman said, "Alvum! Sadie, would you…"

"Did someone say they need some assistance?"

"Rodan!" Nachman would never tell him, but he was actually glad to hear his voice. But there was another in the forefront of his incentum. "Is Novia with you?"

"I'm here, Nachman," Novia responded over the lexcom. Her voice shaky, but she was alive, to Nachman's relief. "Mission accomplished, but the Miga is definitely going to need a facelift." Nachman knew Novia's nerves had had their fill of adventure for a while if she was making jokes. "All Human and Noanoagans accounted for that need to be. Rodan managed to find six vessels within the vicinity friendly to the Vultus and with the same paranoia you and Ro share."

"OK, great, we need the help. Sorry if I sound off, but my head is a little screwy since this new alien was tooling around in there." Nachman did his best not to let anyone hear the quiver of relief in his voice and not to tell Novia to stay away from the rest of the action. Might have been five years, but he still knew better than to give her an order. Nachman quickly formulated a plan of attack. "Rodan, we can't risk any of those ships making it through. These creatures are psychic, and the Vyrinox enhances their abilities somehow. We cannot—I repeat, *cannot*—let any of these ships clear the vicinity of the Aethra."

"Alvum, psychic? Seriously? This first ship doesn't look like it's all the way through yet. Do I blow it now?" Rodan asked.

"No, no, wait until just after it clears the liquid. Don't want to risk blowing the gateway with us on it." Nachman looked at Sadie. She would agree, but Novia wasn't going to like what Nachman said next. "Rodan, if it comes to it, I need you to destroy the Aethra by any means possible. You copy?"

"Copy, boss. It won't come to that, though," Rodan said, a hint of the Creole accent peeking out again. "Um, Nachman, the first one is almost through. That is one damn huge fighter, sleek very sleek...it opened fire! It opened fire! Something like a razor sliced right through the hull of my wingman. The *Dionysus* is down!" Rodan shouted.

"Don't wait. Two fusion torpedoes to the underbelly—that's the sweet spot. Fire! Fire!" Nachman ordered.

The ship exploded. Fire and debris digitized back into the gateway. The rest of the alien vessels continued to push through the Aethra's eye. Rodan shouted congratulations. "Boy, Nach, that exploded nicely. You guys OK down there? Alvum, that was great!"

"Yeah, that was Nachman. But how did you know?" asked Novia.

"Luckily, Sadie has been teaching me a thing or two of counter psi-warfare, and it paid off a bit while that crazy bitch was inside my head."

"Nachman, I have reports of incoming GIA warships," Novia said. "We still don't know who has been compromised within the ranks. We have to hurry."

Nachman didn't get a chance to respond.

"Nach, two more are almost out to the point where the last one fired." Rodan didn't wait for Nachman's order this time; he called out to his fleet using the vessel's call signs: "*Jinn, Orion*, open up on the one on the right. *Mercury*, I know you don't have a lot of firepower but unload on the ship on the left with me on my mark." Rodan continued to command his small fleet and hold the quickening advance of the invasion.

The Krytar broke in and out of Nachman's head like a frequency that couldn't quite get through, *You cannot stop me! The Human skaav will serve me! I will be eternal!*

Nachman shook his head. *Alvum, get out of there.* Nachman took his attention off the space battle above him and looked at Sadie, who was staring right at him. "Sadie, it is very, very creepy when you do that." Sadie didn't smile, didn't even smirk. "Um, Sadie this isn't good. Please tell me we can stop this?"

"We can but—"

"But what?"

"We are going to have to disconnect." Sadie finally broke eye contact, her aura softening to a dull lime green. "And I don't know if have the strength to get back."

Nachman grabbed Sadie's shoulders, flooded with the want to tell his friend never to leave his side for a stunt so insane. But instead, he said, "We gotta do what we gotta do. I'll see you soon, right." Nachman forced it into a statement.

Sadie smiled now. "Right." Sadie always admired Nachman for his insight into situations. Sadie couldn't help but lean in and kiss Nachman on a bearded cheek. "You need a shave."

"Not on your life."

"*Amicus iter tutum*," Sadie said.

"See you soon, Sadie," Nachman said. Then he was alone watching the green mist Sadie left behind fade away. He reached out to touch the dusty Vis; it melted in his hand like a snowflake.

Seconds after Sadie vanished, the Aethra began shutting down. Three more of the Requenoc stellar vessels were partially through when the shimmering liquid sank into the center of the Aethra. The ships were ripped apart; the pieces floated away from the gateway. Rodan and his crew destroyed them promptly. The Krytar screamed one last time; the psionic screech raked through Nachman's head, resonating off the walls of his incentum. He heard her manic howl but ignored it as it faded away. He had the distinct feeling he would see her again. Goody. Nachman saw the Vis tubules go dark; the shimmering Vyrinox lost its halo, becoming the dull ashen color as before. The Aethra was shut down for now. Nachman heard Rodan and the others celebrating their victory but with haste, as the GIA greeting party would be here within the hour. Everyone needed to pack up and leave, but Nachman didn't want to just yet. He took out his lexcom from his ear and drop it to the ground. He could celebrate later if the mood was right. Nachman was grateful the threat was gone, for now anyway. But what was the cost?

Novia came over the psionic link. "Nachman, Nachman, come in! You two did it! Are you and Sadie all right?"

"I can't feel her, Nov. Sadie's gone."

CHAPTER 21

Location Unknown yet Familiar

Sadie felt strange. Not physical pain or emotional terror, just strange, like she was meant to be where she was meant to be but was suddenly pulled away. Pulled away for a purpose, a purpose she didn't know, but she needed to find out quickly as she could feel the tether to Nachman fading fast as soon as she entered the Aethra. The final part of Xon's shutdown algorithm—a Caiet Vis signature.

She remembered entering the gateway mainframe through the main Vistation. A series of brilliant colorful wavelengths vibrated across her aura, and she was automatically transformed into her orb state, green but her orb state. She heard millions of melancholic bizarre rhythms, agonizingly painful sounds, but as soon as she heard them, the sounds became one blissful, rhythmic chant, soothing, if Sadie had to describe it to Nachman later. Then the pull—an immense stretch of her aura. Then she woke up. Where though? The pull was the last thing she can remember.

Sadie couldn't see in the traditional sense, but she could feel she was no longer with Nachman. Sadie couldn't feel his phage, his physical being, and couldn't hear his thoughts. Sadie felt separated from a part of herself but whole in another part of herself. She was in her original orb shape, but now instead of her normal neon green, she was a pearlescent lavender. The only time she was this color, her original color, was just before she was with Nachman, the last time she was in her reality. Was she really here? Sadie's excitement grew as the sensations of grace, fluidic melody, and a peace almost like euphoria. She felt this same sensation when she kept tethered to Nachman the couple of times she sent him here to heal, her realm of reality, her birthplace, what Caiets call the Iun. But as quickly as the elation of being back in her birth realm came it faded. Sadie felt an emptiness; a piece was missing. She wasn't meant to be here. She knew that for a fact.

I am so happy to see you are safe, Sister. You made a great sacrifice to save the Humans from the beginnings of a vile tyranny from the Requenoc.

The voice was deep, bass, a part of a sweet symphony of light and sound reverberating off the thin aura surrounding her orb form. Sadie felt safe, so oddly safe, when the melody cascaded around her orb form. She turned to see the orb speaking to her, this one a blue-green color. When Sadie spoke, her voice flowed with a similar sweetness but a moderately higher pitch. *Who are you? How did you pull me here? The psychic creature is that a Requenoc? Nachman, I can't feel him, how do I get back? Tell me now!*

A swarm of orbs, blue green and lavender, were suddenly at the bass orb's side; an aura of suspicion surrounded the defender orbs instantly. *Calm, sister, calm.* The bass orb spoke to his comrades, *Stand down; she is only fearful because of the circumstance.* The orbs backed off, but Sadie could sense the cautious posture. *So many queries at once, Sadie. We are short on time; we must filter for time's sake.*

Sadie couldn't help but calm herself. No orb here meant her any harm. *You seem so familiar to me, but I haven't felt your presence for so many years. You call me sister; then you claim you are family, yes?*

The bass melody sent off what felt like relief, not offended in the least by anything. *I always knew from the moment you were birthed that you would be kind, graceful with a high level of intuition but the paranoia and suspicion of anyone of your intelligence. A fine combination that I couldn't be any more thankful for in my sweet little sister. I am not surprised you don't remem-*

ber me. However, to answer your question, yes, I am what you have learned to term your brother. My name is very difficult to translate into a Human melodic variation, so I'm afraid I cannot translate for your Nachman, but then again, we have already met, him and I. You and I, however, parted very shortly after the birthing ritual, which happened to coincide with the enslavement of our people by the Requenoc.

I had no idea they existed until our confrontation with their leader, the Krytar. I remember very little of my early years. I was bonded with Nachman in both his and my fourth year, the same year Mo and Po went beyond, but I don't ever remember them speaking of the beings. They did not speak much of the past—or you, for that matter. They did go beyond peacefully, by the way; I sense your worry about that, said Sadie in a smooth, sweet pitch.

Mo and Po are beyond; yes, that I am aware. I was hoping to see them again one day, but at least they went in peace as all beings should. They would have never spoke of those events; all who escaped swore themselves to silence for fear they would project their incentum to the most powerful Requenoc, the Court of Vijsi and their leader, the Krytar. When our species first came into contact with Humans, there was hope again to find a race willing and worthy to know of our existence and live in peace with what they call the Vis. The Humans live with it, manipulate it, and do not abuse the Vis. For now what they see as a tool, we see as an interconnectivity between all the Realms of Reality. We, the Caiets, seek to protect, spread the knowledge, and cultivate the growth between the Realms and their individual people. The Requenoc seek to rule and siphon the Vis for their own wasteful search for power and domination. They enslaved our kind, among many others gaining immense power within their minds and technology. When you shut down the Aethra, you released many of our kind from their bonds. They all thank you. Sadie, we are running out of time; your tether to Nachman grows weak, and as you know you must go back. You are meant to be bonded with Nachman and he with you. You both, only together, are a conduit to the Iun as we have never seen before. With this known, we seek an alliance with Humans and our dear friends the Noanoagans. They don't remember us, but we have known them, long ago. We must all work together; we all have resources that we can use to stop the Requenoc, Sister. Now, go, Sister; your tether with your bond grows weak.

But how will I get back without harming Nachman or myself each time?

Sadie felt a quivering sensation across her aura like a thousand ants skittering across. The sensation didn't hurt, but it was a lot to process. She felt a swath of quantum equations and algorithmic formulas swim over her matrices. *There is so much data to reconstruct.*

Yes, and you now have the time to process. Prepare yourself, Sadie; I am sending you home. We will see each other again very soon. Farewell for now.

Sadie felt the pull again, but this time, she was being pulled back like rubber snapping back to its point. Sadie appeared in the main control room of the Aethra like she had never left. Her luminescent neon-green Humanoid form was fully intact and regenerated, her hair flowed full and a brilliant purple, and she felt as if she had been rejoined with that missing piece. She saw her partner, her bond, her friend kneeling beside his beloved as if his world had been lost in some great abyss.

"Nachman," Sadie said softly as she stepped to his side and laid a hand on his shoulder.

Nachman looked at Sadie, but he had felt her the instant she came back from wherever she had gone. The flood was there, teetering on the edge of sweeping his incentum. But he couldn't be angry, only overjoyed that his friend had returned. While she was gone, he had felt nominal, to say the least, like he could function day to day without her—and she was only gone for mere minutes. Only there was a part of his mind that felt broken, almost impossible to fix, but now that Sadie had returned, Nachman felt everything had been put back in place. Nachman once again felt what she felt, everything she had been through. The Requenoc had enslaved so many beings, including the Noanoagans; she had a brother she never knew was even alive and ready to form a rebellion to take down the Requenoc; and the populace of Caiets want Nachman and Sadie to be ambassadors for their Realm of Reality, the Iun. Nachman had to smirk. *The Iun—so that's where she sent me.* "Hey, there, Sadie. Couldn't stay away, huh?"

Sadie's aura brightened a hue. She knew Nachman was upset about his side trips to the Iun, but like her, Nachman was just glad she was home. "You know you missed me."

"Don't tell anybody, especially my mother." Nachman looked up to where the *Satyr*, their home, had met its end. "So it looks like we need a new ship."

"Yes, that we do." Sadie turned to Novia, who was holding Nachman's arm. Sadie smiled. "And will you be joining us?"

Novia looked up at Nachman, who smiled at her in return. "Yeah, for a while at least."

Nachman and Sadie looked at each other. It was a solemn look, one concerned about the trust between them but one that knew their family was whole once more. Both knew, more importantly, they would be able to remold a family, a trust, a bond that had been present since the first day they were aware of each other. The threats loomed here and half a Celestial away, but with new alliances coming into the fray and old friendships renewed, together they were strong. Together, not just Humanity but the entire Celestial will endure and awaken anew.

EPILOGUE

Ipsum Solaris, Construction Station Rockefeller Orbiting TerraOrbis Nitoomu, Ipsum Solaris HQ
Completion New Stellarcraft Build Labeled *Adonis*, Awaiting Departure Clearance, Four Months Post-Aethra Eventum

Questions, cordons, social angst, political misgivings, distrust in leaders were just some issues raised from the blowback of the Aethra Eventum, as the Celestial media had dubbed the attack. Nachman didn't approve but didn't stop Rodan from releasing his fleet's POV Gnanimus files of the Aethra Incident. Nachman knew the need for public discretion at times, but Rodan never did like keeping secrets from the public. The GIA and Morsus Mihi were facing a social and political blitzkrieg from everyone but surprisingly not placing blame on Nachman and keeping with the truth—well, somewhat. The GIA was covering their tracks, with the civilian sector reassuring public safety but raising fears and a lot of questions in the wake of a near-invasion that wasn't kept as swept under the proverbial rug as they would have liked.

The Morsus Mihi, Noanoagan High Council, and Caiet delegates, through Nachman and Sadie's link with the Iun, had been coordinating a strategic defense plan involving massive amounts of research into the long-abandoned psionic platform that was so sorely needed now that there were hostile psychic aliens waiting in the mist. The Vyrinox in the Aethra was dormant for now and under around the clock surveillance by Naibus and Fala security detachments. Funerals were held for those lost. Tejwenn and Buhai were held in great esteem by the trimoon priests and priestesses. Magnus Xon's funeral was kept to the privacy of the Morsus Mihi. They now know about his manipulation by the Krytar, but they were never truly sure of Xon's ambitions. To the public he was a savior to Humanity. Nachman didn't argue.

After all this was said and done, Nachman knew the tension between all species would be hard-going for a time, but he had regrettably noticed the disconnect between Noanoagans and Humans; distrust was hard thing to get over. After the sudden Aethra shut down, many were injured or killed as a result of the manic state from the abrupt disconnect from the Requenoc stranglehold. Even through the tensions, the Noanoagans were banding together as a people, and the rebuild to their way of life was underway. With the help of the Caiets, who were bonded with them over two thousand years ago, they were able to fully break the Requenoc mind control. The GIA had chosen to set up orbital checkpoints and give the Fala defense forces a Naibus attaché until all were confirmed physically and psychically clear—strictly as a precaution, they claimed. Nachman knew better, and he made sure they knew he was watching as well. With their freedom as a species taking a look toward a new dawn, they had as many questions as everyone but were focused rebuilding their society and the continuing relationship with Humans and Caiets.

Humanity has trust issues within themselves from the Vultus to the higher echelons of the GIA. The hunt for Automatons, Atons, was on, and with the information Sadie returned with from her brother, the GIA scientific community and Caiets were able to severe the Atons' connection to the host Ignivalo without damaging the host's brain or phage. With the invention of new tech and new methods of Vis manipulation, the GIA and Morsus Mihi called it a glorious win for all in the Iun and Celestial.

Now that the Interealm Coalition (Sadie was very proud of the name) was established, Sadie regularly traveled between the Iun and the Celestial for dignitary and now familial reasons. Nachman had noticed the kid sister side more in Sadie now that she had a known family; Nachman had never seen Sadie so happy, and that always made him happy. With the help of Sadie's brother, Nachman found that he had microscopic filaments of Vyrinox interwoven in his fibrous cyber-netic tissues, which had made him more susceptible to the Krytar. No progression had yet been made into finding a way to remove the Vyrinox without doing damage to Nachman. With all the help over the months Sadie's brother had been giving them, Nachman needed to call him something. Sadie finally decided on Ashli after Nachman's father. Nachman did protest the latter but was brought to submission by Delylah, who found it to be a great honor. Sadie was still wary of Ashli; she had an inherent trust in him—but like Nachman, there was always the noda. Novia claimed a little of Nachman's paranoia has imbedded itself in her matrices. Nachman scoffed at the notion, but Sadie tended to agree.

"Well."

"Well, what, Sadie?"

"Can your new addition call me Auntie Sadie or not? Please, Nachman, it would be great. I would show her all the old films, tell her about our adventures—oh, maybe even try to bring her to Iun if I can!" Sadie was very excited about the news of Novia's pregnancy.

"Wait a minute." Nachman looked puzzled, bringing his hand to his beard. "How do you know it's a girl? Alvum, Sadie, we just found we were preggers two standard days ago."

"Just have that noda in the pit, Daddy Nachman."

"Don't call me that." Nachman chuckled, but secretly, he liked the new title. He changed the topic. "But I do say we call up the coordinates to that derelict transport vessel. Rodan sent a lex about an hour ago from the outer reaches of Ipsum. He said he has a takedown squad ready to deploy when-ever we get there." Rodan had been made head of the Aton Search and Rescue Operations for the Ipsum sector. Rodan didn't mind private contracting; he said it gave him a lot of scratch, in more ways than one. Nachman still found the man annoying.

"But, Nachman, we still have about forty-five minutes until the *Adonis* is ready for departure. I think you still need the life support systems," said Sadie.

"How long until the rendezvous at the outer reaches of Ipsum with Rodan's crew for infil of the derelict transport vessel with how many Atons?"

"Two days out and twenty Atons by last Vis scan count from Rodan's recon. But they are still able to mask DNA signatures," reported Sadie. "Do you think we will find Tyrav this time?"

"I can keep hope alive. Like he always says, right?"

Nachman stepped from his maestro's chair at the helm of his new ship, the *Adonis.* He would have to get used to a fixed captain's chair, but the new weapons system, Quantum S9 Tri-engine drive system, and premium Vistation designs that the GIA generously donated were a nice edition. The ship was a little larger than the *Satyr,* a little less durable, and it would take a while before it felt like home. But the people surrounding him...

Nachman looked at his holograph of Novia, now with baby on board; his mother, Delylah; and his kid sister, Sadie. His family. Nachman smiled. *Yeah, I can make this work*, Nachman thought.

"Before you go to get clearance for docking procedures," Sadie said, "I just received a lex from the new Cordrego of Bellatorius Braxus Olivari concerning two unexplained, eerily similar homicides in two Solari within the past few months. They are in need of our expertise and would be extremely grateful if we took a look at the case the Naibus Investigative Division has put together."

"Bet the NID are elated to ask for our help," Nachman responded with a smirk.

Sadie chuckled.

"Well for now, the Institutum is going to have to hold a tic. I'm going to rescue my friend. Gear up, Sadie, let's roll."

The End

Made in the USA
Coppell, TX
21 May 2023

17106132R00194